Deeper
the
Heritage

Deeper the Heritage

By

MURIEL ELWOOD

Author of "Heritage of the River"

New York

CHARLES SCRIBNER'S SONS

1947

NOTE

In this volume I have exercised dramatic license and slightly changed two historical events:

Claude de Ramezay, son of the Governor of Montreal, was killed during the siege of Rio de Janeiro in 1711. While this would have fitted into the story it would have appeared too obvious a denouement, even though it was an actual fact. If any of the descendants of the de Ramezay family are living, I hope they will pardon the liberty I have taken.

In the account of the Walker Expedition, the ships were actually wrecked on the north coast of the St. Lawrence, whereas for the purpose of the story, I have wrecked them on the south coast.

MURIEL ELWOOD.

BOOK I
Antoine

CHAPTER I

APPROACHING WINTER had plucked the leaves from the trees and their nakedness was veiled in a feathery garment of light snow that gave them a transient beauty. Only the balsams and spruce remained live and green, disdainfully shaking the powdery whiteness from their limbs. The azure waters of the St. Lawrence were troubled and grey, reflecting the heaviness of the snow-laden sky above. In another month the rippling waters would be still, locked in an embrace of solid ice that would constrain them for five long months.

The shore was crowded with people anxiously awaiting the arrival of the ship from Quebec—the last that would visit these shores until the following May or June. The cold wind whipped their faces to a rosy red and though inured to the severity of the climate, they stood huddled together in groups. The temperature had fallen suddenly during the night and the many who had waited since dawn, stamped their moccasined feet to counteract the stiffness. As the number of people increased, it became impossible to walk about and as many as could took refuge against the wind behind the bales of cargo. Presently, maybe, the sun would come up and warm them.

There was eagerness in their chatter as they gossiped with one another. They represented a cross section of the various types that peopled Montreal. In the last decade class distinction had become a little more emphasized as the colony had increased in population. The mode of dress distinguished the gentleman from the habitant; in many instances, particularly among the merchants, the finer cloth of the coat and the sword at the side were merely an attempt to appear well-born. For the most part the people were garbed in homespun, topped in nearly all cases by coats of native beaver. Among them mingled the priests in their long black soutanes and in a group together stood several Sisters in habits of dark cloth. Here and there Indians were huddled in their blankets watching with inscrutable dark eyes and expressionless faces, these people with the light skins and strange manners who had brought them Christianity and a new civilization in exchange for the freedom of the forest. For the most part they were Hurons, glad of the white man's protection against their bitter enemies, the Iroquois.

From the taverns nearby, where men took advantage of the cold to have a nip of brandy, could be heard voices raised in argument. Since public meetings of any kind were prohibited by the government, the taverns were the recognized places for discussions. Not far away were the humbler vendors of wines, indicated by a bundle of pine sprigs hanging before the door. This morning these shops were also crowded beyond the thresholds.

The arrival of a ship was always a matter of vital importance to every Montrealer. On this November morning of 1710 it had a special significance, for on board was the Governor of Montreal, returning from one of his rare visits to France. He had been received by his Most Christian Majesty, King Louis XIV, and they had discussed the affairs of the colony. There was anxious speculation as to what success he had achieved. Having founded the colony of New France and established the towns of Quebec, Three Rivers, and Montreal along the shores of the St. Lawrence, the Mother Country had a tendency to leave the hardy colonists who peopled them to strive against the increasing hazards without assistance or understanding. The Chevalier de Ramezay had been Governor of Montreal for the past six years, administering the affairs with a determination and foresight that had made him very popular. Now he was returning—they hoped with many of their problems solved. Because of his expected arrival, the atmosphere was more festive and the elegantly dressed more numerous. Above the voices of the people sounded the shouts of the drivers as carriages and celêches threaded their way through the crowd and deposited the owners in front of Dillon's Tavern. Some had come to meet the Governor or those accompanying him; others had donned their embroidered coats and feather-edged, three-cornered hats in the hope of impressing him. Each time a carriage arrived, every head was craned to see who was in it, and since the distinguished figures were familiar to most of them, the name rippled through the crowd. Frequently the bewigged gentleman would hear the ripple and indicate the fact by a perceptible puffing out of chest or maybe a nod of the head before trying to make his way into the crowded tavern. The arrival of the Intendant and the members of the Council caused a flurry and gave occasion for chatter and gossip.

There were a minimum of well-dressed ladies present, though some could be seen sitting within the shelter of their carriages. As the morning advanced, a carriage came to a stop a short distance from the wharf and a young girl jumped out, lightly touching the arm of the driver standing by the door. She glanced quickly over the crowd and then turned to wait for an older woman who was speaking to the driver.

"Will you find the Sieur, please," she was saying, "and tell him we are here. He will be at Dillon's, I expect." The man nodded and calling to an Indian to hold the horses, departed.

"Madame de Courville-Boissart," some one remarked and the name rippled through the bystanders.

The two women stood for a moment, glancing in a friendly way over the faces turned towards them, looking to see whom they recognized. They were the wife and daughter of a local seigneur and well-known to several who now began to thread their way through the throng to speak to them. Both were enveloped in long beaver coats, the collars of which they pulled up around their faces as the wind whipped their cheeks. In a few moments they were greeting the friends who circled around them, for Madame de Courville-Boissart was well liked. Her black eyes were sparkling eagerly as she said to her friends: "Our son is returning from France today. We are so excited. He has been away two years."

"That would be the elder one?" one woman remarked. It was more a statement than an interrogation.

"Yes, Jean-Baptiste," Madame answered. "Our other son is here with his father. They came into town early this morning. Have you seen them?"

"Here they come now, mother," her daughter said before the question could be answered.

The Sieur de Courville-Boissart hurried towards them followed by his son and when he had greeted their friends, said a little anxiously: "Wouldn't you rather wait in the carriage? There's such a cold wind blowing."

"After a while perhaps," Madame replied. "Is there any news of arrival?"

The Sieur shrugged his shoulders. "Who can say? Any moment the sails may top the horizon."

As they talked, the family resemblance between them was evident. The younger man, like his father, was not very tall and of the same stocky build. Only with the Sieur, the golden-red hair had now faded to a sandy color edged with grey at the temples. It was between brother and sister that the likeness was most pronounced for they were twins, and beneath her fur hat strands of the same bright colored hair emerged. As they chatted and laughed together, the quality of their smiles was the same. Many an eye was turned in André's direction and some of the younger girls obviously wished he would notice them. He was conspicuous among the waiting people, not only because of his good looks and jovial manner, but because of his clothes. He was a *coureur de bois* and wore the traditional garb—a short deerskin jacket and deerskin leggings, both fringed at the seams, with a brightly colored sash around the waist, patterned with arrowlike designs in red, blue and yellow. From this hung a beaded deerskin pouch for pipe and tobacco and a knife in a rawhide case was thrust into it. His round fur cap was perched jauntily on his wavy red hair. To the younger people he was an object of interest, for all *coureurs de bois* had an air of recklessness and adventure, a fact which frequently caused the older folks to disapprove and in many instances to condemn. Though Montreal's main sustenance was derived from the fur trade, the hazards of which appealed to young men more than farming, this desire for the freedom of the woods was frowned upon. If there were disapproving glances André did not notice them. His easy-going good nature always avoided unpleasant things when possible and since his father had once been a *coureur de bois,* André needed neither the approval nor disapproval of any one else. He and the brother for whom they now waited were quite different in type. When Jean-Baptiste had left for a tour of France two years ago, the Sieur had offered his younger son the same opportunity. André would have gone had his father wished it, but when he had remarked he would rather go into the woods, there had been an expression of approval on his father's face that had delighted him. No words had been spoken; there had been no comments regarding Jean-Baptiste, but from that day the bond between André and his father had become very strong.

They had not been waiting long, when the mouths of the people opened to release shouts that gradually ascended to a roar. The top of a mast had appeared upon the horizon, followed by the full-bellied sails of the ship. There was a surge through the crowd as every one instinctively edged nearer to the shore. The noise brought those in the taverns and wine shops hurrying out.

The Sieur and his son protected Madame and Elise as best they could. "Better stand back here," the Sieur said and had to raise his voice almost to a shout to be heard. He guided them towards a stack of cargo that would form a bulwark behind them.

"Looks as though all of Montreal's two thousand inhabitants are down here today!" André remarked with a laugh.

The Sieur looked anxious. Accustomed to the peace of his

own seigneury, crowds bothered him and he was afraid that the good-natured jostling might lead to difficulties as the excitement rose. "It would have been better if you and Elise had remained in the carriage," he remarked reprovingly.

Madame laid her hand gently on his arm. "Don't worry, Paul. It will be all right," she said quietly. As he looked at her his bronzed weather-beaten features relaxed.

It was not until the ship dropped anchor that the Intendant and the Councillors left Dillon's. With some difficulty soldiers cleared the way, making a passage to the edge of the water. Several well-dressed gentlemen took the opportunity to fall in behind, as though they were part of the entourage. The general shuffling of places which this movement occasioned, proved to the advantage of the Sieur and his family who now found they were standing at the far end of the cleared way, and in an excellent position to see Jean-Baptiste when he landed.

André grinned at his sister and nodded with satisfaction at this stroke of good fortune.

"I hear that Claude is returning with his parents," the Sieur remarked, referring to the Governor's eldest son.

"I thought he was in the Navy," Madame commented.

"He is on leave."

"Is that so?" Madame said with interest.

Elise was talking to André. "I'm glad the Governor will be here for the winter. It will mean more entertaining."

"And my sister will be able to display her charms to the Governor's son!" André teased.

"Why only to the Governor's son?" she retorted.

"Claude, no doubt, will have acquired added charm as an Ensign," André teased.

Elise wrinkled her nose. "Claude never attracted me," she replied, thinking of him as the rather overbearing boy of fourteen with whom she and her brothers had played as children. He had always annoyed her because he assumed such superiority on account of his father's position.

"He will probably have changed in five years. Perhaps one

day he will be Governor. You'd like to be the Governor's lady, wouldn't you?" André bantered.

"Not in the least, unless he were attractive."

"Particular, eh?"

She tossed her head as she turned away, though she knew he was only teasing her. Their twin affinity made them very close to each other and though neither would ever have admitted it, each admired the other tremendously.

"Wonder whether Jean-Baptiste will have changed?" André remarked in a low voice.

Elise shrugged her shoulders slightly. "Probably. We shall soon see. Did father say anything to you about the friend he was bringing with him?"

"Not any more than he said to all of us."

"Wonder what he will be like?"

"Probably some fop Jean-Baptiste picked up in Paris. I wouldn't anticipate too much."

Elise gave him a sharp look. "Who said I was anticipating anything? Can't I ask a simple question without your misinterpreting it?"

André merely laughed good-naturedly.

The first boatload to come ashore brought the Governor and his suite. As he stepped on land the men swept him bows and the ladies curtseyed. He was a fine looking man with a simple dignity. With his wife's arm through his he stood for a moment acknowledging the tribute and waving to the people in a friendly fashion. After they had greeted the officials, they passed through the lane that had been cleared for them, stopping every few feet to speak to those they knew. Madame de Ramezay was as popular as her husband. The people were proud of the fact that she was a native Canadian and had given eleven children to the colony. While the noblesse enjoyed the lavish entertainments at the Chateau de Ramezay, the lesser people were equally familiar with the Chateau, for the de Ramezays' bounty was unlimited.

Behind them walked their eldest son, Ensign Claude de

Ramezay, smiling in a friendly way. The few years he had been away had made so much change in him that it was difficult to recognize the boy he had been then. When they reached the de Courville-Boissarts, there were warm-hearted greetings. The Governor and the Sieur had fought side by side in many of the wars against the English and Indians, and after Phips' attack on Quebec, in which both had distinguished themselves, they and the present Governor-General, the Marquis de Vaudreuil, had all found wives in Quebec. This had been a bond between the three of them, though less so with de Vaudreuil than with these two, whose wives had been friends before their marriage.

When greetings were over, Madame de Ramezay linked her arm in her son's and said, "You remember Claude?"

"It would be hard to remember him by looking at him now!" Madame de Courville-Boissart said, smiling as Claude bowed gallantly over her hand. He cut a very elegant figure in his uniform with its heavy gold braid and red facings. He was not really good looking but was tall and well-built and carried his nineteen years with dignity. "I suppose André and Elise also look different to you, Claude?" Madame de Courville-Boissart continued.

Claude's look was in fact one of amazement as he saw Elise. As a child she had always seemed to him a plump, redheaded girl with freckles, who wanted to do all the things the boys did. It seemed strange to be kissing her hand when before it would have been more appropriate to give her a sly slap on the buttocks. When he looked into her face he could not draw his eyes away. Her pretense at haughtiness was counteracted by her green eyes which danced mischievously.

"I would never have recognized you, Elise," he said, embarrassed that his voice quavered slightly. "What have you done to yourself?"

"Just grown up, I suppose," she said, conscious of his admiring looks.

"What have you done with your freckles?"

"Stored them away for the winter." Her eyes now challenged him.

Madame de Ramezay's voice interrupted the compliments that he was about to utter. "Come, Claude, we are blocking the way." She smiled apologetically at Elise. She did not blame her son for the way he was looking at this beautiful young girl.

"We shall meet again, mademoiselle," Claude said as he bowed with a flourish.

"Undoubtedly, monsieur," she replied with a curtsey. The look she gave André when Claude had passed was mocking. "Such elegance!" she whispered. "He fancies himself more than ever." Her lip curled slightly with distaste.

The second boat had discharged its passengers. Among them were two tall young men, dressed alike in the uniform of *officiers des gardes*. Except for their height, they were a direct contrast, one being fair and lean and the other dark and broad-shouldered. The press of the people was so great that it took them some little time to disentangle themselves.

André saw them first and called to his brother, who waved his hat and then was lost again amidst the throng. By a circuitous route they finally reached the family and Jean-Baptiste forgot that he had intended to exhibit his courtly manners, and in an ecstasy of delight at being united again, threw his arms around them. Madame, whose favorite he was, eyed him a little anxiously, and then the anxiety changed to pride at the elegance of his appearance. He did not look like part of the same family, for though his sensitive features resembled his mother's, he was as fair as she was dark. He was the only member of the family who had attained any height, being nearly six feet and towering several inches above his father and brother.

His companion stood discreetly to one side, hat under arm, waiting to be introduced and watching the family with deep interest. When Jean-Baptiste turned to make the introductions, he stepped forward and bowed. His personality was a surprise to all of them, for instead of the dandy they had expected Jean-Baptiste to acquire as a friend, this young man had a frank, sincere countenance, with dark wavy hair that was unruly in the wind.

Jean-Baptiste could now display his elegance. With a flourish he said: "Permit me to present my friend, Antoine de Brievaux —my mother, Madame de Courville-Boissart and my father, the Sieur de Courville-Boissart."

Antoine bowed over Madame's hand with an ease of manner that pleased her. "Your servant, madame," he said and raised her hand to his lips.

"We welcome you, monsieur," Madame replied and her warm smile echoed her words.

The Sieur's handshake was also cordial as he welcomed the guest.

"It is good of you, monsieur, to allow me to come with Jean-Baptiste," he remarked.

"I hope we can make your visit pleasant," the Sieur said.

"I am sure of that," Antoine replied, his gaze resting upon Elise to whom Jean-Baptiste was now introducing him. He kissed her hand and then turning to Jean-Baptiste chided: "And you said all the beautiful women would be in Quebec!"

Jean-Baptiste looked rather surprised, as though he hadn't really noticed his sister's looks before. Then he smiled and said, "You've grown up in two years, Elise."

"Thank you, monsieur," she mocked and dropped him a curtsey.

Antoine admired the ease with which she accomplished it.

"And this is my renegade brother, André," Jean-Baptiste said.

Antoine eyed André with interest. He was such a contrast with his stocky build, bronze leathery skin and unusual clothes. But his handshake was strong and the good-natured smile he gave Antoine made them friends at once. He glanced quickly at brother and sister and interpreting the glance, Jean-Baptiste remarked:

"They're twins."

"I thought so," Antoine said and his smile travelled from one to the other.

"I see you've become a *coureur de bois*," Jean-Baptiste said, his eyebrows raised slightly.

"For the past two years," André replied. He thrust a thumb into his sash and struck an attitude of good-natured defiance.

"He's a fur trader," Jean-Baptiste turned to Antoine. "That's why he's dressed in that incongruous garb."

But the smile Antoine gave André did not match Jean-Baptiste's expression. He nodded with interest and took in the details of dress with keen eyes. "I've heard about that profession. I would like to hear more."

"They live like savages and consort with the Indians," Jean-Baptiste commented disdainfully.

Madame de Courville-Boissart interrupted by urging them all to come along away from the cold wind. As the Sieur took her arm to assist her over the rough uneven roadway, Antoine offered his arm to Elise and was rewarded with the smile which she flashed up at him.

When they reached the carriage, André excused himself because he had business in town.

"And what business would you have, pray?" Jean-Baptiste asked rather mockingly.

André turned to his brother with a half smile. "None that would interest you, my dear brother. It concerns commodities —not the feminine sex."

Jean-Baptiste's reply, if he had been going to make any, was interrupted by the Sieur, who asked André to collect various orders brought by the ship.

"Certainly, monsieur," André replied. Then turning to his brother and his friend asked: "And shall I bring your baggage too?"

"If it is not too much trouble," Antoine said politely.

"Not at all. I brought the cart in this morning."

"Gaston," the Sieur called to his man who came forward with the horses.

Antoine turned to help Elise into the carriage. She paused with one foot on the step and said graciously: "We shall see you at the house, monsieur."

"I shall be impatient, mademoiselle," he replied gallantly and raised her hand to his lips. For a moment their eyes met and so deep was the expression in his, that a slight flush diffused her face, enhancing its beauty. Entranced, he looked after the carriage as it drove away. Then recollecting himself, he adjusted his hat and turned to where Gaston waited with his horse. There was a look of smouldering hate in the man's eyes that startled Antoine. He smiled, but Gaston's swarthy countenance remained immobile. As Antoine mounted his horse and joined the Sieur and Jean-Baptiste, he wondered about Gaston.

CHAPTER II

THEIR PROGRESS along the Rue St. Paul and through the crowded market place was slow, and frequently the Sieur had to call out to prevent their horses trampling on the people. Once through the gate and across the narrow Rivière St. Pierre, the open country lay before them. The narrow path that was the only roadway was slushy from the first snow, and though the horses made fairly easy progress, at intervals the carriage slithered and stuck.

"We'll have to get out the sleighs now," the Sieur remarked. "There will be more snow tonight."

Antoine rode beside him and enjoyed his descriptions and explanations of the farms they passed on their mile journey to their destination. He commented on the long, narrow appearance of each farm, instead of the customary field with home and barns in the center.

"That is peculiar to Canada," the Sieur replied. "Didn't you notice the same thing all along from Quebec?"

"Yes, I did. They looked like narrow strips of ribbon."

"Exactly. There are good reasons for it. The River means everything to the farmers—irrigation, communication and protection. Every farmer, therefore, must have his farm fronting on the River. Often they stretch back several miles and, in too many instances, you will notice the rear section uncleared and uncultivated. With Indian tribes constantly menacing us, this is a considerable danger. This long, narrow plan also has the disadvantage of wasting much time in going back and forth on the farm. But, until we learn to build roads, nothing can be done about it. Another reason for it is that as each son marries he receives his share of the land, which must front on the River, and, as large families are customary here, you can see how the land soon gets cut into narrow strips. It does, however, have the advantage of keeping the farmers close together, which is important in the event of attack."

"Is there still danger of attack?" Antoine inquired.

"Always. The Iroquois menace is less, but might break out again at any time, and then there are frequently marauding bands of other hostile Indians. And, we must never forget the English." The Sieur smiled. Antoine noticed his strong features, with the deep lines set in a skin that was leathery from constant exposure to the weather.

Jean-Baptiste cantered up to join them, waving his arm and pointing ahead. "There's the farm, Antoine," he shouted. A boyish excitement wreathed his features and Antoine mentally noted how much more charming this was than the bored, super-cilious air that Jean-Baptiste had acquired in France. He wondered which of the two attitudes would become predominant.

Directed by Jean-Baptiste he looked ahead, and soon they were entering a gate between the palisades that surrounded the de Courville land. Paul had inherited it twenty years before from the Sieur de Courville, the original seigneur, and though he had joined the seigneur's name to his own, the farm had always retained its name of de Courville. The Manor House stood upon a knoll commanding a view of the entire seigneury. It was not as palatial as its name implied, but the seigneur's house, whether it be cottage or castle, was usually designated as the *Manor House*. Paul had made many improvements since his ownership, not only by protecting the property with sturdy palisades, but rebuilding the seigneurial mansion. It had been about forty years old when the Sieur de Courville died and had begun to show signs of decay. The original stone foundations had been left but the crumbling timbers had been replaced with native stone and a new wing had been added, so that now the appearance was more imposing, though compared with some of the other seigneurs' mansions, it was simple.

Jean-Baptiste and Antoine stood outside on the steps for a few minutes while Jean-Baptiste pointed out landmarks. There were several farmhouses all modelled on the same pattern—square, with small windows and sloping roofs to shed the winter snows.

"The large house which you see to the left," Jean-Baptiste indicated, "is the original farmhouse. My great-grandfather and the Sieur de Courville cleared the land together nearly sixty years ago. For many years that farm and this were the only two houses on the land. There was another small seigneury at the far end, now part of our land, but that didn't amount to anything." He made the last statement rather contemptuously. "Father had the house pulled down and built a new mill in its place." Something in his tone made Antoine realize there was more to the story.

"It all looks prosperous to me," Antoine said, and there was deep interest in his tone.

"Wait until you see it in the spring! You can't really tell anything at this time of the year. And in the summer, it's beautiful. The waters of the River are the deepest blue you ever saw."

The enthusiasm in Jean-Baptiste's voice amused Antoine. He turned to him. "For all your sophistication, Jean-Baptiste, I believe you love the land."

Jean-Baptiste's expression was guarded and there was annoyance in his tone as he replied: "I don't deny it. One usually has a deep-rooted affection for the land where one was born and the home of one's childhood. All the same, I have no desire to be a farmer." Looking at his long, slender fingers it would have been difficult to visualize them handling farm tools. "It's good to return to but no one with any ambition would want to remain buried here all his life. Montreal will never amount to anything. It's almost seventy years old and look at its progress! Tomorrow I'll take you in and you'll see. No," he yawned as though already bored, "the enthusiasm wears off all too quickly. By the end of winter you'll be longing to get back to France."

"Maybe," Antoine said rather slowly, as his eyes roamed over the expanse of the seigneury, taking in every detail.

The interior of the Manor House exuded comfort. The furnishings were a mixture of pieces imported many years before from France and native pieces made by the habitants for the seigneur. Large wood fires burned in the main rooms. Wine had been placed on the table and the Sieur filled the glasses.

"Welcome home, Jean-Baptiste," the Sieur said as he held up his glass. "And to you, Monsieur de Brievaux, a hearty welcome also. I hope you will like it here."

"Thank you, monsieur. I am already finding it fascinating," Antoine replied.

Jean-Baptiste glanced quickly at him. "That won't last long," he said shortly.

"Why?" the Sieur's voice was brittle.

Jean-Baptiste met the challenge. "He's been used to Paris all his life."

"Perhaps that is why I shall enjoy the change," Antoine replied, intercepting the Sieur's answer to his son.

Jean-Baptiste smiled sardonically. "I think I know a little more about it," he said.

"Have you become so enamoured of the gay life overseas that you despise your native country, Jean-Baptiste?" the Sieur asked sharply.

"I wouldn't put it as strongly as that, monsieur. But you must admit that there is much to be said for the culture of Paris."

"It has its uses if properly adapted," the Sieur said, his eyes measuring his son. There was an emphasis in his tone that was a warning.

"Of course, monsieur," Jean-Baptiste answered and his eyes met his father's steadily.

Not wishing to become involved in a family argument, Antoine had turned to study a full-length portrait hanging over the mantelpiece. The room they were in was a small one off the large drawing room, and since the Sieur de Courville's day had been called the library, although it could boast only a few books. The portrait was of an old man with a rough weather-beaten face, haloed by white hair. The lines of the face were deep ravines, and the eyes that looked out from the canvas were vivid blue. The artist had caught a dominating force of character that made it impossible to be in the room long without noticing it.

The Sieur turned to his guest. "He was my grandfather."

"Such a wonderful face, monsieur," Antoine said, his voice full of interest.

"He was a wonderful man," the Sieur replied.

"The great-grandfather you were telling me about just now? The one who was the pioneer?" Antoine asked Jean-Baptiste.

Jean-Baptiste nodded. He was irritated by what his father had said to him. It was the revival of an old argument and the warning that his father had given him the day he left for France. He had hoped to impress them with the changes in him, not be censured for them before his friend.

"He was known to everyone as Old Pierre," the Sieur went on. "He was my ideal." The Sieur was gazing at the portrait with a deep reverence.

"There's something in the picture that makes you feel he is living; as though you could talk to him," Antoine said fervently.

"Yes. And that's surprising, because the artist painted it from memory."

"He did! He must have known him well."

"Old Pierre was known to most people and loved by all. The artist was a native of Montreal."

Antoine continued to study the portrait for a few moments and then said: "He must have been very proud of having been a pioneer here. That is something you can do in a new country like this—build a heritage that people remember." His tone was very serious and again Jean-Baptiste gave him a penetrating look. He had never seen his gay, carefree companion in this mood and wondered whether he was doing it to impress his father. They were now talking earnestly, almost as though they had forgotten he was there.

"Old Pierre was very proud. He loved this land, though he developed it more by his dominating spirit than by actual labor," the Sieur was saying. "It was his only son, my father, who was the builder." Antoine was listening to the Sieur with interest that was far from being feigned. "Old Pierre had many disappointments. He had not been here very long before the Indians captured him and mutilated him so that he could never use his hands again. . . ."

"The Indians captured him!" Antoine exclaimed and turned to scrutinize the portrait.

"But he escaped them. . . ."

"That's unusual, isn't it?"

"Very. We have two in our family who escaped them. My twin sister had the same experience. I will show you her portrait in a moment."

"Wouldn't you like to go up to your room and refresh yourself?" Jean-Baptiste interrupted.

"Presently, Jean-Baptiste. I would like to hear more about Old Pierre," Antoine replied.

Jean-Baptiste shrugged his shoulders. "Whatever you wish," he said.

"Let me fill your glasses," the Sieur said hospitably and when he had done so continued the story.

"You will notice how his hands are dug deep into his pockets." Antoine nodded. "He always stood like that. All but one finger had been torn off by the Indians and his body was a mass of scars." The Sieur sipped his wine for a few minutes. "He came here in 1653 when he was twenty-five years old, bringing his wife and young son. I never saw my grandmother. She died from the shock of finding her husband so mutilated after his escape. They had come here full of hope, but without realizing the many hardships they would have to endure. Our story might have ended there, but my father had become imbued with a love for this country and, though he was only twelve, he carried on."

"They had great courage in those days. . . ." Antoine remarked and there was admiration in his tone.

"The same courage still exists. It will have to if we are to survive. Progress here has been too slow. There is so much yet to be done. We need young, energetic men to carry on."

Antoine looked away from the portrait and met the Sieur's eyes and then turned back again to the portrait, but made no reply, though by his thoughtful expression it was evident he was taking in all that the Sieur said.

"Your father must have been a very fine man, too, monsieur."

"Yes, he was. His experiences had made him hard and he did not have the broad understanding of Old Pierre. It was always to my grandfather that I went when I was in difficulties. Old Pierre always said that my twin sister and I had inherited the characteristics of grandmother's family. We took our red hair from her and presumably the natures that go with it. My father and I did not agree on all things and particularly on the subject of *coureurs de bois*. He had, of course, seen the harm they can do and when, against his will, I became one, he disowned me. He forgave me before he died, but never approved." Paul de Courville-Boissart smiled and as he did so Antoine noticed how much like his grandfather he appeared. There was the same indomitable spirit shining out of his blue-green eyes.

"And now your younger son is a *coureur de bois*," Antoine said.

"Yes, André and also my youngest brother, Philip, whom you will meet in due course. I have been the most fortunate member of the family in that the Sieur de Courville adopted me. He took my side when my father was angry with me for going into the woods. Come into the other room and I will introduce you to the original seigneur."

The drawing room was long and narrow, furnished entirely

by pieces brought by the Sieur de Courville from France. The walls were hung with heavy tapestries to which had now been added three portraits, which the Sieur explained had all been painted by the same artist as the portrait in the other room. One of Madame de Courville-Boissart faced the door and it had the same living quality as that of Old Pierre. Antoine commented upon it.

"The one of my wife is the only one that was not done from memory," the Sieur remarked.

"It is a splendid likeness," Antoine said and paused for a moment to study it and then followed the Sieur to the far end of the room. They stood before the portrait of a fine-looking man, with the same rugged quality as Old Pierre, but instead of the homespun clothes, he was fashionably dressed. His skin had a leathery look, but the lines of the face were those of an aristocrat. The lace ruffles hanging over the hands belied the suggestion that they had ever done hard work.

"The Sieur de Courville," the Sieur remarked, as though he were making an introduction. "He would not have liked the portrait too well. Like the rest of us, he usually wore homespuns and moccasins. He worked on his own land. You will probably find that one of the hardest things to get used to here." Paul glanced at Antoine and then at Jean-Baptiste who stood listening. "They tell me gentlemen are not permitted to work in the Mother Country," Paul went on and a smile played around his mouth. "It's different here, very different. Seigneur and habitant labor side by side in the fields. My grandfather was originally the Sieur de Courville's servant." Again the Sieur's eyes went to his son's face in a challenge. "Not being of the gentry he was not entitled to a grant of land. He was a habitant and as they worked they developed a deep friendship that lasted all their lives. They built this house first. Then my grandfather took a portion of the land on the seigneury and built his own house, helped in turn by the seigneur. It is a system that breaks down social barriers. You won't understand it at first. You may not like it, for you will find it very different from France."

Jean-Baptiste had not failed to notice the glances given him
by his father. He now remarked casually: "There are more
social distinctions today than there were in your day, monsieur."

"That depends," the Sieur replied sharply. "Many of the
merchants in town and their wives enjoy imitating the gentry.
The pioneer families remember their heritage."

Jean-Baptiste's face flushed and he turned away. Antoine
went on as though he had not heard the conversation. "There
appears to be much that is interesting to learn here," he
said.

"There are many opportunities here," the Sieur replied. "If
a man is willing to work hard, he can obtain seigneurial rights
and own his own land. However, I must admit that I was fortunate and did not work as hard as many to obtain this seigneury. The Sieur de Courville gave it to me. His greatest disappointment was that none of his sons would come here. They
were aristocrats and despised the colonies."

"There is much of that feeling in France," Antoine remarked.

"Too much. They forget us until they want something."

"That I can believe, monsieur."

"And now meet another member of the family."

The Sieur led the way to the other end of the long room
and stopped before the partrait of a woman whom Antoine
judged to be in her late twenties. She was seated on a high-
backed chair, the flowing skirt of her pale green dress spread out
gracefully. The color of her dress matched her eyes, which were
the same greenish blue as the Sieur's and complemented the red
hair that fell about her shoulders in soft ringlets. Antoine looked
at the portrait, then at the Sieur, and said smiling:

"An introduction is not necessary this time. She would
obviously be your sister."

"Yes, we are twins."

"She looks like Mademoiselle Elise. . . ."

"Yes, André and Elise are carrying on the redheaded tradition, and they are very much like my sister and I in temperament."

"I'm the different one," Jean-Baptiste interpolated. His lips were curled in the slightly sarcastic expression that he had learned in France.

"Jean-Baptiste takes after my wife's family, in looks at least," the Sieur said quietly.

The conversation was interrupted when a hired man came to inform the Sieur he was wanted.

Antoine continued to study the portrait. He wanted to know more about the twin sister. "She is beautiful," he commented, but Jean-Baptiste did not appear inclined to be informative. "The womenfolk of your family all appear to have splendid looks," Antoine went on.

Jean-Baptiste jerked his head at the portrait of his Aunt Marguerite. "That one would be beautiful to me if she hadn't married an Englishman. As it is, I despise her. It makes me angry every time I look at her portrait."

It was with almost an angry gesture that he took an inlaid snuffbox from his vest and applied a pinch to his nostril. He offered it to Antoine, who refused, still absorbed with the picture and thinking of Jean-Baptiste's statement.

Madame de Courville-Boissart and Elise came into the room. Madame noticed the snuffbox in her son's hand and a faint smile crossed her features. The resemblance between mother and son was noticeable. Though they differed in coloring, the features were similar. Madame's dark eyes dominated her face as did Jean-Baptiste's, and were a contradiction to her sensitive mouth, which in her had a quality of charm, but in her son appeared a definite weakness. She linked her arm affectionately in her son's and his look of irritation faded.

Antoine turned to the ladies, addressing his remark to Madame. "I have been receiving introductions to your family through the portraits," he said.

"They are rather charming, aren't they?" she replied.

"Particularly the one of you, madame," Antoine commented gallantly.

Madame smiled and said, "Thank you. One seldom likes one's own portrait." Then she looked at Antoine a little anxiously. "I am afraid you are going to be surfeited with family. My husband's family is so large and all the aunts, uncles and cousins are eager to see Jean-Baptiste after his absence. So I have had to invite them all to dinner tomorrow. I thought it better to have them all at once than to prolong it over several days. I hope you won't mind?"

"Not at all. I shall be honored to be included," Antoine said reassuringly.

Elise giggled. "There are dozens and dozens of them."

Antoine turned to her. "Then perhaps you will help me sort them out, mademoiselle."

"Even then, you will find it dreadfully confusing."

Antoine looked from her to the portrait hanging above his head and then back again to her. The smile on Elise's face was so similar to that of the aunt in the portrait that the effect might have been studied.

"This lovely lady and you are very much alike," Antoine said and his voice was soft.

"Thank you, monsieur. She is my favorite aunt."

Antoine noted this statement with interest. Evidently all the family did not share Jean-Baptiste's antagonism.

CHAPTER III

ELISE HAD known whereof she spoke when she told Antoine that he would find the family confusing. They began to arrive about an hour before the time set for dinner and came in droves. It was snowing and there was much stamping of feet and shaking of coats as they entered the spacious hall.

Antoine stood by the fireplace in the drawing room talking to Elise who, as promised, remained by him to make the introductions and explanations. While mufflers, coats and heavy moccasins were being removed, Elise began:

"Cousin Pierre and his family just coming in. He has quite a good sized family as you can hear." All the children appeared to be talking at the same time, excited about the first fall of snow. "Pierre's is the oldest branch of the family," Elise went on. "His father was my father's eldest brother. He died about six years ago. Cousin Pierre now lives in the original farmhouse. Understand?"

Antoine smiled down at her. "So far." He was happy because of the opportunity to talk to Elise.

They all trooped into the drawing room. The man whom the Sieur introduced as, "My oldest nephew, Pierre Boissart," was tall and massively built. Antoine was surprised to find he looked only about twenty-five, yet was already the father of six children. His manner towards Antoine as they shook hands was appraising and he did not smile. His wife, Jeanne, was as broad as she was tall and, though not much over twenty, already appeared middle-aged. As she bobbed a curtsey to the guest, she looked scared and with a brief, "How do you do?" turned away to join her husband who was talking to Paul. The children clamored around Antoine and Jean-Baptiste, intrigued with their uniforms and asking rapid questions. Jean-Baptiste had assumed his grand manner, evidently to impress his relatives, and Antoine thought it seemed out of place. In fact, he was feeling very conspicuous in his elegant uniform among these homespun people. This increased as the other men arrived, all dressed in heavy linen shirts and woolen trousers.

Another large group with another brood of children came in. Elise returned to stand beside Antoine. She and her mother both wore light woolen dresses, yet they looked different from the rest. Perhaps it was the way they were made; maybe it was the air with which they wore them.

"Want some more history?" Elise asked and smiled sympathetically.

"Oh, yes please. I know I am going to get horribly confused."

"You will," she agreed and seemed amused. "Even we get confused. There are so many generations and branches of the family, and besides, many of them have the same names."

"*Mon Dieu!*" Antoine exclaimed, though under his breath so that it was hardly audible. "How do you ever know whom you are talking about?"

"We usually distinguish by, Cousin Pierre's Jeanne, or Uncle Etienne's Henri."

"I see. And which group is this?"

He looked towards where a dark man with only one arm was shepherding in several children, followed by a woman whom Antoine assumed was his wife.

"That's Uncle Etienne, father's brother. He lost his arm at the siege of Schenectady many years ago. Two of father's brothers were killed there. That's how father became the eldest of the family, although originally he came in the middle."

Uncle Etienne's attitude was more friendly than Pierre's, and he stood chatting with Antoine as though he were genuinely glad to meet him. He wanted to know whether he was merely visiting or intended to settle in Montreal, and extended a cordial invitation to visit them.

The children were romping around and getting into arguments with each other, so that it was almost impossible for the grownups to hear each other. The mothers would administer an occasional reproof and there would be a momentary subsiding but it soon began again. Over and above it all Antoine now heard a booming voice, just as André came hurrying over to him.

"That's Uncle Philip," he said. "You can always hear him before you see him. He's my favorite uncle and I want you to know him."

It seemed to Antoine that Uncle Philip burst into the room. He gave Jean-Baptiste a sound slap on the back by way of welcome and all his greetings were noisy. He belonged to the stocky group of the family, the tall members, as Antoine later learned, coming from the eldest branch. Uncle Philip's face was large, red and good-humored, with a pair of dark eyes that always appeared to be laughing. It was easy to see why André liked him, for they had the same infectious good humor. Like André, he wore the traditional garb of the *coureur de bois*. The hand he extended to Antoine was large and strong and his grip was not instantly forgotten. Even had André not said anything, Antoine would have liked him best.

"André's been telling me about you," Uncle Philip boomed. "Glad you're going to be with us. Have to take you hunting."

"I would like that," Antoine replied.

"Meet my woman," Uncle Philip turned and said. "Marie —this is Monsieur de Brievaux, Jean-Baptiste's guest."

A round, plump woman with a rosy face wreathed in smiles looked up at Antoine. Something in her jolly manner made Antoine give her a flourishing bow.

"Oh, dear," she exclaimed, "I forgot that we curtsey to the gentry." She grabbed her skirts at each side, descended to the floor and was unable to get up. Loud laughter greeted her in which she joined, so that she could not move, until Antoine took her hand and pulled her up.

"You young devil! What did you make me do that for? I'm too fat to be graceful."

"You are charming, madame," Antoine said and kissed her hand. Then he looked at her and they both burst into laughter.

"I believe you did it purposely to make a fool of me," she reproved him.

"I assure you, madame, I did not!" Antoine protested. "Your charm demanded it."

"Haw! You're a rascal, I can see. Just like this one here." She linked her arm in André's. "And I suppose you'll be trying to make him into a *coureur de bois*, André?"

"He's my brother's guest, Aunt Marie."

"Oh my goodness! Where is Jean-Baptiste? I haven't greeted him."

She looked around quickly and rather guiltily, then waddled off in search of her other nephew.

"She's wonderful!" André said, looking after her. "Always full of fun and always a friend."

"I can believe that."

"You must get to know them better. Some of the women don't quite approve of her. You should have been here one day when she shocked them all by saying she didn't care if her husband slept with Indian squaws while he was on his trips, as long as he didn't bring them home. And then, as though that wasn't enough, she added that it made him appreciate her all the more when he got her in bed."

Antoine joined in André's laughter. "They seem very good-natured," he said.

"Always. Even when things go wrong on the trips, Uncle Philip never gets out of temper."

"He's your father's brother, is that right?" Antoine asked, endeavoring to keep the relatives straight in his mind.

"That's right, his youngest brother. He's eight years younger than father and idolizes him. You see, father encouraged him to go into the woods as he had himself done years previously, because he considers there are too many of us to live off the land. The others don't really approve, because often we are away a year or even two. Father always looks after Uncle Philip's land while he's away."

"You must tell me more about this fur trading some time."

"I shall be glad to, monsieur."

"Shall we dispense with formalities? Won't you call me Antoine, since I'm going to be here all the winter—perhaps longer?"

André flashed him a frank smile.

There was a general movement towards the dining room and they followed. Antoine was relieved to find that the children were to have their dinner in the kitchen, which not only reduced the crowd but minimized the noise. He was placed on Madame's right, with Elise on his other side. They were seated at one long table which extended the full length of the room. With the arrival of further cousins and their children, Antoine lost all count of the family. Voices were hushed and heads bowed as the Sieur rose to say Grace and then the babble started again.

"When we all gather we make quite a colony of our own," Madame remarked.

"Indeed you do, madame," Antoine agreed. "And these are all your husband's relatives?"

"Not quite all. There's a married sister living in Three Rivers. . . ."

"The one of the portrait?" Antoine asked. He had been hoping to see her and had been disappointed.

"No, that's his twin sister, she lives near Albany. She married an Englishman."

"Oh, yes, Jean-Baptiste mentioned it."

"Jean-Baptiste doesn't approve. He's very anti-English for some reason."

"Aren't all Frenchmen?"

"Yes, mostly. But my husband feels that all Englishmen can't be bad, and that this continent is so vast that they and we could easily live peacefully without encroaching upon each other's territory. You see, his sister, Marguerite, married an Englishman because. . . ." She was interrupted by a servant placing a large earthenware crock of soup on the table. Madame looked over the crock and smiled. "I'll have to tell you the story some other time." She began ladling out the soup. "When we all dine together we serve family style," she said, and there was a faint note of apology in her voice.

Similar crocks of soup were placed at intervals down the table and every one helped themselves, excepting Antoine, whom Madame was now serving. He noticed that there seemed to be an abundance of menservants. Later, he learned that women servants were rare in Montreal, since women were in the minority and married at an early age and had homes of their own to look after.

With the removal of the soup, bottles of wine were placed all down the table. The wine was a red claret and both the women and the men drank freely. This, like the food, seemed to be abundant. One dish after another appeared, with a choice of boiled meats, roasts and fowl, followed by a variety of salads.

Antoine ate heartily and while they waited for the table to be cleared, remarked: "That was a sumptuous feast, madame."

"The past season was a plentiful one," she replied.

"Does all the food come from your own land?" he inquired.

"Oh yes. We have to be self-supporting. That is why we do not always fare so abundantly. If the crops are bad, we do not have enough to eat. There have been many lean years. I remember the first years when my husband brought me to Montreal. We had practically a famine then."

Antoine regarded his hostess with keen interest. "You have been here many years, madame?" he asked.

She smiled at him and there was pride in her smile. "Nearly twenty years," she answered.

"And you have not found it difficult?" he questioned.

Her eyes were steady as they met his. "Of course. Particularly at first. It needed much readjustment. But it is a readjustment worth making, I can assure you. Living here has so much more meaning, though perhaps you will not be able to understand that at first."

"Why do you say that?" he asked quietly.

"I was going to say because you are young, yet, I was about your age when I came here. Sometimes women can make adjustments more easily than men." She looked towards her husband at the far end of the table as she added: "But then I had a good reason for wanting to make such adjustments. I have a husband who is a very wonderful man."

Antoine had followed her eyes and when he turned back to look at her he nodded in agreement. "I agree with you. He has already made me feel very much at home."

"I am glad," she said, and again a bright smile lit her dark eyes. "We are a very happy family."

"And are none of these your relatives?" he asked.

Madame shook her head. "I have no relatives. I was an only child and my mother died soon after I was born. I was visiting Quebec with my father when I met my husband. Shortly after we were married, my father returned to France, where he died a few years later."

"You were born in France, madame?"

"In Paris. My father was the Chevalier de Luc."

Antoine raised his eyebrows slightly. "It is a well-known name, madame."

"Thank you," she said simply.

Antoine understood now the difference between Jean-Baptiste and André. There were evidently two distinct sides to the family.

He had thought the meal finished, but dishes of sweetmeats, nuts and fruits of all kinds were now passed.

"Try some of these walnuts," Elise suggested.

"Are these also grown here?" Antoine asked.

"And most of the fruit," she told him.

"And you don't have to import anything?"

"Oh yes! But not much food. All luxuries, articles of dress

and things of that kind have to be sent from France. We make these sort of things ourselves." She indicated her woolen dress.

"You do!" he exclaimed.

"We weave the material ourselves for such dresses as these, and for the men's shirts, and we spin the yarn for their homespuns."

Antoine looked his surprise.

"We do *now*," Madame took up the conversation. "At one time it all had to be sent back to France to be made into cloth, and then exported back here and sold at absurd prices. Fortunately, that ridiculous idea has been discontinued."

"Largely thanks to mother," Elise added.

"Nonsense, Elise," Madame said.

"It isn't nonsense. It was you who stirred up things so that the Governor did something about it, and it was *you* who encouraged the women to weave."

"Well, I was one of those who raised objections," Madame admitted. "It was so absurd when a colony had all the raw material here, to have to export it and then import it again made into cloth."

"It would seem so. I have been noticing the men's clothes. They look very comfortable. In fact, I feel rather conspicuous."

Elise wrinkled her nose. "I like uniforms," she said.

Antoine returned her smile. "Most ladies do. But if I remain here, I shall have to get some homespuns too."

"I'll make you some."

"Will you really?" he asked eagerly. "Is it a promise?"

She nodded her head.

The meal came to an end and the men lit their pipes. Looking down the table, Antoine was astonished to see many of the younger ones who could not have been more than twelve or thirteen, puffing away at pipes. The strong odor of homegrown tobacco soon filled the air and Antoine found it rather stifling. He was surprised that the women did not appear to mind or even notice it, no doubt because they had known it all their lives.

Uncle Philip started a rollicking song and immediately all joined in. His face was flushed with the wine he had consumed and all the food he had eaten, so that Antoine thought he looked as though he would burst.

André, singing lustily, came around the table, an extra pipe in his hand. "Want to try one, Antoine?" he asked, and his expression was mischievous. "Any man living here has to have his pipe, you know."

Antoine returned the friendly smile. "I'd like to, André. May I break it in later? Too many people to watch me now. I have never smoked. But I will. Give me time."

"Certainly. Keep the pipe and I'll give you a lesson later." He slapped Antoine on the shoulder and went away, singing at the top of his voice. Glancing down the table Antoine noticed that Jean-Baptiste was not smoking. In fact he was regarding it with distaste. Poor Jean-Baptiste, he wasn't going to find it easy to make those readjustments Madame had talked about.

Antoine turned to see Elise regarding him with interest. "These are the songs the *coureurs de bois* sing as they travel in their canoes," she told him.

"They are very jolly," he said.

"Yes. Our people love to sing." She appeared to know the songs well. Every verse had a chorus and soon he was able to catch the tune and hum it with her. It was not long before the children burst into the room and joined in with their voices.

The sun was sinking as goodbyes were said. It had ceased snowing and the rays of the winter sun cast a pink glow over the white world. Antoine looked out over the River with its waters slowing down after the race from the Lachine Rapids. The red glow was now reflected in the grey water, turning it to beauty. As he stood there, he thought how different this was from anything he had yet experienced. And with those thoughts came a feeling of inner contentment.

CHAPTER IV

THE FOLLOWING day as they rode into Montreal, Jean-Baptiste suddenly remarked: "I do hope you won't be too bored during the winter here, Antoine."

Antoine turned, looked at him interrogatively for a moment and then said: "Why should I be bored? I am finding it all extremely interesting."

Jean-Baptiste regarded his friend skeptically. "That's because it's all new and very different. But it's the difference that will begin to get boring after a little while."

"In what respect?"

"Well, for instance, family parties like we had to endure yesterday. I found it very trying. You have never been out of France. At least, I knew what to expect."

"What makes you think I enjoyed life in France? Frankly, I found yesterday a most interesting day. Your family. . . ."

"You always were more tolerant than I," Jean-Baptiste admitted. "Probably I take too much after my mother's family. I can imagine how *they* would have felt at such a gathering! I know mother was bored. . . ."

"She didn't appear to be."

"Mother wouldn't show it. She's too clever for that."

"I believe she mentioned she had been here twenty years," Antoine remarked drily.

"What if she has?"

Antoine did not directly answer the question. "The trouble with you, Jean-Baptiste, is that in two years you absorbed just enough of the atmosphere of the Mother Country to make you discontented. You weren't able to gain any understanding of values."

33

"By what right do you make such a remark?" Jean-Baptiste asked haughtily. "You talk as though you were a man of experience instead of being my own age." There was a deep flush on his face.

Antoine proceeded to placate him. "I meant no offense. Time will tell—maybe I shall find you are right."

There was a pause that neither attempted to fill. It had not snowed since the previous afternoon but had remained very cold, hardening the snow so that progress was not too difficult.

"I'm not so sure that we wouldn't have done better to stay in Quebec for the winter, and come on here in the spring," Jean-Baptiste remarked after a while, and Antoine knew that his thoughts were still following the same channel.

"What's the difference?" he asked.

Jean Baptiste's laugh was brittle. "You will soon find out! For one thing, the entertainment in Quebec is much finer and continues all through the winter. Here, except for a few balls at the Governor's chateau, and perhaps a few petits soupers there is nothing to compare with Quebec." Antoine made no comment. "And another thing," Jean-Baptiste went on, "there are no women here to compare with those in Quebec."

"So you said before. I don't agree."

"And what chance have you had to observe?" Jean-Baptiste asked curtly.

"Your own household."

"Sacré nom! You don't mean those you met yesterday?"

"I mean one of them. . . ."

"Which one?"

"Your sister Elise."

Jean-Baptiste looked at him with a half-surprised look but made no comment, and Antoine wished for none. Naturally, a brother would not see in a sister what he could see in Elise.

"I've never quite understood you, Antoine. You had everything in France and yet you deliberately chose to come to the colonies. Why?"

"To answer the first part of your question—what makes you think I had everything? I have no family and . . ."

"But you had entrée everywhere and I know could have made a rich marriage."

"To a woman twice my age!"

"What of it? She was wealthy and a *mariage de con-venance* is very satisfactory. You could have done as you pleased after you were married."

"That depends upon one's viewpoint about marriage. I prefer to wait and marry a girl I love."

Jean-Baptiste's lips curled slightly. "I'm afraid you are too romantic, my dear Antoine."

"Perhaps," Antoine agreed.

"Personally, I disagree with you entirely. The pretty young thing who appears romantic in the moonlight is seldom experienced, and I for one like experienced women."

"So I have observed," Antoine remarked drily.

"As a matter of fact I have always liked older women. They have poise and a zest for life; they bring an exhilaration one seldom finds in a young girl. *Parbleu!* It will be hard to find anybody interesting to amuse us this winter!" He yawned with practised boredom. Antoine did not answer. He was thinking just the opposite.

They were approaching the town, which rose with a gradual slope from the River towards Mont Real from which it derived its name.

"The great town of Montreal, Antoine!" Jean-Baptiste said rather derisively. "Gaze upon it and learn. Don't let any untoward enthusiasm at the sight of new things carry you away."

Antoine was gazing up at the mountain and ignoring Jean-Baptiste's sarcasms which he chose to consider merely banter.

"Have you ever been up that mountain?" he asked.

"*Sacré diable*, no! Why should I want to climb up there?"

"The view from the top would probably be interesting."

Jean-Baptiste shrugged his shoulders. "Except to make pilgrimages, I don't believe any one has since the day the cross was placed there. Anyway, you'd better concern yourself with what's below just now or you may get into trouble. The ground here is very uneven."

They were skirting Pointe Callières, where the former Governor's mansion stood and crossing the bridge over the Rivière St. Pierre. The town presented an artificial cleanliness from the whiteness of the snow that lay over everything. Dominating the scene were the steeples of the churches hovering protectingly over the houses clustered about them.

They turned their horses into the Rue St. Paul, where the gallows, pillory and jail in the Place d'Armes were a sinister reminder of the course of justice. This was soon forgotten, however, as they approached the Market Place, which, as it was market day was a scene of intense animation. The people were eager to procure the additional supplies brought in by the ship. To the din and commotion of those hawking their wares, were added the protesting voices of the livestock brought into the market that morning.

Progress was slow and at times completely at a standstill, so that Antoine had ample time to observe. He had to admit, to himself at least, that the crowd presented a motley appearance. All types and classes were jostling each other.

The Indians in their blankets, with heads shaven except for a single lock, attracted Antoine. Tales of the savagery of the red man were well-known in France. Yet these men wandering about the Market Place with a detached air as though they still wondered what they were doing there, looked harmless enough. Antoine asked Jean-Baptiste about them.

"They've been tamed. They're mostly Hurons who have been converted to the faith. Some may have been taken prisoner at some time, though most of those were burned."

"Burned! Not still?"

"Why not? They burn our people."

"Yes, but we're not savages. They don't know any better."

Jean-Baptiste smiled. "We don't burn many. There have been a few instances, but they were some years ago."

"Have there been any Indian attacks in your lifetime, or was that long ago?"

"We're never free from them, probably never will be. That's why father built the palisade around the seigneury. When he was young they were a constant menace. That's why the town hasn't grown. No sooner would the fields be ready to harvest, than all the men would have to leave to fight off the savages."

"What do these Indians here do?"

"Work in the fields or as servants, though I would never want one. The sight of their faces makes me squirm. I could never trust them. I wouldn't mind having a black servant though."

"You mean Negro?"

Jean-Baptiste nodded. "I've heard that in a place called Virginia, way below here, every one has black servants. Trouble here is they can't stand the climate and most of them die. And, too, father's against slavery, though I can't see why. Some day I'd like to go to Virginia. Only trouble is it's an English possession. Maybe we can get it from them."

Antoine's horse stumbled. "You'd better keep to the center of the road," Jean-Baptiste warned.

"I was trying to but the people seem to like it there too."

"Make them get out of the way."

The street was filthy underfoot. At the sides, refuse was piled high, where it had been thrown from the windows, and as there was no drainage it collected until it rotted away. Now it lay hidden under a white coating of snow which gave an almost picturesque aspect to its sordidness. Underfoot the snow was now black slush in which the feet of their horses slithered.

"We'll stop first at Dillon's and then go to the Chateau to pay our respects," Jean-Baptiste said.

They had almost crossed the Market Place when they heard a shout and saw André standing up on a cart unloading produce.

Gaston was standing beside the cart and it surprised Antoine to see him laughing. As they approached, the smile faded and was replaced by the sullen expression which Antoine had seen the day before and again that morning, when he had brought their horses.

"You look busy," Antoine said. "Want some help?" Gaston shot him a quick, doubtful look.

"Thanks, no." André looked pleased at the offer. "Gaston and I have practically finished."

Antoine looked about and was puzzled. "Are you buying produce?" he asked. "I understood from Madame yesterday that you grew it all."

"We do. And we sell the surplus," André replied.

"Oh, then some people don't grow their own?" He looked around at the sacks of potatoes, beans and fruit piled high upon wooden benches, while others were loaded with chickens and various kinds of meat.

"The townspeople have to eat too," André explained.

"Oh, yes; of course." Antoine laughed at his own stupidity.

"And also many of the farmers don't grow enough to last them all the winter," André continued. "We are fortunate in having good land that produces more than we need. So we bring the surplus here on Tuesdays and Fridays and exchange it for commodities we need. In a few weeks all this will be over." He waved his hand towards the market. "All surplus will have been disposed of and storehouses filled for the winter."

Antoine nodded with interest. Jean-Baptiste tapped his horse and began to move off. "We're going to Dillon's," he said.

"I'll join you there in a little while," André told them as Antoine followed Jean-Baptiste. As he did so, the thought crossed his mind that Jean-Baptiste had made no suggestion of helping his brother. Evidently, André did not expect it.

Dillon's was the most popular tavern in town and it was crowded to the doors so that they had to elbow their way inside. The air was thick with the odor of brandy and beer, to which were added the fumes of *tabac canadien*. Antoine could hardly see through the haze. As he followed Jean-Baptiste he choked on the smoke, thereby marking himself as a newcomer.

They found places at a table against the wall, and Jean-Baptiste immediately called for a bottle of brandy.

"I think I will take beer," Antoine said.

Jean-Baptiste looked rather disdainful as he said: "It's spruce beer."

"I'd like to try it."

Antoine's curiosity about Gaston was aroused and he asked Jean-Baptiste about him.

"He is a strange fellow, I agree. He's my father's bondsman."

"Oh, a bondsman!"

"Yes. There are quite a number here. Salt smuggling was the crime, I believe."

"Is that so?"

"André knows more about him than I do. Gaston seems more morose than ever. He and I used to get along but he hardly speaks to me now. I can guess why." Antoine looked at him for further explanation. Jean-Baptiste took a sip of his brandy. "He hates the noblesse—*aristocrats* as he calls them."

"Oh." Light began to dawn upon Antoine as to why Gaston had seemed so resentful towards him. Shortly after, André came in with Gaston, who elbowed his way to the counter, while André joined them. He gave them a hearty greeting and shouted for beer.

"You drinking beer too," he said approvingly to Antoine. "How do you like our variety?"

"Very good. Rather strong."

"It probably does take getting used to." André took off his knitted cap and ran his hand through his thick hair.

"Had a busy morning?" Antoine asked.

"Oh no, nothing much."

"What's the matter with Gaston?" Jean-Baptiste asked, his tone abrupt.

"Gaston? Is something wrong?" André asked evasively.

"He's not said a word to me except to grunt. Antoine noticed it too."

"Oh, well, I'm a stranger," Antoine said quickly and with a little embarrassment.

André quaffed his beer, wiping his mouth with the back of his hand, to Jean-Baptiste's disgust. "Gaston's all right. You have to get to know him. At one time he was badly treated by what he calls the 'gentry' and he has retained an antipathy towards them. He thinks you have turned aristocrat." He turned to Jean-Baptiste and gave him a playful nudge. "That's probably why he hasn't spoken to you."

"But undoubtedly has spoken to you about it," Jean-Baptiste said with undisguised annoyance.

André smiled broadly. His was the kind of face that wanted to smile all the time and took every opportunity to do so, whereas Jean-Baptiste, even when he did smile, appeared to have to make an effort.

"Frankly, yes," André admitted. "But he'll get over it. He'll realize that you are the same even if you are wearing different clothes."

"And are we supposed to arrange our dress and manners to please a servant?" Jean-Baptiste exclaimed.

"He's not an ordinary servant. In fact, he probably has better blood than we." André turned to explain to Antoine. "Father thinks a great deal of him. So do all of us. It is one of those cases you must have heard about. Probably there are plenty who are guilty of salt smuggling, but according to Gaston, many are sent out of the country on a false pretext. It seems that a half-brother wanted him out of the way. Gaston swears he had nothing to do with any smuggling. Anyway, he was implicated in some way and was sent here as a bondsman. I think it was supposed to be for twelve years. He's been a wonderful help to father. We have always idolized him, especially Elise. I believe he would die for her."

Another thought crossed Antoine's mind. Had his attention to Elise at the wharf caused the angry look on Gaston's face?

"He taught us everything," André was saying. "As children we did nothing without Gaston, did we, Jean-Baptiste?"

"No," Jean-Baptiste admitted reluctantly. "But it was different when we were children. I'm afraid he's going to get very arrogant if he's freed."

"Nonsense."

"What's he going to do? Go back and kill all the aristocrats in France?" Jean-Baptiste asked contemptuously.

"Oh, no. He's dropped that idea." André laughed. "He used to be so resentful when he first came here because of what had happened to him that he could think of nothing but revenge. I think Elise was largely responsible for changing that idea."

Elise evidently has a great influence over the man, Antoine thought. "He's a Breton, isn't he?" he asked.

"Yes. We know little about his actual family except that they weren't peasants. His name is Gaston Renault. Ever hear of the family?"

"No, but then I don't know many Bretons."

They discussed Gaston for a while, André's enthusiasm still unshared by Jean-Baptiste. When André drew out his pipe, Antoine did likewise, receiving a broad smile from André.

"How is it going?" he inquired.

"Not too bad. I can only smoke a little at a time as yet. This tobacco seems very strong."

"It is. If you like I'll crush a little cherry bark into it to make it weaker. That's what the boys do. You won't mind being a boy to start with?"

Antoine laughed. "Not at all. It surprised me yesterday to see them smoking so young."

"Oh, yes. That's the ambition of all of us. I began smoking when I was twelve. We feel we've grown up then. Jean-Baptiste used to smoke. Don't you any more?"

"No. I prefer snuff." He suited the action to the words and took out his snuffbox, putting a great deal of elegance into the gesture. André made no comment. He held no resentment towards his brother for these differences. They always had been different and André's attitude was that each had the right to please himself.

He finished his beer and rose to leave. "We'll meet later," he said and made his way towards the door, calling to Gaston and greeting many friends on the way.

Antoine watched him. "Your brother has a very hearty personality," he remarked.

"He's trying to make a good impression on you and to show me how he's grown up," Jean-Baptiste said languidly.

"How old is he?"

"Eighteen."

"He seems older."

Jean-Baptiste shrugged his shoulders. A few minutes later Claude de Ramezay made his way towards them. On the journey from France they had been together all the time and had become friends. He greeted them and accepted Jean-Baptiste's invitation to join them.

"How are you liking Montreal?" he asked Antoine politely.

"Very much. There is so much of interest."

"Really?" Claude's expression was similar to that which was often on Jean-Baptiste's face. "I'm rather surprised to hear you say that."

"Everything's new at present," Jean-Baptiste remarked.

"Naturally," Claude agreed. Antoine did not feel called upon to say anything further. He had never shared Jean-Baptiste's enthusiasm over Ensign de Ramezay.

"We were on our way to report to 'your father," Jean-Baptiste said.

"Today?" Claude looked rather concerned. "He's deep in conferences with the Intendant and Council."

"We were merely going to report."

"Oh, that can wait. Nothing will happen at this time of year. And if it does, father knows you are here. Anyway you'll be seeing him in a few days. There's going to be an official reception."

"Good. It won't take many days for me to be thoroughly bored here."

"Oh, come now, Jean-Baptiste! This is your home. You shouldn't feel that way," Claude chided him.

"Find me an interesting woman and I won't."

"I shall have to see what I can do. You should have a choice at the reception."

"You think so?" Jean-Baptiste said skeptically.

"We'll hope so anyway. And by the way, what a beautiful woman Elise has grown to be. I was much impressed."

He turned to Antoine. "We were all children together and it's astonishing the difference these few years have made. Elise used to be a chubby girl with freckles and no indication that she would ever grow up to be a beauty." He turned to Jean-Baptiste, "I shall have to turn some attention in that direction."

Antoine felt a twinge of jealousy. On the way home, Jean-Baptiste took him past the beautiful Chateau that was the home of Governor de Ramezay, and Antoine felt despondent. What chance had he, an unknown and homeless man, against this heir of a famous family?

They climbed the sloping, uneven streets to the more fashionable residential districts where Jean-Baptiste pointed out the impressive homes of a few of the prominent residents. Away from the business section and along the Rue Notre Dame, the appearance of the town improved, though Antoine was surprised how little it had developed.

He was thoughtful on the way home, though it was not through any contemplation of the town's disadvantages.

CHAPTER V

THE SIEUR and his wife were sitting in the small library discussing their family and their guest. By force of habit rather than by any definite arrangement, this room had come to be regarded as theirs of an evening while the children used the large room. This brief hour before going to bed was the time Paul and Ann looked forward to each day, and during the busy season was often all they saw of each other, except at meals. It was a habit they had formed early in their married life, when the children were babies and had been put to bed, and as they had grown up, the habit had continued.

Their chairs were drawn comfortably before the fire and while Ann stitched on her embroidery, Paul, with his legs stretched before him, contemplated the flickering blaze and smoked his pipe. He looked tired, for there were many details yet to be attended to on the seigneury before winter closed in. It had been a busy day for both of them, for tomorrow was St. Martin's Day when all the habitants came to pay their dues. Custom demanded that breakfast be served to all and Ann and Elise had been in the kitchen practically all day, superintending the preparations.

Paul looked at his wife and thought, as he often did, that the years had dealt kindly with her. Except that she was heavier and her black hair peppered with grey, she had, in his opinion, grown more beautiful. Hers was not so much beauty of feature as of expression, for analysis would have shown that her mouth was too large and her nose nondescript. Her whole face was dominated by her large, black eyes, which revealed her strong character and contradicted the sensitive mouth. They were both nearing forty and because life had not been easy in the early years of their marriage, they looked their age.

Paul turned back to the fire and then taking his pipe from his mouth, spoke his thoughts. "Do you think Jean-Baptiste has changed?" he asked.

Ann put in several stitches before answering. She had been expecting this question ever since the day their son had returned. "Yes," she said guardedly, "in some ways. It was to be expected."

"Yes," her husband agreed, and there was silence for a few minutes. "Nevertheless," he then went on, looking into the fire as though he expected the answer there, "he hasn't even been over the seigneury, let alone made any offer to help with the work. From his attitude you would think he wasn't part of it. He might be a guest in the house. In fact his guest takes far more interest."

"Yes, he does, doesn't he," Ann agreed. Because she realized Paul was right about Jean-Baptiste she tried to steer the conversation into another channel. She had always understood this firstborn child of hers better than her husband had, and there was a sympathy with Jean-Baptiste's attitude that she would not for anything have let her husband know. "Antoine seems a remarkably nice young man," she commented.

"Remarkably is right. He's not in the least the type of young man I had expected Jean-Baptiste to make friends with. They are so different."

"Perhaps that's why they became friends."

"I can't quite see that. But perhaps it's so." He leaned forward, pushed a brand into the fire and relit his pipe. Ann made no comment. But Paul was not to be distracted from his thoughts about his son. He had been annoyed for days and wanted to get it clear in his mind. "I am rather inclined to remind Jean-Baptiste that it's the seigneury that supports him." His voice hardened with anger. "He acts as though he were a gentleman of means and beneath soiling his hands. It's not going to continue this way."

Ann laid her needlework in her lap. She knew this husband of hers too well not to realize that if something were rankling it was best to let him talk it out. Otherwise, it would lead to an explosion at the wrong time, for his temper was as fiery as his hair had once been.

"By the time winter is over, Paul, he will have settled down. You must remember he has been a gentleman of leisure for two years. . . ."

"Which I am beginning to think was a mistake. . . ."

"I don't believe so," she said quietly. "We can't expect him to readjust himself in a few days. Besides, I don't believe Jean-Baptiste will ever take much interest in the seigneury. He's much more suited to the army."

"Well, I hope this supercilious manner is not going to continue."

Ann laughed. Instead of annoying her, Jean-Baptiste's manner had amused her. "It will pass, Paul, I am sure. He's trying to show us how grown-up he is."

Paul gave a sound that resembled a snort. "I never have understood him as you have." He blew out clouds of smoke, and through them Ann heard him say, "He is so different from the twins. They are much more stable."

"So were we by that time," Ann said softly.

"What do you mean?"

"During the time I was carrying Jean-Baptiste, I was adjusting myself to a new life. I was unsettled, and so were you. Jean-Baptiste reflects that unsettled condition that was then part of us."

Paul put down his pipe and leaned towards the fire. His eyes were deeply thoughtful as he said: "I had never thought of that."

"Those were famine years and you had to go to war. All those things made me restless and unsure."

"No doubt you're right," Paul conceded but he appeared uncertain. "Yes, even admitting this prenatal influence . . ."

"Which many people do not."

"Eh?"

"I say many people do not admit that circumstances prior to birth do influence the child, but I do. I think we have very definite examples in the difference in our children. Jean-Baptiste would like to be like André."

Paul wrinkled his forehead and looked perplexed. "What makes you say that?"

"I have often watched him. I believe he would give anything to have the freedom of nature that André has. He would often like to join in and do the things his brother does."

"They why doesn't he?" Paul said roughly.

"Because he's not sure of himself. He is so sensitive. He's afraid he won't do a thing well and so doesn't do it at all, because with his nature he has to excel in everything he does."

Paul looked doubtful and from his expression showed that he thought his wife was making excuses. "How can you know that it is so?" he asked.

"Mother instinct, perhaps."

"Or mother love wanting to see it that way?"

"No. That's not so. I know you think I have always favored Jean-Baptiste, and to some extent I have. But only because the other two don't need the same protection. . . ."

"Protection!" Paul now looked annoyed. "Are you suggesting we make a pampered fool of him?"

"You don't quite understand, Paul. I'm not talking of physical protection. Jean-Baptiste can take care of himself as well as the others. But sensitive natures suffer so much more. If you could get Jean-Baptiste to admit it, you would find that André is practically his ideal. He would like to be like him; to be able to get rid of that fear of what people think, but he can't and because he can't, he covers it in the way all people do who aren't sure of themselves—he bluffs. He puts on this air of superiority as a protection." Paul still looked skeptical. "You can't understand it, Paul, because your nature is like André's."

"No, I can't understand it. Whenever I have seen him

watching André it has been with an expression of disdain or superiority."

"On his mouth, perhaps, but not in his eyes."

Paul smoked in silence, wondering whether it could be that Ann liked Jean-Baptiste the way he was. Could it be that this son brought a touch of the world in which she had formerly lived? Could it be that she liked having some one around with courtly manners and fine clothes, instead of the roughness of homespuns? Perhaps she was trying to combine the two worlds she had known. Yet those thoughts did not seem quite fair to her. She had adjusted herself so admirably to this new life since her marriage. She had deftly helped him to rise from an ordinary farmer to a seigneur, and in such a manner that no one had ever accused him of being an upstart. With the simplicity of their home she had combined a certain elegance, being as natural at family dinners, as she was when they entertained the noblesse and used fine linens and dainty appointments.

"Why can't Jean-Baptiste adjust himself as you have?" he asked, following his thoughts.

"He will eventually. He is now only the age I was when I came here. . . ."

"But he has lived here all his life and you had not," Paul said impatiently. "Yours needed the greater adjustment."

Ann leaned towards her husband. "Look, Paul. Suppose when you asked me to marry you, I had agreed but on condition that you left Montreal and came to France. . . ."

"I would have done so because I loved you."

"Yes, I know you would, but would you have been able to adjust yourself to that life?"

"Not at first perhaps, but eventually—with your help."

"But wouldn't you, perhaps, have had the same contemptuous expression on your face because you didn't agree with the way people behaved there?"

"That isn't the same, Ann."

"No, it's the reverse."

"But why should Jean-Baptiste have a contempt for the life here?"

"He doesn't. He's trying to adjust himself to two worlds and he can't yet make up his mind which is the better." Paul's silence was disapproval. "It's up to us, Paul, to help him make these adjustments, and he can't do it when he feels you disapprove of him all the time."

"Did he say that?"

"Not in so many words. But before he went to France you remember how restless he was?"

"Yes, and he persuaded you to ask me to let him go to France and now it has made matters worse."

"Your disapproval antagonizes him."

"Mon Dieu! What am I supposed to do? Don't you think he might show me a little consideration? Don't you think that it would at least have been a filial gesture if he had walked over the seigneury with me to see the changes that have been made?"

"Perhaps he would have, had not your first words to him been reproof."

"When?"

"The moment they arrived and were looking at the portraits."

"What did I say?"

"You accused him of despising his home."

"I did not! He was telling Antoine he'd soon get bored and it annoyed me. What did he do, run and tell you about it immediately?"

"Don't let us get angry, Paul," Ann said quietly.

"I'm sorry."

"There's one thing I have never been able to make you understand. Jean-Baptiste seldom discusses things with me; I sense them. When things hurt him he keeps them to himself and talks about them to nobody. I overheard your remarks to him. That's how I knew what you had said."

"And you think that's the reason he hasn't shown any interest in the farm?" Paul asked, a little contritely.

"I think it's probable. If you would try to understand him a little more, he would respond, I'm sure. If you had made some remark about it all seeming very different from what he had known the last two years, or perhaps said you would like him to see the changes you had made or even have asked him for suggestions, he would have felt you weren't antagonistic to him."

"I see. Perhaps I have been rather offhanded."

"Try to understand the difference between the two boys. André is one of those naturally thoughtful boys who always manage to be pleasing. I have no doubt that often Jean-Baptiste is saying to himself, 'If only I'd thought of that.' But he didn't, so he covers up by pretending he doesn't care. I'm only guessing now, but I'm fairly sure I am right."

Paul stretched out a hand towards her. She took it and then slipped over beside him, laying her head against his shoulder. "You're wonderful, Ann. You do understand us all so perfectly. I am so clumsy. You've made me see things differently. I will try to be kinder to Jean-Baptiste."

Ann smiled up at him and then laid her lips against his. She felt him relax, and as she stroked back his hair and looked into his kind eyes, she was happy. She settled herself against his knees, the firelight playing upon her features.

"Antoine will be a good influence upon Jean-Baptiste," she remarked. "In a way he is a combination of our two boys, in type I mean."

"Do you think he means to settle here?"

"I wouldn't be at all surprised. I think he has already found an interest."

"What do you mean?"

"Elise." She turned and smiled at him.

Paul looked surprised. "Is that so?"

"Oh, yes! He can't take his eyes away from her when she is in the room."

"Is she interested?"

"It's too early to say."

"She hasn't mentioned it?"

"Not a word."

"Hm." Paul was thoughtful.

"It would be rather nice," Ann mused pensively.

Paul gave her a quick smile. "Are you turning matchmaker?"

"Well—maybe," she answered with a half smile. "It is time Elise was married. She's growing up and is very restless."

"Do you know anything about the young man? It's strange, but he appears familiar to me. Several times when I have been talking to him he has reminded me of some one and I can't think who. Of course, that is not unusual. But I was wondering whether we met any of the de Brievaux family when we were in France."

"No, not that I remember. I have never heard of the family. He'll probably mention it sometime. Jean-Baptiste did say in one of his letters that both Antoine's parents were dead and he was alone in the world."

"Well, it's not important. He seems a fine young man, with a pleasant personality. Strong face, too." He stifled a yawn.

"You had better get to bed, dear. You have a heavy day tomorrow," Ann urged.

"Yes," he said. But instead of getting up he lowered his head and kissed her. With a tired sigh he relaxed. "You're so lovely, Ann. I'm glad the winter's here. I shall have more time to love you." She held him tight against her, loving the feel of his lips and glad their love had never dwindled to the commonplace.

CHAPTER VI

THE FOLLOWING morning Antoine was awakened early by the din of farmyard noises and the babble of voices beneath his window. At first, with the sleepiness that held his mind in abeyance, he thought something must have gone wrong, for it sounded as though all the animals had escaped from the barns. But as his mind began to function, he remembered the extensive preparations of the day before and Elise's explanation that every November 11th, St. Martin's Day, the habitants of the seigneury came to pay their annual dues—*cens et rentes* as they were called—to the seigneur. It was the great neighborhood day of the year, and on every seigneury throughout the colony, the same scene would be taking place. It was the day that marked the official start of winter, when all animals were in from the pastures and labor in the fields had ceased. After the habitants had paid their dues they would remain to partake of the seigneur's hospitality and gossip with their neighbors, making plans for visiting and entertaining during the long winter months.

Antoine sprang out of bed and went to the window. The strange scene below brought a smile to his face. Men and women, bundled in heavy blanket coats, stood in groups chatting vociferously, while scores of children ran from group to group playing with each other, or tormenting the animals. The grownups for the most part seemed oblivious to the squawking of chickens tied together by the legs or the grunting of pigs huddled together. Baskets of eggs and bundles of wheat were laid about carelessly, until it was the owner's turn to present them as full or part payment of his dues. The whole yard resembled a scene at a fair.

The scene fascinated Antoine and added to the interest which had been growing daily since his arrival. Each day he had found things to interest him and had spent more time with André than with Jean-Baptiste. In fact, at the moment, Jean-Baptiste was annoyed with him. Yesterday, he had invited him to go into Montreal for some amorous diversion but Antoine had declined. Jean-Baptiste had left in a bad humor without him.

He hurried into his clothes, anxious not to miss anything. Elise had kept her promise and had provided him with a woolen shirt and trousers and a pair of moccasins. He put them on for the first time now and felt rather strange but comfortable. Downstairs he found the house deserted, but a babble of voices down the end of a long hall directed him to the seigneur's office. The small room was full of people and a haze of the odoriferous *tabac canadien* hung over all. Antoine stood for a moment by the door, wondering whether he ought to intrude. He could not see any of the members of the family, until a man blocking the doorway moved aside and through the haze he saw 'Monsieur Paul,' as the habitants called the Sieur, seated at a table with André beside him. In front of André was a large ledger in which he was making entries as his father gave him the particulars. Jean-Baptiste was not there, and Antoine doubted whether he was up, for it was still very early. At the door opposite leading into the yard, he saw the burly frame of Gaston, who called out the name of each habitant in turn.

The Sieur glanced towards the door, looked away and then as a broad smile crossed his face, he beckoned to Antoine. "Come on in, Antoine. For the moment I didn't recognize you out of uniform."

André greeted him with a grin. "Now you look like the rest of us, Antoine!" he remarked approvingly.

"Would you like to watch this for a bit?" the Sieur asked. "It's quite an interesting event."

"I certainly would!" Antoine said eagerly.

André started to get up and make room, but Antoine held him down by the shoulder. "Don't move, please. I'll stand here behind you."

"The room's a bit small," the Sieur commented. Then he started to explain the system. "Most of the habitants pay their dues in produce. We have scarcely any money in circulation here. A pig's worth so much, a capon so much, a bushel of wheat or a basket of eggs—each have their value and the amount is calculated according to the number of arpents of land a man owns."

"You mean all pigs and all capons are the same value? What about size or weight?"

"They're all the same. For instance, live capons are valued at twenty sous each. . . ."

"Twenty sous!" Antoine exclaimed.

Paul smiled. "Not much, is it? A seigneur does not get rich on his *cens et rentes,* I can assure you."

"I should think not. How much does an average man pay then?"

"Well, we'll show you. Watch as they come up."

The Sieur shook hands warmly with each habitant as he came to the table and introduced him to Antoine. André knew them all and chatted and bantered with each one. No one seemed to be in any hurry and there was a leisurely aspect about it all, as they talked with the man about his family and his farm. André, in the meantime, turned the ledger to the name of the habitant, and even though the man had probably owned the same amount of land for many years and had been going through this ritual each St. Martin's Day, nevertheless the same procedure was repeated.

"Monsieur Hébard, you have one hundred and fifty arpents. Is that correct?" André asked formally.

"Quite correct, monsieur," the man replied.

André turned to Antoine. "We figure at the rate of one sou per arpent," he explained. Antoine nodded, still further astonished at this infinitesimal figure.

"That will be one hundred fifty sous, Monsieur Hébard," the Sieur remarked. "How are you paying it?"

"Six capons, half a bushel of wheat and three dozen eggs, if that is agreeable, Monsieur Paul?"

"Quite agreeable, monsieur," the Sieur replied. Antoine watched André enter the items against the man's account. The Sieur was shaking hands. "Thank you, Monsieur Hébard. My compliments to your family and a peaceful winter to you."

This procedure was patiently followed with each habitant. Gaston checked off the live stock and produce as André called the items out to him.

"What do you do with it all?" Antoine asked, rather alarmed. It seemed to him that half the stock of the farms on the seigneury must now be quartered in the seigneur's yard.

"Oh, we manage," André said and laughed. "When this is all over, we have to calculate the total and see that it is stored away safely for the winter. Much of it will go to market."

"Oh. And then you get cash for it?" Antoine asked.

"In a way. We rarely use money. Some will be exchanged for other commodities. The rest will be paid in bills of exchange which we use as we need them. If we want things from the Mother Country, then we convert the bills of exchange into bills on France."

"I have a lot to learn, I can see," Antoine remarked.

"It's all very simple really."

The stuffiness of the room and the heaviness of the smoke made Antoine drowsy. Also, he was very much in need of his breakfast but did not like to say so. After he had watched for some time, he told André he would go outside for a moment or so.

"I'll come with you and we'll get some breakfast," André said. "Father will excuse us."

"Certainly, go along. I will join you presently."

André brought some coats and helped Antoine into one, after he had wound a heavy muffler around his neck. "You'd better bundle up well. You're not accustomed to our cold yet. Here, put this on too." He gave him a red knitted woolen cap. Antoine laughed as he looked at it, then pulled it down over his ears with the tassel hanging over one side.

The cold air struck his cheeks and nose, and his breath as it left his mouth looked like smoke. He and André were greeted vociferously by Uncle Philip, waving a flagon of the Sieur's brandy, which was circulating freely among the habitants.

"Have some," Uncle Philip said and thrust the brandy towards André, who took a swig and passed it to Antoine.

"I'd rather have some coffee, if you don't mind," Antoine said half-apologetically.

"Mind? Of course we don't. All the more for us." He held the bottle to his mouth and then smacked his lips as Aunt Marie came bustling up.

"Philip, you'll be intoxicated," she reprimanded.

"I! You've never seen me intoxicated."

"Seldom seen you sober, you mean," she teased.

"That is a lie!" he protested.

"Not during the winter, it isn't."

"Well, what's a man going to do with his idle time during the long months?"

"I'll find plenty for you to do!" she retorted. Then she recognized Antoine, whom at first she had not known because of his different clothes. "Well, if it isn't our gallant lieutenant dressed like a farmer!"

"I was wondering if you were going to ignore me," he said and raised his hand to sweep off the three-cornered hat that wasn't there.

Aunt Marie grabbed his arm. "Now don't you go trying to make me curtsey again, you rascal. If I get down in this snow, I'll have to stay there and catch my death of cold."

"Oh, come now, I wouldn't do that! Perhaps this way would be better." He gave her a resounding kiss on her red cheek. She slapped his face but it was only a light tap and then by way of contradiction said, "That was rather nice. Kiss the other cheek." Antoine readily complied.

"Are you two going to carry on this way all the morning?" André laughed. "I'm hungry and want my breakfast."

"So do I," Antoine agreed heartily. "Have you had yours, Aunt Marie?"

"Listen to the boy! I had breakfast hours before you were up."

"Then you need another one," Antoine said and linked his arm in hers, but she did not move.

"I'm fat enough without two breakfasts! Besides, I have just come from the kitchen."

"You left before giving me my breakfast! Now I *am* hurt. Such neglect," Antoine bantered.

"There's a good-looking redheaded girl waiting to give you your breakfast," she replied.

"She is! Ha! That makes me even hungrier. But don't forget I love you, darling." He encircled her waist and turned her round, giving her another loud kiss, and before she could hit back at him, he was running after André.

The huge kitchen was warm and inviting with its smell of freshly baked bread and steaming coffee. Long tables had been put up the day before and were laden with food and flagons of wine and brandy. Men and women were seated all around, eating heartily. At other tables the children were eating, shouting and wrangling.

Madame de Courville-Boissart enveloped in a large apron was superintending the dispensing of the food. Antoine's eyes roamed quickly around the room until he found Elise. She was carrying a huge platter of hot bread, and Antoine hurried over to assist her. As he took hold of the platter, his hands touched hers and it made his pulse quicken. She peeped round the stack of bread, a surprised look on her face.

"Oh, Antoine, good morning," she greeted him and smiled. For a moment they stood holding the platter between them.

"Good morning, mademoiselle," he said and tried to hold her gaze.

"How nice you look. I like you in those clothes," she said.

"Then I shall always wear them!" he replied.

She laughed, pleased. "But you'd better take off your coat. It's warm in here."

"I will when you have told me where to put this." He lifted the platter from her hands and stood with it poised above his head rather precariously.

"Be careful!" she exclaimed. "If you drop that I'll . . ." She stopped, not knowing what she had meant to say.

"You'll what?" he grinned and his dancing eyes met hers. He held her glance for a moment and then she lowered her eyes.

"You'd better put it down on the table," she said and hurried away to fetch another platter. He laid it down quickly and hurried after her, attempting to take the next one from her.

"Take another," she said. Her tone was quick and he wondered whether he had annoyed her by his behavior. He picked up another and followed her.

"Where shall I put it?" he asked as he passed her.

"On any table that doesn't have one."

They met again at the table and he did not attempt to touch her platter but picked up another. When he returned again, she flashed him a smile, and he was happy.

"Go and have your breakfast, Antoine. You must be starving," she said. At the same moment André shouted to him.

"One moment," Antoine called to him and picked up the last platter.

"Thank you so much," Elise said. "Now come and I will get your breakfast. You have earned it."

Antoine had never eaten more heartily, nor had food ever tasted so good. Even while he chatted with André and the others at the table, he was thinking of Elise and wondering when he would be able to tell her he had fallen in love with her. He did not want to be precipitous but just to give her a hint before Claude de Ramezay got the advantage.

After breakfast he and André stood on the steps and smoked their pipes. From where they stood they had a full view of the seigneury. The previous night it had snowed heavily and now everything was swathed in its winter covering. It all looked very neat and picturesque. Around each farmhouse the trees had been cleared, for they were considered too great a menace, since every tree was a hiding place. Each farm had its barns and outside bake ovens, the latter now deserted and buried in snow. The wooden palisades had all assumed snowy-white conical hats perched on the top of each post. Beyond stretched the primeval wilderness hushed with its own secrets.

"What are those towers at the corners?" Antoine asked.

"Watch towers. When Indian warfare was at its height we had to keep watchers there all the time."

"And that's not necessary now?"

"Only at times. If we get word that the Indians are on the warpath, then we station men in each tower. We never know when they may break out again. The red man has no love for the white man, and you really can't blame him. We came in and took his land and spoiled his hunting. The beaver was his special prerogative."

"And it's the beaver in which you trade?"

"Mainly. Also fox, marten, lynx and otter, but beaver has the finest fur and is most plentiful. Before the white man came the Indian had a monopoly on the market."

"But you've widened his markets, haven't you?"

"Considerably."

"And introduced better modes of living . . . ?"

"That's debatable." André smiled. "We've brought them improvements such as metal cooking utensils in place of their old-fashioned ones of stone or wood; we've given them steel for hatchets and taught them to use guns instead of bows and arrows, but we've also given them a taste for firewater, and that's the worst menace. The red man can't drink much, and when he's drunk he goes on the warpath and that starts the trouble."

"I thought there was a law prohibiting the sale of liquor to them?"

André smiled wryly. *"Coureurs de bois* are accused of breaking most laws! But in this instance what are we to do? If we don't trade them brandy then they take their furs to the English market and trade them for rum. No brandy, no fur trade."

"I see. And these Indians are Iroquois?"

"No. They trade mostly with the English. We trade chiefly with the Hurons and Ottawas, habitual enemies of the Iroquois."

Antoine looked puzzled. "I'm very ignorant. I'd always thought that all red men were friendly with each other and merely antagonistic to the white man."

"Oh, no! The enmity between different tribes is what has been our chief trouble. The Iroquois are the most warlike and have subdued many of the others, especially our friends the Hurons."

"Hm. And where do you go to do this trading?"

"Well, there are various routes. The converging point is Michilimackinac, where there is a large fort."

"And where is that?"

"On the northern tip of Lac Huron."

Antoine was gazing out over the St. Lawrence. "And does this River run into Lac Huron?"

André shook his head. "No. The St. Lawrence starts at Lac Ontario where Fort Frontenac is." Antoine looked puzzled again. "I'll try to explain. You sailed from France to Quebec and then from there to here. You came against the River current. That is, it begins at Lac Ontario, flows over several rapids past here and on to Quebec and out to sea by way of the Gulf of St. Lawrence. Understand?"

"Yes. I understand that. But going west—does it meet another ocean there? What I'm trying to get at is this. I crossed from France by way of the Atlantic Ocean. If we continued on down this River would we meet the Atlantic Ocean again on the other side?"

André smiled. "That, my friend, is what explorers are trying to find out. They say if you continue far enough west, you come to China, but so far no one has determined it."

"Then this land must continue quite a distance farther west? It makes me very curious."

"It does me too. I would like to be an explorer." André's expression was wistful.

"And you have travelled as far as this Lac Ontario?"

"No. We don't go in that direction."

"You don't!"

"No, we follow the St. Lawrence until it meets the Ottawa River, which flows into it from the northwest. We follow it to Nipissing, portage to the Georgian Bay and travel across the northern end of Lac Huron until we come to the Michilimackinac I mentioned."

"And you go all the way by canoe?"

"Yes and no. There are many rapids and as we can't go up these, we have to make portage over land. Some day you must come with me. It's all very interesting and exciting. The return journey is the most exciting because of shooting the rapids. I'll take you up to Lachine in the spring. It's only nine miles from here. Uncle Philip taught me how to handle a canoe over the rapids, and it's thrilling."

"Isn't it dangerous?"

"Very. That's why it's exciting. If you don't twist and turn the canoe properly you are likely to hit a rock, and if you don't smash the canoe to pieces, you will certainly overturn, and a man has little chance against the rapid current. All along the route there are crosses as grim reminders. It takes an experienced helmsman."

"I'm not surprised that you prefer that life to farming. It has so much more excitement and variety."

"Yes, much more." Through his pipe smoke, André's eyes were wistful and longing as one who harbors thoughts that are unspoken.

The habitants were beginning to leave, shouting their farewells to each other and making a great deal of commotion. Some left in carrioles, others in sleighs, but the majority on foot, moving off with practised ease on their raquettes. André came out of his reverie to wave and shout farewells to the departing guests.

"That's another thing I will have to learn," Antoine said.

"What's that?" Antoine pointed to a man fastening on his raquettes. "Snowshoes? Yes, they are new to you. Don't have to wear those kind of things in Paris." Antoine grinned. "I'll teach you. It isn't hard. Awkward at first. Very necessary here."

"I presume so."

They watched the people departing and Antoine remarked: "Do many people have land on this seigneury besides your family?"

"Oh, yes. It's ever increasing as their families grow."

"How is it arranged? I mean, how do they get the land?"

"Well, originally several thousand arpents are granted to a seigneur. He receives it free from the government but on condition that he obtains settlers to clear it. If he doesn't do that he loses the land. To obtain a grant he must be a *gentilhomme*. A peasant can't own land, he can only lease it as a tenant. Some, however, like my father, have risen from habitants to seigneurs. Fifty-four years ago the Sieur de Courville took this grant, and my great-grandfather, Old Pierre, and five other immigrants became habitants. Those five other families, like ours, grew until the entire grant, including another small seigneury to the west that belonged to my Aunt Marguerite, is now all cultivated."

Antoine opened his mouth to ask further questions but Elise came out of the house and they both turned to greet her. She looked worried and Antoine said solicitously: "You must be tired."

She smiled gratefully. "No, but I needed some air. It is stifling in the kitchen."

"Have you been there all the morning?" Antoine asked.

"Since six o'clock."

"Then you need a rest."

"How about taking a sleigh ride?" André suggested.

"It would be lovely. Perhaps I can after a while. I'll see if mother can spare me. But I came out to ask whether either of you know where Jean-Baptiste is?"

"In bed, I presume," André said.

"That's just it. He isn't. He hasn't been home all night. Father's in a rage. Today of all days!"

"He hasn't been home!" André exclaimed. "He went into Montreal last night, didn't he?" he asked Antoine.

"Yes, that's what he said. He asked me to go with him, but I felt I would rather stay here." Beyond that, Antoine did not offer any information. If Jean-Baptiste wanted to explain the reason for his trip to town that was his affair.

"It snowed heavily last night. He probably did not want to risk the roads," was André's explanation.

"Probably. But knowing today was St. Martin's Day, you would think he would have come home early this morning to help," Elise said reproachfully.

"Jean-Baptiste never likes getting up early in the morning." André laughed. "You say father's in a rage?"

"Well, he was looking very angry."

"I'll go and see what I can do."

But Elise laid a restraining hand on his arm. "Mother's with him."

Ann was facing Paul across his desk in the office. His face was set and hard as he said: "And you ask me to be more tolerant! Did you know last night when we discussed this matter that he was in Montreal?"

"No, Paul. I did not," she replied in her soft modulated voice.

He got up from the desk and turned away angrily, glaring out of the window. "The one day of the year when one would expect all the family to be here, particularly as he's been away for the past two years. I'm not even complaining about his not being here to help. I would just have liked the courtesy of his presence."

"I'm sorry, Paul," Ann said and went out of the room. She was as hurt as he but would not voice her feelings.

Paul sat down at his desk again, muttering to himself. All night long he had tossed restlessly, thinking over what his wife had said about Jean-Baptiste. He had risen, still fatigued, but with a determination to understand his son better and to be more tolerant. And now this. . "Adjustments!" he said angrily and banged the ledger shut.

CHAPTER VII

WINTER SET IN, with plenty of hours in which to think. One afternoon, Gaston Renault sat brooding before the fire in his small house. He was not happy; in fact he was very much disturbed. Yet he should have been in one of his happiest moods, for the seigneur had that morning had a long talk with him, offering him his freedom when spring came and, with the freedom, a few arpents of land as a gift. Gaston was devoted to 'Monsieur Paul,' for he had always treated him well, and in making him superintendent of the seigneury had never made him feel that he was a bonded servant. Soon, with a farm of his own, he would be free to take a wife and make a home. Several years ago Paul had permitted him to build this small wooden house for himself, and now, with the land beneath it his own property, he could if he wished pull down the one-room shack and build a better one. All these things Gaston had once planned to do, but there was something important missing in the picture, and that something unattainable. In his brooding he tried to talk himself out of his dissatisfaction; to tell himself that there were many girls who would make him a good wife and that he must forget the red-haired girl who so disturbed him. But the more brandy he drank the deeper his despondency grew. He began to realize that he had loved her since he had first seen her as a pert, freckled child. Almost from the moment of his arrival he had assumed charge of her, teaching her to love and understand horses, giving her her first riding lessons and making her an accomplished horsewoman, teaching her to skate and to handle a gun. She in turn had taught him things, not the least of which had been to allay his bitterness against a society which had robbed him of his birthright. She had tempered his violence and enabled him to be contented. But now the fondness for a

65

child had turned to an intense devotion to a woman. He had not been tortured by it until the arrival of Antoine de Brievaux, and as he noticed his attention to Elise, his jealousy had increased. Now that there were others admiring her, Elise paid less attention to him. He knew that she had understood the glances he had frequently given her, for he had seen her expression change and sometimes she had appeared confused. Again and again on this disgruntled afternoon, he told himself that he was a servant and should not aspire to such heights. Then he would angrily pace the floor and declare that he was not a servant but her equal, and that the events which had placed him in a menial position were not his fault. As a free man he could claim his place in the world. Yet, with all his efforts to convince himself, he did not succeed. Why should a girl as beautiful as Elise consider him, when women of her type were scarce in Montreal and there would be any number of fine offers made to her?

Gaston picked up the flagon of brandy and finding it empty threw it across the floor in a violence of thwarted passion. His was a nature of fierce loves and hates. He could never strike a medium. It had perhaps been this that had caused him to get into trouble in France, for he had hated his half-brother enough to want to kill him, but instead fate had turned against him. This growing love for Elise could not be tempered. It was devouring him so that either she must become his or he must again throw away opportunity and go where he would not be able to see her. He could not be tried too hard.

And it was temptation in all its bitterness that brought a knock at the door when he was at his lowest depth. When he opened it, Elise stood outside. The look in his eyes frightened her. It was the look she had seen frequently of late, focussed upon her whenever they met. She had pretended to ignore it but it had disturbed her. Too late she now knew she should not have come. But it had been a habit of many years, and until this moment she had not realized that what was a habit in childhood could appear very different in a growing woman. As he stared at her with his black eyes pools of smouldering fire, a rush of something she did not understand went through her whole body.

"Oh, Gaston," she said awkwardly. She stopped talking and then began again rapidly. "I did not mean to disturb you. I was passing and thought it would save time if I stopped to tell you I think Bijou has a loose shoe." A bitter wind was blowing and she pulled her collar up round her face.

"You had better come inside," he said tensely. "I will have a look at the horse." He stood back for her to pass. Then went outside and closed the door.

She stood for a moment in the middle of the room wondering why this afternoon it seemed so different. All their lives she and André had come to Gaston's, sometimes alone and often together. More times than she could remember they had spent hours with him, playing games and having fun. Always after she had ridden with him, she had stopped off here for a cooling drink and some cake. But it no longer seemed the same. She threw back her coat and walked to the fire. Drawing off her gloves, she held her hands to the blaze. For all its primitive simplicity the room was comfortable in the firelight. Gaston had made all the furniture himself, the bed in the corner, the couch and the two armchairs that flanked the fireplace. These and a wooden table completed the furnishings, except for rugs and curtains which Madame had made.

Gaston returned. He looked at her for a moment, then said abruptly, "It's all right now."

She turned, and the firelight caught her face. Gaston bit his lip. "Thank you, Gaston. I am sorry to disturb you," she said.

"Why should you apologize?" His tone was curt. "You have never felt it necessary before. You have always come here without apology."

From his massive height he looked down at her, his expression showing the torment he suffered.

She did not look at him as she laughed awkwardly and tried to make light of it. "I know. I don't know why I should feel so apologetic this afternoon."

"You don't?" he said slowly.

"Why, no." She was feeling uncomfortable. She shrugged her coat back on to her shoulders and bent to pick up her gloves. "I must be getting back."

Gaston caught her by the shoulders and turned her to him. "You don't?" he repeated.

She looked up at him and her eyes were frightened but she tried to be casual. "I don't what?"

"You don't know why you acted differently this afternoon? You don't know why it's different when you come here now?"

She tried to free herself from the grip of his hands on her arms, but he would not move. "No, I don't," she replied.

"Then I'll show you."

Violently he pulled her towards him, his arms tight around her and his mouth on hers. His grip was vicelike, making her struggles ineffectual. When he let her go her mouth felt bruised and her green eyes were blazing.

"How dare you!" she cried and slapped him in the face.

He looked at her, his mouth quivering and his nostrils dilating. Her next move astonished and confounded him. With all the contradiction of a woman, she suddenly threw herself against him, burying her face against his shirt. He was so surprised that for a moment he stood like a statue and then realizing she was in his arms and her face turned up to his, he lowered his mouth to hers. She did not move away, and all his pent-up emotions surged over him. He held her hard against him, pressing his lips against her yielding mouth. He could feel her trembling against him, trembling with the first passionate emotion that had ever shaken her. He pushed her coat back from her shoulders and it slid to the floor as he picked her up and carried her to the couch. Her fur cap had slipped off and her red-gold hair spread out in all its glory upon the cushion. Kneeling beside her he kissed her closed eyes and then her mouth. The moments passed as his kisses lengthened and became more ardent. He could see her chest rising and falling

with her quickened breath. Tenderly he laid one hand over the
rounded contour of her breast and felt her stir uneasily. Her
eyes were tightly closed, but though her lips were parted she
uttered no sound. He put his mouth to hers again, taking full
measure of the passion consuming her. Lowering his head, he
laid his cheek for a moment on her breast. She felt his hand
against her bare flesh and then his lips. A violent quiver passed
through her whole body and she gave a sound that was like a
whimper. Slowly he pressed his hand down the length of her
body and felt her respond to his touch. He pressed it against
her thigh and moved it inward and her convulsive movement
tempted him beyond control to draw her tightly against him,
holding her in a full embrace, as again and again he touched
that delicate flesh. Her head rested on his shoulder, her beauty
enhanced by her emotions. His devouring passion tempted him
to take every advantage. She was the woman he wanted more
than anything else, and she was in his arms. But he did not take
the advantage—instead he thrust her roughly from him and
springing to his feet, rushed out of the door.

For a moment or two she lay there, then opened her eyes in
wild surprise. She had expected to see him towering over her,
and when she found she was alone, she sat up abruptly.

"Gaston? Gaston!" she called and received no answer. A
cold draught came through the door which in his flight he had
not closed. She lay back against the cushions again and closed
her eyes. She was still shaking from her experience and dazed
by the unexpectedness of it. She could not yet realize all that
had happened—the full import of what she had done.

"I must go home," she said to herself and slowly got to her
feet. Her legs felt wobbly and she swayed a little. She passed
her hand over her eyes and stood looking at the fire. Then she
noticed her disarranged dress and in confusion fastened it.
Picking up her coat from the floor she put it on and adjusted
her fur cap.

Outside there was no sign of Gaston, and mounting her

horse, she let him take her home. When she was nearly there, she remembered that she had left her gloves on the table but dared not return.

Quickly she slipped up to her room and threw herself on the bed. She was shaking from her wrought-up emotions. At first she did not think of what had happened in relation to Gaston, but in relation to the new sensation she was experiencing. She could not understand it; she did not know its meaning. Gaston had kissed her in a way that was a revelation to her. She pressed her hand to her breast where the feel of his lips still remained. Again a shudder passed through her whole body as though it had been magnetized by his touch. She was miserable, yet she was happy, and that confused her. What had taken possession of her to make her act the way she had? Then she began to think of Gaston. Did this mean that she was in love with him and did not know it? "No, no!" she said half aloud. She could never love Gaston; she would never want to marry him. Yet, she knew that if he walked into her room this moment she would want to fling herself into his arms again. A flush of shame diffused her face when she remembered how she had thrown herself into his arms when she should have walked out of the room. But her hunger had been too great; the longing too intense. "Yet I don't love him," she repeated to herself. Could one feel this intense passionate longing for a man one did not want to marry?

She would be afraid to look at Antoine or even at her brothers for fear that these inner thoughts might be apparent. She pleaded a headache and went to bed early, tossing restlessly all night long. The next morning she saw her gloves lying on the table in the hall and knew Gaston had been to the house. She took them to her room, feeling as though the sight of them revealed her guilt. Musing, she turned them over in her hands and her heart leapt as she felt something stuffed into one of the fingers. She knew without further thought that it was something from Gaston. Unrolling the piece of paper, she read the brief note:

"Does this mean that you love me as I adore you?
Please come to see me again this afternoon. I am in
torment until I know whether you return my love.

G. R."

She crumpled the paper into a ball. She realized now what she
had done. She dare not go near him.

In the days that followed she stayed in the house, helping
her mother with the needlework. They had received invitations
to the Governor's ball and were busy with their dresses which
Jean-Baptiste had brought from France. This gave her a good
excuse when Antoine wanted her to go sleighing with him.
Ann, however, with a mother's instinct, guessed what was
troubling her daughter, though it would not have occurred to
her that Gaston was the cause. She thought that it was Antoine
and rather hoped that the ball might encourage him to speak.
Not that there were not ample opportunities at home, but the
romantic air of a ball stimulated such events. More than ever
was she anxious to get Elise married. She resembled her Aunt
Marguerite not only in looks but in temperament. Ann was the
only one who knew Marguerite's full story, for Marguerite had
confided it to no one but her. In telling her of the birth of her
illegitimate child, Marguerite had confessed that her uncon-
trollable emotions had carried her away and that it was not
entirely the fault of the Chevalier de Favien. Ann watched her
daughter covertly, proud of her beauty, yet afraid of it.

CHAPTER VIII

ON THE EVENING of the Governor's ball, Antoine was the first dressed and stood before the fire in the drawing room waiting for the others to come down. He was particularly eager to see Elise, who he was certain would look ravishing in a ball gown. He had scracely seen her or her mother all day, for this was the first event of the season and both had been busy with their preparations. Antoine stood before the portrait of Aunt Marguerite thinking of Elise, and wondering whether he should speak to her tonight. He was still deep in thought when André came in. It was the first time he had seen him out of deerskins and he smiled with pleasant surprise.

"I hardly recognized you, André," he said.

André made a wry face. "I don't recognize myself. I feel most uncomfortable. I'm so much more at home in moccasins and with a gun in my hand than with a sword at my side."

"You look very well, all the same." Antoine's tone was admiring, for André was handsome in a dark green coat over a full-length embroidered vest of a lighter shade. Furthermore, his legs in light cotton stockings were shapely.

"You look elegant yourself," André replied, and then they both laughed. "Maybe we should save our compliments for the ladies! How about a glass of wine while we are waiting?"

A decanter and glasses stood on a side table and André filled a couple of glasses. A long curl of his wig dangled as he bent over.

"These ridiculous wigs!" he exclaimed. "Don't they bother you or are you used to them?"

"No, they annoy me intensely. It's a stupid fashion," Antoine said.

"I nearly didn't wear one, only they would probably mistake me for a lackey," André laughed.

This question of wigs was a perpetual subject of controversy, particularly among the younger people who seldom wore them except for such dress occasions as this. For many years, Louis XIV, proud of his own abundant hair, had refused to wear a wig but lately in his declining years had adopted the fashion. In the colony it was a matter of personal choice, and while government officials and many of the noblesse wore them, they were by no means general. Furthermore, in these past years, they had reached such absurd dimensions that not only were they uncomfortable and heavy to wear, but also extremely expensive. Madame de Maintenon's sobering influence had eliminated many frivolities, and clothes had become more somber, but several years yet would pass before the wig attained sane proportions. In an era when wars were perpetual, even if more leisurely, male dress reflected the military pattern and though Louis XIV had attempted to standardize the uniforms of his army, there was yet little to distinguish military from fashionable male attire. Certain colors were ordered according to regiment, but the trimmings on them were still governed by individual taste. Antoine, being conservative by nature, had confined his dress uniform to the regulation blue with revers and cuffs of crimson, adorned with a profusion of gold braid and buttons, and a lace ruffle at the neck.

Jean-Baptiste was the next to come down. His uniform, which should have been the same as Antoine's, was much more elaborate. The gold braid was wider and more abundant; the sleeves, which by the dictates of fashion should be wide, were excessively so and the wide skirts of his coat were stiffened with buckram. He wore red hose similar to Antoine's, but with a thread of gold down the seam. Yet no one could have denied that he made a handsome appearance and his long, powdered wig suited him far more than Antoine's or André's. He was in a very gay mood, for he loved these opportunities to dress, and as he sipped his wine, he smiled pleasantly at their compliments.

Standing around the fire, with their backs to the door, they were not aware of Madame until she was halfway into the room. She spoke to them and when they turned they all exclaimed together, for she was beautiful in a gown of pale blue satin brocade. Instinctively they all bowed to her in acknowledgment of her charm and she sank to the floor in a graceful curtsey, lowering her powdered head.

Jean-Baptiste sprang forward, taking her hand and kissing it.

"Most charming and adorable, madame," he said and she smiled happily at him. The other two were not to be outdone and came forward to kiss her hand. Antoine also paid her a compliment but André stood looking at her, his eyes more blue than usual. All his devotion was expressed in that look and he merely said, "Wonderful!"

Ann laughed. "That was very sweet," she said to them, "and now be sensible."

"How can any one be sensible in the presence of such loveliness?" Antoine remarked. She flashed him a smile.

"You boys look very charming," she remarked.

"Yes, aren't we elegant," André said. "Think I'll take to wearing a wig next time I go into the woods. Then when an Indian tries to scalp me, I can just leave it with him and have my head." He grabbed a curl each side and twirled about, cutting a very funny figure that made them all laugh.

Jean-Baptiste brought his mother a glass of wine. "Your father is struggling upstairs," she remarked. "He detests wigs and we had quite a battle before he would agree to wear one."

"I don't blame him," André said. "I was telling Antoine I would'nt have worn one, only I was afraid they would have mistaken me for a lackey."

Jean-Baptiste said nothing. He alone of the men was quite happy and comfortable. The Sieur joined them and there was further bantering.

"What's keeping Elise?" Paul asked.

"The new dress undoubtedly," Ann said. "She will be here

in a moment. She was practically dressed when I came down."

It was, however, almost twenty minutes before Elise made her appearance. The cause of the delay was an unpleasant and unexpected encounter with Gaston. When she came from her room, she found him waiting on the top landing. His presence there at that hour was obviously intentional.

She gave a little gasp and exclaimed, "Oh, Gaston!" Her hand flew to her throat and she was terrified that he would take hold of her again. His face, as he looked at her in all her loveliness, was working with emotion, for she was very desirable. But he remained where he was. Neither did she move. She stood as though transfixed and feeling very guilty yet unable to take her eyes from his face. He appeared an angry giant ready to overpower her, his eyes two penetrating black circles that seared her.

"Don't be afraid. I won't touch you," he said, and his tone was bitter. "Go to your party and find other men to kiss you. You . . ." His lips framed the word but he did not utter it.

"How dare you!" Elise tossed her head haughtily. Her eyes had lost their fearful look and were now blazing.

He took a step nearer. "How dare I what?" he asked between clenched teeth.

"How dare you speak to me that way?"

He was now standing before her. "You know that you deserve it. You know what I would like to call you and that it fits you."

With mounting temper she slapped his face. He waited to see whether she would again throw herself at him, but she continued to glare and did not move. Instead he moved, taking her by the shoulders and shaking her so violently that it loosened the curls she had pinned up so carefully.

"Let me go!" she hissed in a low voice, afraid that at any moment one of the others would come by.

"I'll let you go!" he said scornfully. "Though I know what

I would like to do with you. You have a lesson to learn, young lady, and one day I shall give it to you. Take that now as the first part of the lesson!" His great hand slapped her cheek and he pushed her from him with such force that she lost her balance.

"Oh!" The sound was shaken out of her. "How dare you!" She stamped her foot in wild fury but Gaston had left quickly by the back stairs. She flew into her room and closed the door. She was trembling with rage and pent-up emotion. Sitting before her mirror, she pressed her hands over her eyes to keep back tears of anger and shame. It was the first time she had seen him since that afternoon. When she was calmer she re-arranged her hair, but it was several more minutes before she felt able to face the others. By that time, anger and resentment were uppermost in her mind and she was determined to forget Gaston and flirt all the evening.

She heard her mother calling, and, pulling herself together, went downstairs. As she entered the drawing room, they attributed her heightened color to excitement. There was a stifled exclamation from Antoine. She looked as though the figure had stepped out of the portrait, for her gown was the same shade of green. She stood for a moment in the doorway appreciating their compliments, yet devoid of any ego. She, too, dropped them a curtsey. Immediately Antoine was across the room, offering his hand to assist her. He put her hand to lips that throbbed with longing for her to understand his feelings. "So beautiful," he said very low, and her eyes thanked him. André and Jean-Baptiste exchanged a knowing glance; Paul and Ann, one of satisfaction.

The Chateau de Ramezay looked like a fairy palace, its roof heaped with white snow and every window ablaze with lights that reflected playfully on the glistening crystals that covered the shrubs in the courtyard. The air was filled with the jingling of bells, and the laughter of those waiting in the vehicles mingled with the shouts of the drivers trying to maneuver their horses out of the congestion. The Rue St. Paul and Rue Notre Dame and the narrow side streets were jammed with carriages and carrioles in such confusion that it appeared they would never be extricated. Footmen tried to organize the traffic through the gate and up to the portico. The driveway had been cleared of snow and carpet laid before the entrance to preserve dainty shoes.

The Chateau had been built by the Chevalier de Ramezay five years previously and was the pride of Montreal. It was a long rambling building, well-furnished, with thousands of candles now burning in crystal chandeliers and wall sconces. Festoons of laurel and spruce for the Christmas season added to the appearance of gaiety. Large fires blazed in the grates, and around these the guests gathered in groups. At one end of the ballroom an orchestra was playing softly, waiting for the signal for the dancing to start.

The Chevalier and his wife stood at the entrance of the ballroom receiving their guests. Their eldest daughter, Catherine, was assisting them, as well as Claude, resplendent in his brilliant uniform. The remainder of the Chevalier's large family were too young to be present. Madame de Ramezay's face was wreathed in smiles as she greeted Ann and Paul, for among all her friends they were her favorites. "You look wonderful, Ann," she whispered before they passed on to greet the Chevalier and the Baron de Longueil and his wife, who shared the honor of the receiving line. The Baron, eldest of the famous le Moynes, had expected to be made Governor of Montreal, but had been superseded by de Ramezay because France did not like her officials to be native born. De Longueil was a native Montrealer, and his eminent services to the colony had enabled him to secure a title for himself some ten years ago. His great fortress-chateau on his seigneury across the River and his house in Montreal, a few doors from the Chateau de Ramezay, made him a man of vast importance.

"Darling, you're adorable," Madame de Ramezay greeted Elise. "And Monsieur de Brievaux, it is a pleasure to see you again." Antoine had become quite a favorite with them on the journey from France.

"Welcome to our home," the Chevalier took up the greeting. "Hope you are enjoying Montreal."

"Exceedingly," Antoine replied.

The Chevalier presented Antoine to the Baroness de Longueil, a distinguished lady, who before her marriage had been Lady in Waiting to her Royal Highness the Duchesse d'Orléans. Antoine followed Elise's curtsey with his best leg.

The moment Claude de Ramezay saw Elise and they had formally greeted each other, he detached himself from the receiving line. André and Jean-Baptiste had walked over to greet their many friends but Antoine had remained with Elise, having no intention of releasing her until he had to. Immediately Claude claimed the first dance. Antoine laughingly shook his head.

"Oh, no, that's my privilege," he protested.

There was the faintest note of hostility in Claude's tone as he countered: "On the contrary, I claim the privilege of being an old friend of many years' standing."

"But the lady promised me on the way here," Antoine countered.

"Shall we let the lady settle the matter then?" Claude said curtly, and Antoine knew that he had a rival.

Elise was smiling radiantly. She enjoyed having men vying for her favor. It was gratifying after the rebuff administered by Gaston. It still rankled and on the way she had wondered whether he had deliberately planned it in the hope of spoiling her evening. It made her feel defiant towards him. She would show him he had failed and it was not going to be difficult because even while Antoine and Claude were arguing, a circle of young men began to gather around her. Among them was Charles le Moyne, the Baron de Longueil's son, and hearing Claude claim old friendship, he immediately furthered the same claim.

Antoine watched Elise anxiously. She was for a moment in

a quandary, and her rippling laughter as she tried to please them all, caught many an ear.

"Now, my old friends, you should give way to a guest. I promised Antoine the first dance and he shall have it." Antoine beamed with delight.

"Then you must have supper with me," Claude said quickly.

They all began to clamor at once. Elise reproved them with, "Gentlemen! Gentlemen! Permit me to join my mother." The modesty of the last remark was contradicted by her laughing eyes.

"Not until you have promised me a dance, Elise," Charles le Moyne insisted and the others followed suit.

"Oh, dear!" she exclaimed and then said quickly: "All right. Antoine has the first, Claude the second, you the third, Charles," and going down the line she gave each a number until the first half dozen dances were all promised. Antoine felt a little crestfallen. It looked as though he would not get more than one dance and his disappointment increased as he heard Claude say:

"But I still insist upon your having supper with me, no matter with whom you are dancing before. After all, I am your host, or at least deputy host."

Elise could not refuse, so gave her promise. "And now, gentlemen, please excuse me." She laid her hand lightly on Antoine's arm and he escorted her to where her parents were seated.

"Every one we know seems to be here," she said with apology to her mother as she took the chair next to her.

Ann smiled and there was pride in her smile, for she had not missed the incident, nor had many others. Ann's smile deepened as Antoine said gallantly: "The most beautiful young lady in the room would naturally be besieged."

"Thank you, monsieur," Elise replied and inclined her head gracefully in acknowledgment.

Friends were constantly coming up to greet the Sieur and Madame. The moment Antoine could get Elise's attention he said in a low voice: "And do I have to be content with one dance, Elise?"

"I am sorry, Antoine. It was embarrassing. I didn't know what to do without hurting feelings."

"I understand," he said but the expression of disappointment was still there.

"I'll save the first dance after supper for you," she compromised.

He let his eyes rest steadily on hers for a moment. "Thank you very much. You are very kind."

André joined them, chiding Elise as he said: "And, of course, my very popular sister will have no dance left for a mere brother."

"Oh, André, yes! We must have at least one, even if they have to put in an extra dance just for you and me."

He patted her hand. "That's sweet of you. But we shall see. If I don't get one I shall make you dance all day tomorrow with me."

"You are absurd! But I am going to have one with you tonight."

"Knowing what a bad dancer I am! I'll excuse you." André did not really care for dancing, and when the duty dances were finished, would undoubtedly drift into the card room. Jean-Baptiste, on the other hand, was in his element and no one could have denied his charm. He had a most disarming way with the ladies. At the moment, he was particularly engrossed with a dark and sensuous creature, no longer in the flush of girlhood. She was richly gowned, her dress very décolleté and her jewels flashed.

This was the first opportunity the ladies had had to display their new gowns from France. They were beautiful in their elegance, even if amusing in their efforts to outshine each other. There was an abundance of powdered hair, making the shoulders of the wearer untidy with white dust.

The room was filling up and when the last distinguished guest had arrived, the Chevalier led his wife on to the floor to the soft notes of a minuet. Antoine offered his arm to Elise, proud to have a partner who he considered excelled all other women. He noticed that Jean-Baptiste was dancing with the dark lady with whom he had been conversing so intimately. Later he learned she was Madame de Fontigny, a cousin of the de Ramezays.

The graceful movements of the minuet gave him an opportunity to admire his partner. Each time she came close enough for him to whisper, he paid her a compliment, determined to lay his claim before Claude superseded him.

"You are wonderful," he whispered and was rewarded with a smile. "You dance divinely," he told her, and then just before the dance finished, he took courage and whispered, "I love you." He saw her long eyelashes flicker, perhaps with surprise or perhaps with emotion. She did not answer, and the dance was over before he could say any more.

After that he did not see much of her, for though she returned conventionally to her mother after each dance, Antoine had of necessity to return his own partner. He did manage to maneuver so that he and his partner were in the same set as Elise for the quadrille but he was not successful in securing the place where he and she would have been at opposite corners of the set, so that he would have had an opportunity of executing some of the steps with her. Instead he was on the far side where they could only exchange smiles, but that meant something.

Antoine did not lack partners, for the Chevalier and his wife saw to it that he was introduced to many fair ladies. Most of them were attractive but no one appealed to him as much as Elise. On the contrary, with his pleasant manners and charm, he created quite a flutter among them and they tried coquettishly to make him realize their appeal.

He took Catherine de Ramezay in to supper. She was a year younger than Claude. Charming though she was, Antoine scarcely realized it, for Elise was at the next table and Claude was wasting no time. Antoine's good nature was strained, for he was jealous. And when he saw them leave the room and enter the long gallery, Elise's hand resting on Claude's arm and her lovely eyes turned up to him, his jealousy increased.

The gallery had been arranged with evergreens forming charming arbors, which couples were enjoying.

"Let us walk to the end," Claude said. As they strolled along, Elise chatted away about everything and anything that came to her mind. She was having a delightful time and looked radiantly happy. At the far end they found a small settee, but stood for a while looking out on to the beautiful gardens of the Jesuits, now gleaming white in the light of a full moon.

"Oh, isn't it beautiful!" she exclaimed and clapped her hands like a child. "It looks like fairyland."

"You're beautiful too, Elise," he said.

She looked at him archly and said, "Thank you, monsieur."

"I can't get over the way you've changed," Claude told her.

"Perhaps it's because the freckles aren't so prominent now," she teased.

"It's more than that!" His arm encircled her waist and he buried his face against the back of her ear. She jerked her head away.

"Don't do that!" she said sharply and walked over to the settee. "Let us sit down."

Claude's eyebrows rose in surprise. "No offense, I'm sure," he said.

She gave him a winsome smile. "I know. I didn't mean to be abrupt. Sit down and let us talk of something else."

"But I don't want to talk of something else. I want to talk about you. You've completely captivated me. Five years have made such a difference. I became your slave the moment I saw you on the wharf."

"That was weeks ago," she retorted.

He felt the reproof in her tone but was quick with an answer. "I was waiting for tonight."

"Really! Such nonchalance!"

"It wasn't nonchalance," he said heatedly and leaned

towards her impulsively. She looked into his face and thought how he, too, had changed. There was something about him that reminded her of Jean-Baptiste. He had the same petulant mouth, but where Jean-Baptiste had a certain aesthetic quality, Claude had self-assurance. Even as he tried to make love to her, his attitude was that she should feel flattered. She leaned back away from him as he tried to reach her mouth.

"You've learned coquetry, I see," he said with a smile. "Your mouth is most inviting, my dear, and you have beautiful teeth. Is there a pretty red tongue behind them?"

"You should know! I used to put it out at you."

"Put it out now and I will show you what I will do about it." His grey eyes, now more blue, gleamed. "You're a tantalizing little minx," he said. But she was quicker than he and turned her head swiftly so that his lips caught the side of her throat. "All right, then I'll kiss your throat," he said undaunted. His lips were burning as he pressed them to her throat and then swiftly lowered them. She pushed his head away.

"Behave yourself, Claude." Her tone was faintly irritable.

He raised his head and looked at her. "You mean you don't want to be kissed? Come now, Elise, I don't believe that. We're not children any more and not playing games the way we used to. I've thought of you a lot since my return. I want to marry you."

The statement startled her. It was the first proposal she had ever received, and she had not thought it would be this way. She was disappointed. She laughed.

"It's nothing to laugh about. I'm serious," he remonstrated.

She became serious too. "I'll have to get to know you better. You're so different," she said.

"Well, you wouldn't except me to remain the same as I was at fifteen! We'll have all the winter to get to know each other better. We'll become engaged and I'll begin the lessons right now."

"What lessons?" He was talking a language which in her inexperience she did not understand.

"I can teach you a lot of things I learned in France," he said with bravado.

"Is that so! And suppose I don't want to learn?"

"Don't be childish, darling. Of course you want to learn. Let me show you what I mean."

He pulled her to him again and this time caught her off guard. His lips were pressed against hers and he would not release her until he had forced her tightly shut mouth to relax. She struggled ineffectually but he still held her. With all his ardency he was not rough, moving his soft lips and tongue over her mouth in a way that disturbed her. She had intended to be angry, but when he let her go, she found herself shaken and merely said:

"You did learn a lot in France!"

His smile was one of self-satisfaction. She stood up, looking out of the window again. Standing behind her, he slipped his arms around her, resting his hands on her breasts, but she slapped them away. Strains of music came to her and, turning, she said:

"The dancing has started again! Please take me to my partner."

"In a minute. You haven't answered me. When can we become engaged? I will speak to your father, of course."

"I'm not becoming engaged for the present," she replied and looked him steadily in the face.

"Why not?"

"Because I wish to have time to consider the matter."

His eyebrows went up again. He had not expected to be refused. "As you wish, mademoiselle," he replied in a tone of annoyance.

They walked back through the gallery in silence. Antoine was waiting impatiently and his face was hard and unsmiling as he looked at Claude.

"I believe this is my dance," he said coldly.

"I'm sorry, de Brievaux, we did not hear the music," Claude said.

Antoine bowed stiffly. He wanted to say, "And why not?" but could not trust his feelings.

He and Elise danced in silence. It was the first time she had seen him angry, and strangely enough it added to his charm. She did not want men quarreling over her but she liked them to have spirit.

"Shall we promenade?" he asked when the dance finished. They were the first words he had spoken.

She nodded and he led her back into the gallery. As they passed one of the arbors, Antoine caught a glimpse of Jean-Baptiste whom he had hardly seen during the evening. He recognized him only by his uniform, for his face was buried deep in the bosom of a lady, who though her face was hidden behind her fan, Antoine was certain was Madame de Fontigny. He hoped Elise had not seen them.

They walked to the opposite end of the gallery and found a small settee nestling among the shrubs. There were others sitting around and many strolling up and down. They talked conventionally for a few moments and then Elise asked him if he were having a good time.

"Yes," he answered, "except that the length of time between our dances is too long."

"I know. I'm sorry. I . . ."

He laid his hand on hers. "You don't have to explain. I understand. Only there is something I want to say to you and I had thought tonight would give me the opportunity."

She had not yet gained complete control over herself after her experience with Claude. She was not sure that she wanted Antoine to talk, for she felt certain he was going to speak along the same line. Rather vaguely she said: "Why tonight?"

"Because I can't wait any longer, Elise. Did you hear the last words I spoke to you when we danced the first dance?" His black eyes were looking steadily at her and their expression was gentle. She met them and then looked away.

"You paid me several charming compliments," she said.

"And so undoubtedly has every man who danced with you. I said to you that I loved you. Did they also say that?"

"No," she replied. She remembered then that Claude had made no such statement, though he had proposed to her. Men were so different.

"Then let me repeat. Elise, I love you. I am not the heir of a prominent family," he went on, revealing his jealousy of Claude, "but I can make a home for you if you will be patient. I have made up my mind to remain here. I can build a seigneury and provide for you properly. Or if that is not what you want, we can go to France or Quebec. It will be whatever you wish."

She still did not answer. Two proposals in less than half an hour were disconcerting. He lifted her hand and pressed it to his lips.

She could hear the music and realized that a partner would be waiting for her.

"The next dance has started," she said.

"I know. But can't we let it go?"

"I have a partner waiting," she hedged.

"Let him wait until the next dance. . . ."

"You didn't like it when I kept you waiting just now." Her tone was more teasing than reproachful.

"For the same reason?" Antoine retorted. Elise, to her annoyance, blushed. "You need not answer," he added. His impulse was to get up and escort her back to the ballroom without further comment, yet, if Claude had proposed to her, he was all the more anxious not to leave the field open. While he was debating this point, his face was stern and troubled. Elise did not want to leave with the feeling they had quarreled, for she liked him much more than Claude. So she said:

"The dance will be half over now, so we may as well miss it."

When he looked at her she smiled, and he answered it. The spell had been broken and he tried to recapture it. "I know I am almost a stranger to you, Elise, more so than others you know here. I can only repeat—I love you very deeply. I have never loved any one before. I am not asking you to give me an answer now. You will want to think it over. But I had to let you know my feelings."

There was something so gentle, yet strong about him, something that she had not before realized. She looked up at him and his dark eyes were tender.

"Thank you, Antoine. I shall think over it."

"And don't think because I am staying in your home, I shall bother you."

"Of course not," she assured him.

She wished she had not let Claude kiss her, because now she wanted Antoine's arms around her. She knew that if she had leaned slightly towards him he would have put them there. But she controlled herself, though with difficulty. He looked at her steadily. "How much I love you!" he said hoarsely and then stood up. He offered her his arm, and they strolled back to where her mother and father were sitting. Ann saw the brightness in her daughter's eyes and wondered.

CHAPTER IX

WHEN ELISE wakened the next morning it was with a feeling that something had happened or was to happen. She lay thinking drowsily and then remembered the proposals of the night before. To any woman such a situation was flattering and gratifying, yet at the same time disturbing. She was reasonably certain that to the proposals of Claude and Antoine she· would have been able to add that of Charles le Moyne had he had the opportunity. When she had danced the last dance with him, he had asked to escort her home. When she declined he urged, "I want to talk with you, it's important," but that made her more adamant. She was already confused and a third proposal would have been too much.

What had suddenly happened to make her so desirable? Could it be that the rousing of her emotions by Gaston had brought a new radiance to her that made men want her? The thought of Gaston was the most troubling of all. He had threatened her angrily the evening before and she wondered whether it was just in temper or whether he really would be vindictive. It was going to be very difficult if she had to avoid him. He wasn't in the house much at this time of the year but she frequently had to go out to the barns and could not avoid running into him. Ought she to have a talk with him, apologize and try to make him more reasonable? Yet even as she asked herself this question, she knew that no attempt to talk with him would ever be satisfactory. He was not as young as the others. She did not know his age but guessed he must be nearly ten years her senior. She knew that she could not handle him. Apart from his age, which made her feel a child by comparison, there was that magnetic quality about him that seemed to draw her to him with a devouring passion. The moment his large dark eyes met hers, she felt powerless. Already they were haunting her, so that in the days since the scene in his house, she had seemed to see them always watching. When she closed her eyes, his two piercing orbs came towards her, growing and growing until she was afraid. She wished that among the other three men who now had entered her life, she could have felt more definite so that she could have accepted one proposal and had that protection, not against Gaston so much as against herself and the way she felt about him. But as yet, she did not feel certain about any one of the others.

Mentally she lined them up for review. Claude de Ramezay and Charles le Moyne fell into the same category in that they were both the eldest sons of wealthy families and were, therefore, without question the best matches in the colony. As the wife of either, she could carry on the tradition which her own family had built. Yet both men were spoiled because of the positions they held. Charles was the older by four years. Probably because they had all grown up together, neither man had any romantic appeal for her. But should one be romantic or should one be practical? What of Antoine de Brievaux? He alone of the three had a romantic appeal and had interested her from the moment of his arrival. She had thought about him quite a little in these past several weeks and since last night he had an added charm. Previously she had been misled by his nonchalant manner which she had mistaken for weakness. He had talked of taking land and building a seigneury but would he be successful? He had never done any farming, knew little about it and might fail. So far as she knew he had no family back of him and she knew nothing of his financial position. He had told her they could go to France or Quebec or remain here, whichever she wished, and that would appear to be an indication that he was able to provide for her. Or was he perhaps relying on her dowry, which from what he had seen since he had been their guest, he might presume to be large? She was not sufficiently experienced to be able to judge whether he was just an adventurer looking for a profitable marriage or whether he was really as sincere as he appeared. The more she thought about it the more confused she became. She had to talk it over with some one and throwing on a peignoir she went to her mother's room. Her father was always up at an early hour and usually her mother too, but after parties Ann sometimes rested late.

Elise knocked and at her mother's *"Entrez,"* slipped her head inside the door.

"May I come in?" she asked.

"Why, of course, darling!" Ann exclaimed and held out her arms to this baby of hers who had suddenly, it seemed, developed into such a charming young lady. She kissed her affectionately and Elise sat on the edge of the bed.

"Want to talk?" she asked her mother.

"Of course I do. But you had better get into bed with me. It's too cold out there."

"Ah!" Elise said and quickly slipped in beside her mother, snuggling up to her. "Oh, how nice!" she said and as Ann put her arm under the curly tawny head, it nestled closely against her breast. "Such a nice maman I have," Elise said. After all her struggling thoughts it was so comforting to be able to cling to some one.

Ann kissed her on the forehead. "And such a successful young lady I have for a daughter," she said gently.

Elise looked up quickly. "Was I very naughty last night?" she asked.

Ann laughed lightly. "Now darling, you can probably answer that question better yourself."

Elise's eyes as they looked up at her mother, twinkled roguishly. "I flirted," she said.

"So I guessed. And you did not return dutifully to your mother after each dance." Ann pretended to look stern. "Was that your fault or your partner's?"

"My partner's, of course!" she giggled. Then added: "I had two proposals."

Ann looked pleased as she said: "You did! Am I allowed to ask from whom?"

"Of course; Claude de Ramezay was the first and then Antoine."

"And which did you accept?"

"Neither. I think, too, that Charles le Moyne wanted to say something. He asked if he could bring me home. 'I must talk to you, Elise.'" She lowered her voice to imitate his. Then she giggled. "They all said that."

"Such popularity will turn your head," Ann said, and though she was smiling, there was a note of warning in her tone.

"I don't think so, maman. But I am confused," she confessed.

"I don't wonder."

"What would you do?"

"That's something that it would be difficult for a mother to advise, darling. At least a mother like you have. Doesn't your heart give any indication?"

"That's the difficulty. It doesn't. I'm not in love with any of them." She discussed her various suitors. Ann listened very carefully and when Elise finished said quietly:

"I think then you are wise to wait a while. You will see plenty of all of them during the winter and perhaps by the end, the decision will come of its own."

"Yes, that's how I feel. Only . . ." she buried her face in the softness of her mother's nightdress. "I think it's time I was married." One thing she couldn't mention to her mother was Gaston.

"I do, too, dear."

"Maman, is it wrong to be feeling the way I do?"

Ann's heart gave a little jump at this indication that her guess about her daughter was right.

"How do you feel, dear?" she asked.

"You must know. It all seems to have happened so suddenly. Men never meant much to me until recently. I have always had lots of boys around me as long as I can remember. There were always André and Jean-Baptiste and all their friends."

"And you always were a little *garçonnière!*"

"But I don't feel a *garçonnière* any more—I feel so different now. I . . . oh I don't know." She hid her face again and the back of her neck flushed.

"It's just that you're growing up, dear. You've changed into a woman and have developed a woman's emotions."

"And it's not wrong to feel the way I do?"

Ann thought a moment. "No, dear, not as long as you don't let those feelings get out of control. That's why you should be married as soon as possible. Men, you know, have a way of detecting our feelings and they sometimes use the advantage. Now I don't know any of these boys too well. . . . They have all three been to France and that usually includes a liberal education. I shall have to be a more severe chaperone."

Elise looked up again at her mother who was smiling over her last remark, but her dark eyes were deep wells of tenderness. "Oh, maman, you are so sweet and understanding." The arm around her mother's waist tightened as she hugged her. She was pressing kisses against her mother's cheek and Ann could detect how constrained her emotions were. When the spasm had passed, Elise leaned upon one elbow and looked at her mother.

"Were you and father in love when you married?" she asked.

"Very much."

"And you didn't have any difficulty in making up your mind?"

"Not in making up my mind. But I had difficulties. And I had no mother to discuss things with. My father wasn't much help because he wouldn't interfere or influence me."

"I thought fathers chose their daughters' husbands in those days."

"What do you mean, *in those days!*" Ann laughed. "They

do now, only your father and I don't exercise that prerogative. Maybe we should be more stern and select your husband for you."

"Whom would you select?"

"I should have to speak to your father about that," Ann said and tried to look serious. Then they both laughed.

"And when you met father you fell in love and everything was all right." Elise returned to the subject.

"It wasn't quite as simple as that."

"No?"

"There was another woman, a very beautiful one too."

"You mean father couldn't decide?"

"He had decided the moment we met, so he has always said, but the other woman wanted him and she tried to make trouble for us."

"Then what happened?"

"I'm quite a determined woman." Ann laughed and Elise nodded her head in agreement. "I let your father worry for a while and then when I was quite sure he loved me, well, I married him."

"And the other woman?"

"She married some one else shortly afterwards."

That wasn't quite the way it had been but Ann thought the explanation would suffice. She didn't want to mention her husband's mistress to his daughter.

"And now, child, you had better go and dress. Breakfast will be nearly over."

"I will." She kissed her mother and hugged her. "I feel better now."

As she was getting out of bed, Ann put her hand on her arm. "Always come to me, darling, if you get into difficulties, won't you?"

Elise nodded, and again thoughts of Gaston crossed her mind but she let them go for the present.

Ann lay thinking for a while after Elise had gone. The ball evidently had created quite a few situations with the children.

She and Paul had talked of it the night before. Their two sons had presented a contrast. They had wondered about André, who had spent a large part of the evening in the card room with the men instead of dancing and flirting with the girls.

"I hope he's not going to be one of those men who aren't interested in women," Ann had remarked.

Paul had scoffed at the idea. "When he falls in love it will be serious." There had been defense in his tone which changed to disapproval as he said: "I'd rather see it that way than as it is with Jean-Baptiste, who's always running after some woman."

Ann's tone had then become defensive. "He's had more experience," she had said, "and is only looking for the right woman."

"And I suppose that alluring creature he danced with all the evening was what he considered the *right woman,*" Paul had said as he climbed in beside Ann.

"Don't be absurd. He was only amusing himself."

"Indeed!" She felt her husband's disapproval in the way he thrust his legs determinedly down the bed.

"He will settle down eventually."

"I hope so." Paul's tone had conveyed doubt. "If he's to carry on this seigneury I don't want that kind of woman stepping into your shoes."

"Oh, Paul! Be reasonable. After all, you saw to it that you had your amusement and experience before you married me."

"What do you mean?" His voice had challenged her.

Ann had laughed softly. "A very beautiful lady, also dark and sensuous like Jean-Baptiste's friend last night. Let me see, the name, if I remember, was Hélène de Matier," she had said slowly.

Paul had stared at her. They never mentioned that name. The look he gave her was angry until he saw the teasing expression on her face. Then he, too, had laughed.

"You are a devil!" he had said and without hesitation had gone to the arms she had held out to him.

But later he had thought about her remark. He had said

nothing to Jean-Baptiste about his frequent overnight absences in Montreal. Because he had promised Ann to try to be more understanding, he had controlled his anger over St. Martin's Day and had made no comment. Now, suddenly, he saw the picture in a different light, shed by Ann's reminder of Madame de Matier. He had stayed away from home many a night during his infatuation for her, yet here he was censuring his son for doing the same thing. He told himself he was getting old and losing his sense of proportion. It made him angry with himself and more tolerant towards Jean-Baptiste.

When Ann came down to breakfast she found a heated discussion in progress. Paul wore one of his black looks.

"What's the matter?" she inquired.

"Gaston's had the nerve to go off hunting without asking my permission. Just left a note on my desk and went off. I don't know what's come over him. This is what always happens. You treat a man well, offer him his freedom before it's due, and he takes advantage. But he'll find I'm still master. He's not a free man yet and if he doesn't behave I shan't release him until he has served his full time."

"Well, now, he probably had a reason," Ann said soothingly. Elise hoped her mother could not detect anything from her face. She was feeling relieved yet very guilty, for she knew she was responsible.

"Don't worry, father," André tried to smooth the ruffles. "I'll look after the animals."

"I'll help." Paul looked surprised as Jean-Baptiste made the offer. He shifted his glance to Ann's face. There was a smile of satisfaction there.

"And I shall be delighted to help if you will give me some instruction. It would be a good opportunity for me to begin learning a few things about a seigneury," Antoine said.

Paul's anger faded. "Thanks, boys. It appears I have lots of assistants."

They changed then to a discussion of the ball and all the

people there. Elise came in for much teasing because she had unquestionably been the belle of the ball. Antoine did not join in the teasing nor did he give her any embarrassing looks. His face appeared passive and Elise was grateful to him.

That night Antoine got drunk. While he was helping in the barns, Aunt Marie came by and wanted to know all about the ball.

"I'll come over tonight and tell you all about it, darling," Antoine told her. His cheeks were whipped by the wind and he looked very boyish as he stood by the cart talking to her.

"It's about time you came over! You've been here weeks and have never set foot inside my house. I've been very hurt." Her fat cheeks rumpled into a smile.

"Aw, now! You're not really hurt? You didn't make the invitation definite enough; that's why."

"*Diable!* Do I have to send you a written invitation like the Governor?"

"If you'll give me a kiss I'll accept that instead." He swung up on to the cart as he said it.

"You're a very bold young man," she said but gave him the kiss just the same. André came out of the barn then.

"Well, what's all this?" he exclaimed and laughed.

"I've just been invited over to Aunt Marie's," Antoine said and leapt down from the cart.

"You, too, André! Both of you come to supper tonight."

"That we will!" André's reply was hearty. "Will you have something good to eat?"

Aunt Marie sat with her arms akimbo and pretended to glare at him. "Have you ever been to my house and not had good things to eat?"

"Now, let me think," André said, scratching his head.

"Aw, be off with you!" She tugged the reins and the horse plodded away.

"See you later," the boys shouted.

"Bring *Elegance,* too, if he wants to come," she shouted back.

Antoine looked puzzled until André explained that this was her name for Jean-Baptiste. But Jean-Baptiste had a rendezvous in Montreal.

Uncle Philip's house was the least pretentious of all the Boissart farmhouses. It had one large room that served as parlor and bedroom, with an attic upstairs where the children slept. The over-sized bed, made by Uncle Philip to accommodate their ample proportions, stood in a corner, concealed by a screen. Beside it stood a cradle on rockers—a cradle that had scarcely been empty in the past fourteen years. The rest of the room, for all its rather crude simplicity, had an air of cosiness and was scrupulously clean. Uncle Philip's large bulk was sprawled before a roaring fire that took up half the space at the end of the room. The pots that hung before it glistened in the firelight and a savory aroma that drowned the smell of Uncle Philip's tobacco, welcomed the boys.

André gave a loud "Ah" and almost leapt to the huge pot that swung from a hook directly over the flames. He was about to lift the lid when Aunt Marie's voice boomed from the other side of the room. "Watch out! The lid's hot!" But André whipped out a large hankerchief and lifted it.

"Ooom!" he sniffed. "Aunt Marie, that's wonderful!" Then turning to Antoine, "She can make soup such as you've never tasted in France or anywhere else."

"In France!" Aunt Marie called out scornfully. "What makes them think they know so much!" She was native born and ridiculed the idea that all the best things had to be imported.

This chatter went on while the boys removed their heavy coats and mufflers, and made themselves comfortable before the fire. Uncle Philip immediately pushed a glass of brandy over to each of them. The children had already been sent to bed, though how they could sleep with their father's booming voice was a wonder.

The soup was as delicious as André had said it would be and with the hot bread that Aunt Marie produced, made a most delectable meal. The room was like an oven, for every window was battened down against the sub-zero temperature outside. When the meal was finished, they drew chairs around the fire and Aunt Marie plied them with questions about the ball.

She wanted especially to know all about the women's dresses, but for this she would have to wait until she saw Ann or Elise, for the men were vague. Antoine, however, described Elise's dress and told of her triumph.

"She has certainly developed this year," Aunt Marie remarked. "Few women are going to be able to outshine her. You'd better catch her, Antoine, before some one else does."

"Do you think I've been wasting my time?" Antoine replied warmly.

"That's what I want to know. Have you?"

"No."

She waited but he didn't say more. "Now, come along, tell me. Have you told her you love her?"

André was an interested listener.

"Yes, I have told her," Antoine admitted.

"And her answer?"

"You want to know too much, darling." Antoine grinned at her.

"Of course I do! I don't want to see any of these fandangling young men around here capture my favorite niece." Then she turned on André. "And what are you going to do, André? Sit about and grow fat like your uncle?"

Her husband turned on her. "Now, woman! You leave me alone. You're glad of my fat these cold nights."

"Oh, am I! It's your cold feet that are up my back!"

"And that isn't where I'd have them, either!" he said with a grin, which made his meaning clear.

"*Sacré bleu!* All you men think about is getting a woman pregnant," Aunt Marie retorted.

"Keeps you occupied while I'm away in the summer."

The noise that came from Aunt Marie was indescribable. "While you're amusing yourself with some squaw, you mean!"

"Now, now," Uncle Philip pretended to reprove her. "Don't go giving these young men ideas."

"You're a fine one to talk! What about your introducing André to Indian squaws?"

"Who told you any such thing!" André shouted.

"Who do you suppose? Don't ever think your Uncle Philip can keep a secret. When he gets drunk he blurts out everything."

"I do no such thing!" Uncle Philip shouted, but he looked guilty and uncomfortable.

"Well, don't go bringing any squaws back here, André."

"Now, Aunt Marie, give me credit for a little sense."

"Few men have any sense when it comes to women. And, anyway, we're getting away from the question. When are you going to find a wife, André?"

"Some day when the right woman comes along."

"Oh! You're going to sit back and wait for her to come along!"

"Not exactly. But I haven't found her yet."

"Then you'd better begin looking around. Do you mean to tell me there weren't any women there last night who could interest you?"

"Some, perhaps."

"I'll guarantee your brother found some. I hear he's always in Montreal these nights."

"Oh?" André looked noncommittal. "Who's been telling you stories?"

"Things get around fast here."

"You gossip too much."

"Leave the boys alone, Marie. They'll find their women without your help," Philip grunted.

"Maybe they will and maybe they won't," she answered defiantly.

Philip lifted the bottle of brandy to his mouth and took a large swallow. He seldom bothered with a glass.

"Have you made up your mind yet, Antoine?" Philip asked. "I'm not talking about women—I mean about your life. You going to stay here?"

"I believe so. Think I'll take some land and settle down."

"You'd better come with us in the spring. A trip into the woods 'ud do you good. You need hardening up a bit if you're going to remain here. Do you good to see a bit of Indian warfare."

"And some Indian squaws?" Antoine laughed. He wasn't in the least interested in such but the brandy was making him rowdy.

"Aw! Women!"

Aunt Marie boxed her husband's ears and he gave her thigh a resounding whack in return.

"If women 'ud keep out of this for a bit maybe we could talk," he said.

"Oh. Go to the devil!" she said and went to clean up the dishes.

"Tell me about fur trading," Antoine said.

"Well, I can't tell you much. You have to learn by experience. The Indians trap the beavers and we go to the posts and trade various things for the skins. It takes practice to make a good trader. Otherwise you give too much for the pelts. I remember Paul telling me that one time he was combing his hair and the redskin was so intrigued with the comb that he gave him three pelts for it."

"That certainly couldn't happen to you! You never comb your hair." Aunt Marie's voice came across the room.

"*Sacré enfant du grâce!*" Uncle Philip swore and threw the empty brandy bottle at her. It smashed against the wall and broke.

"Now you come and clean this up, you savage!" she shouted.

"All right, all right." He was a little perturbed at its breaking. "But leave us to talk in peace!"

He heaved his bulk out of the chair and picked up the broken bottle. The next minute he had his arm around her waist and was kissing her. When he came back he had a full bottle in his hand.

"It's a great life, though, Antoine. It'll make you rich if you trade well. It's the future of this land."

"Why do you have to go to the Indians for the pelts? Can't they bring them here?"

"They do. Wait until the end of May and June and the River'll be full of their canoes. But that isn't enough."

"I see. I'd like to go sometime." The thought of this source of revenue interested Antoine.

"Of course," Uncle Philip went on, "if you can't get away —I mean, if you're going to get married and probably couldn't leave for awhile, you can get in on the trading end of things here. Could probably find you some *coureur de bois* who needs money for equipment or supplies. You could go in as partner with a share of the profits he makes. It's a gamble. He might not come back. Still, it's worth a try. Maybe André and I could take you on as a partner. We'll talk it over with Paul. He's a partner too."

They discussed fur trading in detail for some time. It was not until he stood up to leave that Antoine realized how much he had drunk. The moment the cold air hit him, the brandy took effect. He and André had come on snowshoes on which Antoine was now becoming fairly adept. But with his legs none too steady, their progress home was hilarious. André was also far from sober, which always increased his desire to laugh. Each time Antoine would fall, André would pelt him with snow and they would roll over and over like two youngsters. Then André would pull him to his feet and they would stagger on for a while until down they would go again. After several such mishaps they were both so weak with laughter that they just sat in the snow and kept throwing it at each other. André finally staggered to his feet and dragged at Antoine's arm to get him up. When he was almost standing straight, André lost his balance and Antoine came down on top of him. Their laughter and shouts could be heard all over the seigneury. Eventually they reached the Manor House and André took off Antoine's boots and clothes and put him to bed.

CHAPTER X

CHRISTMAS CAME and went and the season was a festive one. The Manor House was gaily decorated with festoons of laurel and spruce and bunches of red-berried holly. Like a light that burns with a false brightness before going out, the town seemed more lively this winter, with many balls, *petits soupers*, skating and sleighing parties. Monsieur and Madame gave a ball at the Manor House for the Governor and the noblesse and also a jolly party for those of the seigneury, at which folk dances were performed to legendary songs sung to the accompaniment of the fiddlers. Elise's popularity continued and there were other men who would have liked to enter the lists and win her, had it not been that the competition between Claude, Charles and Antoine discouraged them. With Claude and Charles it became an open contest to see who could outdo the other and each gave balls and parties in her honor. Ann de Courville-Boissart and Marie-Charlotte de Ramezay were kept constantly busy as chaperones. In such a competition, Antoine de Brievaux was outdistanced. Yet he had the advantage of quieter and more intimate hours with Elise since he lived under the same roof. He made use of this advantage and did not attempt to vie with the other two in the more spectacular way. He approached his courtship with a quiet assurance, though there were times when he was inwardly concerned. Yet, as the weeks passed his advantage increased, for Elise found his quiet consideration something to appreciate. With Charles and Claude she had ever to be on the alert, for their subterfuges to get her alone were often disconcerting and when she found herself in this position, their ardency was not easy to keep in check. She and Claude had quarreled more than once because he had been so insistent and uncontrolled in making love to her. Antoine never annoyed her, though he let no opportunity pass to remind her of his love. He had, however, not kissed her yet, which had meant great restraint on his part. At the house his opportunities for doing so were frequent, but had he taken them, he was afraid his presence might become embarrassing.

Despite her popularity, Elise was neither vain nor flighty, having inherited a serious sensibility from her mother. She could not marry all three men and at least two of them would have to be disappointed. Of the three, Antoine would be the one to take this more seriously. She wished she had not felt so uncertain about his future. When she asked herself why she was concerned about this, she could not answer the question. She did not know; all she knew was that her feelings towards him were deeper, yet something held her back from making the decision. Deeply religious as they all were, she had sought help from her father confessor and had been directed to pray for guidance. Kneeling beside Antoine at Mass on Sundays, she had wondered whether he, too, was praying for the same thing. They all attended Mass at Notre Dame de Bonsecours, built by Marguerite Bourgeoys, the gentle nun who for nearly half a century had guided so many of the lives of the early settlers. Old Pierre Boissart had come to Montreal on the same ship as she, and the entire family had grown up under her splendid guidance. Though Elise had been only eight years old when the Reverend Mother had died, she had retained a vivid memory of her, so that she found herself wishing she were alive today, and could talk with her. Elise did not realize that in so doing she was emulating her Aunt Marguerite, who during the many tragedies that befell her earlier life, had always turned to Sister Marguerite.

The answer to prayer sometimes appears subtly, so that Elise scarcely realized when hers came. It happened one afternoon when she and Antoine and her two brothers returned from skating at the de Longueil seigneury. As they stepped out of the sleigh they began bombarding each other with snowballs and when the fight was at its height, Antoine caught Elise, pretending to rub a ball of snow on her face. Her eyes, alight with excitement, were so luminous and her laughing mouth so desirable, that he held the snowball poised in the air and kissed her. She let her head rest again his shoulder, making no protest, and the brightness of her eyes dissolved to a deep mistiness.

"I love you, darling. I love you," he whispered.

Her gloved hand touched his cheek gently. "And I you, Antoine," she answered. The words had spoken themselves.

Antoine's dark eyes lighted up with victory. "Elise!" The word was uttered fervently and he kissed her again. Jean-Baptiste and André tactfully left to put the sleigh away.

They stood looking at each other for a moment, absorbing what had happened. Without speaking they turned towards the house, hand in hand. Suddenly hers gripped his tightly. Gaston was standing by the back door watching.

"Oh!" It was almost a gasp. "There's Gaston. I didn't know he was back." Her face, already flushed with excitement, became still more deeply diffused.

"Hello, Gaston!" Antoine called gaily.

Elise pulled herself together and called out to him too, but he did not return the greeting. He turned away abruptly but not before Elise had seen the angry expression on his face.

"Looks like something's wrong," Antoine remarked but without concern. "Probably your father has been reproving him." He was too elated to be concerned with Gaston. Inside the door he stopped and asked, "May I speak to your father tonight?"

His words wrenched Elise back to reality. The shock of seeing Gaston had made her forget that moment with Antoine. He was not impatient at her hesitation, though he had not the slightest idea of the real reason for it. She realized that Gaston's return made the announcement of her engagement even more urgent. She looked at Antoine and nodded her head in agreement.

"Thank you, darling," he said.

Supper that evening was very gay. Antoine was in high spirits and kept them all amused with anecdotes. Never before had he seemed so talkative, especially in regard to himself.

"You've always lived in Paris, haven't you?" Madame asked.

"Yes, except for short educational trips such as those with Jean-Baptiste. However, the strange thing is that I was almost born in Quebec which may account for my taking so easily to this country."

"In Quebec!" Several of them exclaimed at the same time.

"You never mentioned it when we were in Quebec," Jean-Baptiste said, and there was resentment in his tone. Antoine had never confided any of his family history to him, and he did not like having to learn it at the same time as the rest of the family.

"No, I didn't," Antoine said apologetically. "And that must seem strange, Jean-Baptiste. You'll hardly believe that I am telling the truth when I say I never thought of it." Jean-Baptiste certainly looked as though he didn't believe it. "You see," Antoine explained, "I have never given much thought to my family until now." He glanced at Elise and went on: "Until I came to visit this delightful family I had not realized how much I have missed." He turned his charming smile on Madame and she smiled back at him.

"I'm glad to hear you say that, Antoine. Family life is a wonderful thing and my husband and I have always wanted ours to be a happy one."

"It is. It . . ."

But Jean-Baptiste interrupted Antoine. "How was it then that you were nearly born in Quebec?" he asked in a tone that indicated he was not going to be put off again.

"Oh. Well, my parents were visiting there at the time, but returned to Paris three months before I was born."

"Maybe we knew them, Antoine," Madame remarked. "You are the same age as Jean-Baptiste, aren't you?"

"Yes, a month older to be exact."

"We were in Quebec all that winter, so it could be possible we knew them, couldn't it, Paul?"

"Yes, indeed. You especially. I didn't know so many people."

"You would have the advantage of me, Madame, if you did know them," Antoine said. "My mother married the Duc de Chamois in Quebec and . . ."

"The Duc de Chamois!" Madame exclaimed and cast a swift glance at her husband but he was idly fingering the stem of his wineglass and did not appear to have recognized the name. "What was your mother's name before her marriage?" she asked quickly and hung upon his reply.

"Hélène de Matier," Antoine answered.

The stem of Paul's wineglass snapped and the red wine made a river down the table cloth.

"Oh!" Elise exclaimed and moved her chair so that the wine would not spill on her.

"It was just an accident," Madame said. "No harm is done."

All eyes were turned to Paul, who was regarding the spilled wine with fixed eyes. It soaked into the table cloth, a red gash on a hitherto spotless surface.

"Hélène de Matier?" Paul turned his eyes to look at Antoine.

"Yes, Paul, you remember Madame de Matier." Madame spoke quickly. "Every one knew her."

"Again you have the advantage of me, Madame," Antoine said. "She died at my birth and my father died when I was two years old."

"Yes, I remember. My father, who knew your mother well, wrote us that she had died giving birth to a son. How strange that that son should be you."

"When were you born?" Paul's voice interrupted. His tone was hard.

"He just told us, dear. He's a month older than Jean-Baptiste."

Paul looked away from her and down at his finger. It was red as with the spilled wine but when he wiped it off, blood gushed out again.

"You've cut yourself!" Ann exclaimed and jumped up quickly to attend to it.

"It's nothing," Paul said irritably as he stood up. "I'll take care of it."

"You had better let me bind it up," Ann said as he reached the door.

"No, I can do it." His tone was sharp, and understanding it, she let him go.

As she resumed her seat she tried to relax the tension that was now in the air. The gaiety of a short while ago had fled. Antoine was concerned, for he sensed that his information had somehow caused the tension.

"What's upset father?" Jean-Baptiste asked.

"It was only an accident," Ann said.

"Shouldn't we take the cloth off?" Elise asked. "It will stain, won't it?"

"I'll take care of it later," Ann said.

"I wasn't referring to the wine," Jean-Baptiste pursued the subject. "I meant, why did he spill it?"

"I said it was an accident, Jean-Baptiste," his mother told him and her tone was firm. Jean-Baptiste became silent, but his look was resentful. He was pleased to know that he had a friend who was the son of a Duc but he would have liked to have been the one who could have bragged about it.

"And so, Antoine, you were nearly a native of this colony," Madame was saying, trying to bridge the awkwardness that had arisen. "Now that I look at you, I can see your mother in you— she had the same dark hair and eyes."

"She did?" Antoine said with interest. "You are the first person I have ever met who knew her. Won't you tell me more about her?"

To be asked to give an account of a woman who had been

her rival and whom she had detested was not too easy. "Yes, I will, sometime," she answered. "I shall have to take my mind back twenty years. She was a remarkably beautiful woman," she said and decided to let the description rest there.

"So I have heard," Antoine said. "I would have liked to have known her. I have always felt so guilty that she died giving birth to me. . . ."

"You could hardly be blamed for that," Elise remarked, and the smile she gave him warmed his heart. How beautiful and comforting that smile could be! How wonderful to be able to watch it for the rest of his life.

"No, Antoine, you couldn't be blamed at all," Madame took up the conversation again. She could have added more to the remark, much that would have been very unpleasant, for if Antoine was Hélène de Matier's only child, it was by accident and not because there couldn't have been many more by a miscellaneous number of fathers.

"Did you know the Duc de Chamois also, Madame?" Antoine asked.

"Only very slightly. I saw him on several occasions."

"I never knew him," Antoine said. "Being left with a newborn child was difficult, of course. I was put out to nurse and when the Duc died, a guardian was appointed. I seldom saw him, either." Antoine laughed, and some of the tension relaxed. "So you see I am very little acquainted with my family."

"Didn't your father have any relative who could look after you?" André asked.

Antoine hesitated a moment. Then in his frank manner said: "Yes, he had a large family. Several sons and daughters by a former marriage. They didn't recognize me."

"Didn't recognize you!" It was Elise who spoke. Antoine's revelation of his family and that his father was a Duc interested her also, but his last statement was rather disconcerting.

Antoine looked at her and then at Madame. "Well, you see, my father was seventy-five years old when I was born."

There was a moment's silence and Elise, understanding the implication, merely replied: "Oh!"

"You have a lot of family comfort to catch up with, Antoine," Madame said in her gentle voice.

His look thanked her.

"But where did you spend your childhood?" Elise asked, quite concerned for him. "Didn't you have any one who cared? Didn't you have other children to play with?"

Antoine turned to her, pleased with her interest. "I was very well looked after. An old nurse who had taken care of many of the children of the family and had been retired, attended to me. . . ."

"But if she was retired, she must have been old!" Elise exclaimed.

"Yes, she was. She had a younger daughter who nursed me. I have no complaints. . . ."

"And you had no love—no family love such as we have had. . . ." Elise was still concerned.

Antoine smiled. "That is true. But what you don't know exists, you don't really miss."

"I think they treated you shamefully!" Elise said indignantly. "People shouldn't have children and then leave them to others to bring up."

Madame interrupted. The conversation had been steered into a safer channel now. "You must excuse me," she said rising. "I must see if my husband has attended to his finger."

Antoine sprang up to open the door for her and she smiled at him as she went out.

Paul was in the library, pacing the floor and facing an awful truth. He had merely wound a handkerchief around his finger and it was already soaked with blood. Ann noticed it and began to scold him. He did not appear to hear. She took his hand and removed the bloodied handkerchief. Then she saw the deep anguish in his eyes and stopped scolding. She took the strip of linen she had brought with her and bound up the wound, talking as she did so.

"Don't take it so hard, dear," she said comfortingly. "After all she . . ."

He interrupted. "You don't understand, Ann. It isn't only that she is his mother. It's . . ." He stopped and passed his free hand over his eyes, pressing them hard into their sockets.

Ann tied the bandage and drew him to his chair. "Come and sit down, dear," she said. When she had stirred the fire into a blaze, she knelt down beside him and tried to comfort him.

"After all, dear, it's so long ago," she said, wanting him to talk to relieve his mind.

"I know now why he has seemed familiar to me," Paul said. "Remember how I told you some time ago he reminded me of some one?"

She nodded. "Yes, he is like her."

"Oh, Ann! Why was I ever such a fool?" It was an anguished cry as he buried his face in his hands.

"I've always understood, dear." Her voice was tender. "I've always known that you were attracted to her. I am happy that her son has grown into such a fine young man and that he found us who knew his mother."

He took his hands away from his face but did not look at her. "But, Ann, that isn't all. I think I am his father!"

"You!" The word was like the crack of a whip.

It loosed a flood of words from Paul. "This has haunted me for years, Ann. It's only in the last few years that I have been able to forget it. I wanted to tell you but it was too sordid and I was afraid you would despise me and I might lose you. It happened the afternoon of your reception after the ball where we met. I came back from the reception full of love for you. She was waiting in my rooms. I hated her then. She would not go away. She insisted I marry her. I tried to get rid of her. I didn't want her. I have no excuse. I hated her, yet I gave in to her insistence. She had a fascination that made fools of men.

She made a fool of me. I didn't want to, Ann. I didn't want to."
He covered his face again. "I gave in to her. I made love to her
and now this is the consequence."

Ann heard his words, yet was thinking all the while of something
else. She answered him with one word: "Elise."

He dropped his hands and stared at her and then with a
groan buried his head in his arms. "Holy Mother!" she heard
him murmur. There was a long silence in which she sought for
some way to comfort him, some ray of hope that might divert
the impending tragedy.

"Perhaps you are mistaken, Paul," she said presently.
"After all, we do know that she distributed her favors over a
wide field. You weren't the only one at that time."

"But the date of his birth, Ann! Did he say anything about
the Duc de Chamois? Does he believe he was his father?"

"No," Ann admitted reluctantly. "He believes to the contrary. He mentioned that the family did not recognize him, as
his father was seventy-five when he was born."

"Where does he get the name de Brievaux?"

"One of his father's minor titles I presume. I don't know.
I did not think to ask him."

"What am I going to do, Ann? Do you think he is serious
about wanting to marry Elise?"

"Yes. In fact, perhaps the reason he mentioned his family
tonight is that only this afternoon Elise decided he was the one
she wanted to marry. She came in and told me before supper.
Antoine was going to speak to you tonight."

"Oh my God, my God!" Paul jumped up and paced back
and forth. "The sins of the fathers!" he quoted. Up and down,
up and down he paced, while Ann crouched before the fire,
silently praying.

"What am I going to do, Ann?" Paul asked again.

"You will have to tell him, Paul. We can't let this marriage
take place."

"What about Elise? She will hate me and have every right
to do so. I shall have wrecked her life."

"Perhaps she won't have to know. I don't know. I must think it out."

She got up. Paul stood before her. "How you must despise me, Ann!"

She looked up at him, her face lined with worry, yet not angry. "No, Paul. We have loved too long for it to change overnight. I can't say I don't blame you. It is too much of a shock yet for me to think clearly. I am so concerned over the children. But I shan't hate you."

She kissed him lightly and went up to her room. Paul did not follow her. All night long he tried to thrash out the question, but when dawn broke through the dark night, no light had broken through his clouds.

CHAPTER XI

THE FOLLOWING MORNING Antoine waylaid Elise as she was on her way to the storehouse to get some supplies for her mother. In her simple work clothes she was just as attractive to him as in her ball gown. There was a sweet naturalness about her that did not, in his opinion, require silks and satins to augment her looks. He drew her into the doorway. "May I have just one little kiss?" he asked.

She frowned, but her eyes were laughing. "Are you going to be one of those persistent nuisances always getting in my way?" she teased.

"Not if you'll give me one kiss."

She held up her mouth and he kissed her gently. "I couldn't get to see your father last night. I waited but the door to the library was closed and I could hear voices. I thought it better not to intrude. And I haven't seen him this morning."

"I haven't seen him, either. He's always busy during the day. Better wait until this evening."

"Yes. I'm going into Montreal now with Jean-Baptiste. We're having dinner at the Chateau. We have to get our assignments for the spring. Seems they are expecting some trouble with the English."

"Oh dear! More fighting."

"Yes, but I'm resigning my commission, though, of course, I shall remain on the reserve."

"Every man has to here."

"So I understand. I am going to speak to the Governor about some land. I would like to get it adjoining here if possible, then you wouldn't have to be away from your family."

She smiled at him and was very happy. "Thank you,

Antoine. Would you do one thing for me before you go into town?"

"Of course. I am your servant to command."

"Thank you. Will you open the storeroom door for me. It is so heavy."

"Why certainly."

He followed her to the storeroom and swinging back the heavy wooden door, blocked it with a stone.

Elise looked out over the white River. "It will soon be melting, Antoine, and spring will be here. I shall be glad. It's beautiful then, with all the trees bursting into leaf."

"I am looking forward to it." He laid his hand on her arm. "I am so deeply and gratefully happy." They looked into each other's eyes for a moment. Then she stood on tiptoe and kissing him quickly, ran inside. "Sure I can't help you with anything? Can't I carry something back with me?" he called to her.

"No, thank you. I am only going to rearrange some things." Her voice came to him from inside.

"I'll hurry back." He poked his head inside the door. She was silhouetted against the light of the candle. "I love you," he said in a loud whisper.

"And I love you," she whispered back.

Elise sang as she worked. It was not only that her love for Antoine was growing but there was relief in having come to a decision. In fact, it was so great, she felt light-headed. "I must go into Montreal this afternoon and offer thanks," she told herself.

Her mother had given her several tasks to do and time flew by as she rearranged shelves and selected various commodities that needed replenishing in the house. She liked working in the storeroom, where the sacks of flour and vegetables, and the sides of meat hanging from the beams, gave her such a feeling of plenty and security. She thought of Antoine and their future, making plans in her mind for the home they would have and wondering the while how long it would take them to build a seigneury that would be as prosperous as her father's. That had, after all, taken over half a century to acquire its present status, but she and Antoine could profit by her father's experience and despite the fact that the colony had developed so slowly, conditions had improved.

She had added the last of her list of supplies to the stack to go to the house, when the light inside faded and her first thought was that the candle had burned low. Then she realized that it was the light from the doorway that was being blocked. For a moment she thought happily that Antoine had come back and she turned to chide him for being a nuisance. But the bulk blocking the doorway was too large for Antoine. It was Gaston, the expression on his face concealed, as he stood with his back to the light. She stared at him, not saying a word, but with fear in her heart, which increased as he roughly kicked away the stone that had been holding the door open. It plunged the room into semi-darkness, leaving only the thin arc of light from the candle at the other end. As he came towards her she felt paralyzed, too frightened to speak. She could not see his expression but there was something in his attitude that was sinister. He had spoken no word of greeting but silently came up to her, and when he stood in front of her, leaned a hand on each side of the shelf, holding her a prisoner. His heavy brows were lowered over dark eyes that glared at her. Never had she seen such a brutal look in any one's eyes. He appeared half mad.

She found her voice and asked: "What do you want, Gaston?" She was annoyed that her voice shook.

"I want you, of course," he said slowly.

"Let me go," she said, her voice scarcely above a whisper.

"Not until I have given you that lesson I promised you. Or did you think those were just idle words?" She did not answer. He brought his face closer to hers. "What I said I meant. I am going to teach you a lesson you will never forget. After this, you won't play with men's affections."

"Gaston, please!" Her tone was terrified and he noticed it, setting his mouth into a straight, hard line that was vicious.

"Now you're afraid. You were so bold before. You thought

you could make me dance to any tune you called. You will see you were mistaken. Once before my life was wrecked over a woman.. It's not going to happen again. This time I'm going to have the satisfaction of avenging myself on the wrecker. Gaston Renault isn't always going to be the one to suffer."

His hands came down on her shoulders, those strong large hands that she had often admired, but which now held her in a vise-like grip.

"Please, Gaston!" she pleaded again. "I didn't mean to hurt you. I didn't realize what I was doing. I was carried away."

He did not reply. His large eyes seemed to grow larger and blacker. She could smell brandy on his breath as he brought his face closer to hers.

"What are you going to do?" she asked, ready to scream as her fright increased.

"I am going to put you in a position where no other man will want you. Then you will have to marry me."

She was trembling so that she could hardly stand. Would he take the knife from his belt and slash her face so that she would be disfigured for life? Her eyes lowered to the knife as this thought occurred to her. He read her thoughts and laughed, an ugly laugh that had no mirth.

"Oh no, I'm not going to mutilate you. You threw yourself into my arms once. You played with me and then scorned me for your aristocratic friends. It is time you learned a few things about men."

"No, Gaston, no!" She struggled as he tried to reach her mouth. She moved her head swiftly this way and that until his hand gripped the back of her head and held it. His lips bruised her mouth as she clenched her teeth and drew her lips tightly together. With an iron grip he pressed her jaw between his powerful fingers until she had to relax. Her only emotion was fear, which rose to hysteria as he jerked her feet from under her and swung her on to some sacks of flour that lay nearby. The horror of what he intended made her desperate. She tried to scream. His large hand clamped over her mouth and when she tried to bite his fingers he gripped her jaw so tightly that it gave her excruciating pain. He was like a madman now, tearing and ripping at her clothes, dragging away anything that interfered with his intentions.

She felt his hands on her body and again tried to plead with him. "Please, Gaston, don't. I'll never hurt you again. Please!" Her words went unheeded. He had lost all sense of reason. His large mouth was over hers again, preventing her screaming. With his strong legs against hers she was powerless to move or resist him. A convulsion of terror seized her and she fainted.

The candle had burned to half an inch and its flickering flame cast distorted shadows across Elise's prostrate form and on the hunched form of the man crouched beside her. As consciousness returned and she saw him, she shrank back against the wall. Then suddenly she leaned forward with a cry, for the candlelight had touched the tawny hair as he lifted his head.

"André!" she cried. And then as he put his arms around her she repeated, "Oh, André!" and a flood of tears broke.

"Are you all right?" he asked anxiously.

"I don't know," she replied. She looked at her dishevelled condition and her sobs increased hysterically.

"Don't cry, dear. It's all right now," he comforted her.

"How did you get here?" she asked between sobs.

"By a lucky chance. I was passing and stopped to get some supplies. I didn't realize any one was in here until I heard Gaston swear and then I saw you. I lashed out at him but he's so big and I landed on the ground."

"Are you hurt?" she asked.

"Only a bump on my head and . . ." he pressed his hand to his temple, "probably a bruise here. What happened? Did he come in here and attack you?"

Elise began to sob again and it was some time before she could control herself enough to speak. Then, somewhat disjointedly, she told him the whole story from the day she had gone to Gaston's house.

André listened, his face set. "So that's the meaning of his strange behavior lately," he said thoughtfully.

"He blames me for wrecking his life. He said . . ." she faltered and then finished the sentence quickly, "he said he was going to make it so I had to marry him."

André stared at her in alarm. After a moment he asked: "He didn't succeed, did he? You know what I mean."

Elise looked confused and did not answer his question. What was he doing . . . I mean when did you come in? I wonder if it was long after I fainted. Oh André, this is dreadful! I'm so ashamed. What am I going to do?" she asked.

"I don't know, Elise. But I know what I am going to do," he said. "He taught me to handle a gun and he will now regret having done so."

"No. Don't do that, André. You might get killed and then I would never forgive myself. He's dangerous. You'd better leave him alone." Her tone became more agitated as she talked.

"I'm not going to do anything hasty, Elise. I owe him at least one punch for this bump on my head and several for you. . . ."

"Oh André—why did this have to happen! Gaston has always been our friend—our special friend."

"I know," André said sadly, ruffling his hands through his hair. "It's unfortunate. Still, something will have to be done about it. I'll never feel you are safe while he's around."

Elise thought for a moment. "Perhaps I had better tell father and mother what has happened. . . ."

"Oh . . ." André exclaimed, "no. No, I don't think I would do that. Father'd kill him."

"What'll we do then?"

"I don't know. I'll have to think. It would be better to handle it ourselves if we can."

"I think so, too. I'd be so ashamed to have to tell mother." She covered her face with her hands. "Perhaps I'll have to anyway," she said without removing her hands. "It was dreadful, André. He was like a wild animal." She pressed her hand against her bruised lips. "Does my mouth look funny to you?" she asked.

"It looks a bit swollen. And your dress is all torn. . . ."

"If mother sees, she'll know something has happened and I'll have to tell."

"Keep your coat on until you get to your room."

The candle sputtered and went out. Elise gave a scream and clung to André in a spasm of terror.

"It's all right, dear. It's only the candle burned out," he assured her. "Stay where you are and I'll light another one." He groped his way across the room and felt along the shelf to where they kept the supply. With a new candle burning brightly she felt more comfortable.

"We must be getting back. Mother'll wonder what's keeping me." She stood up, feeling rather weak, and holding her dress where it was torn.

"What were you doing here before this happened?" André asked.

"Tidying up and getting some supplies. I had just finished when he appeared." She pointed to the stack of things she had collected. "Those are the things that have to go up to the house."

"I'll take them. I'll say I came by and carried them up, which is quite true. Perhaps you can slip upstairs and change your dress without them seeing you."

Elise put her arms around André and kissed him. "You're such a wonderful brother, André. What would I have done if you hadn't come in!" She began to cry again and André said quickly:

"Now, now, dear, don't cry any more. You'll look a sight."

"I do already," she mopped at her eyes. "You don't think I'm very awful, André? You won't despise me?"

"Of course not, dear. Now stop worrying and leave everything to me." He gathered up the supplies. "Put on your coat and I'll extinguish the candle."

In the daylight he looked at her. Her eyes were red and

her nose shining, which with her swollen lips made her anything but presentable.

"If we run into any one, you'd better say you fell down," he said.

"I hope we don't." She looked about anxiously as they hurried along, thankful when they reached the house. In the sanctuary of her own room she gave way and sobbed again.

CHAPTER XII

PAUL NIBBLED at his supper. Antoine had asked to see him afterwards and he dreaded the talk they must have. Yet it had to be faced and when he and Antoine entered the library, Paul braced himself for the ordeal. Quite unaware that anything was wrong, Antoine gave him a smile of assurance as he said: "You probably already know why I wanted to see you, monsieur."

Paul met his glance but did not answer. Antoine was a little disconcerted. He had expected Paul to say in effect: "Yes, I understand, you want to marry my daughter." He had even thought that Paul might continue by saying he was happy about it, for the friendly attitude he had always shown would warrant this. When Paul gave no answer, Antoine continued:

"I am sure you know that I love Elise. She returns my affection. Have I your permission to ask her to be my wife?" Still Paul did not answer and Antoine was puzzled. "You don't have any objection to me, do you, monsieur?" he asked anxiously.

"No, none at all," Paul said quickly. Then he braced himself and tried to look Antoine in the face. They were Hélène de Matier's eyes that met his and he had to look away. "I don't know how to tell you, Antoine. I have a dreadful confession to make to you." Antoine's look of puzzlement deeepened. "I did not know until last night when you spoke of your family, or perhaps I could have prevented things developing the way they have." Then Paul made himself look at Antoine. "I believe you are my son, Antoine."

Antoine leapt to his feet. "Your son!" His voice was a shout. "You mean . . . I . . . you mean Elise and I are related?"

122

"That's what I fear."

Antoine sat down heavily and there was a tense silence before he asked: "But how, monsieur?"

Paul had walked to the window and was staring out with unseeing eyes. He did not turn as he answered: "Your mother was my mistress." Antoine stared at the Sieur's broad back. The scene at dinner the night before recurred to him—the snapping of the wineglass stem, the alarmed look on Paul's face and the tension that had been in the air. Now these were all explained.

"Your mistress?" he said, trying to comprehend.

"Yes. About a month before I married my wife . . . I . . . we . . . met. When I heard that she had given birth to a son and that the Duc was too old to be the father, I suspected then that the child might be mine." Paul turned but remained standing by the window, regarding the boy upon whom he must now thrust his parentage. "There was nothing that I could do at the time. There seemed no need to do anything. With the years I had almost forgotten the matter." Paul paused and then asked: "You had no suspicion that I was your father?"

At the question Antoine's eyes blazed angrily, reminding Paul again of Hélène. "If I had, would I have courted your daughter! Would I even have come here?"

"No, of course not. I'm sorry, Antoine. It was a stupid thought that crossed my mind and I voiced it without thinking. Forgive me."

"Of course, monsieur," Antoine replied and his anger, always quick to fade, was gone.

Again a heavy silence fell, as each man pursued his own thoughts. Words of his guardian's flashed through Antoine's mind. He remembered the cynical expression on his face as he had said: "Your mother had many lovers. The family of the Duc de Chamois refuse to recognize you. They believe your mother knew she was with child when she contracted the marriage. Your only inheritance will be the marriage settlement upon which she insisted. Fortunately for you, that amount has not been touched, otherwise you would be penniless." Antoine thought over these words. "Your mother had many lovers," kept recurring.

"Could it be possible you are mistaken, monsieur?" Antoine asked.

All night long Paul had asked himself the same question. He turned slowly as he replied: "Yes, it could be possible."

"I have been told my mother had many lovers."

Paul looked surprised and a little relief came into his face. "Yes, that is true," he replied. "I did not want to say so because I did not want to injure your mother's reputation in your eyes."

"My mother is dead and I never knew her," Antoine said roughly. "Another lady is going to suffer far more."

Paul's mouth sagged as he thought of his daughter. "Yes," he said in an undertone.

"There must be some way to find out who was my father," Antoine said. "My whole life and Elise's happiness hang upon it. But how to find out?" Antoine held his head in his hands.

"You have no papers of hers?" Paul suggested.

"None. My guardian took so little interest. When he told me about my parentage I asked him that question. He said the Duc's brother had some papers belonging to my mother, but I could never get in touch with him, and now he is dead. The matter never bothered me. I didn't care. If only I had! Perhaps now I might have some proof—*if* there is any. Is there any one living in Quebec who might have known my mother?"

"I don't know. I doubt it. It was twenty years ago."

"Yes," Antoine replied and his tone was hopeless. "How about the Chevalier de Ramezay? Didn't I understand that you and he were married at the same time in Quebec? Did he know my mother?"

"Yes, he did, but I don't know how well." Paul remembered how he had ousted Claude de Ramezay in Hélène's favor. He had been proud of it at the time, but how bitterly he regretted it now! He had been just Antoine's age then and the success had filled him with a false pride.

"Would you mind my speaking to him, monsieur? I wouldn't need to tell him why?"

"I don't mind your telling him if it will help. De Ramezay and I have always been close friends. He would understand."

"Can you think of any one else, monsieur?"

Paul thought of the Chevalier de Favien but he was reluctant to mention the name. De Favien was the natural son of the Sieur de Courville. He had come to Montreal as the Sieur's nephew and had caused much trouble. He had fathered the son of Paul's twin sister, Marguerite, starting a chain of calamities that had clouded her earlier life. Yet now everything must be done to try to straighten out this tangle.

"There is a Chevalier de Favien who came to this country with Madame de Matier. He might possibly know some way in which you might trace information about her." Then Paul shook his head. "No, that wouldn't help. He was in the Bastille at the time."

"In the Bastille!"

"Yes, he had committed some crime. But unless your mother visited him when she returned to France and confided in him, he wouldn't be much help."

"But she might have. She was there several months before I was born. If he were an old friend she might have told him. Is he in the Bastille now?"

"So far as I know."

"Then I shall go to France if I can't find out any other way. I must leave no possibility uninvestigated."

"Only you had better not mention my name to the Chevalier de Favien or that of my wife. It was my wife's father who had him imprisoned. It is too long a story to tell you now."

"It won't be necessary to mention either of you in my inquiries. I can easily say I am inquiring for my own benefit. After all, a man does like to know who his father is." Antoine's tone was bitter.

There was another long silence. Antoine's first feelings towards Paul were resentment and bitterness. Then as he reasoned it out, these faded, for he had had enough experience in

France to have no prejudice again men having mistresses. He could not yet comprehend the full import of Paul's revelation. Could it be that with one sentence all his future hopes had been scattered? Why of all the families in Montreal should it have been this one to which he had come! And what was he going to tell Elise? He asked the question of Paul.

"She must be told the truth," Paul answered.

"But suppose you should be wrong, monsieur?"

Paul shook his head. "I hold very little hope of such a possibility, Antoine."

"But until I have made inquiries, there is nothing to be gained by telling Elise. It might prejudice her against you and that I would like to avoid."

Antoine had risen as he spoke and the two men faced each other. "When I have done you so much harm, you are thoughtful enough to want to spare feelings," Paul said much moved. "I wish I could have claimed you as my son under more happy circumstances, Antoine." These two, who from their first meeting had been mutually attracted, and who under other circumstances would have enjoyed the relationship of father and son, measured each other's worth. Antoine was nearly a head taller, giving Paul the disadvantage of having to look up at him.

"Had it not been for Elise, this would have been a happy revelation, monsieur," Antoine replied. "Instead, it is a tragedy. One that I must go and think out. Perhaps we can arrange something to tell Elise temporarily. When I have had time to think, I will tell you if I come to a decision. We must both have the same stories."

With a slight bow he turned and walked from the room and as Paul watched him go, the dark lines beneath his eyes, deepened and his brow furrowed. All that was finest in Hélène was reflected in her son and much more that she did not possess. Yet even as he stood there watching the closed door through which Antoine had passed, Paul seemed to hear her mocking laugh. His marriage to Ann de Luc after his refusal to marry Hélène, had infuriated her but now she had her revenge. That the cruelty of that revenge fell upon her own son and the girl he loved would not have disturbed Hélène. She believed that love was transitory and something to amuse and entertain. She had loved lightly and frequently, shedding it like a garment when it had ceased to be interesting or useful. Then another thought crossed Paul's mind, one that brought a modicum of comfort and hope with it. On that afternoon twenty years ago, when Hélène had persisted he marry her, could she have then been pregnant? And was her sudden insistence on marriage for the same reason that she had shortly afterwards married the aging Duc de Chamois so hastily? Too soon the hopeful thought faded, for would a woman already pregnant, have lured him into seduction? He could not answer himself and bowed his head wearily.

Antoine could not yet face Elise. He left the library by the door that led into the hall and slipped quickly out of the house before she should see him. The cold air struck him but he did not want to return for a coat. He walked to the side of the house away from the icy breezes. Then he leaned against the wall and sobbed—sobbed for the hopelessness that faced him. It was the first time in all his life that he had cried, at least, so far as he could remember. They were the hard, stifled sobs of a man who cannot let his grief come to the surface. All these months he had clung to a hope, patiently waiting for the woman he loved; after years of indolence he had found a family he could claim as his own, but unfortunately the currents crossed and could not be separated.

How long he stood there he did not know. He was stiff with cold but would not heed it. Indoors, Elise would be waiting, knowing that he was speaking to her father about their marriage. He thought and thought until his mind was as numb as his frozen hands. Suddenly through the haze of the shock that clouded his brain, a light flashed. He saw it but at first gave it no attention. Then it began to penetrate that the light was flames leaping into the air, reflecting a crimson glow upon the snow. It jerked him back to sanity and he rushed into the house shouting that there was a fire. Paul came running from the library and as he dashed outside, the rest of the family followed.

"It's Gaston's house!" André shouted and Elise gripped his arm in the darkness. His arm around her waist signalled to her to control herself. "Come quick!" he shouted, but as they dashed down the steps Paul called to them to stop.

"This may be more serious than you think. It may be an Indian attack. They are restless again. Come inside and get your guns and coats."

They all followed into the house. André went to the gun rack and handed out the muskets. While each man examined the one given to him, Ann and Elise brought them coats.

"One of us had better remain here," Paul said. "They might attack the house."

"That isn't necessary," Ann said quickly. "Elise and I can each handle a gun. Rouse the men and send one of them here."

André was again ready to dash out to rouse the men-servants but again Paul stopped him. "You'd better let me organize this. I have fought Indians before." He turned to Ann. "Are you sure you will be all right?"

"Of course. Now hurry. And be careful. I'll see that the house is barred and bolted. And don't worry about us."

Antoine shot a smile at Elise. That was all he dared do.

The men followed Paul, crouching down against the high banked snow, so as to be less conspicuous in territory that revealed them much too clearly. As they approached the burning building, they could see figures silhouetted against the light. The whole seigneury had been aroused. The men had formed a chain and were passing buckets of water back and forth. Paul's suspicion of Indians appeared a false alarm, though he did not relinquish the possibility until he had despatched men in groups to scour the territory.

"Where's Gaston?" he inquired. No one had seen him. "You're sure he's not inside?"

"We went in before the fire was so bad," his brother Philip replied. "There was no one there."

"How'd it start, Uncle Philip?" André asked.

"Haven't the slightest idea. It was already going when Marie saw the light. Looks like it will be gutted. There's just enough wind to fan the flames."

"Hope it doesn't spread."

"It won't if we watch it." Paul, his sons and Antoine, with others from the seigneury formed another bucket chain but the labor was heavy and the progress slow. Suddenly there was a shout as the wooden roof caved in, pushing the walls outward. The men scrambled out of danger, but Antoine, still unaccustomed to the snow under his feet, slipped and fell and before he could get up, flaming logs from the wall crashed upon him.

"Antoine!" André yelled and with Jean-Baptiste and others rushed to his aid. The red hot timbers burned their hands but they ignored this. Antoine's clothes were aflame and they rolled him over and over in the snow.

"Get him back to the house at once," Paul shouted. Four of them carried him and trudging through the slippery snow, it seemed as though the house moved farther and farther away. Not a sound came from Antoine. Watching from the windows, Ann and Elise saw them coming and quickly pushed a couch into the hall. Ann had laid out bandages and what few medical supplies she had.

When Elise saw that it was Antoine, she flew to his side and knelt down beside him. She called his name, but he did not hear.

"Is he dead, mother?" she asked and there was fear in her eyes.

"I don't know, dear. Get up and let me attend to him. Go and get hot water. André, get a doctor," Ann said. She leaned over Antoine. There were bad burns to be attended to and his dark hair was singed around the hair line.

"Are there any bones broken do you think?" Jean-Baptiste asked. "Heavy logs fell on him."

Ann felt over his body. "It's hard to tell, Jean-Baptiste. I'm not much of a doctor."

CHAPTER XIII

THE PEACE of the Manor House was shattered as surely as the stillness of the River ended with the breaking up of the ice into enormous craggy blocks. As Ann watched from the window, she thought she would always remember this *ice-shove* because it seemed so symbolic of their lives that year. Because of the secret which she shared with Paul and Antoine, she was doing most of the nursing herself, afraid that in his delirium Antoine might reveal the conversation he had had with Paul. Elise was anxious to help with the nursing and Ann tried to limit this to periods when Antoine was asleep. She knew only too well that there was nothing like an illness to increase a bond between people and this at all costs she wanted to prevent.

Antoine had not sustained any broken bones but he was badly burned. What was more serious was the development of inflammation of the lungs, so that he struggled for breath and his body was racked by a hard cough. Checking back over the events which had preceded the fire, Ann found out from Paul and from deductions she herself made, that Antoine had stood outside for a long time without a coat. For nine days the doctor remained at the Manor House, fighting for the life of his patient, as lungs filled up and breath came in hard struggling efforts. Then the crisis passed and his temperature dropped.

The anxiety over Antoine was not the only worry during this time. Two days after the demolition of Gaston's house, his body was found in the forest by hunters. His gun was by his side and there was a wound in his head. Men were so often shot that this did not call for an investigation. His gun might have gone off, or he might have been killed by an Indian, either accidentally or intentionally. André was there when they brought him in and with one look at the position of the wound, he drew his own conclusions and kept them to himself. Immediately he sought Elise, for he did not want some one else to tell her the news. He found her in the kitchen and signalled to her to come outside.

"Gaston has been found," he said gently. Her eyes were dilated with fear as she gripped his arm. "He can't harm you any more," he added reassuringly.

She stared at him for a moment and then said: "He's dead?" André nodded. "Oh André! How?"

"He was shot," he said gently and put his arm around her. "By himself?"

"I don't know," he said, but by his tone she knew what he suspected.

"I killed him," she cried.

"No, no, my dear," André comforted her. Then he felt her sagging against him and braced his arms as she fainted. He gathered her up and carried her inside. Ann was in the kitchen and hurried to him.

"What has happened?" she cried.

"She fainted. I told her about Gaston." That much he had to say and was afraid Elise would revive and start talking. "I'd better take her to her room," he added, and carried her upstairs, Ann following. Elise revived quickly but remained in a daze. Dr. Menoir was in the house and examined her. André was fearful that Gaston might have harmed her, but he could not voice that fear to the doctor. When the doctor gave his report there was nothing to indicate that André's fears might have foundation and he was relieved.

"Exhaustion, probably," Dr. Menoir remarked. "Too much excitement these past days. Better keep her in bed."

She lay there for days, with André her self-appointed nurse. Just as Ann feared to have Elise in the room lest Antoine talk in his delirium, so André wanted to keep the others out for the same reason. Each room held its secret, without the other knowing that anything untoward had taken place. That André should insist upon remaining with Elise did not seem strange. They had always clung to each other with their twin understanding. Paul and Jean-Baptiste did what was asked of them, neither of them very useful with the household all disrupted. Aunt Marie was the first to come over and help and Ann welcomed her bustling efficiency. Madeline Boissart and the other women of the seigneury also came with offers of help.

André particularly welcomed Aunt Marie and was glad to have her relieve him. Somehow he felt that if she learned about Elise and Gaston, she would understand. After the first two days Elise remained quiet, lying in a coma that puzzled them all, although her childhood fondness for Gaston provided some explanation.

What went on in Elise's mind during the days she lay there so still and quiet, no one knew. Not even André. He would talk gently to her but her eyes that were burning as though with fever, would only fill with tears. Again and again he would admonish her not to worry. Gaston had been their particular favorite for so many years and in the stillness of those hours André thought of the loss of his friend. He had had so many happy times with him. He did not blame Elise for what had happened, for André was not one to pass judgment. Then, too, he knew the violence of Gaston's nature and had many times argued with him about it.

One afternoon the curé called. The kindly old priest had been a friend of the family for many years and his arrival gladdened them all. Since the passing of the crisis, Antoine was making slow but steady progress. Father Joseph visited him but Antoine was still too weak to do more than smile faintly.

When Elise heard that Father Joseph was in the house she asked to see him. He had been her father confessor all her life and she needed him desperately now. It was the cry of an anguished soul seeking comfort. During the days she had lain there she had been able to think of only one thing—that by her foolishness she had sent a man to his death. Over and over

she tormented herself by remembering Gaston's kindness to her
during her childhood. This kindness she had repaid by driving
him to put a gun to his head, after burning down the home
which he had built.

Father Joseph listened quietly. His gentle face showed no
sternness or disapproval. He was not there to judge but to comfort. He could see how much she had already suffered for her
thoughtlessness. He talked with her a long while, gently advis-
ing her and at her request promised to say a special mass for
Gaston. When he had gone she knew comfort and peace
again.

When André returned to her room, he felt the calmness
that had now come to her.

"Feeling better?" he asked with a smile.

"Yes, André. I told Father Joseph the whole story. He was
very understanding."

"He always is," he said. Hesitating a little he asked: "Did
you tell Dr. Menoir what had happened?"

She looked at him with alarm. "No. Should I have?"

"You know best, dear."

"I don't believe there is any need to worry, André."

He looked relieved. "I'm glad of that."

"I am, too. It has worried me."

"You're sure you know?"

"Practically."

They left the subject there and fortunately there was not
again any need to bring it up.

Ann sat beside Antoine's bed wondering what they would
do when he recovered; how they would handle the situation.
She hoped his going to Quebec or France might hold matters
in abeyance for a while. But what should Elise be told? As she
recovered she asked repeatedly about Antoine.

Antoine was sleeping, his face thin and hollow from his
desperate struggle. Ann watched him and thought of the circumstances of his birth. Parents were so careless about the

hardships which they brought upon children. Ann felt no antipathy towards him because Hélène de Matier was his mother. On the contrary she felt sympathetic because he had had such a woman to bring him into the world. It was surprising that he had developed into such a frank, good-natured man, when such qualities were so alien to his mother's nature. Had he inherited them from his father? With a twinge Ann realized that these were qualities in her own husband. She asked herself if, had Elise not been involved, she would have minded having this natural son of her husband's? Had the circumstances been different would she have accepted Antoine with a good grace? She answered herself. Had he come to the house, determined to claim his birthright, she might have resented it. But coming as a guest of her son's and discovering his relationship to them by accident, she knew she would have been able to accept him graciously, for by this time she had grown fond of him. Another son added to her family would have been acceptable, even under the circumstances—except for the complications over Elise.

She sat stitching upon her embroidery. Outside it was raining heavily, washing away the accumulated snows of the winter. Antoine wakened and he, too, was thinking the same kind of thoughts as he looked at her. The lamp reflected on her face and greying black hair and he who had never known a mother, wished she had been his. Because he had never known a mother's tenderness he did not, as others might have done, long to feel her caresses as in childhood. He had never known such things. Nurses and governesses had cared for him and among them there had never been a motherly soul to foster his love.

Ann looked up and met his eyes. The fever had left them and they were now clearer. She smiled at him and laid her hand on the covers.

"Feeling better?" she asked.

"Much, thank you. I have given you a lot of trouble, I'm afraid," he said apologetically.

"You have been very ill."

"What happened?"

She described the night of the fire and his injuries.

"I did stand out in the cold without a coat. I am sorry. It was foolish. But it was such a shock, I hardly knew what I was doing." He wrinkled his forehead and troubled lines played around his mouth.

"I know, Antoine."

"Monsieur told you?"

"Yes," she said softly.

"Do the others know?"

She shook her head. "No, only my husband and I."

"I am so sorry I brought this unhappiness upon you." He looked very distressed.

"You can scarcely be blamed, Antoine."

"No—but . . . I have complicated your lives. I hope, er . . . I hope this won't spoil the happiness of this family. I mean before I came and this odd twist of fate. . . ." He stumbled over his words, not knowing quite how to put it. "What I'm trying to say is, before I came, you and your husband were so devoted. It won't make any difference, will it? I mean knowing that your husband and my mother . . ."

Ann laid her hand on his and smiled kindly at him. "No, Antoine. My husband and I have been devoted too many years. I wouldn't let anything interfere with that."

"You're very understanding. Had I had even the slightest suspicion, I would not have come here. You do believe that?"

"Of course, Antoine."

"Some people might believe that I knew about it and forced myself into the family to get recognition or something of the sort. I assure you I did not."

"Please don't let it worry you, Antoine. We have grown very fond of you. . . ."

"But you can't be any more. However you look at it, I am some one you will want to forget. No one wants to be reminded that there has been an irregularity in the family. You all seem so understanding of one another. It is the first time I have ever been associated with family life. I have always gone my own way. I used to think I liked it; I enjoyed what I thought was freedom. It wasn't until I came here that I realized how much I have missed."

"Aren't we rather responsible for your having missed it?" Ann said quietly.

Antoine looked surprised. "How could you be?"

"Surely my husband has some responsibility towards you."

"Oh no! Please do not feel that. No." He spoke emphatically. "I don't want you to feel the slightest responsibility. I have no claim, nor would I ever make any. I have looked after myself all these years and can continue to do so. The moment I am able I must go away."

"We shall be sorry to see you go, Antoine. I hope you will be able to return soon."

"That depends upon what I am able to find out about my birth."

"You think . . . it is possible my husband is mistaken?"

"I can only hope. You knew my mother. . . ."

Ann looked a little alarmed. She did not want to discuss Hélène de Matier, but the alarm gave way to relief as Antoine went on.

"The Duc de Chamois' family and my guardian both mentioned that she was a lady who distributed her favors widely." Ann nodded without answering. Paul had told her that Antoine knew his mother's reputation. "If only I had not been so nonchalant about it!" Antoine said. "I might then have found out more and have been able to furnish some proof. As it is, years have been lost and people who knew her have died or scattered elsewhere." There was silence for a few moments and then he said, "And now I have to hurt Elise. I don't know what to tell her. I can't bring more trouble upon you by telling her the truth and possibly turning her against her father."

"Yet, perhaps she should know the truth," Ann said.

"No!" His tone was decisive. "Monsieur said that. It must not be. I must go to Quebec and perhaps to France. I shall tell her I have to investigate some family affairs. That would be best."

"She has been ill."

"Ill!" Antoine looked alarmed. "What . . . ?"

"Gaston was killed."

"In the fire?"

"No, he was found shot in the woods."

"By whom?"

"We don't know. It is a mystery. He was found two days after his house burned."

"Oh, I am sorry! Elise was fond of him, wasn't she?"

"She had known him since she was a little girl."

"Is she still ill?"

"No, she is better now. I have made excuses to keep her away from this room. She has sat here sometimes while you slept."

"She has?" His expression was thoughtful. She had sat there watching him and he had not known it.

"I thought it better you should not have to talk while you were still weak."

"That was very thoughtful of you. The last time we talked to each other was the night I went to speak to Monsieur about our being married." His mouth quivered slightly. "She knew I was speaking to him and I have never mentioned it since. I must tell her I am going away. How soon can I leave?"

"The first ship should reach here in about two weeks. We can never tell exactly. It depends on the break at Quebec."

"The break?"

"The ice-break. The ice has melted here and as soon as it is clear up to Quebec, the ships will sail."

"The ice-break," he said and his tone was rather wistful. "I had hoped to see that. They told me it was an interesting sight."

"Maybe you can see it another year."

He shook his head doubtfully and did not answer. Raising himself on one elbow, he looked out of the window. The rain beat against the panes and he could not see much.

"The spring rains washing away the snows," Ann said.

"Spring." He sank back and closed his eyes. He had hoped for so much when spring came. The grant of land he had obtained from the Governor would now probably have to be relinquished. He had thought to start working on it when spring came and to build a home for Elise. Tears that he would not shed pricked his eyelids.

CHAPTER XIV

IT WAS NOT ONLY in the Manor House that the peace and gaiety of the winter had been shattered, but throughout all Montreal. That gayest of winters had been brought to a sudden end as rumors become more alarming and then were confirmed as a fact. The English were preparing for an attack on New France—an attack, it was rumored, that would be a combined sea and land assault. The previous year Port Royal had fallen into the hands of the English, with scarcely any resistance from the French. It was not that the commander of the garrison lacked spirit but he did not have the men and the supplies with which to resist. What men he had were half starved, his defenses crumbling and despite repeated pleas to the Mother Country, no reinforcements had been sent. There were those in New France who regarded this fall of Port Royal as insignificant. No place had changed hands so frequently and it could change again. The less optimistic regarded it as a bad omen, a forerunner of what was to come. The English had renamed the place Annapolis Royal after their Queen who was now casting greedy glances in the direction of these French colonies, while Louis XIV saw no reason to send any help to strengthen them. He had insisted upon the colonization of this territory and then his only interest was the revenue it brought him.

As the rumors increased, the Governor of Montreal became more uneasy. With the news came word that the Indian tribes were restive, with their faith in France diminished by the loss of Port Royal, so that they were accepting lavish gifts from the English and going over to their side. The Chevalier de Ramezay had dispatched the Baron de Longueil to Onondaga, the home of the Iroquois tribes. No man had more experience with Indians than de Longueil. Since the Treaty ten years ago, the Iroquois had kept their word and had remained reluctantly faithful to the French. Now they were threatening to break the Treaty as they had done innumerable times before. De Longueil was received with friendly stoicism and when quantities of wampum had been exchanged, he sat round their Council fires with them, listening to the Chiefs harangue and make promises they had no intention of keeping, for the redman had little regard for the truth. He loved words and used them, without feeling obligated to stand by his assurances. He had no love for the white man and played one nation against the other, in the hope of gaining the best of the bargain. When the Chiefs had finished, de Longueil, who was a master of rhetoric, also spoke for a long time, knowing the redman would thereby be impressed. He warned them that if they now sided with the English, the tribes of the north and west, their habitual enemies, would descend upon them and show no quarter. When he returned to Montreal he brought back deputies who assured the Governor of their loyalty, while those at home parleyed with the English, who scoffed at the French threats and promised protection and gain. When the delegates returned to Onondaga, Montreal was even more uneasy.

Though there had been peace for the past decade, the inhabitants remembered only too well the devastation of Indian warfare. There was scarcely a pioneer family that had not lost many of their menfolk in these ravages in the past. Tales of Indian tortures were not just stories to scare recalcitrant children. Many had witnessed them and had lost their dear ones in this awful manner.

So ominous did the Governor-General consider the threat that he came over the ice from Quebec to confer with Governor de Ramezay. The friendship between these two men had lessened with the years owing to political jealousy, but each respected the leadership of the other. The relative strength of Montreal was reviewed and found sadly lacking. Every able-bodied man was ordered to be prepared to answer the call to arms. Again the colony was faced with the loss of the crops, which would mean a shortage of food in the winter, and perhaps famine. Men made ready to leave and, while they awaited developments, hurried to get the ground ready for sowing. If they could get the crops sown, those who remained behind, aided by the women and children, could take care of the cultivation.

Antoine sat at the window of his room convalescing. From here he had watched the newborn season, the imperceptible budding of the trees, the deep azure of the River. It was a new world that he had not seen; a world so different from the white-clad winter in which he had arrived. From his window he watched the May Day celebration—the day when throughout the colony the habitants paid homage to their seigneurs. Paul had had no heart for this joyous day to which he had hitherto always looked forward, but aided by Ann he managed to get through it. Again Antoine's anticipated participation in a custom which he had never before witnessed was spoiled. He watched the raising of the gaily decorated fir tree and listened to the merry shouts of the children; he heard the firing of the muskets to blacken the tree and the murmur of voices from below as the people breakfasted in the Manor House; but it only made him sadder because he could not look upon it as part of his future. He appreciated Jean-Baptiste's coming to sit with him to explain the details, but it embarrassed him because he had to force himself to appear enthusiastic. His embarrassment increased when Elise joined them and remarked that perhaps next year he would be having the same celebration on his own seigneury. Fortunately, Ann had followed closely upon Elise and she covered up the remark by cleverly changing the conversation, but Elise noticed Antoine's lack of enthusiasm.

There were several such awkward situations and Antoine knew he could not put off speaking to Elise much longer. With Ann as his adviser, they had decided that it would be best for him to keep to his room until just before he sailed. This would be any day now and no one in the family had yet been told. Antoine did not want to tell Elise until the last moment. While he remained in his room, personal conversation was limited, since propriety dictated that whenever she visited him, it was in company with one of the others. Her visits always left him dreadfully depressed, because she was so desirable but out of reach. He hardly dared meet her eyes. Elise noticed the change in his manner and mentioned it to her mother.

"After all, we are practically engaged," she said. "He spoke to father the night before he was injured."

"Did he, dear?" Ann said vaguely.

"You know he did. I told you that night that he was going to. Didn't father mention it?"

"No," Ann said evasively. "Perhaps their talk was interrupted by the fire."

"He was with father a long time before that happened." She looked perplexed. "He seems so quiet."

"You must remember he's been very ill," Ann admonished.

"Yes. Do you think it could have affected his memory. Some illnesses do, don't they?"

"Some do. But I don't think it has Antoine's. Wait until he is stronger."

"He does look weak. His face is so drawn and worried," Elise said anxiously. "Oh dear, why did this have to happen! We were so happy."

Ann did not make any comment. She could not. She had scarcely slept for nights and the strain was beginning to tell upon her. Those words, "we were so happy," cut to her heart, knowing how unhappy her child was going to be.

Paul was silent and brooding. He and Ann had talked of the matter until there was nothing more to say. He stopped in each day to see Antoine but stayed only a short time. Ann told him that Antoine was leaving on the first ship and on his next visit Paul spoke to him about it.

"You must let me pay your expenses," he said.

Antoine shook his head. "No, monsieur, that is not necessary," he insisted.

"I want to, Antoine. It is the least I can do. You must let me make some amends."

Still Antoine was adamant. "I have no claim on you, monsieur."

"But you have," Paul argued.

"I wish you would not feel that way, monsieur. I would prefer you would forget me."

"We could not do that, Antoine." It was Ann's voice that answered. She had come in during the conversation. Antoine smiled affectionately at her. "I would not want to think that you were going away from here and entirely out of our lives."

"I wish it did not have to be that way, but I see no other way. I could not come here and see Elise without being very unhappy. And it would not be fair to her. Perhaps you will some day come to France. But, I shall never forget your kindness to me."

"Kindness!" The word cracked out sharply from Paul. "I fail to see where you have received any kindness. . . ."

"Whatever happens, Antoine," Ann said, "you will always know that you are deep in our hearts, even more so for the manner in which you have taken all this. Have you spoken to Elise yet?"

"No, but I must do so. Things become more difficult every day. I would like to wait until the day before I leave. But if that isn't possible, I will speak to her and then go and stay in Montreal until I sail."

As if in response to his remark, André hurried into the room with news that the ship had arrived. Antoine looked out of the window to hide his face.

"You can't see it from here," André remarked and Antoine was glad that this was the way he had interpreted the gesture.

Paul and Ann asked questions about the arrival—who had come by it and what supplies it had brought. Also, what news?

"Mostly about the war. It looks as though it is imminent. They say the English fleet is on its way to Boston," André told them.

A few days before this Jean-Baptiste had come in to see Antoine, quite excited over the prospect of their seeing action. He had been very attentive during Antoine's illness and had sat with him for hours at a time regaling him with stories of Montreal. He had also confided to Antoine that he had a mistress there—a fact which probably accounted for his good humor of late. With his own complex situation in mind, Antoine was in no mood to be very sympathetic upon the subject of mistresses.

Jean-Baptiste came in now, his face aglow with the news. "They say in town that all the regulars and militia are to be called. That'll probably interfere with your plans, André. They'll want you *coureurs de bois*. You're tougher than most men."

It was the first time Jean-Baptiste had paid any tribute to *coureurs de bois* and André acknowledged it with a smile. "We were just discussing the news. Looks like our plans for the woods are going to be spoiled." André's face clouded with disappointment.

"You'd better hurry and get well, Antoine. They'll need officers," Jean-Baptiste said.

Antoine's face was serious. He looked quickly at Ann and then moistening his lips said: "I shall probably not be here." Jean-Baptiste and André both looked at him with surprise. "I have to leave for Quebec immediately on some private business."

"Trouble?" André asked solicitously.

"A family matter," Antoine said evasively.

"Get word by the ship?" Jean-Baptiste asked.

"Yes, indirectly," Antoine said, not sure whether this lie could stand.

"When'll you leave?" Jean-Baptiste asked.

"When the ship returns."

"You'll have to get permission," Jean-Baptiste remarked.

"I suppose so. I shall see the Governor. If you're taking the cart into town tomorrow, may I go with you, André? I don't feel up to riding just yet."

"Why, of course," André said.

"I'll take you in the carriage," Jean-Baptiste offered. "I can see the Governor at the same time."

But this Antoine did not want. He had to see the Chevalier de Ramezay alone. He left the matter where it was, relying upon Ann to arrange it for him. He changed the subject by saying, "Please don't mention my departure until after I have seen Elise. I would like to tell her first."

"That reminds me," André said. "She sent you a message. It's quite warm outside and she wanted to know if you would not be better sitting in the sun for a little while."

Ann turned, ready to help him with an excuse but he stood up saying, "I think that would be a good idea." His glance met Ann's and she understood.

"You'd better wrap up carefully, though. This May air is treacherous," she said.

He smiled at her and nodded. He had lost so much weight that his coat hung loosely on him. His weeks of illness had made him very unsteady on his legs and André and Jean-Baptiste helped him down the stairs. When Elise saw them, her eyes were gentle with concern.

"Oh, Antoine, how nice!" she exclaimed, and then added solicitously, "You're still weak, though."

"Only my legs, I haven't used them much lately. They'll soon strengthen."

But she continued to look at him with concern and the sweetness of her expression increased his unhappiness. He wanted so much to rest his head on her shoulder, feel her arms around him and her delicate hands stroking his aching head. He sat rigidly wondering how he should begin. They were sitting outside the house looking over the River. It was an afternoon of peace and beauty, with deep blue sky, birds singing merrily and all the trees bursting with new life. It was a perfect setting in which to talk to the woman he loved of future plans and ambitions. Instead he would at any moment see those gentle eyes cloud with disappointment. How would she take it? Would she cry or be angry? They talked about the new season and Elise tried to steer the conversation into a personal channel by remarking:

"I had André take me over your land the other day. There's

a lovely rise in the ground where you can build the house." The property he had obtained adjoined the de Courville seigneury on the west.

She glanced covertly at him as she said it and was surprised to see his face flush and then drain of all color. As he did not answer, she said quickly, "You don't mind, do you?"

He turned to her and the deep distress in his eyes puzzled her. Had he changed his mind? Was this why he had been so strangely silent of late? She asked herself these questions as she waited for his answer. But he did not answer her question.

"Elise, I have to go away," he said and could not go on because of the look of disappointment and alarm that came into her face.

"Away?" she queried sharply.

"I have to go to Quebec—maybe to France. . . ."

"Without me?" she nearly queried, but before she could speak he added:

"I have to find out some details about my family."

"About your family?"

"It seems there are some complications I didn't know of. I . . . er, I . . . can't marry until I have straightened them out."

"You're telling me you don't want to marry me?" she asked coldly.

His heart cried out. "Oh, Elise, if only you knew!" But in a controlled voice, he said, "I could never *not want* to marry you, Elise. I want it with all my heart. But I *can't* marry you until I have disentangled my parentage."

"Was this father's idea?" she asked suspiciously. "Did you speak to him that night?"

"Yes, I did. It was then that I realized I owed this to you."

"I don't understand." Her tone was petulant. "Do you mean because you don't think the Duc de Chamois was your father?"

"Yes, that's the reason." He grasped at a straw.

"But, Antoine, does that matter? This is not France and we don't need to examine family trees."

"It wouldn't be fair to you otherwise."

"That's nonsense! After all both father and mother knew your mother. They said so the night you mentioned it at supper."

Antoine was getting in deeper than he could stand. He wanted to exclaim. "Indeed they knew my mother! That's why I have to find out who the man was." His tone was unconvincing as he answered, "Yes, but they didn't know my father."

"What does it matter? They're both dead. And if you are, well, illegitimate," her tone was apologetic as she said the word, "it isn't important."

"But it is important to me, Elise. I must know."

"You're either keeping something from me or you've changed your mind about wanting to marry me," she said doubtfully.

"Oh, Elise!" It was a cry from his heart and he covered his face with one hand. "I love you desperately. You must trust me."

Her face softened. In these weeks her love had grown deeper and now without any doubt she knew he was the man she wanted to marry. Others had ceased to interest her. But the softness in her face changed as she heard him say:

"I will release you from your promise to marry me."

"Then you *don't* love me! If you did, you couldn't say such a thing!"

There was a moment's silence. Then he said: "But I may not come back." She jumped up and started towards the house but his cry of "Elise!" was in a tone of anguish. She stopped and looked at him. He, too, was standing, swaying a little on his weak legs.

"Don't leave me in anger, Elise. You must trust me."

He came towards her unsteadily and put his arm around her, bracing himself so that he did not lean his weight upon her for support. "Oh, darling, I love you so," he cried. His face rested in her neck but he did not dare move his lips to her mouth. He crushed her to him and then hurried, stumbling as he did so, into the house.

CHAPTER XV

THE NEXT MORNING André drove Antoine into Montreal. His baggage was in the back of the cart and he had said goodbye to all except Jean-Baptiste, who had remained in Montreal overnight. Antoine sat deep in thought, moving his head occasionally to glance regretfully at some landmark. He had talked for a long while the previous evening with Ann, his only comfort being her assurance that she would do all she could to relieve Elise of suffering. Together they had decided it would be better for him to leave in the morning, and either go on board ship, or stay in Montreal, until the ship sailed. After he had left, Ann had gone to Elise's room and, with difficulty, had tried to make her see that this change in plans was not Antoine's fault, nor did it signify any lessening in his affection. On this last point, however, she dared not be too emphatic. She did not want to cheer Elise by holding out hopes that would only have to be dashed later. Antoine had said goodbye to her in the presence of her father and mother. To have to leave the woman you loved by merely kissing her hand was heartrending. He had not dared to say anything to her—not even to meet her eyes. He had seen the abruptness with which she turned away to the window, her unhappiness evident by the droop of her shoulders, and that was the picture that haunted him now.

It was necessary to say something. He could not drive all the way into Montreal without a word, even if André, with his usual consideration, might attribute it to the unhappiness of lovers' parting. André, as a matter of fact, suspected that something was wrong, for otherwise all the family would have come to see their guest off. Also, he had noticed his father's silence lately.

"I want to thank you," Antoine said, "for your kindness to

me while I have been here. You have made me feel very much at home."

André turned with his frank smile. "You will promise to come back, won't you?"

Antoine hesitated and then said: "I wish I could. I had made up my mind to settle here. Family affairs may change that."

"I hope not. I looked forward to your developing that seigneury next to ours."

Antoine did not answer.

"If there is ever anything I can do, you will let me know, won't you?" André said kindly and then added. "Twins have an understanding you know. So if I can help about Elise, I shall be anxious to."

For a moment Antoine was tempted to tell André the truth but there was his father to be considered. So he answered: "Help her not to be too unhappy."

"I will," André assured him and asked no further questions. Instead he changed the subject. "This war is a nuisance. It means a great loss of money to all the *coureurs de bois,* too."

"It must. You'll have to go? Can they stop you leaving for the woods?"

"Yes and no. We could sneak off but it would mean we would have to take our furs elsewhere. We couldn't return here without being arrested. And no one wants to become an outlaw. Actually we break enough rules or edicts as it is. I can't tell you how many times they have tried to condemn *coureurs.* But, that's not really the point. Neither Uncle Philip nor I would go off and leave the others to defend the place alone. How do we know that the English will not land here? It may mean that every man has to fight to defend his home and family. That's the drawback to colonial life. No sooner have you built up a heritage than wars come, and it is all lost. By missing the trading this year it will probably mean the pelts will go to the English traders and that means bad years ahead for us." Instead of his usually happy expression, André looked worried and disgruntled.

"You really enjoy trading, don't you?" Antoine commented.

André then revealed something that was surprising. "I want to make it my life, Antoine."

"What about the seigneury?"

"I love that, too, but not in the way most people suppose. I love it as a duty. I don't ever want to settle down as a farmer."

"I'm surprised to hear you say that," Antoine told him.

"Every one else would be too. I have never mentioned it to any one and I probably shan't. I'm telling it to you confidentially."

"I respect that."

André drew off his wool cap and let the wind play through his hair. "I want to be more than a trader. I want to be an explorer. I want to see what this vast land contains. I met the Sieur de Cadillac once. I was only a young lad but he made a deep impression upon me. He founded Detroit, you know. I would like to do things such as he has done."

Antoine looked at him and saw his face aglow with eagerness. "Wouldn't your father be disappointed?" he asked.

"No. He has never believed in all the sons remaining on the land. He never intended to himself, only circumstances changed things. I haven't mentioned this to him, not in so many words at least, but I feel he understands. For one thing, he never says anything to me about marrying and settling down with my own portion of the land. A wonderful man, my father."

"He certainly is," Antoine agreed and was glad he had not yielded to the temptation to confide his own trouble to André. He could not help wondering, though, what André would have said had he remarked: "He's my father, too." He asked André:

"Don't you intend to marry?"

"Oh, probably, sometime. But if I intend to wander, it wouldn't be fair to any woman. It would worry me to have a wife and family I wasn't looking after."

"Your Aunt Marie seems to get along all right."

"Oh yes, but there aren't many women like her. No. It's best that I remain free for the next several years anyway. Jean-Baptiste's more fitted for that and he can carry on the family."

"But Jean-Baptiste doesn't like farming. . . ."

"He would like being a seigneur, though. Things are changing, and probably by the time he takes that position, seigneurs won't work the way my father does."

"And you think Jean-Baptiste will marry the kind of woman who would carry on the traditions here?"

"I don't know why not. My mother was an aristocrat. The Baron de Longueil's wife was also. Jean-Baptiste is restless now but so much the better. He'll have had a good experience and be all the more ready to settle down. You have to know Jean-Baptiste. He is always surprising. Why only the other day when he found we were all working desperately to get the fields ploughed and sown before we have to leave, he came out and worked as hard as the rest."

"He did!"

"Surprising, wasn't it? But when he saw the desperate need, he did his share. He's like that."

"I hope to see him before I leave."

"We'll probably run into him in town."

And that they did. He was in the sailing office where Antoine went first to arrange about passage.

"Why Jean-Baptiste, what are you doing here?" Antoine and André exclaimed together.

Jean-Baptiste looked a little confused. "Oh. I am doing an errand for a friend," he said hastily.

"Oh, I see," Antoine said and smiled. "I thought maybe you had obtained permission to go to Quebec." Jean-Baptiste looked surprised and Antoine continued: "You did mention coming with me, didn't you?"

"Are you leaving?" Jean-Baptiste inquired.

"Yes, when the ship sails."

"Have you seen the Governor?"

"I'm on my way there as soon as I have made arrangements here."

"Then you had better reverse the procedure. This morning the Governor refused me permission to leave."

Antoine looked alarmed. The thought of having to stay in Montreal, with the hazard of running into Elise, was disconcerting. He tried to appear nonchalant as he said, "I'll make the arrangements, anyway. I can always cancel them."

"You are optimistic, my friend," Jean-Baptiste said, and seemed anxious to get away, no doubt to the friend for whom he was doing the errand.

"Au revoir, if I don't see you," Antoine called to him.

"I'll see you. At home tonight, probably," Jean-Baptiste called back, laughing, and before Antoine had time to think of an explanation he was gone.

"I'll tell him later," André assured him.

"He seemed in a hurry."

"His lady love was waiting, no doubt."

André was right. Jean-Baptiste stepped into a carriage around the corner.

Antoine wanted to go alone to see the Governor, so he turned to André. "This may take some time and then I have to go to the Governor. You have many things to do. Why don't we meet later at Dillons?"

This was agreeable and André went on his way. Antoine had to wait a while to see Governor de Ramezay, and when he was admitted he was apologetic for taking up the time of a man who obviously had more than he could handle. The Governor was cordial, but anticipating Antoine's mission asked: "Have you come with the same request as Jean-Baptiste?"

"What was that?" Antoine asked, pretending not to know.

"That I give you permission to go to Quebec."

"Not entirely, monsieur. I have come to consult you on a private matter and for that I must apologize. I wouldn't bother you at such a time—only it is urgent."

"I see," the Governor said kindly.

There was a slight pause and then Antoine said: "I believe you knew my mother, monsieur—Madame Hélène de Matier."

The Governor looked surprised—almost startled. "I did not know you were her son."

"I had no idea, monsieur, that the information would prove to be such a coincidence. It seems that my mother was very well-known here. Until the Sieur de Courville-Boissart told me, I was not even aware that she had ever visited Montreal."

The Governor was studying the objects on his desk, obviously very much on guard.

Antoine continued: "My mother died giving me birth." The Governor looked up with interest, and then down at his desk again. "She was married at the time to the Duc de Chamois, but his family have never recognized me as his son."

De Ramezay raised his eyebrows with surprise, and said, "No?"

"He was an old man. The reason I am bothering you with all this is that I am endeavoring to find out, if possible, who might have fathered me." The Chevalier now looked uncomfortable. "Let me add, monsieur," Antoine went on quickly, "that I know my mother's reputation. I have discussed this with the Sieur de Courville-Boissart and he suggested one or two people who might help me."

"You mean, Paul thought *I* might have been your father? He. . . ."

"Oh no, monsieur. He merely suggested that you might remember the names of some men who. . . ."

De Ramezay laughed awkwardly. "Did Paul mention himself? He knew the lady better than most of us."

Antoine felt himself perspiring. He felt he was bungling the whole thing. "He mentioned that, monsieur. He was married before this event could have taken place," Antoine lied.

"Well, I married a month before he did," the Chevalier said a little huffily.

"Please don't misunderstand me, monsieur," Antoine pleaded. "You have mistaken my inquiry. I was not suggesting for a moment that you might be my father. I am only trying to find out if you remember any of the names of those who knew my mother at that time. I want to marry and don't feel I should until I know."

Despite Antoine's efforts to shield Paul, and though he did not mention the name of the lady whom he wished to marry, Claude de Ramezay saw through the thin veil to the true situation, but kept his own council.

"I'm afraid I can't be much help, Antoine," the Governor said.

"You were in Quebec, though, the winter my mother married?"

"Yes," de Ramezay said thoughtfully, "but I was courting my wife and did not notice other people very much."

"You can understand then, monsieur, how it would have been had there been an obstacle to your marrying. This is so very important to me."

"Yes, of course."

"Monsieur Paul mentioned the name of the Marquis de Vaudreuil."

De Ramezay looked dubious. "I doubt if he could help you. He was also getting married at the same time."

"He might remember something that would give me a lead."

"Can't the Duc de Chamois' family tell you anything?"

"They may be able to. I have written to my guardian. If necessary I shall go to France to make inquiries. Meanwhile, monsieur, won't you please give me permission to go to Quebec to continue my inquiries?"

"When I have just refused Jean-Baptiste?"

"But he hasn't the same need to go, monsieur. If I wait, then the winter may be here again and my hopes lost."

"What do you expect to find out in Quebec?"

"I don't know," Antoine said abjectly. "I can only hope that perchance I may be able to find a clue."

The Governor did not look very encouraging. "Well, I can give you a letter of introduction to the Governor-General, but

I doubt that it will help much. And you will have to put it right with Jean-Baptiste. I don't like to grant a request to one and refuse it to another."

"I appreciate that, monsieur, and I would not ask you if it did not mean so much to me. This may change my whole life."

The following morning Antoine sat on board ship, waiting for it to sail. He had found a remote spot and used a coil of rope as a seat. He was in no mood to see people. Since his talk with Governor de Ramezay he felt completely hopeless. He realized from the confusion of that conversation that even if de Ramezay and the Marquis de Vaudreuil knew anything, they probably would not reveal it. Consciences were too guilty and they were afraid of giving themselves away. Furthermore, he was fearful of involving Paul. He was not even sure that he would use the letter of introduction to de Vaudreuil which the Governor had given him. It would be better to go to France as soon as possible and perhaps make inquiries there where Paul was not known, or, as his despair told him, to drop the whole matter and give up all hopes of Elise. No one with her beauty would be long in finding a husband and in time she would forget him.

"But I can see no reason for you to return to Quebec." The sound of Jean-Baptiste's voice startled Antoine. Peering round from where he was hidden, he saw him standing, talking to Madame de Fontigny. He had not seen Jean-Baptiste since they had met at the sailing office. Should he step out now, say a brief goodbye and disappear? The moment was embarrassing and still more so as he heard their further conversation.

"We argued that all night, *mon chèr enfant*," the lady was saying. "I have to return to my husband and there's no use arguing any further."

"But you could go later," Jean-Baptiste insisted.

"I could not! It is only by luck that I have been able to remain here during the winter. The letter I received yesterday was peremptory, and my husband is not a man whose will I would dare to cross."

"Then you don't love me the way you profess to," Jean-Baptiste said peevishly.

"Don't act like a child!" she replied crossly. "You should know that a husband is merely a convenience. I have let you love me. . . ."

"Let me!" Jean-Baptiste replied and his tone was angry.

"All right, darling. I have enjoyed it, too. But I need a husband to support me. You are only a baby yet and can't give me the things I have to have."

"Very well, go!" Jean-Baptiste said angrily and started to walk away. Antoine was helplessly caught. He dared not reveal himself now and let them know that he had overheard their conversation. Yet, the position of eavesdropper was most unpleasant. He made himself as small as he could and tried not to hear. But that was impossible. The lover's quarrel was now being made up and Antoine was afraid to move. All he could do was to suffer his discomfort and embarrassment, for Jean-Baptiste was a passionate lover, and they were behaving as though they were in the privacy of a boudoir. They both appeared oblivious to the fact that at any moment passengers or crew might appear.

"If only they had let me go to Quebec, darling! But I shall follow you the moment I can," Jean-Baptiste was saying, and then there were murmured words of familiar endearment.

When they finally parted and Antoine was certain he would not be seen, he untwisted his cramped legs and stood up. He did not remember having a more distasteful experience. At the same time he found himself wondering bitterly whether his mother had been a woman like this Madame de Fontigny.

CHAPTER XVI

On arrival in Quebec, Antoine obeyed the Governor's orders and reported immediately to the Commander of the Forces. The town was in a state of nervous excitement, the latest news being that the English ships had arrived in Boston, and that two thousand trained soldiers were assembled in New York. The defenses of Quebec were much stronger than in Montreal and all was ready to withstand a siege. There was nothing further to be done but await developments.

Antoine sent a note to Madame de Courville-Boissart, informing her of his safe arrival, and asking her to explain to Jean-Baptiste as best she could why the Governor had permitted him to leave for Quebec. He told her, too, of his despair and suggested she encourage Elise to consider other suitors.

After two weeks, he decided that he would use his letter of introduction to the Governor-General. Although he dreaded the interview and the necessity of repeating his story again, he still clung to a vain hope that the Sieur might be wrong. It was several days before he received an answer, giving him an appointment.

The Marquis de Vaudreuil received him courteously and without the impatience that Antoine had anticipated. He apologized immediately for bothering him with a private matter at such a time, and was relieved when the Governor-General waved the apology aside with the remark that he was glad of a diversion from the subject of war.

As briefly as possible Antoine explained the purpose of his visit, without revealing the name of the lady he wished to marry. He wanted to be sure he did not make the same mistake he had with de Ramezay and give the impression, that he thought the Marquis might have been one of his mother's lovers. So he picked his words carefully.

"My only reason for consulting you, monsieur, is that you were in Quebec at the time and might have known some of my mother's friends," he concluded his story.

The Marquis smiled and said: "Wouldn't it help if you told me your mother's name? So far you haven't mentioned it."

Antoine had been so careful to avoid names that he had overlooked the fact. "Madame Hélène de Matier," he said.

The Marquis' face flushed. How Antoine was coming to hate the change of expression on men's faces whenever he mentioned the name!

"Well, er, well, yes," the Marquis blustered. "I think we all knew her. Remarkably beautiful woman. Hm, yes. And you're her son? Well, didn't know she had a son. Were you born here?"

"No, monsieur, in France." Again Antoine explained the difficulties of his birth.

The Marquis took out his snuffbox and slowly occupied himself with it. "Complicated for you, very complicated. Quite a few men in the same position, though. Won't the lady you wish to marry accept you by the name you bear?"

"Yes, monsieur. But I wish to find out for my own satisfaction."

"Rather unnecessarily particular, aren't you? It's been done before. What I mean is, well, here it doesn't matter so much. 'Tisn't as though there were an inheritance involved, or is there?"

Unable to explain, Antoine merely said: "No, but I wish to know."

"Well, that's your affair. What year did you say it was?"

"The winter of 1690."

"That was the year I married. Let me think back. It was the time of the Phips' siege. There were several of us here. De Ramezay also married, and, why yes, Paul Boissart. He was the hero of the siege and married the Chevalier de Luc's daughter. He subsequently became the Sieur de Courville-Boissart." Antoine kept his face rigid. He had purposely not mentioned his association with this family. "Why, that's probably your man!" the Marquis exclaimed, and looked delighted with himself. "Let me see now, it seems there was a little scandal connected with Boissart's marriage, or perhaps I should say, connected with him before his marriage. My wife would probably remember it. Women, you know, and gossip. I'll check with my wife. If I remember rightly, Madame de Matier, your mother, wanted to marry Boissart. Yes, that was it, and I remember the talk about his being only half her age. Your mother, I would say, would then have been in her forties; Boissart was only a lad about your age. Can't remember now what happened. Anyway they didn't marry, but I do know that Paul Boissart had been her lover in Montreal." He leaned over the desk confidentially. "I know because I was making my first visit to Montreal at the time. We were all quite interested in the affair and I can tell you why. We all wanted to take Boissart's place!" He laughed, revelling in the recollections of the past.

"But Boissart became her favorite," he continued. "There's no doubt, he's your man. And I'll tell you why I'm sure." He coughed and then assumed a confidential expression again. "She left Montreal and went back to France, returning here just before the siege. I hadn't then met the lady who became my wife and when I learned Hélène was here, I tried to get back into her graces." He laughed at the recollection, preening himself. "And again I found Boissart had superseded me. It was then, if I remember, that she told me of her forthcoming marriage to him. It's so many years ago now, one's memory becomes vague."

He sat back thinking for a moment, tapping his cheek with one finger, a pleased smile on his face. "I had forgotten it all until now," he said. "Maybe I hadn't better mention it to my wife, come to think of it." He slapped the desk and laughed.

Antoine tried not to reveal his feelings. Each word the

Marquis uttered had pressed the knife deeper into the wound. He rose and thanked him. The Marquis patted him on the back.

"Looks as though you have come all the way to Quebec, when the man you wanted was right in Montreal," he said and appeared to find it amusing. "I may have to go to Montreal soon and if I do, I will arrange for you to go on the same ship with me," he added affably. "Then you can see de Courville-Boissart and get it all straightened out."

"Thank you," Antoine said, feeling the net tightening around him. "I appreciate your helping me, monsieur."

"Not at all. Glad to help a son of Hélène de Matier's."

"May I ask you to keep all this confidential? It is very important to me that nothing be said until the proper time."

"Of course, my boy, of course," the Marquis assured him. "Your secret's safe with me."

"Perhaps it would be better not to mention it even to Madame, your wife," Antoine reminded him.

"She's in France. Don't worry. I'll not mention a word."

Antoine bowed. Outside the door, he stood for a moment, steadying himself. The effort not to betray himself had been an immense strain. The full import of the Marquis' words struck him and he felt weak with despair.

The Marquis kept his word. A few days later Antoine received a message from him that he was leaving for Montreal, and that Antoine could accompany him. The Marquis had given considerable thought to the conversation he had had with Antoine, his surprise at this sudden appearance of a son of Hélène de Matier's increasing. And with the surprise of this revelation, his curiosity also increased. He thought of Paul de Courville-Boissart and his family, and wondered how they would take this sudden appearance of a natural son. His mind travelled back two decades and he remembered the annoyance he and many members of the aristocracy had felt over Hélène's preference for "the farmer's boy," as they had called Paul.

That he was an attractive red-headed lad they were willing to admit but Hélène had always had such a contempt for the lower classes. Yet now, de Vaudreuil felt rather grateful to Paul. He realized that had Paul not been the favored one, he, the Marquis Philippe de Rigaud de Vaudreuil, might now have been involved. Antoine had made a good impression upon him and he hoped to get to know him better on the trip to Montreal. It was, therefore, disappointing to receive a reply from him, thanking him for the opportunity but declining the invitation. It puzzled the Marquis, for he had felt gratified that he had solved Antoine's riddle for him. He would have been further puzzled had he known that the ship carried two letters of Antoine's—one to the Sieur de Courville-Boissart and one to Mademoiselle Elise de Courville-Boissart.

Montreal was in a doleful condition. Word had come that the English fleet under Admiral Sir Hovenden Walker was ready to sail from Boston, while General Nicholson, with an army of several thousand was proceeding to Albany, preparing to march upon Montreal. The Chevalier de Ramezay had mustered three thousand soldiers and militia and a few Indians and had placed them under the command of the Baron de Longueil, who was preparing to set out for Chambly and await General Nicholson there.

The priests called upon the people to repent, blaming the frivolities of the winter for this menace that now threatened them. Penitential processions marched through the town, the Montrealers walking barefooted with cords around their necks. The women vowed not to wear ribbons or laces for a whole year. The Sisters of the Congregation made a vow that, if they were saved they would build a chapel in honor of the Mother of God, and name it Our Lady of Victory. Every day crowds of people knelt before the statue of the Virgin at Notre Dame de Bonsecours and prayed for help. This statue was regarded as the Guardian Saint of all sailors. It had been brought over from France by Sister Marguerite Bourgeoys in 1653, and from its position on the roof of the Church, looked down the River. Gift offerings were brought every day, but that alone was not enough. Special intercession was sought from a recluse who was regarded by many as a saint. This was Jeanne le Ber, who had voluntarily chosen to live in solitary confinement in a little room behind the altar in the Church of the Sisters of the Congregation. She had been a wealthy girl but had renounced all worldly interests and to the great sorrow of her family, remained for nearly twenty years in her little cell, denying herself everything, wearing the coarsest garb and with only a bed of straw to lie upon. She occupied herself with fervent prayer and in making exquisite embroidery for the church. She saw no one, not even her family. Only once had she left her cell. When her brother lay dead in an adjacent room, killed in a fight with the English, Jeanne had suddenly appeared before her astonished Sisters, stood for a moment in silent prayer by the body and then left, without uttering a word.

Frantic now for help in this crisis, an appeal was made to her. She gave the Sisters of the Congregation an image of the Virgin on which she had written a prayer for protection against the invaders. Other persons, anxious to have the same protection, sent her images to write upon, but she declined. One of the disappointed applicants subsequently stole the inscribed image from the Congregation.

At the Manor House everything was in preparation for the impending disaster. The stockade around the seigneury had been checked and strengthened and day and night, men manned the watch towers. Paul was unable to go with the Baron de Longueil because of an old wound in his leg, received at the siege of Schenectady, which made long marches impossible for him. He was, however, left in charge of home defenses. Jean-Baptiste and André had both left for Chambly, as well as Uncle Philip and cousin Pierre. The long, tedious wait had been trying for them all, although it had enabled the men to leave their fields in good condition. André and Uncle Philip fretted as they smoked their pipes together each night and looked longingly at the River, down which they had hoped to paddle months ago. May and June had passed, and it was the beginning of July before they received the order to proceed to Chambly. Jean-Baptiste had likewise found the interim of waiting very trying. At first, he had been furious when he had learned that Antoine had left for Quebec, and was bitterly resentful towards the Chevalier de Ramezay, whom he felt was a family friend and could have granted his request. Some of his resentment lessened when his mother explained as well as she could, that Antoine had an urgent reason for going. As Jean-Baptiste could not mention his reason for wishing to go to Quebec, and was somewhat embarrassed when his mother expressed surprise that he should want to leave his family at such a time, he threw off his bad humor and once again surprised them by helping with the seigneury.

Paul was in his office when he received Antoine's letter. Elise, though she had never seen Antoine's handwriting, guessed that her letter was from him and with her heart beating with excitement, hurried to her room to read it alone. Antoine's letter to Paul was brief. It related his conversation with the Marquis and what he felt was undeniable proof that Paul's surmise had been correct. "Therefore, monsieur, I must accept the fact and bow my head in resignation. As soon as possible I shall leave for France and try to forget. A letter to Elise comes by the same ship," Antoine concluded his letter. Paul sat for a long while, thinking, trying to review in his mind, the events of twenty years ago, and de Vaudreuil's participation in them. Ann came in, and he handed her the letter to read.

"I don't believe he can be any more certain than you, Paul," she commented, when she had finished reading the letter.

"Nor do I," Paul agreed. "He arrived by the ship this morning."

"The Marquis?" Paul nodded. "Will you mention the matter to him?"

"Do you think I should?"

Ann thought for a moment and then said decisively, "No." Paul looked relieved. "He may mention it to you, of course," she added.

"I don't believe he will unless I mention it first. Furthermore, I probably shall not see him."

Ann was reading the letter again. "I must go to Elise. This will upset her very much," she said and hurried away.

Elise was standing before the window, her letter held in a hand that hung limply by her side. Her attitude was one of utter dejection as she tried to realize that everything between her and Antoine was finished. She could not believe it. In the weeks since he had left, she had gone over every word that had passed between them; and as she had accepted the necessity of his making these inquiries, she had become more certain that he would soon be back. The letter, she had felt sure, was to tell her of his early return. And now—it was all over. She read the letter again. The salutation was formal. She did not know that Antoine had started it half a dozen different ways—running the gamut of "Elise darling," "My own darling," "Dearest Elise," and "Elise dear," until he decided that none of these would do. It read:

MADEMOISELLE:
This letter is very difficult to write and I have spent days wondering how to tell you that I cannot return. My investigations regarding my family have disclosed evidences that will prevent my marrying. It is all the more difficult because I can give you no reasons, since to do so would involve others whom I would not injure. I can only ask you to believe that I shall always love you with my whole heart.

Thank you, Elise, for having honored me with your love. Try to forgive me. I shall never forget our happy days and shall always remain,

Your devoted,
ANTOINE.

Ann put her arms around her daughter. The eyes that looked into hers were wells of anguish, and Ann knew the suffering to be harder than if she had been shaken with sobs. Without a word she handed her mother the letter and walked away, staring with fixed gaze at a small statue of the Madonna and child that hung over her *prie-dieu*. When Ann had finished reading the letter, she glanced over at Elise, wondering whether she prayed, or whether that fixed glance was the vacancy of a dazed mind. Ann, herself, was praying fervently for the right words to say, words of comfort that were so difficult to find.

Elise met her mother's eyes. "What can it mean, mother?" she asked. "What could he have found that would prevent his marrying?"

"I don't know, dear," Ann lied and wanted to say something more but words would not come.

"Are you sure Antoine didn't explain things to you? There must be something more. I feel there is something that you and father know. Father has been strange lately. He looks at me so peculiarly sometimes."

A feeling that was near panic spread over Ann. She had always been able to handle family difficulties and to help, but now she was helpless because her lips were sealed. She did not dare answer Elise's last remark because whatever she said would only complicate things. "All we know is that the Duc de Chamois never recognized him as his son. . . ."

"That's such a weak explanation!" Elise said and her green eyes flashed angrily. "He is merely making excuses and hasn't the character to tell me he doesn't want to marry me. All these family complications he keeps talking about are only an excuse. His so-called family have probably contracted for him to marry some Duchesse!"

"I don't think that attitude is fair, Elise," Ann reproved. "If you read the letter again you will find words that contradict such a possibility."

"Words!" Elise retorted, still angry.

"Being angry won't help, dear," Ann remarked gently.

"No, it won't," Elise said and as her voice broke, she flung herself on the bed and sobbed. Ann was relieved. She sat beside her but did not attempt to stay the tears, nor could she withhold her own. At that moment as she watched her child's anguish she hated Hélène de Matier bitterly, and in that hatred, her own husband was momentarily included.

"I love him so much, mother," Elise sobbed and Ann's tears mingled with hers. "I didn't know it at first but when I did realize it, I knew it so very certainly. He was so gentle and so understanding. He never bothered me like other men. And he loved me, mother. I know he did. Oh, what could have come between us? Can't I go to Quebec and tell him I don't care what there is in his family—it couldn't make any difference between us. It couldn't." The hysteria in her voice ended with a sob and was muffled by the pillow in which she buried her face.

What answer could Ann give? How could she hold out any hopes? How could she comfort her, other than by telling her the truth? And would the truth help? It would exonerate Antoine, but it would implicate Paul, and it was her father she would be seeing in the future years, and not Antoine. The truth could not bring her and Antoine together. If it could have, she would have told her, but it would merely have added hatred and resentment to a situation already complicated enough.

The Angelus sounded and they both knelt to pray, imploring God to send them a solution to what appeared an insoluble problem.

The weeks passed and some comfort was found in work which was heavy with so many men away. Fruit trees burst into bloom, adding their pastel colors to the fresh green of the fields, scythes were sharpened, ready for the cutting of the hay that was ripening. Soon, every one able to swing a scythe would have to go into the fields and swelter in the blazing sun until the hay was stacked in the barns. And no further news came from the waiting armies.

It was on a hot July afternoon that Paul asked Elise to come into his office and told her Claude de Ramezay had asked for her hand in marriage. Claude's position had been a difficult one. When his leave expired he had been unable to return to his naval post in France, owing to the presence of the English ships in the Atlantic. The Governor-General had instructed him to await orders, but these had not come. Now, he was leaving for Quebec, to sail immediately he could obtain a safe passage. Elise had seen him only a few times since Antoine's departure, although he had sent her many invitations which she had declined on the pretext that she was needed at home. She had been to dinner at the Chateau twice with her parents, and each time Claude had renewed his proposal of marriage. Now, he had taken matters into his own hands and spoken to her father. At any other time she would have been annoyed but since receipt of Antoine's letter, nothing seemed to matter. In answer to her father, she merely shrugged her shoulders and said: "Very well."

Paul's worried expression deepened as he looked at her. Her innate *joie de vivre* was gone. She now seemed listless and there were dark circles under her eyes. Her father put his arm around her, wanting so much to say something comforting.

"Don't decide in a hurry, dear," he said.

"He has asked me many times already," she answered. "I might as well marry him."

"That doesn't sound like love," Paul protested.

She shrugged her shoulders again and said: "It will do," and walked out of the room. Her father watched her, the lines on his bronzed face deep with anxiety. As always when in trouble he sought out Ann.

"I've killed her happiness," he declared.

"Claude is a fine boy and will make her happy, I'm sure," Ann said. "Before Antoine came, it is what we always hoped."

"Before Antoine, yes, but it is he whom she loves."

"She will forget—in time."

Later that afternoon Claude called to see Elise. The sad

look she gave him was not very encouraging. "Are you angry with me?" he asked.

She merely shook her head and then realizing he knew nothing of her unhappiness over Antoine, she rallied and tried to smile. "Persistency wins," she said.

"You mean you will marry me?" he exclaimed and as joy radiated his face he looked very attractive. His usual arrogance was missing and he appeared almost humble. "I didn't believe you would ever say *yes*, Elise."

She couldn't tell him she loved him, so she said nothing, and let him do the talking.

"I have to leave for Quebec tomorrow. It's all rather hurried and not the way I wanted it. When this war is over we can celebrate properly. Could we announce our engagement tonight?"

"We had better go and speak to mother and father."

"In a minute." He turned her towards him. "I do love you, Elise, very much. I will try to make you happy."

"Thank you, Claude," she answered and let him kiss her.

That night as the two families toasted the betrothed couple, Elise exerted herself to be charming. Marie-Charlotte de Ramezay's happiness over the occasion was infectious, for it was what she had always wanted. Elise tried to forget the ache deep inside her and was touched by the affection of her future mother-in-law. After all, she told herself, to marry the Governor's son was something to make any girl happy. She was fond of Claude and as her second choice he had much to recommend him.

When she waved goodbye to her fiancé the next morning, there were tears in her eyes, tears that she refused to analyze.

BOOK II
Henry

CHAPTER XVII

HE STOOD IN THE BOW OF THE SHIP, the sullen, unhappy expression on his face marring his good looks. He was a tall, wiry lad looking much older than his sixteen years. His fair hair, tending towards a reddish tint, caught in the wind and several times he pushed it from his face with an irritable gesture. It felt dirty and sticky from the salt air. How he hated the sea! Hated everything about this English ship which was his prison. He hated the guns bristling with death. He did not want to take life but to save it. His ambition had always been to be a doctor and now that ambition was lost in despair. This urge of men to kill other men in order to gain power for themselves was alien to him, an attitude nurtured in him by his parents. With an English father and a French mother he had been taught that there was seldom any reason for one nation to fight another; that on this vast continent there was room for people of all nations and that they could live in peace, without encroaching on each other's territory. It wasn't the people of the colonies, it was the home governments that caused the unrest, and he hated those governments. He was colonial born and he loved the colonies. Right now he had a bitter and savage hatred of the English, because of the arbitrary methods which had placed him on board this ship.

If only he had been able to let his parents know what had happened to him. But when he had recovered from that sudden blow on the head, it had been to find himself bound hand and foot in a world that heaved and tossed. How it had happened he would never fully remember. He had gone to Boston on some business for his mother. Though she had not said so, he was reasonably sure she had sent him away from Albany so that he would not be called upon to join the army under General Nicholson, forming for the attack on Montreal. He had only just stepped ashore and was walking along tending to his own business, when, suddenly, the world had begun to reel and all had gone black. From the bump on his head he could to some extent reconstruct what had happened. He had heard of these press-gangs that forced men into the service of the British Navy, but he had always understood they pressed only people who frequented the low life. His shipmates had since told him that on the journey from England, they had lost so many men with dysentery, that the press-gang method was their only recourse.

As he stood brooding on deck, he thought of the anxiety of his parents. He could picture his adored mother, her prematurely white head bent over her needlework and his tall, lean father smoking his pipe and watching her. The devotion of his parents to one another, despite their different nationalities, was something that had always impressed him. The three of them had been united in an unusually close bond. His mother, he had been told, had lost two sons from a former marriage, which had made him all the more precious to her. Henry stifled a groan. And now she would think he, too, was lost! He could picture her small frame shaken with sobs as she leaned against his father. For her sake, he must try to escape, or if that did not prove possible, at least to come through the fighting unharmed. He had learned that they were on their way to attack Quebec. Montreal had been his mother's home, where her people still lived. At least in attacking Quebec he would not be actually fighting his own relatives. But he didn't want to fight any one!

His face clouded angrily again. These past weeks on a disease-ridden ship, eating food alive with weevils, and denied water in which to wash, so that he felt filthy beyond conception, had been a nightmare to him. The habits of the dirty, lying scum with whom he had to associate below decks had frequently forced him to turn away and retch. The nauseating stench of that hell-hole they called the crew quarters, was something unbelievably vile. Only on days when they worked on deck could he get away from the foul smell but even this was often denied when he was assigned to work in the cook's galley, and sometimes there were days on end, when he never saw daylight.

He had worked hard because he did not relish the cat-o'-nine-tails that was held ready for application to any bare back that wasn't bent to work. Henry had not yet felt its sting but he had seen others writhing under it, and on more than one occasion had seen these lacerated bodies dangling from the masts.

He saw the coxswain's mate coming towards him but did not move. He knew he had no right to be standing idle on the upper deck but he was in a rebellious mood. When the mate struck him in the face, he managed to get in at least one telling blow before his arm was twisted nearly out of its socket, and a kick sent him reeling backwards on to some tackle. The blow stunned him so that he was only half aware of what happened afterwards. He heard the mate's bullying voice shouting orders and felt himself being dragged across the deck by the legs. A rope was twisted around his wrists and jerked so tightly that it cut into his flesh as he was triced to the mast. Even before he felt the stinging cut on his back he knew what was coming. The vicious thongs of the "cat" cut again and again into his flesh, feeling like red hot irons drawn across his back. He heard the angry hisses of the mate as with mounting temper he wielded the whip. He would have liked to have taken the punishment without a sound but it was not humanly possible. At first he only groaned but as the pain became unbearable he screamed. On and on the brute lashed at him, losing all sense of reason in his sadistic joy. Unconsciousness mercifully enveloped him.

When later he wakened he was in darkness. The place was dank and evil-smelling. He was lying on his face and when he tried to turn, a pain as of a thousand knives cut into his back. He dropped back on to his face and groaned. As he did so a voice whispered: *"Qui va là?"* but he did not hear it. All his courage had drained from him and he sobbed in weakness and pain. Never again would he see his home; never would he get away from this cursed ship. A rat ran across his back digging its sharp claws into his lacerations and he screamed and cursed. There was the sound of chains dragging over the floor and again the voice asked: *"Qui va là?"*

Henry held his breath, surprised to find he was not alone. He was more surprised as he realized the voice had spoken in French and in the same language he asked: "Who is it?"

"French prisoner, Paradis," came the reply and then in an eager tone. "You are French, too?"

"Half-English, half-French," Henry replied, the words coming slowly and painfully.

"You are injured?"

"Beaten to death," he groaned.

"The cat?"

"Yes."

"I am sorry I can't help you. My chains won't permit me to come any nearer. Have courage."

"It's all gone. I want to die."

"You must not give up," the voice urged.

There was a long silence and then Paradis asked: "Are you all right?" He was afraid that life had already ebbed.

"If I lie still it doesn't hurt so much. But I am so stiff and want to move." He stifled another groan and then asked: "How long have you been here?"

"I have lost all count of time. It's probably only weeks but it seems months."

"Why are you here?"

There was a hard laugh. "Because I'm French."

In a voice that could hardly be heard, Henry muttered: "I'm so thirsty."

"There should be water near you."

"But I can't move," Henry muttered, "and my hands are tied."

"I'll try and push my bowl over to you. Can you see me?"

Henry lifted his head from his arms and strained his eyes into the darkness. He could make out a form and heard the grating of a metal bowl on the floor.

"Can you move a bit closer? I think then you could reach it," Paradis said. His voice had a soothing quality.

Painfully Henry dragged himself along, stopping every few inches in a paroxysm of pain. It was a slow process and only by stretching his ankle chains to their full length could he reach the bowl and then he was too exhausted to drink. He lay there racked with pain, the sweat pouring off his forehead and into his eyes. Paradis stretched his legs until the clamps cut into his ankles, but he managed to push the bowl nearer. Gathering all his strength, Henry lifted his head and pressed his face into the water. For a moment he lay there, the tepid water soothing him. He sucked some water into his mouth and let it trickle down his parched throat. It tasted foul, but it was better than the dryness. Then his head dropped, hitting the side of the bowl and upsetting the contents over his face. Paradis, whose eyes were accustomed to the darkness watched him, pitying but helpless to assist.

Hours passed by as he lay there in semi-consciousness from which he only roused when a stream of light from the opening door shone on his face. Two soldiers came in and unlocked Paradis' chains. He spoke to them in French, asking where they were taking him but they did not understand. At the same time two sailors came in and when the soldiers had left, spoke kindly to Henry. One of them treated the lacerations on his back and untied his wrists. These they left free but according to orders had to leave the chains on his ankles. They brought him fresh water, which was still foul, as was all the water aboard, and gave him some food—weevil-ridden bread.

"What did you want to go and lose your temper for?" one of them asked, not unkindly. "You know what striking a superior means."

"What will it mean?" Henry asked.

"If you don't know, mate, then the better off you are," the man replied.

Henry had long hours in which to think. Only now as his head began to clear did he remember what had happened. Just whom he had struck he did not clearly remember. He could have learned all the various ranks of the officers and their subordinates but he had not cared. He had taken his orders sullenly and resentfully, and had made no effort to learn anything about seamanship. Back in his mind somewhere was the recollection that striking a superior called for the death penalty. Perhaps this was the end. He broke out in a cold sweat as he thought it over. What would they do with him? What death penalty did the Navy demand? Would they string him up to the mast and leave him to die slowly? Would they make him face a firing squad? He prayed for that. A word crossed his mind that he had heard somewhere, and it made him shudder. Keelhauled. He had never witnessed it; for that matter he had seen no drastic punishment except flogging, which seemed part of a ship's routine, and that was drastic enough. Captain Goddard, he had heard, was a stern disciplinarian but not a man who liked violence. Admiral Walker, it seemed, was more concerned with himself than with petty details of law and order aboard the ship.

Henry sat up and tried to lean his back against the wall but the motion of the ship made it impossible to find a place where he could be comfortable. His back pained him terribly. The heat and the stench were abominable and he gasped for breath. There was no means by which even the smallest breath of air could get into the hell-hole where he was confined, and in frantic desperation he lay face downward again, and tried to brace himself so that he would not roll from side to side.

When night came he had no way of knowing, for it was night all the time in his pitch-black hole. He slept but he did not know for how long. The gnawing in his stomach forced him to nibble the bread. The first bite he spat out but soon he could no longer endure the hunger and despite the foulness had to chew the bread and swallow it. It seemed to drop into the hollow of his stomach and achieve nothing in the way of satiating his appetite.

His solitary confinement came to an end and he was ordered out to work, still wearing chains on his ankles. Punishments were meted out once a week, and, near as Henry could calculate from the previous ones, there were still two or three days yet before the next allotted day. Painful though it was, he preferred working to confinement. Each day, the wounds on his back broke out anew as he was forced to move his arms and strain his back. He learned that it was the coxswain's mate whom he had struck, a man named Brown, whose sadistic nature revelled in brutalities. A belaying pin or knotted rope was always in his hand and he lost no opportunity of laying it on Henry's back every time he came near.

Henry wondered what had happened to the French prisoner, since he had not been returned to the brig. He did not see him anywhere. On the third morning as he swabbed decks, the coxswain's mate came to him, a heavier scowl than usual on his face. Henry met the scowl defiantly. Although he realized this man had the power to kill him, he did not intend to give him any advantage by showing fear or trying to pacify him.

"Come with me," Brown said curtly and led the way to the other end of the ship.

Henry followed in silence, telling himself that this was the moment when he would have to face his officers and hear what punishment he would receive for his misdeeds. Somehow he did not care; he was too weary and miserable. The sooner it was over the better, only he hoped it would be a quick death and not a long, drawn-out one. Even as he thought of it he glanced up at the mast and could not repress a shudder.

At the companionway leading to the quarterdeck, Brown stopped.

"Raise your leg," he grunted angrily. Henry supported himself with the rail and raised one leg as high as he could. To his surprise Brown unlocked the manacles about his ankles and threw them aside. There was fury in the gesture. "Put on a shirt," he said abruptly.

"I don't have one," Henry replied.

Brown gave him a threatening scowl and sent for one. It was much too large but for this Henry was grateful, for it did not hurt his back too much.

They proceeded up the companionway, towards the Captain's cabin. It was the first time Henry had been on the quarterdeck and he looked around curiously. At the Captain's door, they stopped and Brown knocked. Henry stood erect, towering over the squat figure of the coxswain's mate. A voice from inside answered the knock and they entered. The limited space within was filled by four men, three of whom, in the uniforms of British officers, were bending over a table studying a chart. The fourth presented a contrast. He was a short man dressed in a dirty jersey and ragged trousers, his sparse hair reaching to his shoulders and his chin covered by a straggly beard. His eyes were half-closed to shield them from unaccustomed light but, as Henry entered, they opened wide for a moment and smiled a friendly greeting. But Brown did not acknowledge it.

As the man whose back was to him straightened his broad shoulders, his head nearly touched the deck beam above. He turned to them, glanced from the mate to Henry, appraising him.

"Henry Walker, sir," the mate said and touched his forelock. The swaggering, bullying attitude had now disappeared and Brown was subservient.

The Captain continued to look at Henry for a further moment and then sat down, the officers discontinuing their study of the chart and also staring. All three men wore wigs, Captain Goddard's heavy wig framing a hard, rough face, tanned like leather. The features were large and well-formed, with a beaklike nose that dominated the face. The eyes were cold and calculating and in an instant appraised any one they regarded with a judgment that seldom erred. It was the face of a man who has experienced the roughness of life; yet, despite the firmness of the lines and the tight lips, there was a warmth, perhaps of understanding, that radiated from his personality.

He regarded Henry again and for a fleeting second his expression changed from puzzlement to curiosity and then was a mask again.

"Henry Walker?" he queried. Brown pushed him forward. Despite the pain in his back, Henry stood erect before the Captain, expecting to hear that sentence of death had been passed on him, and yet surprised that it was not done before the entire crew of the ship. Perhaps, he thought, they pronounced it privately first, and then publicly. Knowing nothing of the procedure in such matters, he could only wait and see. His head nearly reached the deck beam, his lanky frame emphasizing his height. He faced the Captain with an easy dignity, with no suggestion of servility in his attitude.

"Walker?" the Captain repeated. Then with a flicker of a smile he asked: "No relation to the Admiral, are you?"

Henry was surprised at the easiness of the Captain's tone. "Not that I am aware of, sir," he replied. "My father is Eric Walker of Albany."

The Captain nodded. "What is your position in the ship?" he asked.

"Ordinary seaman, sir."

"What do you know about sailing?"

"Nothing, sir," was the frank reply.

The suggestion of a smile again crossed the Captain's face. "Just joined the expedition for the adventure, eh?" he said.

"No, sir. I did not join it. I was pressed into it." Henry replied in a measured tone. Captain Goddard studied him. He liked straightforward people.

"What trouble had you been in?" was the next query. "You look young to have been frequenting waterfronts."

"I hadn't been in any trouble, sir. I had just arrived in

Boston and was on my way to attend to some family business when I was seized." The mate standing behind Henry had an angry scowl on his face. Henry met the Captain's eye steadily and saw the forehead wrinkle into a heavy frown. The steel-blue eyes were piercing as they turned to the mate.

"Mr. Brown, will you explain this?" he said in a brittle tone.

"We were told to get fifteen men, sir," Brown replied. "We . . ."

A volume of oaths from the Captain silenced him. "You blubberheaded fools! Isn't there enough scum frequenting the ports? Do you fools have to press into service people who are attending to their own affairs? God's truth, this isn't the first time this has happened!"

So it was Brown, or his men, who had given him that blow on the head!

"He must have been loitering about or they wouldn't have pressed him," Brown said rather defiantly. Henry turned sharply at the lie and saw the fury in Brown's eyes, but no comment was necessary. Captain Goddard was talking again. He had always been bitterly opposed to the press-gang method of obtaining crews. Now, he vented his dislike of the method upon the mate.

"If your men don't know the proper method of obtaining crews, then they'll have to be taught, and I'll give them a lesson they won't forget. Any man who knows his job could tell the difference between waterfront riff-raff and educated men."

"We don't usually have time to question them about their education," Brown answered sarcastically and added, "sir," as an afterthought.

"Get out!" Captain Goddard shouted and banged the table with his fist. The stale rum breath and the reek of the man's body had begun to fill the crowded room and though Captain Goddard was not fastidious, the stench combined with his short temper, after an irritating morning, made him feel he wanted to hit somebody.

Brown turned to the door and Henry started to follow. "Not you, Walker," Goddard said. "I sent for you for another reason." Now would come the condemnation, Henry thought. He turned and faced the Captain again.

Captain Goddard mopped his forehead with a fine cambric handkerchief, holding it to his nose for a moment or two. There was silence in the cabin. Then he hunched his shoulders and settled back into his chair, and when he spoke his voice was controlled. "Paradis tells me you are half-French and half-English," he said to Henry.

Then it dawned upon Henry who the dishevelled man was. In the darkness he had not been able to tell what he was like. He realized now that the friendly nod had been for him when they entered. He looked at the man again and keen blue eyes smiled at him.

"Yes, sir," Henry replied to the query.

"Paradis was taken on board because he is an experienced pilot and we shall soon be entering treacherous waters. He has undertaken to guide us. He does not, however, understand English and neither my officers nor I speak French. He says you speak both languages."

Henry wondered how Paradis could know this, since they had conversed only in French. Maybe he had just surmised it.

"Yes, sir," Henry answered.

"Do you understand both languages well enough to act as interpreter?"

"Certainly, sir," Henry answered and could not keep the delight out of his voice. "I understand both languages equally well. I have spoken both since childhood. My mother is French and my father English."

"Who did you say your father was?"

"Eric Walker of Albany, sir."

"Mm," was the Captain's only comment but his thoughts were troubled. The name wasn't familiar to him; he could only hope the father wasn't a man of prominence who would be able to cause trouble over this pressing of his son into the service. He dismissed the matter from his mind for the present and gave his orders. "Quarters will be fixed for you on this deck. You will not leave it at any time. Is that clear?" He addressed both of them. Henry repeated the sentence in French to Paradis. Captain Goddard listened and seemed satisfied. One of his officers understood a little French and nodded with approval. "You, Paradis, will be responsible for the safe conduct of this ship to Quebec." Henry interpreted again and Paradis bowed and replied: "Oui, monsieur."

"When you repeat an order, Walker, you must be absolutely sure that it is the same and that Paradis understands you."

"Yes, sir."

"Any deviation or misunderstanding might be fatal. I shall hold you responsible under penalty of death." Though his words were harsh, his tone was not.

"Yes, sir," Henry replied.

"Very well. Mr. Richards, you will see that my instructions are carried out and the necessary arrangements made."

"Aye, aye, sir." Lieutenant Richards saluted and signalled to Paradis and Walker to follow him.

Not a word had been said about Henry's misadventure. He left the cabin, marvelling. He could not wait to ask Paradis how it had all happened.

CHAPTER XVIII

IT WAS NOT UNTIL THE FOLLOWING MORNING that Paradis and Walker were summoned to the Admiral's quarters. In the meantime both of them had changed in appearance. Paradis' first request had been that he be allowed to wash, for he had not been given the opportunity during his confinement, except when he could spare enough drinking water to swill over his face. At the same time he asked for a shirt and a pair of trousers to replace the rat-eaten ones he wore. When he had washed and changed, he asked Henry to cut his hair, and he trimmed his beard to a neat tuft on the chin. He then looked very different from the shambling old man in the cabin. Despite his long confinement, he still retained some of the ruddiness that forty years of sea life had ingrained into his skin. He was short and stockily built with the bandy legs of one who has spent most of his life walking a deck.

Henry watched him curiously, wondering what his story was. He was surprised to find that he now looked much younger and not more than fifty years of age. Paradis also commented upon Henry's youth. When Henry told him he was sixteen he exclaimed: "That's young to have had such a rough start. I could tell by your voice when we first met down below that you weren't very old. Still to look at you, I would have judged you to be about twenty-five."

Henry gave him the pleased smile of youth that likes to be credited with maturity. They were both sitting on the deck, stripped to the waist, and enjoying the feel of the warm August sun upon their skin. Paradis exclaimed at the sight of Henry's back. It was beginning to heal with deep-ridged scars, which would always tell a story. Some of them were still red and angry looking. Paradis was not the only one who saw them. Lieutenant Richards in assigning them their new duties, noticed them. His dignity as an officer prevented his exclaiming, but Paradis' sharp eyes saw the horrified look on the young man's face.

"Does it still hurt you?" Paradis inquired solicitously.

"Yes, but if I don't have to do hard labor it will have a chance to heal better."

"With this job you won't have to work hard."

"How did it all come about, Paradis? I mean, how did I come into it? I know nothing about navigation "

"You're not supposed to. You are to interpret orders to me. I don't understand English." Paradis threw back his head and laughed. Then he looked round cautiously and lowering his voice, said in perfect English, "Paradis, if you will guide us through the treacherous waters of the St. Lawrence you will be given your freedom."

Henry stared and then started to exclaim but Paradis held a warning finger to his lips. "You do speak English, then?" Henry whispered.

Paradis nodded and then speaking in French explained, "When I found out that Lieutenant Richards was the only one who knew any French and that very inadequately, the idea came to me. I purposely spoke very rapidly to confuse them and then I mentioned you. The scheme worked. You must not remember I know English. Never for a moment must you remember it."

"I won't. But how did you know I spoke English?"

"You had told me you were half-English and I just made a guess."

"I am very grateful," Henry said again and then asked: "How do you happen to be on board? I know you are a French prisoner, but why did they bring you?"

"Because I am an experienced navigator. Do you know the St. Lawrence region at all?" Henry shook his head. "It is very dangerous. Strong currents, many islands, shifting sandbars and reefs. The English have pilots aboard, of course, but a man has to know the region to be able to navigate a ship safely. I have been sailing these waters for many years. For bringing them safely to Quebec they will give me my freedom."

"And you will do that?"

"Why not?"

"But the French are your people and that way you guide an enemy to attack them."

"Attack them, yes, but not necessarily with success. You are too young to remember Phips' attempt twenty years ago— in fact you weren't even born. The English attack on Quebec failed then—why should they succeed now?"

"But if they fail, where will that leave you?"

Paradis smiled. "I can take care of myself and you. The moment we sight Quebec we make plans to desert. I have many friends there. They will look after us."

"Where is your home?"

"Home?" Paradis looked pensive. "It used to be Three Rivers, between Quebec and Montreal. These last years it has been my ship—but that is gone."

"Gone?"

"They sank it," he jerked his head to indicate the English. "I was caught by them on their way to Boston."

"And that is how you were made prisoner?"

Paradis' face was sad. "Yes. A skipper should be allowed to go down with his ship. I wasn't so lucky."

"I still can't see why, if they brought you along as navigator, they should have had to keep you in irons in that rathole below," Henry said indignantly.

Paradis shrugged his shoulders. "*Ça fait rien!* The rats and I came to know each other very well." He laughed and Henry was amazed at his philosophical nature.

"What are we supposed to do now?" Henry asked.

"Chart the course for them . . ."

"But what am I supposed to do? As I said, I know nothing about ships."

"You translate for me so that I understand," Paradis grinned. "And be sure you do it so that I do understand!" He laughed again.

"Is it difficult to navigate?"

"One has to learn. I will teach you the rudiments of it, if I have time. One must know the stars and their positions." He looked up. "Tonight I will tell you about them. Ah! It will be good to sleep beneath them again."

Lieutenant Richards had been much perturbed as to where he was to put them, for the quarterdeck was filled to capacity. Paradis had quickly solved the problem by asking permission to sling hammocks on deck. After weeks of confinement, he could not get enough air and this suited Henry equally well.

And so when night came, Henry lay in his hammock and watched the stars. For the first time since his capture he felt happy and breathed pure air. New hopes filled his heart and as he said his prayers he included special aves for Paradis, to whom he was already growing attached. Though their ages were far apart, they had found much in common, perhaps because they were both in adversity. Paradis had recalled memories of home when he had called him *Henri*. All his life he had been called both *Henry* and *Henri* because his mother, try as she would, could not master the English aspirate. When she tried to say Henry it was always " *'enery*" and that his English father could not stand. So with her it remained *Henri*.

Admiral Sir Hovenden Walker was pompous and arrogant. Captain Goddard's greeting that morning was reserved but friendly, especially towards Henry. When he presented him to the Admiral and commented upon his bearing the same name, Sir Hovenden disdainfully ignored the remark. Nor did he appear to consider Paradis' services of importance, and was extremely irritated that all his remarks or inquiries had to be translated through Henry, who could hardly keep from smiling every time he translated a phrase that Paradis had already understood perfectly. Admiral Walker had all the disdain of an Englishman for any language other than his own. Captain

Goddard repeatedly pointed out the hazards they would encounter when they had passed Gaspé. The Admiral's reply was to puff and snort, which blew the snuff to which he had frequent recourse, in a brown cascade down the front of his uniform. Once when Goddard made a futile effort to impress him yet again with the difficulties they were likely to encounter, the Admiral exploded with: "Are you trying to teach me how to navigate a ship?" and Captain Goddard remained silent.

They saw little of the Admiral. All orders were conveyed to them through Captain Goddard and it was with him that they spent much time studying the course.

For the first time Henry looked at the ship with interest and no longer regarded it as a prison but as a new experience. Every minute he could learn something from Paradis and though much of it was complicated to his land-bred mind, nevertheless he was an apt pupil. From Paradis he learned the names of the different masts and sails, studied the rigging, observed some of the rudiments of tacking and sailing and began to understand the flag and light signals to other ships. For the first time he became interested in the fleet as he learned there were fifteen men-of-war, and forty-six transports and store ships making up the armada sailing towards Quebec.

A strong head-wind drove them into the Bay of Gaspé, where they sheltered for two days until the wind shifted to the southeast. Then they set sail again and began the perilous voyage down the St. Lawrence River. From then on they ran into difficulties battling a strong east wind and fog so that it was frequently necessary to tack about in order not to be driven on to the treacherous shoals. So many times did Paradis find it necessary to change the course that the Admiral's bellowing could be heard through the door of his cabin. Henry was kept scuttling back and forth with messages between the pilot and Goddard, while the Admiral insisted that all this maneuvring was unnecessary and a trick on the part of Paradis to tire out the crew. To this comment Paradis merely smiled grimly and attended to his difficult task, but to Henry he muttered: "Does the old fool want to be shipwrecked on a reef? What he knows about navigation I could put into my pipe and blow out in smoke."

Those nights were grim, for only Paradis knew the full extent of their danger, as he peered through the dense fog and strained to keep the ships from crowding on to each other in the narrow waters. There were moments when the fog would break and the moon would peep through only to be eclipsed a moment or two later. Perhaps no one but Paradis realized the crisis through which they were passing—no one but Paradis and Henry who appreciated his sincerity. The Admiral suffered no misgivings whatsoever. He was, in fact, elated over the fog and told his officers so as they sat at supper. He boasted of a knowledge of the River which some believed and others doubted, Captain Goddard among the latter. As the wine made him mellow, he became voluble upon the surprise the French would get when the English ships appeared at Quebec, their arrival having been completely eclipsed by the fog. In his mind he already saw himself donning his most elegant uniform and accepting the surrender from the Governor-General of the colony. He informed his listeners that he was confident this could be done with the firing of a few guns just to frighten the inhabitants. He laughed and spilled his wine, belching loudly at the same time. "Defenses of Quebec!" he ridiculed. "They're nothing more than so many sticks of wood!"

"I've always understood the town stands upon a precipitous rock," Captain Goddard remarked drily.

The Admiral turned bloodshot eyes to the speaker. "Have you never heard of strategy, Captain?" he asked, and Captain Goddard made no reply. When supper was finished, Goddard went on deck and remained there. His feelings were uneasy and foreboding. It was the night of August 22nd, 1711.

Before getting into bed, Admiral Walker inspected his uniforms and decided that before he made his report to Queen Anne, he would have a new and more elaborate one made. He puffed out his chest and studied himself in the mirror. Yes, this achievement, no doubt, would be the zenith of his career. Probably it would gain him an earldom and certainly much acclaim.

Henry was at the helm, while Paradis stood with the compass, his face drawn and set as he gazed frequently into the thick fog.

"Bad night," Captain Goddard commented as he came to stand beside him.

"Very bad. And I don't like the Admiral's charting either. We're too close to land to be safe," Paradis remarked, and Henry repeated the statement in English. They were silent, tense in a muffled world. Then Paradis said: "It's no good, sir, we'll have to turn back. The whole fleet will be led to disaster if we continue this way. Won't you please speak to the Admiral?" Henry translated.

Goddard demurred. "He's already gone to bed," he said.

"Bed—on a night like this!" Paradis growled. "Then you'd better waken him, for I'll not continue. Either he listens to reason or I disobey his instructions. I'm the pilot and I'm not a fool."

Goddard listened to him and then turned and went towards the Admiral's quarters. He hesitated a moment and then rapped sharply on the door. Stertorous sounds were the only answer. Again he rapped more loudly and when there was still no reply, he opened the door and went in, bracing himself for the tirade that would undoubtedly greet him when he wakened the Admiral. He did not underestimate it. He had to shake him several times before he aroused him and then loud curses greeted him.

"What now? Can't I be left to sleep in peace?" the Admiral bellowed.

"Not the way things look, sir," Goddard answered firmly. "We are in danger of striking a reef. The fog is so thick you can't even see the length of the ship. The pilot asks permission to turn back."

"Turn back!" the Admiral shouted. As he sat up, his nightcap lurched to one side, while his bloated cheeks puffed out. Angrily he adjusted the cap. "We will not turn back! We have already maneuvred and maneuvred until we're off our course. What is that fool Frenchman trying to do? God damn it, he will carry out my orders or I'll have him put in irons. Tell him to keep a southerly course and remain in that direction." And with that he plumped his head down on the pillow and turned his back.

Goddard returned to Paradis and gave the orders. "South! He means north." In his excitement Paradis spoke in English and sharing his concern, Captain Goddard did not at the time notice it. They were already so close to land to the south that the slightest move in that direction would be disastrous. At that moment, as though to substantiate his statement, the moon broke through, showing a range of coast with breakers directly ahead. Paradis shouted for signals to be sent to the other ships to wear and bring to with heads northward. It was no longer a matter of orders, it was a matter of life and death. Without waiting further, Captain Goddard dashed to the Admiral's cabin again, wasting no time in knocking but rushing in and shaking him violently by the shoulder, and shouting:

"For God's sake, sir, come up on deck or we shall certainly be lost."

"God damn you for a fool! I have already given you my orders to steer south."

"But south is land, sir!" Goddard urged. "There are breakers all around us."

Scarcely were the words out than there was a thunderous sound, not a deep rolling noise, but crackling and splintering, and a violent lurching of the ship. Overhead could be heard the trampling of scurrying feet and confused shouting. Only then did Admiral Walker jump out of bed, and in dressing gown and slippers come on deck. It was a scene of fright and confusion.

Meanwhile Paradis had made a quick decision. "We are

not going to stay here and drown like rats, Henri. Quick, over the side and swim with all your strength. Head south and you will make land. God go with you."

"What about you?" Henri said anxiously.

"I follow. Quick. Don't waste precious time with words."

Henry dashed to the side and climbed over, clinging to the ship until he saw that Paradis was following. At that moment the Admiral stormed out and collided with Paradis.

"What now, dog?" he bellowed. "Why aren't you at the helm?"

"Sacré bleu cochon!" Paradis swore at him, and then in English he said. "Do you take me for a fool! Go and paddle your own canoe!" Only now did Captain Goddard notice that Paradis spoke English, but this was no time for comment. "Listen to that!" Paradis was shouting.

And through the fog came the sounds of splintering wood and voices raised in terrified screams. Pandemonium broke loose as officers yelled conflicting orders. Through the shifting fog, they caught glimpses of foundering ships, their masts locked in a deathly embrace, as ship piled upon ship, crushing against each other, inextricably entangled. The fog muffled much of the sound but added to the confusion.

"You French bastard! This is your doing!" the Admiral screamed and lunging at Paradis he struck him a blow that sent him lurching against the side. His head struck the bulwark near where Henry was clinging. He saw Paradis crumple into a heap and began to climb back to rescue him. But it was too late. The ship gave a violent lurch. Henry lost his grip and plunged into the water.

CHAPTER XIX

HENRY REVIVED IN A WORLD that was deathly still. For several moments he could not recollect where he was or what had happened. He felt around him and his hands came in contact with a hard slimy surface. The movement of the ship was no longer there. He sat up quickly and then fell back again, for his head throbbed and swam. He put his hand to his forehead and it was wet and sticky. When he tried to see the sticky substance, everything was misty so that for the moment he thought his eyesight was affected. As his brain cleared again he realized that the mistiness was not in him but that he was surrounded by the densest fog. He sat up again, slowly, and then saw that his clothes were soaked and the stickiness on his hand was blood. He groped in his pocket for a sodden handkerchief and wiped his forehead, wincing at the pain from the gash. He tied the handkerchief around his head and turned to look around him but the motion made him dizzy. He lay back again and slid into unconsciousness.

When later he wakened, the scene had changed. The fog had lifted and a warm sun had dried his clothes. The sight that met his eyes when he looked around was one of unspeakable horror. Bodies were strewn all along the shore, piled one upon the other, in attitudes of agony. Some were in red coats— others were women, who according to custom had accompanied the soldiers. Their hands were clasped in each others and terror was on their lifeless faces. Stunned, Henry gazed at them and tried to recall what had happened. Slowly the meaning of the horror came back to him. He remembered hitting the water and striking out for land as Paradis had told him. But after a few yards he had become entangled with struggling bodies and

192

hands that dragged him under in their efforts to gain a hold. A frantic mass of terrified humanity trying to get away from the wreckage of the ships, and floundering to watery graves in a pitch-black world. There had been no time and no space in which to lower boats. To save his own life, Henry had had to strike out, tearing the hands away from his own body and trying desperately to find space in which to reach the shore. Paradis had told him to strike southward for shore but in the darkness he had lost the course. For hours it seemed he had swum about until exhaustion threatened him. He could not now remember when he had struck land but from his position it was evident that he had been the first to reach it.

And then he thought of Paradis. Where was he? He must find him. He scrambled to his feet but fell back as everything around him whirled dizzily. He held his aching head between his hands. From the gash on his forehead he must have struck it forcefully. When the dizziness had passed he got to his knees, waited a moment and then stood up, swaying uncertainly. He stood alone in a world of corpses, hundreds of them, some half in and half out of the water. Beyond lay the wreckage of eight large ships, their incongruous attitudes mute evidence of the ignominy of an English sealord whose obstinacy and ignorance had sent thousands to their death.

Henry then remembered seeing Paradis crumple against the side of the ship. Where was the Admiral's flagship? Perhaps he could yet save Paradis. Where was it? He stumbled along, trying to avoid the bodies but with the uncertainty of his legs, often falling. "Paradis!" he shouted but no answer came from that world of death. He strained his eyes trying to distinguish among the wreckage a ship that looked like the flagship. He could not see it. No, he could not, because the Admiral had extricated his ship and a few others and fled back to Boston, there to face not triumph but disgrace. But before that, Paradis had been flung overboard to a grave in the deep.

Henry sank down in despair, tears of weakness welling up as he cried out to God. Why had he been spared? What was he doing alive amidst this scene of carnage? Perhaps there were yet others who lived. He crawled to his knees and bracing himself stood surveying the scene and watching for any sign of life. The breeze played tricks with him and the fluttering of drying garments would deceive him as he stumbled hither and yon, calling out as he went and poking among the dead to find the living. In the pocket of a soldier he found a bottle of rum, and drained the remains in one gulp. The warm liquid was comforting but it also reminded him he was hungry. Food? Could there be such a thing among this desolation? He climbed on to the nearest wreckage and began a search but, except for the upper deck, all was submerged in water. Wading knee deep he entered an open cabin and found a few biscuits and gnawed on them.

He returned to land and again the horror of his position overwhelmed him. The deep blue sky overhead and the warm sun, a mockery amidst such a scene! He, whose ambition was to preserve life lay amidst death. And from here, where? He had no idea where he was. His throat was parched.

The stench of bodies beginning to rot in the sun was nauseating and panic seized him. He must get away from this awful world. Perhaps beyond there would be help. The sun began to sink and he shivered. Though he hated to touch these dead, he stripped a red coat off a soldier and threw it over his thin shirt. That he was still in French territory he felt sure and the conspicuous coat would be dangerous, but it was all he could find. Later, maybe, he could dispose of it. He looked about for some firearms. There were guns on some of the men but he had no powder. On one sailor he found a knife and stuck this in his own belt. With it, perhaps, he could find some food to still the gnawing ache in his stomach.

He turned and stumbled away from the scene of death. The days that followed were a nightmare. On and on he tramped through completely uninhabited country, without the slightest idea of where he was going, except that he tried to keep a southerly direction. Day after day he prayed that he might come upon some hut or house, trusting in his bi-lingual proficiency to pose as either French or English. Some days he found a spring from which he could drink and on other days there was nothing with which to slake his thirst. He lived on berries and roots that he found in the forest, which sometimes made him sick, and occasionally he snared a rabbit or squirrel. Sometimes when he stumbled and fell, he lay there too weak to get up. Nor did he want to. He prayed for the release of death, for that it must come soon he did not doubt. Fate had wrecked him in territory that appeared never to have been discovered by man. The nights were a terror, haunted by the sounds of wild animals and the fear of snakes. Each day when he awoke and found himself still living, he groaned. "How much longer, oh God!" he would cry, yet on he wandered. It was death by slow degrees, a lingering, despairing death, with strength ebbing each day. Some days lightheaded and delirious he raved of home and at other times thoughts of it came to him in dreams. His lanky body was a frame of bones and his haggard face was disfigured by the ragged scar on his forehead.

When at last he heard voices he was too weak to move. He felt his body being lifted and borne along and was only relieved that he did not have to make the effort. Something hot and burning was poured down his throat and he choked on the taste of brandy. Between snatches of consciousness he heard French voices and vaguely realized that he had been captured. Only when he heard the words *habit-rouge* and *soldat anglais* did he remember the coat he was wearing and which he had intended to discard, though when exactly he had meant to do this, he could not remember. Food brought back some strength and at last he was able to take stock of his surroundings. It was night and they were grouped around a campfire, eight red men, their faces streaked with warpaint. The sight struck horror into him, for he had heard from his mother how the Indians fed their victims and healed their wounds, only to take them to the village for indescribable tortures. He lay on the ground in the shadows, but when he tried to move, found his arms and legs were tightly bound.

He slept. When he wakened it was early morning and several French soldiers and an officer were standing near the group of Indians. The officer in charge appeared to be having trouble, as the soldiers protested while the Indians did the same in a series of grunts. Henry studied the officer. He was a young lieutenant and his expression was at the moment one of resentment. As far as Henry could fathom, the men were all dissatisfied with his leadership. Furthermore, he gathered, they had lost their way and considered it useless to drag along just one prisoner.

"We've got to have something to show for this expedition!" he heard the officer remark petulantly. Henry judged him to be about twenty-five, perhaps younger. Some of the men with him were about the same age, others older. Henry wondered why he did not ask the men for suggestions as to the best course to take, but evidently he was too inexperienced to realize the efficacy of this. His next remark proved this fact.

"I'm the leader and I'll take the lead!" he exclaimed angrily.

"If you have any one to lead!" an older man retorted.

The officer's mouth was a thin line. He gave the man who had made the remark a withering look and turning on his heel went into his tent.

The men all began to talk at once, until one of the older men silenced them. They withdrew from the circle of Indians, too far away for Henry to hear what they said. Evidently, they came to some agreement, for he saw the man who had silenced them go into the officer's tent. When later he emerged, he went and spoke to the men again. From the expressions on the faces of the men they still appeared to be disgruntled.

That day they made him walk, his hands still tied behind him. He was placed between two husky Indians whose tomahawks made him decide he had better go peaceably. He did not relish having one of those weapons close to his scalp. Nobody had as yet said a word to him. He had expected to be questioned now that he had recovered, and had decided on his story despite the red coat. But they would give him no chance and when he asked to see the officer, they ignored his request. It seemed to surprise them when he spoke in French but apparently they were all too concerned with finding their way back to take any interest in the prisoner.

That evening towards dusk came the first ray of hope. Below them lay a small village—a few houses huddled together within a stockade. There were shouts of delight from the men as they halted.

"Wait here. I will make inquiries," the young officer said. "At least we can now find out where we are," he added with relief.

"Better go carefully," an older man warned. "They may be English."

Henry watched as the officer approached the nearest house but before he reached it a shot rang out. It missed its mark as the officer sprang out of range behind a house. The next moment pandemonium broke loose as the Frenchmen, followed by the Indians, dashed into the enclosure, firing their guns. The officer shouted to them to go back but they either did not hear or would not heed. They were all bored with the past few weeks and the Indians in particular were thirsting for action. For a moment Henry saw a chance to escape but it was soon gone. An Indian lashed him to a tree and left him there, a helpless witness to the massacre. He twisted and writhed in his ropes, but only succeeded in bruising his wrists already raw from being tied so long.

It was all over in what must have been less than half an hour. Uttering their bloodcurdling warwhoops the savages dragged people from their houses, severing their scalps and holding the bloody objects up to gloat over before attaching them to their belts. The officer tried frantically to stop it but his efforts were useless. The Frenchmen plunged into the houses, looting each one, dragging out food and wine and stacking it in the center of the enclosure. When each house had been looted, it was set afire and soon the darkening sky was illuminated with a deep red glow. What at dusk had been a peaceful group of people, now lay dead or dying or taken prisoner.

Henry watched with horrified fascination. By the light of the fires he could see the redskins dancing gleefully each time a helpless victim was discovered and dragged into the open to be murdered. Then for the fraction of a moment everything seemed to stand still before it broke into frantic pandemonium in another direction. A redskin had a young girl by the hair, his tomahawk raised to strike. She was a child of not more than fourteen and too horrified to utter a sound. The next moment the redskin dropped, killed by a bullet from a musket held in the officer's hand. He had been unable to stand the sight any longer and had turned the gun against his own men. The redskin's hand still gripped the girl's hair, dragging her down with him. The officer wrenched her away and thrust her behind him where she fell in a heap. It was a matter of a few moments only, and then the Indians rushed at the officer to revenge their comrade. Again, it was a few moments before the Frenchmen realized what was happening—not until the officer had felled another savage. There was no time for him to reload his musket and he had to depend upon his sword. He smashed it against a raised tomahawk, knocking it out of the savage's hand and then cleaved the head in two. Another moment and the officer would have been overwhelmed, but three shots rang out and the savages dropped to the earth.

An unnatural silence followed. The officer, his face drawn and deathly pale, stood with his sword gripped in his hand, surveying the scene.

"*Sacré bleu cochon!*" A Frenchman's voice broke the silence. "A fine kind of officer you are, killing your own people!"

The officer seemed dazed. He looked at the faces of the remaining men, their countenances evil in the light of the burning houses. "You fools! You idiots! You've killed a lot of innocent people and burned their homes, for what? What has it gained you?"

"Some food, wine!" shouted one soldier who had already imbibed plenty of it. "Come on, what are we standing around here for? Do you want to get your whiskers singed?" He laughed raucously as he raised the wine bottle to his lips. Another man snatched it from him and drained it. The others pounced upon the heap of food and wine and began carrying it away. An old man knelt piteously by the body of his slain wife, oblivious to what was going on around him. A soldier jerked him to his feet. "Come along, grandpa. No good crying." The old man pulled his arm away.

"Leave me here to die or kill me now. I have no wish to live." But he spoke in English and the soldier did not understand. He pushed him roughly ahead of him, up the hill to where they were camping. The girl saved by the officer had recovered consciousness and started to run away but a soldier caught her. As he looked at her he made a crude remark to his companion, for she was a pretty child with long golden hair and large eyes. She did not understand French, so did not know what he said but the movement of his hands was sufficient indication. She shrank back. Henry writhed in his bonds.

The officer had now recovered and issued orders sullenly. There were four prisoners now—the girl, the old man and another woman, as well as Henry. They tied the hands and feet of each and pushed them in a heap. That night the men were all drunk, all except the officer, who retired to his tent and remained there.

Lieutenant Jean-Baptiste de Courville-Boissart was suffering from intense shock. This was his first experience with warfare, if such could be called warfare. He tried to analyze what had happened. It was easy to say the English had started it by firing that first shot, and probably if the men had not attacked immediately he would have been killed. But this brought him little comfort. They could easily have fired a few warning shots and have surrounded the village until they surrendered. To have murdered so unmercifully seemed out of all proportion. He had been uneasy about the Indians from the start. He did not understand them and had never liked them nor trusted them. He felt relieved that they were all killed. He had not wanted them in his company but the Baron de Longueil had been insistent that each party consist of Frenchmen and Indians. Several such parties had been sent out when news came that the English under General Nicholson were retreating. Not certain whether this rumor was correct, de Longueil would not leave Chambly until it had been confirmed. It might be a trick to make them give up the strong defense they had established. What had happened to the other patrols, the Lieutenant did not know. He had hopelessly lost his way and the Indians who were supposed to be such good guides had been of little help.

The camp was quiet now, but before retiring he decided to make the rounds to see that all was in order. It was as well that he did, for he surprised the man who had made the obscene remark about the girl creeping towards her.

"What are you doing?" the Lieutenant asked sharply.

"What I please to do," the man answered insolently.

The officer lashed out with his fist and sent the man spinning.

When the officer had gone, Henry wriggled over so that the girl was between him and the other two prisoners. He had tried to comfort her a little as they lay there and now she slept from exhaustion. He had learned that her name was Rosalind Booth.

CHAPTER XX

PAUL CROSSED FROM THE BARNS and came up the back steps of the house. He moved with a heavy gait, for these past months had aged him beyond his forty years. His sandy hair showed more white and his ruddy face was seamed with anxiety. Try as he would, he could not reconcile his own conscience. Every time he looked at Elise he felt guilty. Her quiet, subdued manner was a torment to him and he missed her laughter that had always echoed through the house. She reminded him too much of how his sister, Marguerite, had been at the same age when the laughter had also gone out of her eyes. And he thought of Antoine as he looked towards the far end of the seigneury, where a large acreage was held in his name. He wondered what Antoine would do about it. Land could not be held by grant and remain undeveloped. The Chevalier de Ramezay had mentioned the matter to Paul only a few days before. He had written Antoine in reply to his letter, offering to do anything he could to compensate him. "If you cannot be my son-in-law then you are my son and I owe you the devotion and care due to a son. Let me at least do something that will help you and perhaps in time salve my conscience," he had written. But Antoine had not answered and he did not know whether he was still in Quebec.

He worried, too, over Jean-Baptiste from whom they had not heard for many months. The others had all returned safely. All they knew was that Jean-Baptiste had been sent out in charge of one of the patrols and it was feared was lost. Ann said little now that her first grief had passed but he knew that she brooded over the loss even more deeply than he. André was their mainstay with his quiet understanding of their problems. Paul wished he would find a wife. But he seemed more intent upon looking after Elise, and Paul could understand this devotion for he had felt it towards his own twin sister. He missed her dreadfully, far more than his sister, Marie, living in Three Rivers. But then they had seen her several times since her marriage, for Three Rivers was not as far away. And now Marguerite was bowed down again with grief. One of her rare letters had come through a few days ago, the loss of her son overshadowing her joy because the attempted invasion had failed. "If only there could be peace between the nations so that I could come to visit you," she had written. "I never thought when I went away that so many years would pass without my seeing my beloved brother. Pray for peace, Paul, pray without ceasing."

He looked out over the seigneury that was his pride. Peace. What it would mean to have a lasting peace between nations that man might survive and prosper. They had been fortunate, indeed, this year that the threatened war had not ruined the crops. The men had returned in time for harvesting. The spring had come and gone in the fullness of its beauty; the cherry trees and the plum and apple had blossomed in their glory and had yielded an abundance now stored away for future use; the golden grain had ripened and had been harvested. Now the fields were all plowed and the restful beauty of autumn, which had painted the maple and elm in rich tones, seemed to defy any one to disturb the peace. The River flowed along, proud of its deep azure waters which reflected the glory of the setting sun, a glory that seemed more beautiful here than in any other place. The rays of the sinking sun touched Paul's hair, restoring it momentarily to its former color. Yet, though the peace around him was soothing, he turned away with a sigh.

He should have been happy; they should all have been happy, sharing in the rejoicing that gripped the town. The full horror of the tragedy that had wrecked a portion of the English fleet and sent the rest into retreat was not yet known. Many believed that Divine intercession had caused the wreck and prayers of petition changed to prayers of thanksgiving. Hundreds knelt every day before the Bonsecours Church, atop which the image of the Virgin Mary watched always over the safety of those at sea. Others ascribed the happy turn of events to the prayers of the saintly Jeanne le Ber. General Nicholson, in charge of the land army moving on Montreal, could not believe the despatch which brought the news of the disaster at sea. He had been the greatest promoter of this expedition but did not dare attempt to attack alone. In a rage he tried to tear his wig and then threw it on the ground and trampled on it crying: "Roguery! Treachery!" When the rage had spent itself, he glumly ordered the forts he had built to be burned and marched back to Albany, there to vent his spleen upon the name of Admiral Walker.

They sat down to supper that evening without waiting for André, who was in Montreal. Before they had finished they heard sounds of his arrival but he did not go to the stable with the cart. Instead he hurried in, his face radiant with excitement. Elise noticed it immediately but before she could question him, he went to his mother, and with his arm across her shoulders said, in a voice he could not entirely control: "Jean-Baptiste has returned, mother."

Their exclamations were simultaneous and Elise began asking questions eagerly. Ann seemed stunned, unable for the moment to accept the reality of having prayers answered when she had schooled herself to believe that such an answer was beyond hope. André heard her whispered exclamation that was in itself a prayer: "Thanks be to God." Then she turned to him and asked quietly: "Where is he, André? Is he injured?"

Paul had already asked the same questions and André answered them both together. "He is at the hospital. He isn't injured but is very weak. His feet are so swollen he cannot stand."

"At the hospital? Can't he come home?" Ann asked anxiously.

"That is why I hurried out here—to see what should be done," André said. He turned to his father. "He would be more comfortable here . . ."

"Why not take the carriage and get him?" Paul said.

"That's what I was going to suggest," André replied.

"You'd better eat your supper first. I'll go and hitch up the carriage."

"I left the cart outside. I couldn't wait to give you the news."

Paul left the table, pausing to kiss his wife as he passed. She looked up at him gratefully.

"It's too wonderful to believe," Elise remarked. "I feel dazed. I just can't believe it. It's so wonderful."

"You must prepare yourself for a change in him," André warned. "He's dreadfully emaciated. But food and rest will soon restore him," he added cheerfully. Then he saw that his mother had covered her face and he and Elise both went to her. She was sobbing quietly and as they put their arms around her, the tears became more unrestrained. They had seldom seen her so moved. It was only a moment or two and she was again controlled. "I'm sorry, children, I didn't mean to be so foolish. We should be laughing, not crying."

"You've been under such a strain," André said, sympathetically. "You'll feel better now you've had your weep."

Ann hugged them both to her and kissed each of them. Paul came in, wrapped in a heavy fur coat and ready to leave.

"What's this?" he said and smiled.

"I'm just being stupid, dear, a silly, weepy woman." As she stood up he put his arms around her and gave her an understanding smile.

"All over now?" he asked.

She nodded. "All over. Elise and I will get his room ready. Hurry back."

It seemed to the two women that the hours were endless before they heard the sound of the horse's hoofs. They rushed to the door and watched anxiously while Paul and André half carried Jean-Baptiste into the house. His appearance was more shocking than they had expected and he smiled wanly at them as he saw the looks on their faces. His eyes appeared to have sunk far back into their sockets and burned with fever. His cheeks were hollowed and he was dirty and unshaven. The elegant uniform was stained and ragged and hung on his thin, emaciated frame. His shoes were tied to his feet with rags through which his swollen feet could be seen.

"Oh, my darling!" Ann cried, as she enveloped him in her arms. "What have they done to you?"

"Don't worry," he said, his voice hardly above a whisper. They helped him into bed and fed him some hot soup, but after a few gulps he lay back and fell into an exhausted sleep.

Downstairs they talked it over anxiously. André had been able to glean a little news, but only that they had been lost and that some of the men had been killed.

"The men don't seem to be nearly as weak as Jean-Baptiste," André said, and he was puzzled.

"They were probably huskier," Paul remarked.

"Jean-Baptiste has never been very strong," was Ann's comment.

"No, but he used to be wiry. I remember when we were boys, I was huskier but he used to be able to outdo me in energy," André remarked.

It was a few days later that Paul discovered what had reduced Jean-Baptiste to such a condition, and by that time many things had crowded into their lives to complicate it. Paul sat by Jean-Baptiste's bed talking to him.

"I am too weak to be a leader, father," he said. "They

wouldn't heed me. They scoffed at me. I tried to understand them but they were mostly older men. And the Indians with us despised me."

"Indians despise most white men," Paul said, trying to find words to ease the boy's torment.

But Jean-Baptiste's mind would not be eased. His pale blue eyes were full of agony as he said: "But the massacre, father. Innocent people dragged out of their houses and murdered for no reason."

Paul laid his solid hand upon the thin, tapering one that clutched at the sheet. "You weren't weak," he comforted him. "I saw the same thing at Schenectady and I couldn't stand it."

"But Schenectady was different! Then it was their lives or yours."

Paul started to debate the point but Jean-Baptiste was living the agony of his experience over again. "They were hurting no one. It was dusk and they were probably preparing supper. It was not only the Indians who dragged them out and scalped them—the other men went in and killed—killed old men and women and children. I shall never forget it and never get the sight out of my mind."

"Those experiences are hard to forget," Paul agreed.

"All I wanted to do was to inquire where we were. The Indians were supposed to guide us but they knew nothing or wouldn't tell. When I tried to stop the men from pillaging, they ignored me, some mocked me. How can men, men who are our neighbors, kill people like that and not think anything of it?"

"I have wondered about that too, Jean-Baptiste. At Schenectady I stood behind a house and vomited at the sights. One has to be heartless to stand it. Perhaps now you can understand, son, why I have never hated the English the way most Frenchmen do."

Jean-Baptiste fixed his eyes upon his father's face. Then again returned to the thoughts he could not reconcile. "But if we didn't attack the English, they'd attack us. These people, father, weren't attacking anybody. They were a small, isolated community. I don't even know where it was, or how they came to be there. And now all that is left are charred ruins of their houses and whitened bones. We didn't even have the decency to bury the dead. I suggested it. The men looked at me contemptuously and one said something about getting ourselves killed for our trouble."

He lay back and soon exhaustion hid the horrors of his memory and he slept.

Paul watched him, thinking of this son whose nature was so complex, whose desire to achieve was thwarted by a weakness he could not overcome. He thought over what Jean-Baptiste had said and from his own experiences could reconstruct the scene of the massacre. Then he looked intently at the sleeper, whose long, narrow face seemed longer because he was so emaciated. His cheeks were flushed with fever and the corners of the petulant mouth were drawn down as the thin lips compressed together. He whimpered in his sleep and began to mutter and toss. Where there had formerly been irritation in Paul there was now only pity, pity for a man who had failed and who knew that he had failed. Again Paul questioned why this son should have these qualities; what was it that he as a father had done or had not done? He thought back to Jean-Baptiste as a little boy and wondered whether they had spoiled him, but he could not find the answer. For all that he could reconstruct of those days, Jean-Baptiste and André had been treated alike, yet had matured so differently. There was no question but that Jean-Baptiste had sustained a shock from which he would not easily recover, and as Paul thought of this, he wondered about the boy's future. He was the one who must carry on this heritage and would he be able to do it? Paul wondered what Old Pierre, his beloved grandfather, would have advised. Old Pierre, rugged and uneducated, yet possessing a knowledge of people, and particularly young ones, which Paul would have given anything at this moment to be able to use.

CHAPTER XXI

Two DAYS AFTER Jean-Baptiste's return Paul received a note which astounded him. It was scrawled illegibly on a scrap of paper and read:

> MONSIEUR,
>   Unfortunate circumstances have brought me to Montreal as a prisoner. I am the son of your twin sister, Mme. Eric Walker, and for her sake, I beg of you to arrange for my ransom, the amount of which my father will gladly reimburse you.
>   Your obedient servant,
>   HENRY WALKER.

The note had been brought by messenger and after a brief word with Ann, Paul hurried to Montreal. He was excited at the prospect of seeing his nephew for the first time, and concerned over the situation. He went first to see Governor de Ramezay, who knew the circumstances of Marguerite's marriage to an Englishman. When he learned that the prisoners had been brought in by Jean-Baptiste and his men, he was perplexed that Jean-Baptiste had not known his own cousin.

"They've never met, of course," Paul said to de Ramezay.

"But the names! Surely they would have known that!" the Governor exclaimed.

"Just what I have been thinking," Paul agreed and shook his head. "Jean-Baptiste didn't mention anything about prisoners, either. He seems more concerned over the mutinous attitude of his men."

Claude de Ramezay stroked his chin. "I can't quite make out why they took these people prisoners. Seems to me a waste of time and trouble, particularly when they were short of food. Gives me a lot of bother, too. Shall have to have a talk with this son of yours as soon as he's well again."

"There'll be no difficulty about the ransom?" Paul asked anxiously.

"No, we can arrange that between us. Have to ask you to pay a nominal sum, or there'll be protests that I'm showing the English favors." There was a frown on the Governor's face. "You may come in for some unpleasant comments, Paul."

Paul swore. "He's my own sister's son and the least I can do is to look after him. She's lost two boys already and is nearly frantic over the loss of this one. I'll have to send a message to her. Have you a good Indian who could be trusted with a message?"

"Can find you one. I'll send him to you." The Governor paused and then asked: "Are you going to take the boy to your house?"

"Of course," Paul said tensely. "Until I can get him back to his parents anyway."

"What about Jean-Baptiste?"

Paul shrugged his shoulders. "That'll have to take care of itself."

The prisoners had been confined in the jail. There were only three of them now, for the old man had died on the journey. A note from the Governor admitted Paul without question. The jailer, whom Paul did not know at all, gave him a sharp look as he admitted him. Henry was lying on a pallet of dirty straw, too weak to get up. His long, narrow face as he looked up, was so haggard that the cheekbones stood out in ridges. The light from the small window high in the wall, cast an eerie look about the place, which smelled intolerably.

Paul hastened over to the pallet and knelt down beside the boy.

"I'm your Uncle Paul," he said kindly.

Henry held up a hand and smiled wanly. "It's good of you to come. It's only for my mother's sake."

"Of course, my boy. I have arranged with the Governor for your release."

"Thank you, monsieur." Though the cell was cold and damp, the hand he held was hot.

"You have a fever. We must get you out of here at once. I am taking you home "

"Oh, thank you, monsieur," Henry answered and his eyelids drooped over his eyes.

Paul had intended mentioning Jean-Baptiste but decided to delay the questioning until later.

"I am sending an Indian runner with a message to your mother," Paul told him. A look of relief crossed Henry's face.

"Thank you so very much, monsieur. She does not know what happened to me. The press-gang caught me."

"Press-gang?" Paul exclaimed. Henry moistened his cracked lips and tried to go on but Paul laid a hand on his. "Tell me later, Henri. There will be plenty of time. Let me get you out of here first."

As Paul stood up, Henry put out his hand and started to speak. He seemed to be having difficulty in finding the right words. He closed his eyes tightly and then looked up at Paul, afraid.

"Something bothering you?" Paul asked.

"The other prisoners," Henry began and stopped. "One is a young girl—her father and mother were killed in the massacre. Could you do something for her?"

"I'll try, Henri. We'll see about that later."

This did not appear to satisfy Henry. He closed his eyes again and his expression was worried. Paul dropped on one knee again and leaned over him, tenderly. "There's something more?" he inquired. "Don't mind telling me."

Henry looked at him hesitantly. "I promised her I would look after her. She is so helpless. I want to take her back to my mother. She will understand and look after her."

"Of course," Paul said, sympathetically. "I will go and make inquiries now." A look of relief and gratitude came over Henry's face.

"I will return in a minute," Paul told him as he hurried from the cell. The warden knew him by name at least and was very courteous. He took him to another cell where the two women were incarcerated. Paul could understand Henry's anxiety as he looked at the pale child who lay on the pallet as though every hope had gone out of her life. Her eyes were open and staring up at the ceiling and she did not move them as the two men came into the cell.

"Pitiful, isn't it?" Paul whispered.

"And unnecessary," the warden answered, "but don't quote me."

On the other pallet lay the older woman and no sound came from her either.

Paul arranged with the Governor to take Rosalind also to his home, and the other woman was taken care of by the Sisters of the Congregation. Fortunately, André was in town and Paul was able to find him. Together they got them to the Manor House. Paul was concerned for Ann in bringing her two more sick people but she waved it aside.

"Don't be absurd, dear. Of course we'll take care of them," she said. And when she saw them she was much concerned over their condition. Elise helped her undress Rosalind and wash the sores on her little body. The girl made no comment. She watched them with scared eyes but their gentleness and kind words, even though she did not know their language, soon reassured her. As they pulled the clean, fresh clothes over her, tears trickled through her closed eyelids.

"Thank you," she said in English and drifted into sleep.

When the patients were cared for, they held a family conference. Paul explained the story he had heard and the difficulties they would probably run into when the prisoners and their captor met.

"After all, Henri is our nephew," Ann reassured him.

"I must get that message off to Marguerite at once. I had better mention the girl. Henri wants to take her home with him. Seems her father and mother were massacred before her eyes."

The two women shook their heads at the horror. "Marguerite can understand that better than any one," Ann commented.

In the days that followed, Henry and Rosalind made quick recovery under Ann's expert care. Paul heard Henry's full story and was particularly interested in his tale of the shipwreck. He relayed the story to the Governor. It was the first detailed account of what had happened and was important to them all. When he came to the story of the massacre, Henry was bitter, but withheld too much comment, because he did not want to hurt French feelings.

"You didn't know the name of the young officer you mention?" was Paul's question.

"No, sir, I never heard it."

"But he must have known yours"

"No, sir, they did not ask me. The officer was in disagreement with the men and particularly with the Indians he had with him. He didn't want that attack and did everything to prevent it. I felt sorry for him, for he was helpless. I don't believe he even wanted to keep me prisoner. The others, well, their homes had been burned and to leave them there would have been to leave them to die. It was this officer who saved Rosalind's life. An Indian was about to scalp her when the officer shot him. He nearly lost his own life, then, because all the savages turned on him. It turned into a fight between the red men and the white."

Every word that he uttered was important to Paul. "Thank you for telling me this, Henri," Paul said quietly. "That officer was my son, your cousin."

Henry jumped as though he were going to leap out of bed. "Your son!" he exclaimed, and then mortification covered his face. "Oh, monsieur, why didn't you tell me before? I wouldn't have said so much."

"But what you have said is a vindication of the officer."

Henry was thoughtful. Then he said, "Yes, it was, and it is true. He did try to prevent it. The men were mutinous. He had difficulty in handling them." He turned a very anxious look to Paul as he said, "Monsieur, I shouldn't have come here."

"That is all right, Henri," Paul reassured him.

"But it isn't, monsieur! And I asked you to have Rosalind, too! This is awful!"

"Don't worry now. My wife and I want it this way."

"But your son? What will he say when he sees us?"

Paul half smiled. "I don't know. We haven't told him yet. He is very ill."

"And I added two more sick people to your household!"

"We have plenty of help. And Madame is a very good nurse."

"She is wonderful," Henry said gratefully. "We must get away from here before your son knows."

"Not at all. I intend he shall know. I shall wait for the right moment to tell him."

But the right moment was not found before Jean-Baptiste unexpectedly put in an appearance. By that time Henry and Rosalind were both able to be up and André and Elise had made them welcome. As Rosalind could not speak French, Henry acted as interpreter. This, naturally, meant that she spoke little. She was a sweet child, not yet fourteen, and still dazed at finding herself alone in the world. Henry was very tender towards her and since he could speak her language, they talked frequently together. Unfortunately their return presented a problem, for winter was setting in and it was impossible for them to travel without adequate protection. They were waiting for a reply from his parents and were discussing the matter one evening when Jean-Baptiste appeared. They had not known he was up but he had felt better and had decided to put on a dressing gown and join the family. André, Elise, Henry and Rosalind were grouped round the fire; Paul and Ann were in the library.

Elise saw him first and exclaimed, "Why, Jean-Baptiste!" and hurried to meet him. "It's wonderful to see you up, dear."

"Thought I would come down for a little while. I am sorry, I did not know we had company. I am not properly dressed."

He did not at first recognize his former prisoners, now that the dirt and grime had been removed and they were wearing borrowed clothes. He walked slowly towards the fire, Elise's arm through his. Henry and Rosalind had risen and their anxiety was written on their faces. André came to Elise's assistance, taking Jean-Baptiste's other arm.

"Sit here by the fire," André said solicitously.

Jean-Baptiste paused before the guests and André began making the introductions. "Mlle. Booth, this is my brother, Jean-Baptiste and this is Henry Walker, our cousin."

Jean-Baptiste's already pale face turned ashen as he looked from one to another. Elise still holding his arm felt him stiffen as he now recognized them.

"What is the meaning of this?" he asked, his voice low.

"I will explain." Paul's voice came across the room and he followed it. "It was our intention to tell you about our guests, Jean-Baptiste, but we were waiting until you were feeling better." He smiled rather anxiously at his son. "But you surprised us by coming downstairs sooner than we expected."

Jean-Baptiste's face was a mask. Ann put her arm around his waist and took up the explanation. "Henri has told us the whole story, Jean-Baptiste. It was strange that neither of you heard the other's name . . ."

"Other's name?" Jean-Baptiste said vaguely.

"Yes, Henri is your Aunt Marguerite's son." She felt Jean-Baptiste become tense. "He had been forced into the Navy by a press-gang. The red coat was one he took off a dead soldier after he was shipwrecked."

Jean-Baptiste still made no comment. He shifted his eyes to Rosalind and they were inquiring. "This young lady is going back with Henri to his home," Ann continued the explanation.

Jean-Baptiste's delicate nostrils quivered slightly as he looked at Rosalind, for he was reminded too poignantly of the scene of the massacre She stood beside Henry, her eyes lowered to the floor and they could see her trembling.

Jean-Baptiste turned slowly. "I had better go back to my room. I don't stand shock very easily yet," he said weakly. Ann took his arm and together they walked from the room and upstairs, the others watching anxiously.

CHAPTER XXII

ANTOINE DE BRIEVAUX stood upon the ramparts at Quebec and looked out across the waters that flowed into the Gulf of St. Lawrence and thence to the sea. He was a solitary figure huddled in a great coat and feeling as gloomy as the heavy grey sky that would soon unburden itself with the first fall of snow. As he stood there his troubles, however, did not unburden themselves but seemed to weigh increasingly upon his mind. He had spent many miserable months in Quebec and now had to face a weary winter of equally unhappy days. Though he did not know it, he was standing at the same place where, some twenty years ago, Paul Boissart had stood, equally miserable and thinking in the same unhappy strain about the same woman. Paul had thought of Hélène de Matier as a menace to his marriage with Ann, and now Antoine thought of her in the same relation to his desire to marry Elise. Had Hélène been alive, her deep throaty laugh would have rung out provocatively, for she had been as heartless as she was beautiful. Antoine tried not to let his thoughts of resentment turn to hatred of the woman who had given him birth, yet at times it was difficult not to do so.

For weeks he had tried to forget his unhappiness by frequenting the taverns in the Lower Town. He had consumed brandy until his mind refused to function any more. Sometimes he had wakened in the morning to find his head resting on his arms at a table where he had fallen into a stupor the night before; other times he had wakened in a strange bed and had wondered how he had come to be there; on several occasions he had found his pockets rifled, though fortunately he had enough sense not to carry much upon his person. After several weeks he had become disgusted with himself for such behavior. His usually clear complexion was blotchy and his dark eyes streaked with red. He had pulled himself together, annoyed that after a life of ease and freedom from worry, he should have behaved in such a manner the first time he had met with trouble.

He had been glad when ordered to duty with one of the expeditions sent to find out what had become of the English fleet. Their jubilation upon seeing the wrecked vessels was marred by the sight of hundreds of decomposing bodies. From the wrecked ships they salvaged enough spoils to fill five ships and when the hapless victims had been disposed of, they returned in triumph to Quebec. Activity had restored Antoine's equilibrium and his good nature once more asserted itself.

On the return journey to Quebec he had decided that he would obtain permission to return to France. Unfortunately, his ship reached port too late, for the last ship for France had departed two days previously. There was nothing he could do but wait through the long winter until navigation opened up again.

Quebec became very gay, as every one burst their bonds of anxiety, now that the threatened invasion was over, and plunged into celebration of what the French regarded as a victory. There was plenty of opportunity for a young man like Antoine, but he seldom accepted the invitations. Women were attracted to him but he was in no mood to be gracious to them. He could not treat love lightly as Jean-Baptiste would have done. Had he wanted proof of the fickleness of women, Madame Aimée de Fontigny, Jean-Baptiste's *amoureuse* could have supplied it. Scarcely had the ship left Montreal than she had tried to attract Antoine's attention and failing in that direction, found others for whom she could display her charms. Several times Antoine had seen her in Quebec but seldom with her husband.

Standing brooding upon the ramparts, he wondered about his future, something upon which he had never wasted a thought while he lived in France. He had then been perfectly content to live each day for what it brought. Not until he had stayed at the de Courville Manor had family life meant anything to him and he had never missed it. Having sampled it, he realized what he had been denied and how much it could mean to him. He had begun then to dream of a future and a similar setting for his own life, but that had melted away like the snows, only no new spring had come in their place. He tried desperately now to readjust himself and accept life with his former nonchalance, but he could not seem to do it.

Paul in his reply to him had accepted the Marquis de Vaudreuil's deductions with reservation, pointing out to Antoine that they furnished no proof. His guardian's reply to his inquiry was a curt note in which he stated emphatically that the Duc de Chamois' family knew nothing of Madame de Matier's affairs, nor were they interested. Furthermore, he was warned to discontinue his inquiries in case they should prove embarrassing to the de Chamois family. Despite this, Antoine was determined to make one last effort when he reached France. There still remained the possibility that the Chevalier de Favien, whom Paul had mentioned as being in the Bastille, might know something. Though he had now schooled himself to accept the loss of Elise, he yet hoped to obtain proof of his parentage.

A clock rang out the hour and he turned towards the Citadel to keep an appointment with Colonel François de Truite, Commandant of the Forces. He had again applied for active duty, asking to be sent to one of the distant forts for winter service. It was the only thing that he could think of that might keep him at least partially busy, even if it were lonely in some outlandish spot.

Though he had an appointment he was kept waiting in an anteroom for over an hour. When he was admitted no one had come from the room, and he suspected that the Colonel liked to keep people waiting. One look at Colonel de Truite's unpleasant face seemed to confirm this. Though Antoine was not in a mirthful mood, he could hardly repress a smile when he looked at the officer, who so much resembled the fish whose name he bore. The face was thin, with protruding eyes, a large nose and a receding chin—in fact, it was hardly a chin at all.

The big desk behind which the Colonel sat almost eclipsed him. Antoine, his hat under his arm, stood rigidly at attention waiting for his superior officer to notice him. When he did look up he snapped: "Yes, what is it?"

Antoine saluted and replied: "Lieutenant Antoine de Brievaux reporting, monsieur."

"De Brievaux?" the voice snapped back. "Very well, come in and sit down."

Antoine took a chair and waited for the Colonel to speak. He was examining a paper which Antoine presumed was his request for service. Colonel de Truite stared at him and then asked: "What's the matter with you?"

"I beg your pardon, monsieur?" Antoine said puzzled.

"Why do you want to bury yourself in some outlandish fort?"

"I prefer duty to having nothing to do in Quebec all the winter."

"Nothing to do! It's the first time I ever heard of a man of your age not being able to find amusement enough here in the winter. It's usually the other way."

"That's what I thought, monsieur. I might be able to change places with another officer, who is anxious to be stationed in Quebec during the winter. In the spring, I wish to obtain leave to go to France on the first ship. I, unfortunately, missed the last one sailing for France."

"Why do you want to go back to France? Isn't it good enough here for you? You're like all the young men, always wanting to go to France." Antoine did not answer. He was finding the man before him so repulsive, he wanted to make the interview as brief as possible.

"Well?" snapped the Colonel. "What's your reason? You needn't think that because the English fools drowned them-

selves this time they'll keep on doing it, and we're not sending our men back until we find out what they're going to do
in the spring. *Nom de dieu*, we have few enough men here
now!"

Antoine let the Colonel rant and then said quietly, "I have
important family business I must attend to in France."

"Oh you have!" de Truite said sarcastically. "And I suppose you think none of us has? What important business can a
young man like you have? Some wench you're running after
I'll be bound."

The Colonel's manner was becoming increasingly irritating,
and his harsh voice rasped on Antoine's nerves.

"Yes, it does concern a lady," Antoine said crisply. "Indirectly at least."

"What do you mean? Must you talk in riddles?"

Antoine did not want to go into detail with this man, but
there appeared to be no alternative. The Colonel was glaring
at him waiting for an answer.

"I'm trying to find the name of my father," he said shortly.

"Your father? Don't you know?"

"If I did, monsieur, I would not have to make inquiries,"
Antoine said a little acidly.

"You mean you're a bastard?" Colonel de Truite barked.
Antoine's jaw set in a firm line. He resented the remark
even if it were true.

"Probably," he answered coldly.

"Where did you get the name *de Brievaux* then?"

Antoine wanted to reply that it was none of his affair but he
was duty bound to answer questions politely so he said, "It
was one of the Duc de Chamois' minor titles."

"The Duc de Chamois!" The Colonel's expression changed.
It was a name to be reckoned with.

"How do you come to be carrying his name?" the questions went on.

"He married my mother," Antoine answered wearily. He
seemed to be getting more and more involved and so unnec-

essarily. He wished he had never mentioned returning to France.

"Married your mother! Then wasn't he your father or had she been married before? Speak up, man. Don't keep me asking a string of questions!"

"But does this all matter, monsieur? It has nothing to do with my request to be sent on duty," Antoine said impatiently. It was the wrong thing to have said. The Colonel was an exceedingly inquisitive man and enjoyed other people's affairs. His face went crimson.

"Young man, if you're impertinent, I'll have you spend the winter in one of the dungeons below this, fort," the Colonel bellowed.

Antoine flushed. "I beg your pardon, monsieur, I didn't mean to be impertinent."

"Then answer my questions in the proper manner."

Antoine girded his patience. "The Duc de Chamois did not recognize me as his son," Antoine said in parrot-like repetition of what he had said so many times before.

"Why not?"

"The Duc was too old to have been my father."

The Colonel sat forward eagerly, scenting a scandal.

"You're talking of the old Duc, of course, not the present one."

Antoine nodded. How he hated inquisitive people! "Yes, monsieur. The one who died some eighteen years ago."

"The Duc de Chamois," de Truite repeated, stroking his shallow chin. Then he looked up sharply, stared at Antoine steadily as though trying to recall something. His eyes widened and then narrowed as he asked: "Who was your mother?"

Antoine hesitated but dared not refuse to answer. His look was rather defiant as he replied. "Madame Hélène de Matier."

He had seen men's faces change at that name but never in the manner he now witnessed. The pale grey eyes bulged and the face went purple. For a moment Antoine thought the man was going to have apoplexy. He could not understand it. Surely this horrible fish-like person couldn't have been one of his mother's lovers! The idea made him want to laugh. The Colonel was now having a fit of coughing, induced Antoine felt, to cover up the change of countenance.

Antoine's tone was malicious as he asked: "You knew my mother, monsieur?"

There was no answer. The Colonel was pouring a glass of wine, which he drained before turning to stand before a portrait on the wall. From the distance Antoine presumed that it was a portrait of the Colonel at an earlier age and thought how artists always flattered their subjects. Undoubtedly, the name of Madame de Matier had occasioned the reverie and produced the silence in the room. The Colonel took his time, taking out his snuffbox, carefully selecting a pinch which he applied to each nostril, sneezed and blew his nose. Antoine coughed as a reminder that he was in the room.

Colonel de Truite turned and remarked: "Portrait of my brother."

With a puzzled expression, Antoine got up and went over to get a closer view of the portrait, since the Colonel's manner seemed to indicate that this was expected. It was of a handsome man in a chasseur's uniform. The features were well-formed, with dark eyes that looked frankly from the canvas. The portrait was only head and shoulders which, by their build, indicated that the man had been tall and well-built.

"Chevalier de Vinont," was written below and Antoine read the words aloud. While he studied it, the Colonel's eyes had not left his face and the gaze became steady when Antoine said the name. But the Colonel made no comment. To Antoine the whole thing seemed irrelevant to the conversation they had had and he could only conclude that it was the Colonel's intention to change the subject.

"From the distance I thought it might be a portrait of you, monsieur," Antoine said, since he felt he must make some comment.

The Colonel laughed, hard and bitterly, and then said

irritably. "Flattering young fool! You know that I could never have looked like that, even when I was twenty years younger. No, they distributed the looks very unfairly in my family."

Watching the fish-like face, with its meanness and bitterness, Antoine could only agree and so kept silent.

"They gave him all the looks and all the good luck," Colonel de Truite remarked sourly.

"Yes, he is very handsome," Antoine agreed.

"Had several sons. Thought you might have run across them in France."

"Vinont? No, I don't know the name."

"Very old name, all the same," de Truite said testily.

"I am sure it is, monsieur," Antoine said politely and wondered how he could turn the conversation back to the purpose for which he had come. Yet he had already been reproved once, so he waited politely but impatiently. The protruding greenish eyes were fixed intently upon his face. He turned and met the gaze so frankly that the Colonel turned abruptly and sat down at his desk again. The contempt that Antoine could not conceal had been mirrored in his eyes and brought back to de Truite unpleasant remembrances of a woman who had had the same contemptuous expression in her eyes.

Now the Colonel began to bluster and said abruptly: " 'Tisn't important, not important at all."

Antoine was sorely tempted to ask: "Then why bring up the matter?" but he let it pass.

"I'll think over your request for a transfer. Leave your address and you will be communicated with."

Relieved that family discussions were at an end, Antoine bowed politely and said: "The address is on my letter, monsieur. Are there any further orders?"

Something still seemed to be bothering the Colonel, for he gave Antoine another scrutinizing look and when it was again met steadily, he looked away and said quickly: "No, no, that's all."

Antoine saluted and left, very much dissatisfied with the

interview. He felt certain that the man would not grant his request, not because it couldn't be easily arranged, but because he was the type who could only show authority by being mean.

When the door had closed, Colonel de Truite poured another glass of wine and stood a long while before his brother's portrait. Then he swore violently, banged the wineglass on the tray so that it smashed into several pieces and throwing himself into a chair, sat scowling at the room.

CHAPTER XXIII

FRANÇOIS DE TRUITE paced the floor of his study. He had been doing so for several hours, stopping from time to time to gaze at another portrait of his brother and then at the other end of his pacing, picking up a bundle of papers and examining them. He muttered to himself as he walked and when again he stopped before the portrait, directed his remarks to it. "How I hate you, have always hated you!" The words hissed through his thin lips and he was answered by the confident smile on the face of his brother. This portrait was full length. His reason for having one in his room and another in his office, was the opposite of what it would appear. He enjoyed the torments he experienced every time he looked at the portraits. At times he worked himself into a terrible rage over it, expending it on whomever might then cross his path. "Why should you have had everything?" he raged at the picture. "You with your good looks, your fine physique, your charming manners, your beautiful wife! Everything! And what have I? Nothing. A life that has been a void." He paced the room again, picked up the bundle of papers, looked at the fire and hesitated. "He wants a father," he muttered. "Why not I?" His eyes gloated at the thought and he wetted his lips apprehensively. "A son— a son of my own! He could be here with me. Perhaps I could make him love me." Then he shrugged his shoulders. "No one else ever has." He thought of the wife who had hated him so; hated him to the day when she had died with a smile of triumph on her face because she had cheated him. No woman would ever have voluntarily accepted his proposal of marriage. To all of them he was too repulsive. But Renée d'Edincourt had had no choice. Her family had sold her to the highest bidder and that was François de Truite. They were impoverished, he was rich and it was an excellent arrangement, for all except the woman concerned. Yet she had had her revenge. He had wanted a large family, one so large that out of it he would surely have been able to find one who would have loved him. How much he had craved love all his life! But Renée had given him no children. Even the night of their marriage he had had to force her to consummate it. She had become pregnant but she had lost the child, and gloried in telling him that she had purposely brought on the miscarriage. For nine years he had insisted upon his rights as a husband but she had died cheating him.

And now, did he dare pretend that Antoine was his son? It would revenge him for some of the insults Hélène de Matier had heaped upon him. He moved uncomfortably as he thought of her. How he had adored her! But when he had told her, she had laughed as though it were something amusing. It had necessitated many subterfuges before he could get an opportunity to tell her. He remembered that night so well when, using his brother's name, he had decoyed her to this very room. She had stood there by the fire, exotically beautiful and exquisitely gowned. "Why, François, how utterly absurd you are!" Those had been her words; he could hear them now—hear them as he had so many times all these years, spoken in her deep throaty voice, the sound of which had always excited him. He looked again at the portrait and the hatred he was feeling made the veins stand out in his forehead. "Yet she came to you when you didn't want her," he hissed.

He went to the fire, the bundle of papers in his hand. "A son of my own," he muttered and stared into the flames. Why had he saved the papers all these years? No one knew he had them. He had found them among his brother's effects and had told nobody. When he had found the secret they contained, he had not turned them over to his brother's children. At first he had read them many times, gloating over his discovery, but latterly he had not done so, not until the night after Antoine had called upon him. It was not out of consideration of his nephews and nieces that he had kept the secret. They had never had any consideration for him. It was because he did not want to share the secret with any one. And now, why not destroy the evidence and change the story? He crouched down before the fire and stirred it into a blaze.

There was a knock at the door and a servant announced: "Lieutenant de Brievaux."

Quickly the Colonel straightened up, holding the bundle of papers behind him. His expression was guilty as he returned Antoine's bow. Then he came forward, his hand extended and his manner cordial. It was so different from his former attitude that Antoine could scarcely conceal his surprise. In fact, he had been wondering all day what was the meaning of the summons, not to the Citadel but to the Colonel's private residence. For four days he had been waiting for his orders, wondering at times whether his request was going to be ignored. For all the Colonel's cordiality now, he was still repulsive to Antoine, whose manner was polite but aloof.

"You sent for me, monsieur?" he said coldly.

"Yes, my boy, I wanted to have a talk with you. Sit down and have a glass of wine. Devilishly cold tonight. Below zero they tell me." He held his hands towards the blazing fire. "Come and warm yourself." For the first time Antoine saw a smile on his face. It was like the grin of a gargoyle.

Antoine did not sit down but stood by the fire watching his host and becoming more curious every minute. He took the proffered glass of wine and sipped it.

"Been keeping yourself busy?" the Colonel asked congenially.

"No. I'm waiting for my orders," Antoine said crisply and looked directly at de Truite.

"Yes, yes. We'll talk about that presently. I have something else I want to talk over with you. Have been doing a lot of thinking these past few days." He had begun pacing again. "Think I might be able to make you an offer that would be quite an advantage to you—quite an advantage." He looked

quickly at Antoine whose face was a mask. "You know," he
went on, "I'm a lonely man. Live all alone in this big house.
I've lived here over twenty years. Used to be married—wife's
dead. I haven't any children, wanted some badly, but,
well, . . ." he cleared his throat. It was an irritating habit of
his. "Wife couldn't have any, it seems. It has always been a
bitter disappointment to me. I'd like to have a young man
like you about. Make me feel young again." Antoine was
listening with alarm. "I'm a very rich man, you know," he was
saying. "A young fellow like you could do a lot with plenty of
money." He looked directly at Antoine and was disconcerted
by the cold stare he received in return. "You could live your
own life, do as you liked. Just give me a bit of consideration.
Can't go by looks always, you know. I'm quite warmhearted
when you get to know me." He looked at the portrait now. The
light caught the eyes and they mocked him. It seemed to trouble
him. He stopped talking and cleared his throat again. His self-
confidence began to ebb and Antoine heard him utter an oath.
The thought he had had that day in the Citadel, confirmed
itself; this man undoubtedly had some strange mental quirk.
His behavior was so odd. The next moment it seemed still
more so.

"Go and stand by that portrait," he said, and it was in a tone
of command.

Antoine looked from him to the portrait. "Another portrait
of your brother?" he remarked.

"Yes, yes," the voice was testy. "Go and stand by it."
Antoine walked over and surveyed the picture, his back to the
room. "No, turn around with your back to it." Antoine did so.
"Now hold your left arm the way he has his." Antoine's bewilderment increased but he turned to see how the Chevalier
was standing. Then turned back and stood with his hand on
the hilt of his sword. François de Truite studied him, his expression changing from gloating to anger and then to hopelessness. "All right, you always did win!" he muttered. Antoine
asked him to repeat the remark, not understanding it, but the

Colonel, whose mood was again snappish, replied, "I wasn't speaking to you."

"I beg your pardon," Antoine said, and dropping his sword to its normal position, walked back to the fireplace. He was completely puzzled and quite bored.

"Have another glass of wine," the Colonel said. Antoine was helping himself to the wine as de Truite remarked, "You are thinking my behavior very odd. It is. I have puzzled over something for several days. You must bear with me while I tell you some family history." Antoine made no comment. "My brother and I were the only sons. I was the elder. How I hated him!" Antoine looked his surprise and wanted to ask why the portraits were everywhere. "He had everything; I had nothing, except the things that money could buy. You can see how we differ in looks." His tone was bitter. "I was very jealous of him. Perhaps I could have stood it, had some one cared for me. No one did. He had a beautiful wife and nine children. As if that were not enough, every woman adored him, with his charm and looks, while the woman I adored ignored me." The Colonel stopped his pacing and faced Antoine. Then he said slowly and deliberately: "That woman was Hélène de Matier."

Antoine jumped as though the Colonel had struck him. His worst fears seemed about to be realized. "You were my mother's lover?" he exclaimed, and the horror that his tone expressed brought an ugly look into the Colonel's face.

"Surprises you, evidently," the Colonel said with a smirk. "I told you looks weren't everything. I've known many handsome men who were very inadequate lovers. Nature has its compensations. Because my face is ugly, it doesn't signify that I wouldn't make a delightful bed companion. Women know those things. Your mother was very beautiful—gorgeous creature and such charms." From the corner of his eye he watched Antoine's revulsion. There was a sensuous gloat in his tone as he said: "Any one of dozens of men might have fathered you. She had so many of them. It might have been I."

Antoine looked at him with disgust, and again it was the expression that he had seen on Hélène's face. It was her eyes that mocked him now. "Yes, you hate me, despise me and she did, too." He gripped Antoine's arm in a frenzy. "I would have given everything I had to possess her, even if for only one half hour, everything, do you understand. It was such an obsession that I could not sleep or eat. I wanted her, craved her. But she laughed at me, stared at me as you do now, with cold eyes. I longed for her but she wouldn't even listen, but he . . ." he flung out an arm towards the portrait, "he never gave her a second thought yet she went to him, gave herself to him when he didn't want her."

Despite his dislike for the man, Antoine felt a little sorry for him because of his agony. Moreover, from the man's babblings he was relieved to find that he had only been his mother's lover in his own imagination.

The Colonel was standing at the desk, deliberating over the papers he held. He turned, glanced angrily at the portrait and then shouted, "All right, have it your own way, both of you," and tossed the package to Antoine. The package fell at his feet and he stooped to pick it up.

"What are these?" he asked.

"Read them," the Colonel shouted.

"Now?"

"Yes, now." De Truite flung himself in a chair, exhausted after his tirade. He shielded his eyes with his hand.

Puzzled, Antoine sat down and untied the bundle of papers. There were legal documents dealing with land in Quebec; the Chevalier de Vinont's commission in the chasseurs and several other documents; to all of which Antoine gave a cursory glance. He disliked looking at other people's papers and when he came to personal letters he hesitated. "Am I to read these letters?" he inquired.

"Yes," the word snapped at him.

He unfolded them and began to read. Several were *billets-doux* and he hurried through them. Then he opened one written

in a scrawly handwriting. It was dated December 30, 1690 and
began without salutation.

"It will undoubtedly be some satisfaction to your ego-
tistical nature to know that you are the one man in all my
experience who has made a fool of me. When this reaches
you I shall have changed my name by marriage since the
circumstances in which you have placed me make it im-
perative that I take this step. The man I am marrying is
too old for it to be very convincing that he is the father
of the child I am carrying—a child which is yours. Some
day I hope that this trick which you have played me will
rebound to you and that you will suffer for it. If the child
is a boy I shall call him Antoine after you. If perchance one
day you should come across him, or it may be her, then I
hope you will do the decent thing for I shall probably
not be alive. At my age, and for other reasons, bearing a
child will probably take my life. Console yourself, my
dear conceited Antoine, and know that I died for you, but
not because I love you. I hate you now as deeply as I once
loved you,

Adieu,

Hélène."

The moments ticked by loudly as Antoine read and reread
the letter, trying to absorb it all and yet afraid to believe its
contents. His conversation with the Colonel had upset him so
that he was not sure that it might not be a trick. The letter,
though, was yellowed with age. He read it again, then looked
up at the Colonel who was still sitting with his eyes covered.
His short body was huddled in a chair.

"Monsieur," Antoine said.

A muffled voice replied, "Yes."

"This letter signed, *Hélène*. It was written by my mother?"

"Yes," came another muffled answer.

"And the Antoine she is writing to was your brother?"

"Yes."

"Then the child she mentions is I?"

"Yes."

"Then I have found my father!" Antoine's voice rose excitedly. "It is not Monsieur Paul." He caught himself and corrected, "It isn't the man I thought."

The Colonel looked up then, "Whom did you think it was?"

Antoine ignored the question. He was so excited. "Monsieur," he exclaimed. "Do you realize what this means? The problem is solved. I can marry Elise. Oh, monsieur, I am so grateful to you! Where is your brother? I must see him."

"The Indians scalped him and spoiled his beauty." The tone was malicious.

"I'm sorry," Antoine said and then jumped up excitedly. "I may take the letter, monsieur?" he asked anxiously.

"Oh yes, take it," the Colonel said bitterly.

"Thank you, monsieur. I am too excited to express my appreciation now. You don't know what this means. I must go to Montreal at once."

"Aren't you forgetting the time of the year?"

"I'll hire a sleigh and cross the ice."

"Impossible. You'd never get there."

"I shall try."

"I haven't given you permission to leave."

"I shan't need it. I am resigning my commission."

"Don't act so hastily." The Colonel had risen and tried to restrain him. "There's no hurry."

"But there is. You don't know. The girl I love may marry some one else."

"Then she must love you very much!" the Colonel said sarcastically.

"It's too long a story to tell you now. Forgive me, I must go. I have to think about this. Thank you, monsieur, thank you."

Antoine ran out of the room before he could be restrained.

Colonel François de Truite looked after him bitterly. "How I would have liked to have revenged myself on you by telling him he was my son!" he said to the portrait. "I would have, if I could have furnished some proof. I could then have been even with you. I, the father of Hélène's son!"

He shook his fist at the portrait. All the week he had tried to find some means of changing that one line in the letter. *I shall call him Antoine after you,* but his name was François and he would not have been able to substantiate the lie.

CHAPTER XXIV

JEAN-BAPTISTE grew steadily weaker. Except occasionally to sit by the fire in his bedroom, he did not leave his bed. The exposure he had sustained had affected a chest already none too strong and a serious lung condition developed. For months there was little they could do for him as he slowly wasted away, racked by a cough that left him exhausted. Sometimes for days he lay with his eyes closed, while Ann watched anxiously by his bed. Paul and André would relieve her and frequently Aunt Marie. They kept Elise away, not wanting to expose her to the disease. Paul would have preferred that Ann should not remain in the room, but to this she would not listen. Having her near seemed to comfort Jean-Baptiste, and often she sat with his hand in hers, listening while he relieved his mind of the things that worried him. He was the gentle little boy of former years and all the affectation, which for a time he had assumed, had now disappeared. He could not forget the horror of the massacre and cried out in his sleep, reliving the anguish he had suffered. At other times he would talk to his mother about it, telling her of his inadequacy to cope with the situation. With her understanding she knew that it was better for him to talk of it and relieve his mind. She found words to comfort him, as did Father Joseph, who came each day.

They talked also of Henry and Rosalind and at Jean-Baptiste's request Henry came to see him. This was a relief to them all and particularly to Henry who felt an intruder in the house. When Henry left the room his eyes were bright with tears that a man could not shed. The greatest comfort to Jean-Baptiste was Henry's insistence that he had done all that was possible to avert the massacre. "I saw it all," Henry assured him and grinned as he added: "I was tied to a tree and had a fine view."

"How exactly did it all start?" Jean-Baptiste asked. "What did I do that began it?"

"You did nothing," Henry consoled him. "A shot was fired at you from one of the houses."

"Yes, that I remember," Jean-Baptiste said.

"Then hell broke loose among your men." Henry described the whole incident. "And Rosalind knows that you saved her life. I told her all about it."

"Rosalind?" Jean-Baptiste looked perplexed.

"The young girl you saved by killing the Indian."

"Oh yes, she's with you here."

"Yes, I asked your father to ransom her also. I did not know when I made the request that you were the officer in charge of the expedition," Henry said apologetically.

Jean-Baptiste's brow was wrinkled in perplexity. "But I don't understand why you did not tell me you were my cousin . . ."

"I didn't know."

"But surely your mother must have mentioned my father by name?"

Henry laughed. "Of course, but I did not know your name."

"Didn't the men mention it? You speak French . . ."

"I seldom spoke to them. They gave me little opportunity. And when they referred to you it was usually as *the Lieutenant* . . ."

"Or by some other opprobrium," Jean-Baptiste said bitterly.

Henry did not answer the remark, but went on. "Once I asked to speak to you but they ignored my request."

Jean-Baptiste turned his face away. "I don't know why they insisted upon taking you prisoner. It was so futile."

"Perhaps, but it saved my life."

Jean-Baptiste turned to him with surprise. "How?" he asked.

"If you hadn't found me, I would have died of exposure and hunger." Then he related his experiences and subsequent shipwreck. Jean-Baptiste listened to every word with keen interest forgetting his depression for the while. When Henry had concluded the story, he exclaimed:

"*Mon dieu!* You certainly underwent hardships. And you say the men were kind to you?" He even half smiled as he added: "I must admit I hardly noticed you. I was too pre-occupied with my own troubles. *Sacré diable,* will you ever forget that homeward journey! How we ever found the right route again, except by luck, I'll never know."

"Nor I."

Jean-Baptiste lay back exhausted by talking. As Henry rose to leave, Jean-Baptiste opened his eyes and asked: "You really feel sure that I could not have averted the massacre?"

"I do," Henry assured him. Jean-Baptiste was relieved yet not fully convinced.

"And this—Rosalind did you say her name was?"

"Yes."

"Her parents were killed then?"

"Yes," Henry said and quickly added, "but I am going to look after her. I'm taking her back to my mother. The snows have held us here for the winter."

Then Jean-Baptiste held out his hand and the former enemies clasped hands. "I'm glad you're here, both of you. It is some recompense," he said.

"I'm glad too, Jean-Baptiste. Now that it's all over, we must forget it."

"I wish I could," Jean-Baptiste said and shook his head. "Thanks."

The elements having no respect for any situation had complicated matters. Before arrangements could be made for them to leave for Albany, winter had closed all communications and means of travel. It would have been possible to cross over the ice and André and Uncle Philip had offered to go with them, for they were used to rugged travel. But there was also the return journey, with its hazards and penetration into enemy territory. Paul saw no reason to take the risk. A letter had come from Marguerite in which she agreed that it was better for them to remain if it did not compromise Paul too much. "Perhaps by spring we shall have peace, or is that hoping for too much?" she wrote. "There are rumors here that after the recent ignominious defeat, the two governments are more inclined to come to terms. Oh, Paul, I do hope so! Then perhaps Eric and I might come to Montreal and see you before taking the children home." Paul had been able to get an Indian to take back a reply, reassuring his sister and they had all settled down.

As a matter of fact, Henry and Rosalind became attached to the family. Elise, in particular, enjoyed having another girl in the house and when Rosalind had been able to master enough of the language to converse, they had long talks together. With André and Henry, they spent the long winter evenings, learning each other's languages.

Rosalind began to laugh again and forget some of her tragedy. She was timid by nature when with other people, but with Elise she lost much of it. Rosalind's attitude towards Elise was one of great admiration. Although Elise was only five years her senior, she had led a much broader life. Association with her brothers and their friends had prevented men being strangers to her. Rosalind was, too, much impressed by the fact that Elise was engaged to the Governor's eldest son. Elise's engagement had not been very satisfactory to her, even though there was some gratification in the prestige it gave her. She had received two letters from Claude in which he talked of being home in the spring and elaborated upon the plans they would then make.

With Jean-Baptiste so ill, André was now glad he had not left for the woods. From Chambly he also had been despatched with a group to find out what had happened to the English, but probably because he was more used to the rough life or maybe because he had a more efficient leader, he had suffered little hardship and had returned safely. He spent as much time as possible with his brother, sometimes just sitting with him and at others talking. One afternoon Jean-Baptiste turned his eyes, bright with fever, and fixed them on André.

"You'll have to carry on in my place, André," he said haltingly. "You're better fitted for it anyway."

André tried to conceal the alarm he felt. "Sure I will carry on until you are better, Jean-Baptiste," he said reassuringly. "Don't worry about that."

"I'm not going to get better," Jean-Baptiste replied and the face lying on the pillow was drawn.

"Of course you are!" André said. "As soon as this cold weather goes, your strength will return."

Jean-Baptiste shook his head and almost imperceptibly murmured: "No."

André watched him anxiously and waited until a paroxysm of coughing had passed. The handkerchief Jean-Baptiste drew away from his mouth was spotted with blood. Alarmed, but trying to appear calm, André asked if he would like him to get the doctor. He shook his head.

"No, André I am not deceived. It will be the priest I shall need, not a doctor." André half rose, but Jean-Baptiste held up a protesting hand. "Not yet, André. Don't leave me. I feel I want to talk to you. I haven't always been the brother I should have been. When I came back from France I was an impossible bore . . ."

"We all go through a foolish period," André tried to comfort.

"You were all so patient with me. I thought I was being important. I have always felt so inadequate—so weak. André, I couldn't control my men!" It was a pitiful cry, but before André could say anything he went on: "They shouldn't have sent me in charge of that search party. I didn't know how to handle it. I sent all those innocent people to their death. We murdered them." He leaned back exhausted and André laid a hand over his brother's.

"You're torturing yourself unnecessarily, Jean-Baptiste. Henry has described it all to us. You weren't to blame."

"But I was!" he cried hysterically. "I was in charge, I should have been able to control them. Oh God, I'll have to answer to you for so many crimes."

"God knows that you did everything you could to prevent it," André consoled him.

"I hope so," he said weakly. He turned towards the shuttered window. "Open the shutters, André. I want to see out."

André went quickly to the window and fastened back the shutters. March winds had banked the snow in high drifts and a gleam of white came into the room, striking sharply upon their eyes. It was a bleak day with the wind whistling around the house. But to Jean-Baptiste it was not bleak—it was a scene he had often looked at. As he raised himself upon one elbow, André put an arm around him to support his emaciated body. Jean-Baptiste watched in silence for several moments and then said softly: "It's all white. It looks so beautiful, it *is* beautiful, yet I never properly appreciated it before. Some day, André, you will succeed father as seigneur. If you have sons, don't ever let them forget what this heritage means." He leaned his weight against André's strong arms. "I love it so," he said hardly above a whisper. "I don't want to leave it. I want to make amends—but . . ." His voice trailed off and as he closed his eyes, his long lashes were wet.

André's jaw was set to control his feelings. Jean-Baptiste jerked forward as another fit of coughing seized him. André supported him, agonized because of his helplessness to do anything. When the paroxysm had passed he eased him gently back on to the pillows, and closed the shutters again. When he returned, Jean-Baptiste was gasping for breath. André grabbed a spare pillow and pushed it on top of the others to give him a more upright position, but he could not lie back. For long moments he struggled to breathe more easily, André again holding him in his arms. Jean-Baptiste gripped his brother's hand, with both of his, clinging to him for the strength that

André prayed desperately he might be able to transmit to him. He was afraid to leave him, yet knew that the curé should be summoned without delay. Not wishing to alarm Jean-Baptiste, he waited a moment or two more, but the breathing did not ease. André called and then a second time, and Elise heard him. She hurried in and instantly took in the situation. Her lips formed the question and André nodded.

"Father and mother too," he said in an undertone.

Elise hurried away and in a moment running footsteps sounded upon the stairs, stopped outside the door and then quietly Ann and Paul came in. Ann's dark eyes were bright with fear for a moment and then she controlled herself. She put an arm around Jean-Baptiste and laid his head on her shoulder. She had been warned by the doctor not to kiss him on the mouth, so she pressed her lips to his forehead. His long, tapering fingers closed over her hand. His breathing was less labored, but came in short gasps.

"Mother," she heard him murmur and pressing him against her, she answered: "My beloved son." Her lips were compressed as she struggled not to give way to her feelings.

Paul watched anxiously, tormented by the remembrance of the many irritable thoughts he had had about this son. He understood now. Taking Jean-Baptiste's other hand, he was relieved to receive a pressure in return.

Father Joseph arrived with Elise in time to administer the last rites. As the short gasps came more slowly, the strained look left the drawn face and as life ebbed, gave way to a gentle smile.

Henry and Rosalind sat together downstairs. This was a family matter in which they felt they should not intrude. Though they scarcely knew Jean-Baptiste and had had no reason to love him, yet both felt grief at his passing. Neither of them held any resentment. Henry was a Catholic but Rosalind had been brought up in the Protestant religion, a fact which the de Courville-Boissarts had kept secret because Protestants were not allowed in the colony.

Rosalind looked very dejected now, sitting before the fire, dabbing intermittently at her eyes in sympathy with those upstairs. Henry stood looking out of the window at the white world veiled in winter silence. He thought of his mother and father and felt homesick. A sob escaped from Rosalind and he turned to look at her. Her loneliness touched him and going over, he knelt beside her, for the first time putting his arm around her. She leaned her head on his shoulder, her long golden hair falling down the side. He took it in his fingers, caressing the soft golden strands. Somehow she always made him think of a little bird that had been stolen from its nest. He hoped she would some day let him build a new nest for her.

They stayed for some time in this position, exchanging no words, yet gathering comfort from each other. Presently Rosalind said quietly, "You've been so good to me, Henry. I don't know what I should have done if it hadn't been for you."

He turned then so that he could look at her. He smiled and his light blue eyes became a deeper shade. "I love you, Rosalind," he said, his voice hardly above a whisper. She did not shrink or start. She merely nestled a little closer. It was a strange time to be making a proposal when death had entered the house. They would never be able to tell any one just when it had happened. It would seem too callous. Yet that very thing seemed to make them realize how closely they were linked; how much apart they really were from these other people. "I just had to tell you now."

"Thank you," she said simply.

He kissed her then, because it seemed the natural thing to do—a kiss that was protecting in its tenderness and devoid of passion. Yet with it there was all the emotion born of a quietly dawning love that was true in its simplicity.

CHAPTER XXV

With the coming of April, most of the population went down to the River each day to watch for signs that the ice was beginning to move. There was always much speculation as to when this would happen. The bright March sun had sent cascades of water tumbling down from the melting snows on the hill tops. Then the ice on the River began to crack with a roar like thunder, as though this vital element in the lives of these people, had given a huge yawn waking from its winter lethargy. Great jagged blocks began pushing against each other, piling up on the wharf and against the houses. Ditches and hollows became rivers and lakes, and men labored to direct the slush and water away from their homes.

Watching the *ice-shove*, André wondered what he ought to do about his future. Jean-Baptiste's death had changed everything. No longer could he feel free to live independently and become an explorer. Now he ought to contemplate marriage and the continuance of the heritage. Having missed going to the woods the previous year, Uncle Philip was anxious to get an early start this spring, but there was no longer Gaston to assist his father with the seigneury. André had voiced his indecision to Uncle Philip who had advised him to speak to his father. "He understands how we *coureurs de bois* feel," Uncle Philip had remarked.

André decided to take Uncle Philip's advice. His father was in his office and when André asked if he could spare a few moments to talk, he answered readily: "Why, of course, my son. What's troubling you?"

"I should like to talk over future plans with you, father."

Paul listened quietly. "I'm wondering whether I ought to go with Uncle Philip . . ."

"I don't see why not," Paul answered immediately.

"But you no longer have Gaston, and Jean-Baptiste's death . . ."

"We can manage, André," Paul interrupted. "You were not able to go to the woods last year and I wouldn't want you to miss it again this year. In fact"—he smiled and tapped a ledger in front of him—"I was just looking over accounts here and thinking about your expedition. Philip told me yesterday that he contemplated leaving early and taking four canoes. I would like to see you take double that number. I will advance you what you need for your share."

"That's very good of you, father, but . . . aren't I being very selfish in leaving you and mother at such a time?"

Paul laid his hand on André's shoulder and as they stood side by side, their resemblance to each other was very marked. "No, André. I know how much it means to you. I remember how I felt when I saw my hopes fading because my father did not want me to continue being a *coureur de bois*. It was your great-grandfather and the Sieur de Courville who advised me then. It will be several years yet, I hope, before you will have to feel responsible for the management of this seigneury."

The happy expression on André's face reflected the reply he would make. He was so relieved that he could only grin broadly and Paul's face reflected the same expression. He was very proud of this son.

"Of course, I ought to be getting married, I suppose," André remarked, looking sideways at his father.

"Yes, you ought to," his father agreed. "You're twenty now and subject to a fine if you don't marry."

"But is it fair for me to marry and then go off to the woods and leave a wife?"

"That's always the problem. Unless you have some one you really want to marry . . ."

"I haven't . . ."

"Then I wouldn't worry about it, André. Pay the fine if you have to and do as you please. Of course, you'll come in for some censure from the curé, but then you get that every time you talk to him, and will, as long as you persist in being a *coureur de bois*. He lectures me, too, because I encourage you in a life of vice and recklessness as he calls it."

"But it isn't . . ." André began to protest.

"I know," Paul said reassuringly. "I have every confidence that when it becomes necessary for you to settle down and take up the reins you will do it and do it well."

"I hope so." André's voice was anxious.

"There are some men like Charles Péchard, who was my partner, who never settle down. Restlessness is in their blood and try as they will they cannot lead any other life. I don't believe you are that way but I do suggest that you watch yourself."

"I will. As a matter of fact, father, my desire to go to the woods isn't restlessness. I love it here and would be quite content. I like farm work and you know how much the seigneury means to me." He ruffled his hand through his red hair. "It's just that I feel I want to . . . to see more of life before I settle down. And when I say life I mean, well, life beyond here. I have a terrific desire to explore. To see what there is farther west."

Paul was thoughtful before he answered. Then he said: "Yes, that is a worthy ambition. Perhaps you might sometime be able to link up with some one like the Sieur de Cadillac, or d'Iberville."

"That is what I had in mind."

"We must think of it. I want you to feel free to do whatever you wish for several years to come. I've plenty of good years ahead of me yet, I hope. Live each year, André, to its fullest extent, for you never know what changes life is going to bring. We have seen that this year. It is foolish to try to plan a whole life. Take it as it comes. Go with a clear conscience, my boy, and God be with you."

So it was that at the end of April, a flotilla of eight sturdy canoes, paddled up the River, laden with goods and trinkets to trade for furs. They left several weeks before the other fur traders in the hope of being able to retrieve their losses of the previous year. This would mean a more dangerous trip because, instead of going to the trading posts and waiting for the Indian trappers to bring in the pelts, they would travel beyond Michilimackinac and forestall the trappers. Uncle Philip was able to speak the language of many of the tribes and thus could meet them on a more friendly footing.

As the canoes went by, the men singing their familiar songs to the rhythm of the paddles, all the family watched and waved them goodbye. There were tears in Elise's eyes for she always missed André. Rosalind and Henry watched with them, fascinated by a sight they had never seen before and perhaps would not see again. André's departure would leave a great gap, for it was he who had the knack of drawing every one together, of always making everything seem brighter because of his ready humor and quick perception.

Paul stood for a while after the canoes had disappeared and the others had returned to the house. Despite the many years that had passed since he had been a *coureur de bois,* he always felt a twinge of envy when he saw the canoes going by. It was a rough life but one that appealed to any man who liked adventure. It was exhilarating and exciting with the dangerous rapids to maneuver and the long portages made hard work, but at the end of a day there was a satisfaction in having accomplished a job well. He had meant to devote many years to it but circumstances had changed this plan. For this reason he was determined that André's career should not be interrupted. As he looked over the seigneury he felt he had been well compensated. The snows had gone and the world had changed from white to fresh green. The River was no longer bleak and frozen, but deep azure blue that twinkled in the sunlight.

In whatever direction he looked, men were busy in the fields and every farmhouse buzzed with industry. The many children playing around each homestead gave an assurance that the seigneury would be carried on indefinitely, unless disaster befell the colony, and this was becoming more remote with every year. No longer was there such grave danger that large families would be depleted of their men before they had even reached middle age, as had Paul's family. Where there had once been a wilderness of uncleared land on the seigneury, now the problem was to find enough land to subdivide among the increasing families. It would have been better had some of the inhabitants with large families, moved to a new seigneury where they could expand. But this no family would do. They would have scorned the idea of leaving a place where their roots had first begun to grow. The land was their pride and where their grandparents had started they would remain.

The following day was the first of May and there was the traditional May Day ceremony. This was the official opening of the spring season and on every seigneury the habitants donned their gala attire and came to pay homage to the seigneur. The people loved their Saints Days and holidays, which were the only days during this season except Sundays that they were not working from dawn to dusk. They played as hard as they worked.

At dawn on each May Day, a tall fir tree, especially selected, was set up before the Manor House and after it had been appropriately decorated there would be dancing and feasting. Because of Jean-Baptiste's death, a suggestion had been made that the ceremony should be dispensed with, but Ann was adamant. For over half a century this ceremony had been performed on the seigneury and she could not bear the idea of the chain of years being broken. She was too sensible a woman to let sorrow hang like a pall over the house. So the ceremony took place and she was immensely proud as she stood on the steps and heard her husband thanking the people for their loyalty. When he had responded to the homage of his habitants, he took his gun and fired at the Maypole which had previously been stripped of all its branches so that the trunk gleamed white. After the Seigneur, his wife took the gun and fired. And so on through the family and all those of the seigneury, until the tree was completely blackened, for the more powder used on the Maypole, the greater the compliment to the seigneur. A huge breakfast followed, ending with songs led by Paul.

Then the seigneury settled down to seven months of hard work, with the men in the fields all day and the women at their bake-ovens or spinning wheels. The Manor House had a huge indoor oven, added when Paul had improved the house, but most of the farmhouses had outdoor ovens which were never idle. Every available man was needed in the fields and Henry asked Paul if he might help. Ann and Elise had few idle moments and were glad of Rosalind's help. She had been capably brought up by a pioneer mother and though when it came to cooking, her English methods were different, she quickly learned their ways. It was a happy household, with no time to think of personal sorrows.

Such was the activity one morning when a *calèche* stopped in front of the Manor House. A tall, lean man jumped out, followed eagerly by a petite woman who could hardly wait for him to assist her. She gripped his arm and her glistening eyes roved slowly over the seigneury taking in every detail. Her face was tense with emotion and her husband did not speak, but smiled at her with an expression of understanding. For some minutes they stood there as she absorbed it all. Then she turned to him and cried:

"Oh Eric! How wonderful it looks! It's grown so! Look at all the houses and there used only to be half a dozen!"

"The sapling grown into a sturdy oak," Eric said quietly.

Then she turned and looked up at the Manor House. "And Paul has enlarged the house so much. Oh dear, and I missed seeing it all grow." She turned away to gaze over the River, a little ashamed of the tears that coursed down her cheeks. She did not want her husband to think her ungrateful for all his care, but this sight of her beloved home was too much for her emotional nature.

Eric produced a handkerchief and with a kindly, "Now, now, don't cry," handed it to her.

"I'm sorry, dear. I did not mean to be such a fool!"

"That's all right. Only you don't want them to see you with red eyes. Besides, your face is dusty and the tears are leaving streaks!"

"Oh dear!" she exclaimed, "I must look awful! Why did I have to go and cry!"

She began rubbing her cheeks. Her husband took the handkerchief from her and wiped her face carefully. She smiled at him through misty eyes. "Thank you, Eric. Forgive me."

His answer was a quick kiss. "Now you look better," he said.

"They're all in the fields. Won't they be surprised!" she said and ran lightly up the steps, followed by her husband. At the top she paused again and turned for another intent look. "Wonderful!" he heard her say.

Then she opened the door—no door was ever kept locked in Montreal. She slipped her head inside and then drew it back to say to her husband: "They must be in the kitchen." She stepped inside and called. "Ann! Ann!" and waited. In a moment the door leading to the kitchen quarters opened and Ann appeared enveloped in a large apron. She looked puzzled for a moment and then cried: "Marguerite!" Marguerite flew to Ann's outstretched arms raining kisses on her face; then they stopped to look at each other and kissed again, both of them crying with joy. "Oh, Ann darling!" was answered by, "Marguerite darling, after so many years!"

Eric Walker stood in the doorway, smiling and understanding. When last he had entered this house he had been wearing the red coat of a British officer. Coming to Montreal as a member of a peace commission, he had taken the opportunity of calling upon the girl whom he had rescued from the Indians. Nine years had elapsed and the boy had matured to a young man, who at sight knew that he loved the red-headed girl. Two days later they had eloped. Now another seventeen years had passed and his fair hair had grown thin and the delicate lines on his face had deepened. There was the same esthetic quality about him and a sensitivity marked by a quiet strength. He was a man who listened while others talked; who thought much more than he ever put into words.

It was Ann who first thought of him and as she embraced Marguerite, held out a hand to him. His wife turned and included him in the embrace.

"You remember Ann, Eric?" she said.

"Indeed, yes," he answered and bowed over Ann's hand.

"I am so happy to welcome you both. And Paul will be elated," Ann said.

"Ann, if you knew what it means to be back here!" Marguerite exclaimed. "It all looks so familiar and yet so different. You have made so many improvements!" She walked into the drawing room as she spoke and then stopped with an exclamation. Eric and Ann had followed her and saw that the exclamation had been caused by coming face to face with her own portrait.

"Paul wrote you that he had had it done, didn't he?" Ann asked.

"Yes, but . . ." Marguerite gazed at it intently. "Yes, he did," she said quietly.

Eric was also gazing at the portrait with a rapt expression, recalling a scene of years ago. It was exactly as he had seen Marguerite in this very room at that time.

Her expression was rather sad, as she slowly pulled off her hat, revealing that the red-gold hair of which she had been so proud was now snow-white. Ann started to exclaim, but smothered it.

"How the years have changed me!" Marguerite said quietly.

"They've changed us all, my dear," Ann remarked.

"You don't look very different . . ."

"My hair is grey."

"Has Paul's hair gone white?" Marguerite asked.

"No, but it's going grey. I must send word to him at once. He'll be so happy you are here. And Henri too." Ann put her arm around Marguerite again. "We've grown so fond of Henri, dear. He's such a fine boy."

"We're proud of him. Tell me, Ann, has he suffered much from his experience?"

"I don't believe so. He was weak at first but he's well now. Excuse me and I'll send word to both of them. Please take off your coats and make yourselves comfortable. I won't be a moment."

As Ann hurried from the room, Marguerite turned again to the portrait. "That was how I looked when you first saw me, Eric." Her tone was wistful.

"Not when I *first* saw you. You were then wearing a ragged nightgown and not a beautiful silk dress."

"No, I didn't mean the time with the Indians, I mean when you first saw me here."

"I know what you mean, dear. I wanted to tease you."

He helped her out of her coat and removed his own. She was still looking anxiously at the portrait.

"Did I really look just like that when you first knew me, Eric?"

"Exactly. And you are still beautiful, so don't look so worried."

"How you do prevaricate!"

"Madame, I never prevaricate!" he said with a broad smile. He turned her to him, looked intently into her eyes and kissed her. "Conceited woman! Worrying about your looks!"

"Most women do!" Ann's voice spoke from the doorway. Elise was with her, but was too excited to speak for the moment. Her favorite aunt had come home. It was a moment for which she had longed through the years. For the fraction of a moment Marguerite stared at her, while her husband quickly drew in his breath. Elise was so like Marguerite that he was seeing his wife again as she had looked seventeen years ago.

"You remember Elise, Marguerite?" Ann was saying.

Marguerite and Elise moved towards each other.

"My little Elise!" Marguerite exclaimed. "And she has grown into a beautiful woman! I *am* proud." She kissed her niece on both cheeks.

Elise glanced up at her aunt's portrait. "They have always told me I resemble you," she said, breathless with excitement.

Marguerite laughed and Ann noted it had lost none of its old merriment. "As I *used* to be dear, perhaps," she said and passed her hand over her hair.

Ann turned towards Eric and said: "And this is Monsieur Walker, my daughter Elise."

"Monsieur Walker!" Marguerite exclaimed. "Oh no, please, he is one of the family too." She linked her arm affectionately in her husband's. "This is your Uncle Eric, Elise."

Elise included him with her warm smile and curtseying, held out her hand. He bent over it gallantly. "I am charmed to have such a niece," he said and then added. "You are indeed the image of my wife. As you stood there you looked just as she did years ago, standing in that same doorway."

"Thank you, monsieur, or I should say Uncle," she replied and they all laughed. Then suddenly Marguerite's laugh faded as she noticed Ann and Elise were both wearing black dresses.

"But . . . you're in mourning!" she exclaimed anxiously.

"Yes, Marguerite, we had a great loss this winter. Our son, Jean-Baptiste, died." Ann said quietly.

"Oh no!" Marguerite cried, and threw her arms comfortingly around Ann. "Jean-Baptiste. How did it happen?"

"He caught cold while on an expedition. I will tell you about it later."

"I am sorry, my dear. I know what it means to lose a child," Marguerite said.

"Thank you, dear," Ann said quietly.

Rosalind had heard the voices and guessed who had arrived. She hurried up to her room by the back stairs. Her heart was beating fast and she felt a little faint. The moment had come. Apart from the anxiety of meeting her future mother-in-law, her shyness made the meeting of strangers an ordeal. She had

once told Elise her fear of meeting Henry's parents and Elise
had exclaimed: "But Aunt Marguerite's a darling, you'll adore
her."

"But you haven't seen her for many years," Rosalind had
reminded her.

"No, but still you needn't worry. I'm supposed to be very
like her."

But Rosalind had remained unconvinced. Now she was
shaking with nervousness and wanted to go and hide. She
pulled herself together and realized that she must look her
best. She took down the dress that Elise had helped her make
and put it on. She combed her tresses that reached nearly to
her waist and waited, every minute seeming longer than an
hour.

Henry was in the barns and reached the house before Paul,
who was far out in the fields. He bounded into the room
and was enveloped by both parents. Marguerite broke down
again, weeping so that Henry had all he could do to control
her.

"It's all right, mother," he said. "I'm all right and we're all
together again."

She looked up into the face of her tall son, smiling through
her tears. "I do believe you've grown," she said. "You're as tall
as your father now."

"He'll be taller," Eric said proudly, his arm across his son's
shoulders.

Marguerite ran her finger down the scar that went from
his hair line to one eyebrow. "You were injured?" she said
anxiously.

Henry laughed. "I was lucky that was all. I was the only
survivor from the shipwreck."

"Oh, darling, it must have been dreadful for you," his
mother cried. "I want to hear all about it."

"You shall in good time, darling. Here's Uncle Paul."

Running footsteps sounded outside and Paul burst in,
paused for a moment and then rushed to his sister. Their twin

likeness was not so apparent now that it was a grey head mingling with a white. They held each other in a long embrace, unable to speak, and both crying unashamed.

"Paul, darling, oh Paul!" Marguerite finally was able to say. "I'm back at last. I can hardly believe it's true. I have dreamed of this moment so many, many times."

"I, too, dear," Paul answered. He pulled himself together and held out his hand to Eric.

"Thank you for bringing her, Eric," he said. An Englishman and a Frenchman clasped hands, performing an almost unprecedented gesture. "This is a great day in our lives," Paul remarked. "And how do you think Henri is looking?"

"Fine. We are both very grateful to you for having looked after him for us."

"I've had a wonderful time," Henry remarked. "I'm learning to be a good farmer and thoroughly enjoying it."

"Thought you wanted to be a doctor," his father said with a smile.

"So I do, sir, but even a doctor has to know how to take care of his land."

"True, very true," Eric agreed.

"I am sorry our son is away," Ann said.

"Oh yes, André!" Marguerite exclaimed.

"My twin brother," Elise explained to Eric.

"He's a *coureur de bois*," Paul said and his tone was proud.

"*Coureur de bois*," Marguerite remarked. "Just like you used to be, Paul."

"Only he will be a more experienced one than I. I only had a couple of years of it. He is with our brother, Philip."

"How much I have to catch up on!" Marguerite exclaimed.

"Don't you think we should have some wine, Paul, to celebrate this momentous occasion?" Ann prompted him.

"Why yes, of course. I'll go and fetch it." He hurried away. It was, of course, Henry who thought of Rosalind and whispered to Elise.

"Oh Rosalind!" she exclaimed. "We've forgotten the poor child. I'll go and get her." She went to the kitchen and not finding her there ran up to her room. When she burst into the room, Rosalind was standing facing the door, agitation written on her face. Elise put her arm around her. "Don't be afraid, darling. It's all right. Really it is. She's very sweet. Come along down." She could feel Rosalind trembling.

"Do I look all right?" she asked nervously.

"You look adorable. Now smile and don't tremble so."

Henry was waiting at the bottom of the stairs and he took Rosalind's hand in his, smiling encouragingly. He led her to his mother.

"Mother, this is Rosalind," he said simply.

The timid girl with the long golden tresses and the frightened blue eyes would have melted a much harder heart than Marguerite's. Immediately she felt sorry for the child and taking her hands, kissed her on both cheeks. Rosalind felt encouraged. "You poor child. You have been through an ordeal. I know. I went through the same thing. We shall take care of you."

"Thank you so much," Rosalind said, her voice a whisper.

"And this is my father—Rosalind," Henry said. Rosalind looked up at the tall man and bobbed a curtsey.

"How do you do, sir," she said in English, too scared to remember the French she had learned.

Eric Walker's smile was also encouraging. Before he could say anything, Henry blurted out: "Rosalind has promised to be my wife." The abruptness of the announcement was not entirely the impetuosity of youth. Henry knew that he should have waited until the excitement of his parents' arrival had subsided and then have spoken to them in private about Rosalind. But she had looked so frightened and he did not want her to feel a stranger outside the family circle.

The shock of the announcement was apparent on every face except Elise's, who was the only one acquainted with the secret. She now slipped her hand behind Rosalind's back and gave her a surreptitious squeeze. Rosalind was standing with her eyes to the floor and looking such a lonely little person that Marguerite quickly recovered and putting her arms around her said kindly:

"Then we shall all be one happy family. We shall soon get to know each other, dear."

Rosalind raised her eyes full of anxiety and met the green-blue eyes of her future mother-in-law. They, too, were anxious but kind. She said, faintly: "Thank you, madame."

Ann broke the tension by exclaiming: "How lovely! I am so glad for you two dear children," and kissed them both. "We must celebrate it properly just as soon as we can arrange it."

Paul returned with the wine and was told. When they had welcomed Marguerite and Eric, there was a toast to Rosalind and Henry.

There would be no more work that day. All were too excited. Marguerite wanted to talk to Paul and Henry at the same time about entirely different things and would ask one a question and before she heard the answer, would be asking another question of the other. Ann took over. Supported by Eric, she insisted that Marguerite lie down. They had had a long arduous journey and with the excitement, Marguerite had deep circles under her eyes and looked desperately tired. She protested. There was so much she must know. She wasn't tired. But when Ann had her in bed, she dropped into an exhausted sleep almost immediately.

CHAPTER XXVI

THE EXCITEMENT AND THE JOURNEY had fatigued Marguerite more than she realized and Ann was insistent that she remain in bed the following day. When Eric added his voice to the insistence, Marguerite complied and found she was very glad not to have to exert herself. It was pleasant to lie there propped against pillows and be waited upon. It was many years since she had been able to indulge in such luxury. Henry and Rosalind came in to see her and Marguerite began to warm towards her future daughter-in-law, whose simplicity she found appealing. They were going into Montreal to watch the first ship come in from Quebec, and Marguerite gave them a list of purchases to make for her.

Her next visitor was jovial Aunt Marie. As Philip had married the year following her elopement, this was their first meeting. Marie's good-humored face was wreathed in smiles as Ann introduced them. As she plumped down on the chair Ann placed for her, she threw back her short jacket and remarked that the weather was beginning to get warm. Marguerite studied the neat, homespun woman before her and knew she had an ally. Marie wanted to know all about the journey and Ann filled in with comments and explanations.

"It will be hard for me to recognize my own family," Marguerite said and there was a note of apology in her voice. "I've been away so long. I'm a stranger to most of you."

"Not altogether, my dear," Marie said kindly. "You're something of a heroine to many here." Marguerite looked at her inquiringly. "The boys never tire of hearing about the aunt who escaped from the Indians," Marie told her.

For a moment Marguerite's heart had jumped. She had

been afraid in that moment that Marie was going to say, "the aunt who ran off with an Englishman," and was relieved when it was the Indian story.

She returned Marie's smile. "Don't tell me you use me to scare the children!" she chided.

Marie threw out her work-scarred hands. "Bless me, no! But it does help to make them obey."

"What do you tell them? If you're not good, the Indians will get you like they did Aunt Marguerite?" Her eyes danced as she said it and then clouded for a moment as she remembered she had used this technique with her little son, Pierre, but it had never scared him. He had been killed falling from the lookout tower as he played.

"It takes a lot to scare my brood," Marie was saying. "Their father believes in bringing them up to be hardy."

"You have eight children, haven't you?" Marguerite inquired.

"Yes, eight boys and another on the way, as you can see," Marie said and laughed.

"You *do* have a large family. That will make nine!" Marguerite said admiringly.

"And it will probably be nineteen!" Marie said resignedly but her laugh was hearty.

"It would seem to me nine was plenty," Marguerite remarked.

"Not for Philip Boissart! There would have been eleven, I lost three. A woman can't be married to a man like him for sixteen years and have only nine children. I believe he's the most virile man on the place!"

"And you don't mind?" Marguerite inquired.

"Mind! God bless my soul, no! It keeps me occupied when he's away and it will be all the more to look after me in my old age. I would like this one to be a girl, though," she said wistfully. "There's too much masculine about the place. There're three of them making all that noise downstairs and with five more like them . . ." she threw up her hands.

"Could I see them? Those downstairs, I mean?" Marguerite asked.

"Why, of course, if you want to."

Marie went to the door and called: "Boys come up here." Footsteps clattered on the staircase. "Can't you be quieter?" she reproved them, and Marguerite had a vision of what the house must be like with all eight of them and their energetic parents there too. But when the three boys came in they were quiet.

"This is my eldest—Philip," Marie said, introducing a tall lad. With the innate politeness of these people, he held out his hand to his aunt, giving her a small bow at the same time.

"How do you do, Philip?" Marguerite said. "You look exactly as your father did when I last saw him." Then turning to Marie, "He is like his father, don't you think?"

"You can probably see it more than we," Marie agreed. "My husband's fat now." She turned to the next boy. "And this is Paul, he's the second oldest." Paul imitated his older brother with a little bow.

The third, aged only four, was already climbing on the bed before it came to his turn to be introduced. "Get down, Charles," Marie said and cuffed him, but he got right back on the bed.

"It's all right," Marguerite said. "And you're Charles?" She smiled at the curly-headed boy whose big blue eyes were staring at her.

"Why've you got white hair?" he asked.

"Don't go asking a lot of questions, now," his mother admonished, but he wasn't heeding her.

"Are you old?" he was asking.

Marguerite smiled. "Not so old. It went white after the Indians caught me." She mentioned this because she knew it was their chief interest in her. Charles' large eyes widened.

"You're the one the Indians caught. Tell me about it."

"I will later, Charles. When I get up you and I will have a special time together."

"Without the others?" he said eagerly.

"Well, we shall have to see." She had visions of having to relate the story to each one separately if she were not careful.

"I want to hear it alone." Charles was insistent and received further reproof from his mother. "Why're you in bed? Are you ill?" came the questions.

"No, just tired. I shall be up tomorrow."

He had gradually eased himself higher up the bed. "May I touch it?" he asked.

"Touch what, darling?" Marguerite asked with a smile.

"Your hair."

His mother remonstrated but Marguerite let him do it. The little hand that touched her hair was surprisingly gentle, and Marguerite could not resist taking him in her arms and hugging him.

The other boys did not say much. They felt very grown up beside their little brother. Philip had his own importance as the eldest, and with his father away had already had his share of responsibility.

"And are you going to be a *coureur de bois?*" Marguerite asked him.

"I hope to be, madame. Father says perhaps I can go with them next year."

"How old will you be, then, Philip?"

"Fourteen, madame."

"Say Aunt Marguerite, not madame," Marie corrected.

The boy looked at his mother but did not repeat her words.

"And you, Paul, are you going to be a *coureur de bois* too?" Marguerite asked.

Paul was shy and did not answer immediately. His mother gave him a nudge.

"I don't know," he finally answered.

"He wants to be a soldier," Philip answered for him.

"Who said so?" Paul found his voice and looked defiantly at his brother.

"You did the other day," Philip said, and his tone dared his brother to argue the point.

"I want to be a soldier, too," young Charles interrupted, determined not to be left out. "I want to fight the Indians." And scrambling off the bed, he began to suit the words to the action by racing around the room uttering war-whoops. His mother silenced him.

"He reminds me of my Pierre," Marguerite said to Ann. "He was always hunting Indians." Then she turned to Marie and explained. "He was the little boy who was killed by an accident."

"I heard about that, my dear. You have a fine boy now, though, to compensate you," Aunt Marie said quickly.

"Henri? Yes. He is a great comfort."

"He has been over to see me once or twice."

"Haven't your boys resented his being English?"

Marie hesitated, and Marguerite replied for her.

"Of course, they have."

"Well, yes, to some extent," Marie admitted. Then turning to the boys, she said: "Run along now and wait for me downstairs."

"May we go out to the barn?" Paul asked.

"Yes, as long as you don't get in Uncle Paul's way. And don't make a lot of noise."

"I'll come down with you, boys," Ann said. "I think there's some cake in the kitchen."

This was all the encouragement they needed. When they had gone, Marguerite turned to Marie and remarked: "I'm awfully afraid of meeting the rest of the family, Marie!"

"Aw now, why?" Marie protested.

"You know why, my dear. You must have heard the whole story. And I haven't seen or communicated with any of them since I ran away. They won't accept my husband or my son. You must know that. They haven't accepted Henri while he has been here, have they?"

"They haven't seen much of him, my dear. He has been

very tactful and when he has worked for Paul it has been right here. He has never been out in the fields. He wouldn't have come over to see me only I urged him."

"You're very understanding, Marie. Paul said you would be."

"Pshaw! I haven't time for all the gossip around here. You're our own family, and from what Paul tells me your husband's a fine man."

"He is, Marie. Even if he is English," she added with a smile.

"There must be exceptions in every nationality. After all, no one could honestly say that all Frenchmen are fine people. There's good and bad among us all. I don't know why God had to go and make so many different nationalities to complicate the world."

"We'd much rather have it all French, eh?" Marguerite said, and as they laughed she forgot what had started to worry her.

Marie hoisted her rotund body out of the chair as she said: "I must be getting back to my work now. But don't you worry about the family, *chérie*. You lie there and get rested and in the meantime, I'll get in a few words to pave the way for you."

She leaned over and gave Marguerite an affectionate kiss on each cheek. Marguerite impulsively threw her arms around her. "You're a dear," she said. "Thank you so much for coming to see me. You've made me feel so happy."

"Old Marie'll help you," she replied.

"Who's old?" Ann came in, laughing.

"Me, I'm getting old and much too fat."

"Nonsense, Marie. You haven't a grey hair in your head. Look at mine!" Ann argued.

"You'll never look old!" Marie exclaimed. "You're too good-looking."

"Just as if that had anything to do with it! I'll be forty next birthday."

"Haw! I'll be that, too, very soon."

"Nonsense, you've another ten years yet."

The banter went on and Marie's genuine affection and admiration for Ann was apparent. As she left, her hearty laugh remained to echo through the house.

"She's a darling!" Marguerite said enthusiastically.

"Isn't she. She means a lot to me. If ever we have any trouble Marie is right here and doesn't have to be asked. I love her," Ann said warmly.

"How old is she actually?"

"Not much over thirty."

"Really! She looks older."

"Marie is the type that wants to mother the world. She will always seem older."

The object of their discussion was, at that moment, doing just what they said. She had both arms around a young man and was hugging him to her. There were tears in her eyes.

"Antoine! I'm so glad to see you!" she cried.

"And I you, Aunt Marie!" He gave her another smacking kiss on her cheek. Then he put his finger to his lips. "But don't let the others know yet. I want to see Monsieur Paul first."

"I didn't think you were coming back. They said you'd gone back to France."

"I thought I would have to, but things worked out better. Tell me, how is every one?"

"Oh, lots of things have been happening here. Did you know Jean-Baptiste had died?"

The color drained from Antoine's face. "Jean-Baptiste dead?"

Marie nodded her head. "Died in March. Exposure during the war caused lung trouble. They'll tell you all about it. And Marguerite, my husband's sister, is here—arrived yesterday?"

"Marguerite? The beautiful one in the picture?"

Marie nodded again. "And her young son, Henri, is here. In fact every one seems to be arriving. When did you arrive?"

"Half an hour ago. I hired a horse from Dillon's and raced here. I couldn't wait. How's Elise?"

"Fine, fine," Marie said, but her eyes were anxious. She did not know whether she should warn him by mentioning Elise's engagement. She decided she had better leave matters alone.

"And André?" Antoine asked.

"Gone to the woods with my husband."

"Oh, I'm sorry." Antoine's expression showed his disappointment. "But then, of course, he would have left by now."

"They left early this year anyway."

"And how's all your family? How's Philip and Paul and the rest and the baby?"

"All fine. Paul and Philip and Charles are around somewhere. They're over at the barns I believe. Why don't you come over with me and find them? They'll be delighted to see you."

"Later I will. I have business to talk over with Monsieur Paul first."

"All right, but mind you come and see me soon," she said.

"I will. The very first opportunity."

Aunt Marie went off towards the barns to find her children. Antoine waited until he saw them all on their way to their own house. He looked around while he waited, the emotion he felt, visible on his face. He had feared he would never see this place again. It held so many happy memories for him. He hoped he would be able to find Paul without running into any more of the family, particularly Elise. He walked cautiously over to the barns and looked into each, but could not find Paul. He had just decided to go up to the house when they came face to face.

"Monsieur Paul!"

"Antoine!"

They exclaimed together. Paul's first reaction was one of delight as they clasped hands. Then a look of anxiety replaced the happy expression. Antoine saw it and said quickly: "It's all right, monsieur. I mean I don't . . . I can't call you *mon père*."

"What do you mean?"

"You're not responsible. I have found out who my father was."

"You have? You're sure?"

"Absolutely." Antoine looked around. "Could we go into the barn for a moment? I have a letter I want to show you."

"Come in here." Paul led the way to the storehouse. As they entered Antoine thought of the day he had kissed Elise there. He wanted so much to speak of her, but held his anxiety until he had explained the situation to her father.

When they were inside, he handed Paul the letter Colonel de Truite had given him. There was silence while Paul read it and reread it.

The months since Antoine had received that letter had been an agony of waiting. He had tried to hire a sleigh and guides, but had been unsuccessful and so had had to wait impatiently until the ice melted. The sojourn in Quebec had been dreadfully irritating, not only because of his impatience but because of the idiosyncrasies of Colonel de Truite. Antoine had called again to thank the Colonel in the proper manner. It had been a disagreeable shock to realize that this repulsive man was his uncle and, as far as he knew, his only living relative. De Truite had tried every way in his power, which was considerable, to prevent Antoine resigning his commission and leaving Quebec. It was fortunate for Antoine that he had made the acquaintance of the Governor-General to whom he confided his discovery. The Marquis de Vaudreuil was kind and most understanding when Antoine explained his difficulties with his new found relative. He had managed to get away without an open break with de Truite, but only because of his own even temper and tact.

Paul folded the yellowed letter and handed it back to Antoine. "Who was this man?" he asked.

"The Chevalier de Vinont," Antoine told him.

Paul frowned. "I don't ever remember meeting him. But then I didn't know Quebec society very well."

Antoine explained how he had stumbled on the discovery and Paul listened quietly. "It certainly was a lucky chance," Antoine concluded.

"I am so relieved, Antoine," Paul told him.

"So was I, because I had given up all hope. On the journey here I was thinking what explanation I should make to Elise." Paul's heart skipped a beat. How could he tell Antoine he was too late? Antoine was talking of the story he had thought up to explain things to Elise.

Paul shook his head. "Tell her the truth, Antoine," he said quietly. Antoine began to protest, but Paul held up his hand. "It is better that way. She may not understand otherwise. I appreciate your wanting to protect me but . . ." He shook his head. "Too much harm has been done already. I may never be able to repair the damage I have done."

"But it's all straightened out now, monsieur."

"Not all, Antoine."

"What do you mean, monsieur?"

"Elise is engaged to Claude de Ramezay."

The happy expression left Antoine's face. All the fears he had lived through were expressed in the word, "Oh." He walked out of the storehouse, his back to Paul so that he should not see the shock he had sustained. "I am too late," he said slowly. "If I only had not had to wait for the ice to break. I tried to get a sleigh."

"It still would have been too late."

"When did it happen?"

"After she got your letter. Last summer."

Antoine felt deflated. The fear had haunted him all the time, but he had optimistically clung to the hope that his good fortune would stay with him.

"Should I go back without seeing her?"

"Oh no! We can't let you do that," Paul said quickly. "Come up to the house. My wife will know what to do."

The swinging strides with which Antoine had crossed to the barn were now gone. So many times he had visualized this moment of arrival—the look of surprise on Elise's face; the quick explanation and then her capitulation as she kissed him. The picture crumpled up as though it had been dropped into the fire and all that remained were the ashes of his hopes.

Ann was in the kitchen and Paul called to her through the open door.

"Yes, dear," she answered and then stopped suddenly in the doorway as she saw Antoine. "Antoine!" Hers was a quiet exclamation and when he would have bent to kiss her hand, she took his face between her hands and kissed him on the cheek. "This *is* a wonderful surprise!"

"But one that is ill-timed, I find," Antoine said despondently.

"We're so happy to see you again, Antoine, that it could never be ill-timed."

"Too late then," he said. Ann looked at him questioningly. "I have discovered who my father was and would have been free to ask Elise to marry me, but I have lost her."

"Oh, Antoine. I am sorry." Ann put her hand on his arm and led him towards the drawing room. "Come in here and tell us."

But before the explanation could be given to Ann, Elise walked into the room from the library. Ann had not known she was in there. They all saw the color drain from her face, while her mouth trembled and then set in a hard line. Antoine looked at her, unable to avert his face, and for a moment their eyes locked.

Ann quickly slipped into the breach. "Antoine's come back to see us, Elise," she said, but diplomacy could not bridge the gap.

"So I see," Elise replied coldly, though she extended her hand for him to kiss.

Antoine rose determinedly to the occasion. "May I have your permission, monsieur, and yours, madame, to speak with Mademoiselle Elise alone?"

Paul and Ann both started to assent but Elise interrupted

with a haughty: "There is nothing you can have to say that cannot be said before my parents, monsieur."

"But there is, mademoiselle." Antoine met her gaze with one that was equally steady. "They know what I wish to discuss."

"There is nothing I wish to discuss," she repeated and her green eyes flashed defiance as she turned to walk from the room.

"Elise." Paul's tone was firm. "You will please wait and hear what Antoine has to say to you. He is entitled to an opportunity to make an explanation."

"You cannot force me to remain," she replied defiantly.

"I am not forcing you to remain, Elise. I am asking you to do so for my sake."

Elise looked quickly at her father, perplexed by the pleading look in his eyes. She turned to her mother.

"Hear what Antoine has to say, Elise. You'll then be in a better position to judge," Ann said.

"Very well," Elise said petulantly. She was annoyed that Antoine had won the argument. She walked back into the room and sat down, her back to the light. Paul and Ann left them. Antoine did not sit down. He was not feeling nearly as calm as he pretended. It was difficult to know where to begin.

"Thank you, Elise," he said quietly, hoping to ease the tension, but she wasn't in the mood to help him.

"Don't thank me, thank my parents," she said crisply.

"It is because I have always thought so much of your parents that I have placed myself in such an unfavorable light with you," he said, his eyes fixed upon her face.

She did not understand and there was a puzzled frown on her face as she asked for an explanation.

"It is your father's wish that I tell you the truth," he said.

"You are speaking in riddles, but I suppose it is all right," she said and shrugged her shoulders.

"I am doing so because what I have to say is not easy." His

voice was brittle and she noticed it. "You might try to help me, instead of acting so coldly."

"I have already said I am not interested in any explanation of yours and I still am not interested," she said angrily.

"I would keep my temper if I were you," Antoine warned, "or you may have words to regret."

"I have nothing to regret," she said in the same angry tone. Getting up she walked to the window, her back to him. "Your behavior was inexcusable. You went off to Quebec and then invented some story about your family. I wish you had stayed away!"

"I shall be going away again."

"I hope so."

Her words cut him and he bit his lip to prevent saying what came to his mind. He did not answer for a moment and then said, "Would you have admired me had I gone through with our marriage not knowing whether I was your half-brother or not?"

She swung round to face him. "What are you saying?" she exclaimed.

"I will tell you if you will be a little more sympathetic. Since it was not my fault, I can hardly be held responsible."

She came and sat down again, her expression a little kinder. She noticed that Antoine was no longer wearing an officer's uniform. The cloth of his suit was of the finest quality, embroidered sufficiently to give it good taste without dandyism, and he wore a sword at his side. His dark eyes were steady as he looked at her and though his expression was a little angry, she had to admire the strong determination of his features. She was feeling rather ashamed of her behavior, but she had not dared behave in any other way.

Antoine stood by the mantelpiece, his back to the portrait he had always admired so much.

"What I have to say is very difficult because it involves your father and . . ."

"My father!" she was becoming more and more confused.

"Yes, your father. Do you remember the night at supper when I mentioned my parents—the night I wanted to ask your father for your hand?"

"Yes."

"I mentioned then that my mother was Madame Hélène de Matier." He paused a moment, wondering just how he should put the next sentence. "When I spoke to your father the following day he told me that he and my mother had been . . . very close friends." He looked at Elise to see whether this explanation had brought any light. It had not.

He went on. "In fact they were *more than friends* . . ." He hesitated and as she looked up sharply, he saw that she was beginning to understand.

"When was this?" she asked.

"When he was a young man. Before he married your mother, of course."

"I see."

"Do you see now, without my going into further explanation, the complications that your father feared?"

"I think I do. He thought . . . you were his son . . ."

"Yes. I went away to try to find proof if I could. I have found it."

"And . . . are you my . . . half-brother?" she asked.

"No." He waited to see her expression change to relief and pleasure and it did, adding to his anguish. "No. I found proof that my father was the Chevalier de Vinont."

"And all this has been about nothing?"

"Yes. But I had to find out for sure."

"Of course." She covered her face with her hand. He wanted so much to go to her but remained rigidly where he was. This was the moment when in his dreams they were to have renewed their protestations of love; the moment when he was to have felt her lips again upon his. Instead he could only watch her in silence, seeing the drooping shoulders and gaining a modicum of comfort by realizing from her attitude that despite her engagement to another man she still felt deeply for him.

She looked up, remorse on her face.

"I am sorry, Antoine. I behaved disgracefully just now."

"*I* am sorry all this has been found out too late."

"Yes," she said in a low voice.

"Had I known of your engagement I would not have returned. I did not know until your father told me just now." He paused and then asked: "When will you be married?"

"As soon as Claude returns. We expect him on an early vessel."

He looked away from her as he asked: "You love him?"

"Of course," she replied.

There was a long silence. Then Antoine said: "You mustn't let this make any difference between you and your father . . ."

"I understand," she replied.

"I wouldn't want to feel, when I have gone away, that my having come here as a guest, had caused a rift in your family."

She shook her head.

"Your father is a fine man. He has suffered very much over all this, suffered more because he made you unhappy."

She understood now the look she had often seen on her father's face. She did not speak.

"I shall return at once to Montreal . . ."

"Please don't hurry away, Antoine. My parents . . ."

"I couldn't stay in the house knowing I had lost you. It would be a torment I could not endure. I have been through too much agony already on account of this. I love you more than any one in the world, Elise."

She looked up at him, her eyes full of tears. Then she ran from the room, the tap of her shoes echoing on the stairs.

CHAPTER XXVII

PAUL AND ANN WERE WAITING anxiously in the library. Paul had told her of Antoine's discovery and they, too, tried to look into the future. If Elise should wish it, could the engagement with Claude de Ramezay be broken? It could, but only at the risk of breaking a long family friendship. During the months of the engagement, Marie-Charlotte had more than once told Ann of her long cherished hope that the two families would be united through their children, and she had expressed her devotion to her future daughter-in-law.

"We must see what can be done," Ann told her husband. "It is a difficult situation and I don't know what to advise. I shall have to give it much thought."

When they heard Elise run upstairs they came out of the library. Antoine's hunched shoulders told their own story and Ann shot a distressed look at her husband. She hesitated a moment as to what to do and then went over to him. He did not hear them until she spoke his name. He jumped up quickly and turned, embarrassed that they should have discovered him with his face in his hands. His agonized look touched Ann's motherly nature and she put her arm around him.

"I am sorry, Antoine. I wish there were something we could do. Perhaps there will be." She tried to make her voice sound hopeful.

Antoine shook his head and his smile was feeble. "No. It's all over. I'm too late," he said.

"Did she understand?" Paul asked.

"Yes, monsieur, she was very understanding. I am too confused to be able to say any more now. I'll be getting back to

271

Montreal." Paul and Ann both began to protest. "But I can't remain in the same house with Elise. I just couldn't bear to look at her and be reminded of what I have lost." He turned away abruptly to hide his emotion. He was embarrassed because he wanted to cry.

"We owe you too much, Antoine—at least I do," Paul said firmly. "If it had not been for my foolishness you would have been married to Elise by now. I don't know exactly what to suggest at the moment. This has all happened so suddenly. But I shall find some plan."

"It is nearly dinner time, anyway," Ann said in her practical way. "Stay and have dinner with us and then you and Paul can talk it over this afternoon."

Antoine yielded to their persuasions. The presence of others helped to ease matters. Marguerite, who decided to come down for dinner, was given a brief outline of the situation by Ann. Antoine was able to shake off his depression a little at the pleasure of meeting the lady whose picture had always fascinated him. As he bowed over her hand he told her this and they instantly became friends. Henry and Rosalind had returned from Montreal full of excitement at seeing the ship come in. Rosalind gave him a little bob curtsey and was shy as he took her hand and kissed it. She had not been trained in courtly manners and it left her speechless. Antoine immediately put them at ease by showing that he had no antipathy towards the English, and when Paul and Eric joined them, the atmosphere was gay with chatter.

Ann had gone to Elise's room and was distressed when she saw her red eyes. They talked together for a while, but Elise would not yield to her mother's persuasions to come to dinner.

"I couldn't eat, mother," she pleaded, "and I want to be alone for a while to get things straight in my mind."

Her mother did not argue with her. She knew that in like circumstances she could not have faced the family, let alone being at the same table with Antoine.

"All right, darling," she said and kissed her. "Try not to

upset yourself too much." She looked towards the *prie-dieu* and added: "Pray quietly for guidance, dear. It is the best way." And as she went out of the door: "I will send you up a tray. Try to eat a little."

Antoine tried to do justice to the food set before him but with little success. When dinner was over, Paul took him into the library and offered him a pipe. Though Antoine had smoked little since leaving Montreal, he took the pipe and filled it.

"Sit down, Antoine, and let us have a talk," Paul said. "There's no situation which we can't surmount, or at least make an effort to. In the first place, what about your grant of land?"

"I don't know, monsieur. I have held the grant over a year and have done nothing with it. It may have reverted to royal domain."

"No, you still own it." Antoine glanced at him quickly and despite his despondency there was surprised interest in his expression. "I spoke to the Governor some time ago and he agreed to let the grant remain in your name until we heard from you."

"That was very good of you, monsieur."

"I felt that one day you would come back and claim it."

"I had great plans in my mind, but they've all collapsed now," Antoine said and shook his head.

"Not necessarily, Antoine. If Elise marries Claude de Ramezay she will live in Montreal, or maybe Quebec or even France. What will you do if you don't remain here? I notice you are not in uniform."

"I resigned my commission."

"So I thought."

"I can buy it back probably."

"But you had intended remaining here?"

"Yes, monsieur, I had. When I was here before, it seemed to me the ideal life. I know nothing about farming of course. . . ."

"We can teach you. I don't believe you would be afraid of hard work—and it is hard work, particularly at the start."

"That I would welcome. These past idle months have been very trying. I wish I knew what to do." He ran his hands through his thick wavy hair.

"Will you follow my advice?" Paul asked.

"I'd like to, monsieur."

"Here is a suggestion I would like to make." Antoine fixed his eyes upon Paul's face and listened. "Carry out your original intention of settling down here. Marie is very fond of you and I am sure would be glad to have you live with her until you can build a place of your own."

"Just a shack would do to begin with."

"It would, but you're not used to fending for yourself as we were. You'd have to do your own cooking and I warrant you know nothing about it." Paul laughed and Antoine answered with a smile.

"No, but I could get along."

"Why make things harder if it's not necessary? Marie's farm is the nearest point to your land and therefore convenient. I know she would be delighted to look after you."

"We've always been able to get along very well."

"Suppose then we leave that point there. Then about your land. I will help you get experienced woodsmen to clear it. I would like to help you myself. I'm a good woodsman. Ever chop down a tree?" Antoine shook his head. "It's hard work but good exercise," Paul said with a smile. "Develops the muscles and you'll need those if you're going to be a farmer."

Antoine looked at his soft hands that had never done any labor. "Yes, I have much to learn," he said and getting up, gazed out of the window, thinking deeply. He wanted so much to lay his foundations here. The thought of returning to France and beginning that empty life again was very distasteful. He presently turned back into the room and sat down again.

"I believe, monsieur, I shall take your advice and go

through with my plans, despite my disappointment. I am tired of wandering about and an idle life now bores me. With a lot of work to do, I might be able to forget."

"I think you would be doing the wise thing," Paul told him.

Antoine studied the carpet thoughtfully and then said: "On the journey here from Quebec I thought out a few ideas. Would you permit me to discuss them with you, monsieur?"

"I would be delighted," Paul said, brightening at the prospect of Antoine's remaining and giving him an opportunity to help him. "Light your pipe."

When they had their pipes going again they were more relaxed. "Well, monsieur, I have a small fortune that was left me by my mother." This was interesting news to Paul and he studied Antoine thoughtfully. "I inherited it on my eighteenth birthday and I still have about three-quarters of it intact. Would you be willing to combine, to some extent, the advantages of the two seigneuries?"

Paul smiled broadly and with the lines on his face relaxed, the strained look which had settled there lately was gone. "That idea had occurred to me, too," he said.

Antoine looked pleased. "I'm pleased to hear that," he said. "I am not a rich man but I have enough," he added modestly.

"You don't need much once you're established."

"From what I saw on the St. Martin's Day I was here, the revenue from tenants can hardly be counted."

"No, it amounts to very little. But if you plant your crops well and have a normal year without too many setbacks, you should receive enough return from them to support yourself and a family. As the years continue you should have enough surplus after your own needs to send sufficient to market to exchange for other things you require. It's all barter and exchange."

"Yes. André explained that to me when last I was here. I miss André. . . ."

"So do I. I am sorry he's not here. He will be very happy to see you back. He thinks a lot of you."

"And I of him." They had already discussed Jean-Baptiste's death before dinner and Antoine did not now refer to it again.

"Coming back to our discussion of crops," Paul said, "I have always wanted to branch out into other things—tobacco, for instance. We grow some, enough for our own use, but why not plant whole fields of it and send it to the market?"

"That sounds interesting!" Antoine said enthusiastically. "Is it difficult to grow?"

"No more than anything else. The Indians are very fond of it and it is a very useful commodity for trading with them. The *coureurs de bois* never can get enough to take with them. You could devote your fields to growing tobacco and we could supply you with produce from our surplus here. In that way we would both benefit."

"Excellent idea!"

"And then I have always wanted to expand my sheep farming. It is very profitable."

Antoine nodded with approval and his depression began to lift. "What about horse breeding, monsieur?" he asked presently.

"Restricted at present. Some day that may change. As it is now we are not permitted to keep more horses than we need for our own farm work. We're not really supposed to use them for riding, but I do," Paul said and smiled.

"Why is that?" Antoine inquired.

"Well, in the first place, they are expensive. During the winter they have to be kept in the barn and eat up all the profits. But the real reason is that the government doesn't want the people to acquire the habit of riding. They want them to walk. Our strength lies in our adeptness on snowshoes. It strengthens the leg muscles and enables us to travel long distances without getting tired. This has proven a great advantage to us in warfare."

"I understand. But we can hope there won't always be warfare."

Paul laughed. "That we have hoped for years, but we can never be too confident. One of the first things you would have to do is to protect your land with strong palisades. Uncultivated land is always a menace to us. Enemies can hide too easily in it and particularly redskins. I never feel we are safe from their attacks. Even if the tribes in general are friendly, there are always marauding bands of them. The far side of your property, just as mine is now, will have a boundary of wild forest. . . ."

"But with mine built up, you will not have that menace. . . ."

"No, I'll pass it on to you!" Paul laughed. "And you will have to watch it. Have to build watch towers for protection."

"That I would do."

There was a pause for a while as they both pursued their thoughts. Then Paul said: "And we lack a granary. As it is now we have to sell our crops before winter sets in, and usually at a loss. With a granary we could store them."

"Then I should build a granary. Couldn't it be built so that both seigneuries could use it? It could be on the side where the two properties join." Antoine's voice rose in eager enthusiasm that Paul did not fail to notice.

"It could," Paul said. "And in return you could use my mill. It is a good one. I tore down the old one some years ago and built a new one. It is one of the few hereabouts that is operated by water power. All the others have to rely on the wind, and that doesn't always oblige when needed."

Antoine's eyes were now bright as one idea after another tumbled over in his mind. "And perhaps, monsieur, in time we could build our own church. Then we wouldn't have to go all the way into Montreal for Mass. Maybe we could have our own curé who could also teach the children."

Paul nodded with approval and there was a faraway look in his eyes as he said: "Yes—I would like to hear the Angelus from our own church instead of ringing in the distance as it does now." Then he leaned forward intently, puffing hard on his pipe. "These ideas you have voiced—they have been my dreams for years. Ever since I became seigneur over twenty years ago, I have wanted these things. I have never been a rich man; I had nothing until I married. It was my wife's dowry that enabled me to make the improvements I have." Then realizing that this might bring back recollections of Elise, he asked quickly: "Have you seen the Baron de Longueil's seigneury?"

"Yes, the winter I stayed here."

"That has always been my incentive. He has done so many wonderful things. . . ."

"Perhaps eventually we can do the same, monsieur."

Paul smiled happily. "Then you will remain here?" he asked.

Antoine's expression was rather wistful. "I believe so, monsieur," he said. "I must think it over. I have to have something to interest me."

"I would like to make another suggestion," Paul said. "You have never seen the de Longueil seigneury when it was working. It is very different in the summer from the winter. I would like to take you over there tomorrow."

"I should be delighted."

"The Baron can give you much good advice."

"I shall need plenty. I am very ignorant." He stood up. "And now, monsieur, as I don't wish to embarrass Mademoiselle Elise, I think it would be wise if I called on Aunt Marie to see if she will let me stay with her."

"I'll go with you," Paul said.

The de Longueil seigneury lay on the opposite side of the River directly across from Montreal. As they paddled over, Antoine asked Paul questions regarding the seigneury's history.

"The Baron came from humble stock," Paul told him. "His grandfather was an innkeeper in Dieppe and came here a poor boy. He made his money by fur trading as many men here have done."

"The thought has occurred to me that perhaps I should go into the fur trade before settling down," Antoine remarked.

Paul was a little alarmed as he saw his ambitions in danger. "Do you mean by going to the woods yourself or as a silent partner, as I am now with André and Philip?" he asked.

"No, I meant as André does; perhaps by joining him. It would take me away until Mademoiselle Elise is married."

"But you couldn't do that and settle your seigneury too," Paul reminded him.

"No, I realize that," Antoine said uncertainly.

They paddled in silence for a while. "If the Baron came from humble stock how did he obtain his title?" Antoine asked presently.

Paul laughed. "Some think he was overly ambitious but I don't share that point of view. His father rendered splendid service to the colony through his understanding of the Indians. He was rewarded with letters of nobility and made Sieur de Longueil. About ten years ago, His Majesty conferred the title of Baron on the present de Longueil. Some say he bought the title. I don't know. I have never heard the full story. I do know that he has served the colony very well and lost an arm while doing it."

This information increased Antoine's interest as the Baron came to greet them. He was a powerfully built man nearing sixty, with a bluff manner that made them feel welcome. When Paul explained the object of their visit, he looked pleased, for nothing was so gratifying to him as to have his seigneury admired, and when Antoine asked him for advice, it increased his cordiality. He first took them over the large chateau-fortress which had been erected a decade before. It was an impressive edifice flanked by four towers and complete with guard room and barracks. It was lavishly furnished with pieces and tapestries imported from France and everywhere armorial bearings were in evidence. He conducted them through his farm and stables and showed them his sheepfold and dovecotes. They entered the church and met the curé and then went over some of the farms belonging to the habitants. It was one of the largest and most prosperous seigneuries in the colony, and the Baron had reason to be proud.

As Paul had foreseen, Antoine was much impressed and on the return journey talked rapidly and at intervals sank into reverie. Nothing more was said about the fur trade and Paul let the matter rest.

That evening as Antoine sat outside with Aunt Marie, smoking his last pipe before going to bed, he told her of the ideas he had discussed with Paul. She had not only readily acquiesced to the idea of Antoine's living with her but had welcomed it. None of her children was yet old enough to be a companion, and though she usually went to bed when they did, she really liked to sit up a while and talk.

Antoine had suggested to Paul that there was no need for any one on the seigneury to be told the real reason for his having gone to Quebec and Paul was glad to agree. All that any one need know was that he had gone on family business.

When Antoine had finished telling Aunt Marie of his future plans, she said: "It all sounds fine, Antoine, but a man needs a woman to raise a family."

"Yes, that's true," he answered vaguely.

She was not to be put off. "I'm disappointed. When you were here before I was sure you were going to propose to Elise. Why didn't you?"

Antoine hid his face in a cloud of smoke from his pipe. He was tempted to tell her the true story but decided against it. "I was too slow," was all he said.

There was a snort from Aunt Marie. "And now she's gone and engaged herself to the Governor's son. You're a fool, Antoine! You might have known that if you left here without speaking to her, some other man would. She's the most attractive girl for miles around. Did you know she was engaged?"

"If I had I wouldn't have returned," he admitted.

Aunt Marie looked at him sharply: "Then you did come back with the idea of marrying her?"

"Yes," he said.

"Pshaw!" Her tone was cross. There was a long pause and then she said: "What are you going to do about it?"

"There is nothing I can do," he said rather bitterly.

"You love her, though," she thought but she kept silent. Before she left him to go to bed, she kissed him on the forehead and remarked: "Maybe things will turn out all right yet."

Antoine sat outside a while longer, smoking in silence. He had let his enthusiasm carry him along, but with it there was a despairing void.

CHAPTER XXVIII

FOR SEVERAL DAYS Elise battled her problem alone. Ann did not discuss it with her, knowing that when Elise was ready she would open up the subject. Her father's participation in the matter had shocked her. She was well aware that men often had mistresses, though she had thought this mostly confined to France. In their talks with each other as they sat at their looms or embroidery, her mother had told her many things about the Court, considering it part of her daughter's education that she should have a broad view of life—a broader view than most people would have within the narrow confines of Montreal. She had talked many times on this subject to Elise since she had become engaged to Claude de Ramezay, foreseeing the kind of life she would ultimately lead.

Elise realized her father would be anxious over her reaction to Antoine's disclosure and the following morning she sought him out in his office. When she opened the door and came in, he looked up at her, his expression troubled. When she smiled, the weight lifted a little. She came and sat upon the arm of his chair and his arms tightened around her.

"I'm sorry, Elise, deeply sorry," he said.

"It's all right, father, I understand."

"But it's not all right, Elise. It's far from right. I would have told you the truth when Antoine first went away. I should have. But it seemed to me then that it wouldn't help; it wouldn't have brought Antoine back to you. I was a coward. I didn't want you to be ashamed of your father."

"I'm not ashamed of you, father. Don't think that."

"That doesn't put things right, though. I know you love

282

Antoine, and now you're engaged to Claude." She did not answer. "I think the best thing would be for me to see Governor de Ramezay and explain the whole situation to him."

"Perhaps we had better wait until Claude gets back. He should be here any day now."

"Whatever you want, dear. But it won't be right for you to marry him feeling as you do about Antoine."

"I know. I must think it over, father. I'm too confused at present. I just wanted you to know that—well, I still love you the same."

She kissed the top of his head and left. Paul was still unhappy. He scored himself for being a complacent fool all these years. The things he had wanted had come to him too easily— a seigneury, a charming wife and lovable children. He had taken it too much for granted that good fortune would continue. It had given him a considerable shock to find that the Biblical warning regarding the sins of the fathers should be evinced in his family.

Except for the first spasm Elise had not shed many tears. She was confused and weary from turning the matter over and over in her mind. After talking to her father she had gone into Montreal and had spent several hours in church seeking guidance. When she came back she felt more at peace, but still undecided as to what she should do.

It was with her Aunt Marguerite that she finally discussed the matter. Eric and Henry were doing some work for Paul while he went into Montreal with Antoine to secure woodsmen. Elise came to the door and Marguerite called to her.

"Can't you come and talk with me, Elise?"

"Mother has gone over to a neighbor's but Rosalind is helping, so I think I can be spared for a little while," she said. She pulled over a stool and sat down. "The Lameaux's baby is ill and mother took over some broth."

"She is a wonderful woman. I admire so much the way she has adapted herself to the life here."

"Yes, she is very wonderful," Elise agreed.

"I remember when Paul brought her here. I was so anxious in case I shouldn't like her. But the moment she stepped off the ship we became friends. She has such a warmth towards every one. She was so understanding, too, when I was in trouble."

Elise looked at her aunt. There is always something intriguing about a person who has had adventures and difficulties. It had added interesting lines to Marguerite's face and though they were lines of suffering, they gave her a vivid personality that contrasted with the blank expressions that Elise was accustomed to seeing on the faces of most other women she knew. Marguerite felt Elise's eyes upon her and turned to meet them. Spontaneously she put out a hand and laid it upon Elise's.

"What are you thinking, child? You were looking so serious."

"That it is nice having you here. I have always wanted to know you," she replied frankly.

"Why?" Marguerite asked with a smile.

"Probably because they have always told me I was like you."

"Don't become too much like me, dear. I made a muddle of my life. I wouldn't want you to do that. Our redheaded temperaments aren't always easy to manage."

"No," Elise agreed and thought of Gaston.

"Don't rush into a wrong marriage, dear," Marguerite cautioned. She did not want to force any confidence from her niece, but wanted to talk over the situation with her in the hope that she might be able to help. She felt quite relieved when Elise said:

"I would like to talk to you about it, Tante Marguerite."

"I was hoping you might." Marguerite smiled at her affectionately. "Your father has told me all the details."

"Oh, then that helps. I didn't know whether you knew."

"Yes, he told me a few days ago. He and I have always shared our confidences. . . ."

"Like André and me. I wish he were here. He'd tell me what to do."

"You feel towards him as I did towards Paul when we were your age. I am sorry I shall not see André."

"I am too. He is such a dear. They say he looks like father when he was young. He is always so full of life and energy. It's impossible to be dull with him around. Do you remember Jean-Baptiste?"

"Only as I remember all of you—as children. He was always a sensitive child and you two were the noisy ones."

"We grew up just that way."

"So I expected."

"You knew Jean-Baptiste went to France for two years?"

"Yes."

"It was he who brought Antoine here. . . ." She stopped talking and there was a faraway look in her eyes which were directed towards Antoine's seigneury.

"You love him, dear, don't you?" Marguerite said.

"Antoine? Yes," Elise answered, without changing the direction of her gaze.

"Then you should marry him," Marguerite advised quietly.

Elise did not answer at once. "Do you remember Claude de Ramezay?" she asked presently.

"Only as a child."

"Yes, of course. I forget all the years that have elapsed."

"You are fond of him, too?"

"Yes, but not in the same way. He's quite different from Antoine."

"What's he like?" Marguerite encouraged her.

"Good-looking and—well, much more elegant than Antoine. Oh, I don't know. . . ." She broke off suddenly.

"Let me tell you a little about myself, dear. It may help to clarify your own thoughts," Marguerite said kindly.

Elise turned to her. "I wish you would, Tante Marguerite."

"You knew that I once had a child without being married?" Marguerite asked.

"I have heard it," Elise said carefully.

"I presume every one has. Those things become a legend

that is never allowed to die. At that time I was restless. I wanted to become a grand lady and not a farmer's wife. De Favien flattered me and I was a fool. Did you ever hear of Charles Péchard?"

"Wasn't that the seigneury that is now part of this?"

"Yes. Charles asked me to marry him and I eventually did. I didn't love him but thought that it would work out somehow. He was a strange man, half-savage, eccentric in many ways, brutal at times, yet very lovable at others. We had a son who was killed by falling from one of the towers. That you have probably heard also." Elise nodded. "The reason I am telling you this, dear, is that through it all I was reaching for something I could not get. I made one mistake after another because I wanted love but couldn't get it. We think that other things will compensate, but they don't. We throw all our love into our children, but that isn't the same. Living with a man you don't love is misery; on the other hand, you can endure a lot if you have a husband you do love. That is why marrying Eric was worth all the other heartaches."

"I know that I would never be the only love in Claude's life. He is too sophisticated. . . ."

"Yet you became engaged to him?"

"Only when I thought Antoine wasn't coming back. . . ." She stopped and then added: "I wanted to get married." Again she thought of Gaston but did not mention him. It was in the past now and there was no need to resurrect it. She thought, too, how near she had been to repeating Marguerite's experience. Suppose she had had a child by Gaston? They would then have been able to say with much more emphasis, "She's so like her Aunt Marguerite."

Marguerite covertly studied her as she sat deep in thought. She had inherited Ann's delicate refinement, making her much more beautiful than her aunt had been at her age. She had not known the roughness of life that Marguerite had and because of this was not as restless and discontented. She did not have to make the choice between becoming the wife of some simple farmer or marrying beyond her station. She had not had to live the life of a rugged pioneer, yet she possessed the depth of character that would have made her a good one.

"Think it over very carefully before you decide," Marguerite said.

"I have, Tante, I have," Elise said desperately, "and I get more and more confused. I hate to hurt people."

"You'd be hurting Antoine. He will take it more seriously than Claude. From what you tell me Claude would soon find some one else."

"I haven't been thinking of him so much as his mother."

"His mother!" Margerite exclaimed. "But that is foolish!"

"I know it is. But she has been so anxious for this marriage to unite the families."

"Nonsense," Marguerite said harshly. "If that's what's keeping you undecided, then I would forget it."

"I suppose so," Elise said thoughtfully. Yet it was not going to be easy to face Madame de Ramezay and see the look of intense disappointment on her face. At the time she had lost her last baby, Elise had sat with her a long while and this forthcoming marriage had been the one thing that had made her brighten. She sat staring into space and wondering how she would ever be able to muster enough courage to tell her.

Marguerite leaned forward and took both of Elise's hands in hers, looking earnestly into her face. "You have been happy with your life here on the seigneury, dear, haven't you?" she asked.

"Oh, yes, Tante Marguerite. I love this place."

"Then why leave it? If you marry Claude your life will be entirely changed. You will live in the artificial atmosphere of a petty court; you will not have the freedom of life here. You will not be able to wear simple clothes like you have on now. Perhaps you won't mind that. Perhaps the prospect of having many fine clothes and being a grand lady is what you want. Maybe that's what's making it hard for you to decide."

"No, it isn't," Elise said quickly.

"I thought I would never mind leaving here but my heart has never stopped aching and never will," Marguerite went on. "When we live so close to it, perhaps we don't realize the full depth of this inheritance that grandfather Pierre founded for us. The life may be hard, although yours is less rugged than mine, but it becomes part of you. You have the freedom of the open spaces, the joy of seeing things grow and develop. Old Pierre always maintained that someday this place would grow far beyond our imaginations, and he was a man of foresight. With Claude you might not even be living here. He would probably want to go to Quebec or France. And if he is the type of man you have portrayed, you would become a woman with probably many worldly possessions but a lonely heart. You would have to smile and look happy when you were yearning to be back here. Claude would leave you alone maybe night after night while he courted a mistress and left you with only the comfort of your children. I may be painting a picture that is all wrong, but I don't believe so."

"I don't believe so, either," Elise said quietly.

"Your mother knows more of that kind of social life than any of us. She often used to speak of it to me. You would miss her and your father and André. With Antoine you would not have to leave them. He would build you an inheritance that you would be proud of."

"But would he? He's never lived this kind of life. He's not a farmer," Elise said uncertainly.

"But he will become one. Why do you doubt him?"

"How can you be so sure? You know him very little," Elise countered.

"That is true. I don't know how I know, but I do. Without you he might get tired of it, but with you I don't believe he would."

Elise studied her aunt's face. It was alight with earnestness as she talked.

"Even though many of them here are prejudiced against me, I love them. They have an earthiness that is real." Marguerite leaned her head back and closed her eyes. In trying to convince Elise, she had intensified the longing in her own heart.

Elise went to her and crouched by the chair. "You're a very brave woman, Tante Marguerite," she said softly and smoothed back the wavy white hair.

Marguerite opened her eyes and looked into the other pair that were exactly the same color. "No I'm not, dear. I'm a woman who has failed miserably."

"I don't think so," Elise said earnestly and bending over, kissed her. "Thank you for talking to me. I will think over all you have said very carefully."

They heard Ann's voice calling to Elise and she got up quickly. "Thank you," she said again and hurried inside.

Marguerite's closed eyelids were wet. Desperately she struggled with the nostalgia that was overwhelming her, determined that this should be the last time that she would let it upset her. It was not going to be easy.

She heard Paul's voice and quickly pulled herself together, forcing a smile upon her face. He was talking to Antoine and did not see her. He invited Antoine to come in to dinner and she heard him reply:

"Some other time, monsieur. Thank you very much."

"Is it because of Elise?" she heard Paul ask and then add: "You will have to meet some time."

"I know, monsieur, but later on," Antoine said. Marguerite could see his face and was sure her judgment of him had been correct.

Elise also saw Antoine but from her bedroom window. She watched him as he walked along the River bank; watched the movement of his broad shoulders as he swung along; watched him stop to speak to neighbors and throw a ball to a group of children. With every movement there was a confidence, a sureness in himself that made her want to call out to him or run after him. She leaned her face against her hand that rested on the window frame, pressing her eyes hard to keep them from filling with tears. How she would have delighted in going over the property with him and planning where the house would be and how they would lay out the garden and the fields.

She watched him until he disappeared into Aunt Marie's house and she still stood there, thinking over Aunt Marguerite's words. She could not go through with this marriage to Claude knowing that she loved Antoine. She would have to tell Claude as soon as he arrived. It would not be pleasant.

CHAPTER XXIX

WORK BEGAN ON Antoine's seigneury. They had only been able to hire three woodsmen and when Eric and Henry offered to help, Antoine accepted their offer without hesitation. When Eric told Marguerite she gave him a penetrating look and asked:

"Antoine didn't object?"

"Object? Why, no. What do you mean?"

"Because you are an Englishman," she said in a steady voice.

"He's never shown any objection at all. In fact, he's been most friendly from the time we first met."

"Yes, he seems very fair minded," Marguerite remarked and nothing more was said.

But if Antoine had no objection, others had. On the morning that the woodsmen arrived, Eric and Henry were already at work. Paul was showing Antoine how to handle an axe. When Paul swung the axe and made a deep, straight cut and then swinging again, made a slanting cut to meet it, severing a clean wedge at the base of the tree, it did not look difficult. But when Antoine tried he lacked the precision and the two lines did not meet truly. Antoine looked at it wryly and Paul laughed. "It takes practice," he said.

"It looked so easy!" Antoine said despondently.

"Watch us for a while. You'll soon learn. You must be careful to make the cut so that the tree will fall the right way and whatever you do, watch where the other men are. We don't want any accidents."

The men were introduced to the Walkers and as they both spoke French fluently, no comment was made. Antoine had asked Paul to oversee the work, since he was experienced. Paul set the men to work and the first morning progressed well. During the morning Etienne walked over but when he saw Eric and Henry he turned abruptly and left. Arrangements had been made with Aunt Marie to feed the men and at noon she brought over their dinner. Antoine protested and said that the men would fetch it themselves but in her good-humored way she waved him aside. "I like to come over and gossip. Besides I want to see how you are getting on," she said.

"But you shouldn't be carrying heavy pails," he protested, for he had observed her pregnancy.

"When I can't, Philip can carry it over," she argued. "You stay on the job, young man, or you'll never get this wilderness cleared."

Antoine looked around and from where he squatted on the ground with a plate on his knees, it did not look very encouraging. "It does look hopeless, doesn't it?" he said rather despondently. "And I'm such a novice."

"Wait until you've been at it a week instead of a day. You'll be more heartened," she said. "Can you imagine what this must have looked like to our fathers and grandfathers?"

He shook his head. "They certainly had courage. At least I can look at Monsieur Paul's land and know what I am aiming to do."

"And you will. You'll have a fine place some day," she encouraged.

Paul, Eric and Henry took their dinner with the rest so as not to waste time and afterwards they all worked until sundown. They were all very tired but it had been a good healthy day.

They had selected a rise in the ground where the house would be built with a wide view of the River. Paul's plan was to clear a space around this, sufficient to start planting, and to protect it with a temporary palisade. When this was completed, the entire seigneury would be enclosed with sturdy palisades selected from the best cut timber, with watch towers at the two farthest corners.

The hired men were to camp on the land until their work was finished, and they set up their tents before going to supper. They had friends among the habitants and after supper went visiting.

The next morning when Paul arrived with Eric and Henry he found the men grouped around Antoine and an argument in progress. He laid down his axe and went over to them. As he approached, the conversation stopped abruptly.

"Something wrong?" he asked. There was silence. "Well?" he asked sharply.

Antoine started to explain but one of the men interrupted with: "We can't work here, monsieur."

"Why not?" Paul asked, his tone still sharp.

"We don't work with Englishmen," he was told decisively.

The bronze of Paul's skin went deeper and his green eyes were piercing. "What harm are they doing you?" he snapped.

"Englishmen have done us plenty of harm," the same man replied.

"Then they can work on the other side of the seigneury where you won't see them," Paul said.

"We don't work with Englishmen," they all said together in firm voices.

Paul lost his temper. "Very well, then, get back to town," he said and walked away from them. But Eric stood in his path.

"I overheard the conversation, Paul," he said quietly but so that the men could hear. "Don't dismiss them. You'll only make trouble for yourself and Antoine. Henry and I understand."

"It's all stupid prejudice," Paul protested angrily.

"Perhaps it is," Eric agreed, "but you can't fight it. I've experienced it many times before in the past years. It's best to accept it."

Paul glared before him. Antoine stood by saying nothing. It was too much a family affair for him to interfere. The men looked awkward but determined.

"Come along, Henry," Eric said.

"We'll talk of this again, Eric," Paul said as they departed.

"Please forget it," he said and waved a friendly hand. As they walked along the River bank, many a back turned towards them and when they had passed, the gossip began.

Marguerite saw them come in and hurried to them. "What's the matter? Has something gone wrong?" she asked.

"No, my dear, we're not working today," Eric replied.

"Why not?" she asked, and her tone was suspicious.

Eric turned to Henry. "Why don't you go and finish splitting those logs we were working on the other day," he said to his son.

"Yes, father," he said and left after giving his mother a kiss.

"What is it, Eric?" Marguerite asked anxiously.

He put his arm around her. "Nothing to worry about, darling; nothing, I assure you."

"I want to know what happened," she said stubbornly.

"You remember, my dear, that we have sometimes had difficulties with our neighbors at home," he began.

"You mean that the men won't work with you because you're English," she said bluntly. "I knew this would happen," she added bitterly and turned away to hide her feelings.

Eric went after her and turned her facing him. "I tell you there is nothing to worry about, Marguerite. We are used to this by now. . . ."

"I shall never get used to it." Her voice broke on the words.

"It is the cross you have to bear for having married an Englishman, my dear," he said in his gentle voice.

She threw her arms around his neck. "I didn't mean to hurt you, Eric. I'm sorry." She buried her face against his shirt until she had controlled her desire to cry. "I have tried to be so good, but sometimes it gets beyond me."

"I know," he said, understanding.

"It was the same the other day when I visited the family. Except for Marie they wouldn't accept you. Etienne quite frankly told me he wouldn't have you in his house."

"I know," he said again.

"How do you know?"

"I didn't expect anything different. Think it out, Marguerite. How can you expect it to be any different?"

"I don't know. But I had hoped it might be. Let us go back home, Eric."

"Whatever you want to do, my dear." She could not tell whether he was hurt or not, for he seldom showed his feelings. "Oh, why do there have to be all these differences and prejudices!" she cried. "Was Paul very upset?"

"He was angry and wanted to dismiss the men. I asked him not to. It would only cause him trouble."

"But they worked with you yesterday."

"They probably had not realized we were English. Evidently some one told them last night."

"Those wretched gossips! I hate it all!"

Eric ignored her protests and said: "Paul has been very kind in allowing me to come here and in taking care of our son. We cannot repay his kindness by causing him trouble."

"No," she agreed. "That's why we had better leave before more trouble is caused."

"I think you are right."

"What about Antoine? What did he say?"

"There was little he could say."

"I did hope it was all going to work out all right." All the dejection she felt was mirrored in her face.

"Now stop worrying, my dear. I shall have a talk with Paul when he comes home tonight. Run along now and finish what you were doing and forget it. I'm going outside. There's plenty of work around here I can do to help Paul."

He kissed her and went out. She watched him striding along. There was something so strong and comforting about him. Just because he was a different nationality why should there be so much resentment? Would there ever come a day when all men could live in peace?

That same day something else occurred over at Antoine's

seigneury. Aunt Marie was busy preparing dinner for the men when Elise came in and offered to help. When it was ready she helped carry it over and Aunt Marie made no comment. Antoine was leaning on his axe and resting. He was stripped to the waist and sweating in the noonday sun. Elise saw him before he realized she was there. As she watched him he had never seemed more attractive. He had lost his genteel appearance and his dark hair was matted with sweat. But she was accustomed to men who worked and sweated. As she came up to him he was rubbing his head vigorously with a towel, his back towards her.

"Hello, Antoine," she said. He turned quickly at the sound of her voice. Then he became a little embarrassed and covered his chest with the towel.

"Oh! Excuse me," he said.

Elise laughed, and the sound of it made his blood rush. "Don't be embarrassed. I'm used to it. I have seen men working, stripped of their shirts, all my life."

"I suppose you have," he said, and smiled back at her. All the same he continued rather self-consciously rubbing his chest with the towel. "Excuse me," he said again, and turning his back reached for his shirt that was hanging on a nearby tree.

"Let us be friends, Antoine," she said quietly.

He pulled his shirt over his head and as his face emerged, he said: "Did you think we would be otherwise?" His voice was a little unsteady.

"I didn't know," she answered him. "I was rather disagreeable to you the other day."

He looked at her steadily, and there was tenderness in his dark eyes as he said: "I hope we shall always be good friends, Elise."

"Thank you," she replied and struggled with the thoughts in her mind. Should she tell him now that she was going to break her engagement? The men were talking nearby, jesting and making a noise, and it was not a propitious moment for confidences.

Antoine broke the silence that these tangled thoughts had occasioned by asking: "You don't mind that I have decided to remain here?"

"Mind!" she exclaimed. "Of course I don't. I would have been very unhappy had you changed your plans."

"I will never bother or embarrass you. Please be assured of that."

"But . . ." she hesitated, wanting to tell him but unable to. "Please don't feel that you have to avoid me. Come up to the house and visit us."

"I will—later on. I have a lot of work to do here. How do you think it is beginning to look?" It was rather a pointless remark with so little progress made, and he realized it as he looked over the small space they had cleared. "Of course, you can't tell much yet."

"No, but it won't be long. Where are you going to build the house?"

He pointed to the knoll. "There—eventually. I don't think I'll build it this year. I can't make up my mind about it."

She met his eyes then and knowing what was in his mind, did not answer.

"Your dinner's ready," she said.

"And I'm hungry!" he exclaimed, hoping that such a mundane thing might bring the conversation down to a safe level. "This work gives a man an enormous appetite." He tried to smooth down his unruly hair but it would not respond.

Aunt Marie had been watching them covertly. Paul, who had been working over the other side, saw them and was anxious. That morning he had received news that the ship with Claude de Ramezay on board was expected the next day. He had told Elise and had also given her an invitation from Madame de Ramezay to spend the night and go with them to meet the ship. He supposed Elise had wanted to see Antoine before meeting Claude again, and his supposition was correct. She had made no comment to her father when he had given her the news. It was while she was helping her mother that she said rather abruptly:

"Mother, I think I'll go and give Aunt Marie a hand. I want to speak to Antoine before I go into Montreal this afternoon."

"You haven't seen him since his arrival, have you?" Ann asked carefully.

"No, I have been waiting until I felt more sure of myself," she replied and then asked: "Do you think I would be wrong to break my engagement with Claude?"

Ann stopped what she was doing and gave all her attention to her daughter. "I think it would be wrong to marry Claude if it's Antoine you love. You must be sure, though. Engagements cannot be broken lightly."

"I know. Should I tell his mother first?" She was not looking forward to spending the night with the de Ramezays, knowing the trend that the conversation would undoubtedly take. They would expect her to be excited over her fiancé's return and it was difficult for her to pretend.

"I think you should see Claude first and talk things over with him," Ann advised.

That evening when they were finishing up their work Paul asked Antoine if Elise had mentioned Claude's return.

"No, she didn't," he replied and it set him wondering. Was this why she had come that day? Was it in the nature of a last visit before she prepared to become another man's wife? Long after supper he sat alone smoking his pipe and going over their conversation. His thoughts were despairing. Though he was growing fond of this place of his own, he sometimes wished he had never started it. What joy would there be in living here alone? There were, of course, other women and no doubt eventually he would find some one who could share his home, but it was an empty thought.

This disturbing day was not to be concluded in peace. After supper Ann and Marguerite joined Henry and Rosalind in a game of picquet, while Paul and Eric sat in the library smoking their pipes and talking. Eric's rationalism counteracted Paul's anger and obstinacy to some extent and he was forced to agree that Eric's viewpoint was the more sensible. But he would not agree to their leaving within the next few days.

"I don't want Marguerite leaving here feeling that she has not been wanted. I want this to be a happy visit," he argued.

"And it will have been," Eric tried to assure him.

"Not if she leaves with this matter uppermost in her mind."

"Can she avoid feeling that way? She herself told me that the day she visited her family they made her aware that with an English husband she was not acceptable. She only told me this today, but I had already surmised it."

"But surely we can find some way in which she can leave on a happier note," Paul said hopelessly. "You know Marguerite. She broods over things. We both do. She cannot come out and talk about what is worrying her."

"I know that. All these years she has been brooding because she misses you and this place so much. Sometimes I think I have done her a grave injury by taking her away."

"I don't believe so," Paul said quickly. "Time might have healed things, but it is doubtful whether she would have married here and have been able to be happy."

"Well, it's too late to worry about it now," Eric said philosophically. "I must try to find some way in which I can divert her mind so that she does not think so much of what she has lost. Perhaps when Henry marries and has a family it may change things," he said with a smile.

"It probably will. At least we can hope so."

Further conversation was interrupted when a hired man came in to tell Paul that there were a group of habitants wishing to see him.

"At this late hour?" he said with annoyance. "I attend to business in my office in the mornings. Who are they?"

"Monsieur Pierre Boissart and three others," the man replied.

"Pierre?" Paul thought for a moment and then said: "Perhaps I had better see them." A suspicion of what might be the cause crossed his mind. He apologized to Eric and went out. With Pierre were three of the senior habitants of the seigneury.

Paul greeted them in a friendly way and asked: "What can I do for you, messieurs?" He addressed the remark to the older men but Pierre replied:

"We would like to talk to you, Uncle Paul." He was looking uncomfortable and Paul was sure his suspicions were correct.

"Come into my office, then," he said a little tersely and led the way. He seated himself at his desk and lit his pipe, suggesting that the men light theirs. Then he asked: "What did you wish to see me about, messieurs?"

Evidently Pierre, although the youngest of them, had been appointed spokesman. "There is resentment, Uncle, over your harboring Englishmen here."

Paul's face hardened. "They are our relatives and . . ."

"And no credit to us," Pierre said boldly. Paul fixed his green eyes upon his nephew, but Pierre was undaunted. "We didn't mind so much when you ransomed the boy and girl. That was understood, but we resent having the man here and his wife."

The rudeness of his tone angered Paul and his temper flared up, but before he could blaze out the retort that came to his lips, one of the older men attempted to handle the matter more tactfully.

"We understand your position, Sieur, and it is because we felt sure that you would understand ours that we have come to you." With the softer words Paul began to cool down a little. "My father and two of my brothers were killed by the English, and we can't forget it. They've never been permitted in the colony and it will give us a bad reputation. We know you're friendly with the Governor, Sieur, and no doubt have his permission. . . ."

The suggestion of favoritism by the Governor annoyed Paul, and he said irritably: "My being friendly with the Governer hasn't a thing to do with it. Madame Walker is my sister and . . ."

"That is your misfortune, Sieur," another man remarked coolly.

"This is all stupid, narrow prejudice!" Paul said, raising his voice. "I grant we have suffered at the hands of the English and so have they at ours. I was at Schenectady and saw innocent men and women dragged out of their beds and murdered. Monsieur Walker's parents were both slaughtered at that time. They were colonists like ourselves and attending to their own business."

"Then let these people go back and attend to their business," a man answered in a steady tone that would give no quarter.

"We're practically at peace with the English. . . ." Paul tried to argue.

"Until they attempt to slit our throats again," one of the men scoffed.

"A treaty is being drawn up now. . . ." Paul persisted but was interrupted again.

"So have other treaties until it suits the English to break them and conquer our territory!"

Paul puffed on his pipe sullenly. He had always prided himself upon understanding the people of his seigneury, and in all the years he had owned it there had never been a difficulty that had not been settled amicably. At the time that Marguerite had eloped with Eric Walker, he had had to face some criticism, but because he was popular as a seigneur, it had died down. It had, however, prevented his taking any official position in the government, as Governor de Ramezay some years previously had tactfully told him. This had not bothered him, for he had no ambitions to hold office, nor had it made him change his viewpoint. But now that it had been revived upon his own seigneury, the harmony of which was his pride, he knew that he must compromise.

There was a long silence as they waited for him to speak. He was determined they should not go away thinking that they had forced him. He did not feel as angry with the three men as he did with Pierre whose taciturn manner always irritated him. Moreover, he felt that Pierre as one of the family, should not have been with the deputation.

"Don't think I do not appreciate how you gentlemen feel," he began, addressing himself to the three men. "I do. But you must also appreciate that Madame Walker is my sister—my twin sister and my favorite one. This is the first time she has visited me in seventeen years, and I have no intention of making her feel unwelcome." He regarded them steadily. "Flesh and blood are deeper than prejudices—or they should be," he said, letting his glance rest momentarily upon Pierre. "Perhaps we can hate a nation as a whole, but we can regard individuals with tolerance. I happen to know Monsieur Walker's point of view and know that he is a man of fine integrity and also has liberal views regarding our people. He would not have married my sister otherwise, nor would he have embraced her faith. Furthermore, when he rescued her from Indian torture, he did not stop to consider that they were different nationalities—he thought of human kindness first. For that reason, if for no other, I shall think of human kindness, and I think you could do the same. Surely you could consider the circumstances relating to this case. If one of your family had to choose between death and being rescued by an Englishman you wouldn't spurn that rescuer." He paused a moment to let his words sink in and then said deliberately: "I have no intention of asking my guests to leave until they are ready to do so."

Long after the deputation had left, Paul sat brooding over the matter, wondering what he ought to do. The men had not been unfriendly when they left, but Pierre had looked sullen.

Still nothing had been settled. He had asked them to leave the matter to him, but he did not know what he could do.

It was a weary man who crept in beside his wife that night. She cradled his head in her arms and waited for him to talk and when he did, it was late into the night before they finished. She had known that something had gone wrong when Eric and Henry had returned but as always she asked no questions until he was ready to tell her. Eric had joined them in the drawing room and had later taken her place at picquet. He had mentioned that Pierre had come with some men and she did not need much perspicacity to know that something was wrong.

"Leave it to God, dear. He will find a way and no one will be hurt," she tried to comfort Paul. She herself could not find a solution.

"I wish I had your faith, Ann. You always take these things so calmly."

"Getting upset and lying awake never solved any problem, dear. Now try to put it out of your mind and go to sleep. You'll be too tired to work tomorrow, otherwise," she replied.

CHAPTER XXX

JULY ON THE ST. LAWRENCE could be more beautiful than anywhere else, or so those who lived there thought—even those who had known Julys elsewhere. In summer the River wore its deepest blue and encouraged canoe and picnicking parties; the trees were in full bloom and the fields were radiant with ripening wheat and maturing hay. Soon the haymaking would begin and the air would vibrate with the laughter of the children to whom this brought such excitement. It was a time when hearts were happy contemplating the promise of a successful harvest, and though labor was heavy, the longer evenings offered a brief respite before bedtime when every one sat outside to gossip for a while in the warmth of the evening. These were evenings that young lovers cherished, catching the joy that was in the air.

Elise sat at the window of her bedroom in the Chateau, her youth calling to her to be happy. She was impatient to be done with unpleasant tasks—to clear the way for that moment when she could go to Antoine and tell him she was no longer pledged to marry another. The day had been a difficult one. Since they would all have to rise early in the morning, she had been able to make an easy excuse to retire to her room. Yet, she had little desire to go to bed, even though she was weary. But it was a mental weariness. All the afternoon and during supper, she had tried tactfully to avoid complications. She had listened with concern to Madame de Ramezay's enthusiastic suggestions for an early wedding.

"You will want it to be soon, dear, I know," she had said confidently. It was a statement rather than a question, yet it required an answer.

"It depends upon Claude," Elise had hedged, and the remark had been regarded as deference to the wishes of her fiancé.

Her sleep that night was haunted by confused dreams in which both men figured in complicated situations.

The next morning as she sat with Madame in the carriage, waiting for the ship to be sighted, she was nervous and tired. The shore was jammed with excited people, but the excitement did not convey itself to Elise. She found the long wait nerve-racking. Many people came up to the carriage to chat, and she forced a set smile upon her face. Those who knew them well would remark: "And you're waiting for your fiancé! You must be excited. How long has he been away?" And to the reply would exclaim: "Over a year! Such a long wait for you!" And off they would go to gossip with friends that Elise de Courville-Boissart had come with the Governor's party to meet her fiancé, and womanlike they would begin to think of getting a new dress for the wedding that undoubtedly would be the event of the season.

It was nearly noon before the passengers began to land. Claude was among the first to be rowed ashore and Elise felt faint with the rapid beating of her heart. How should she greet him and what should she say to him? She had to admit his attraction as he stood up in the boat and waved his hat to them. He was resplendent in a new uniform on which buttons and braid of real gold glittered in the sun. Yet, even as she reluctantly admired him, the memory of a strong muscular figure, bronzed by the sun, clouded her vision.

He embraced his father and mother and sister, Catherine, and then turned to his fiancée, surveying her keenly with blue eyes that flashed. Conventionally, he bent over her hand as she curtseyed to him. She was conscious of many eyes watching them but with an admirable poise he ignored it, retaining her hand in his and saying in a lowered voice:

"More beautiful than ever! It has been a long wait, Elise, too long."

"I am glad to see you back, Claude," she said and withdrew her hand, which was clammy with her nervousness.

"Really glad, I hope," he said, as though he had felt something of her hesitation.

She allowed a smile to be her answer.

Many people had grouped around them, some old friends and most of them those who were anxious to appear intimate with the Governor. De Ramezay was smiling radiantly, his good-humored face reflecting the pride he felt. Claude had distinguished himself at the capture of Rio de Janeiro and was the recipient of many flatteries which he acknowledged with a faint arrogance.

At dinner the whole family were assembled, with Claude naturally the center of attention. His younger brothers plagued him with questions about the naval battles in which he had been engaged, and were constantly interrupted by the sisters, who were more anxious to know what presents he had brought for them. They threatened to usurp the entire conversation until admonished by their mother. Even then it required some sharp reproof from their father as well, before they attended to their dinner and became quiet.

Sitting next to her fiancé, Elise had been glad of their chatter. After dessert the younger children were sent away and Madame and the older girls lingered for a while before leaving the men to their port.

The moment had arrived. Governor de Ramezay rose to his feet and proposed a toast to Claude and Elise. Claude had slipped his hand into Elise's, and now he lifted it to his lips. She felt beads of perspiration break out on her forehead. Should she rise now and make her announcement? Her legs felt too weak and she remained in her seat, mechanically acknowledging the warmth of their good wishes as glasses were drained.

Claude stood up and with glass in hand said: "To my fiancée. The most beautiful woman in Montreal—more than that—in the world."

She bowed her head, drawing her lips together. She was

trembling. She had to acknowledge it in some way, for every eye was upon her. She looked up at him nervously and murmured, "Thank you, Claude."

Madame de Ramezay approved of this sweet modesty and thinking to help her, at once began suggesting that they settle the marriage date.

"I must talk to Claude first," Elise managed to say.

"Don't be so impatient, mother. I haven't had one word with her yet," Claude said, laughing.

"Of course, my dears," she said, and smiled at him. "Come along, girls. Let's leave the men alone." She bent and kissed the top of her son's head. "Don't be too long, darling. Elise will be waiting."

The moment they were outside, Elise excused herself and ran up to her room. There she buried her face in her hands but did not cry. She tried desperately to control herself, to calm the rapid beating of her heart. She must not dally any longer. The moment she and Claude were alone, she must tell him, even if it were necessary to blurt it out bluntly. It was the only way, for even now doubts again began to assail her. Was she a fool to refuse all this honor and become the wife of a man who was not established? Her mind argued that she loved Antoine, and that would mean everything. She thought of the beauty and richness of this Chateau; of the prestige of such a marriage; of going to Quebec and France and being the center of an attentive circle of admirers. Would this become hollow, as Aunt Marguerite had warned her? Claude appeared to be in love with her, but how many other women had he looked at in just that way during the time he had been away? Should she tell him that she had changed her mind and then leave him to tell his family? What would they think of her for having accepted their hospitality and then repudiating it? She had still clarified nothing when a knock at the door admitted Madame.

"Claude is waiting for you, dear," she said and then added: "What is the matter? You look so pale."

"I have a headache," she replied.

"It's the excitement. I have, too. And Claude says his head is aching. We have all been under such a tension. I'm going to lie down." Madame kissed her affectionately as she left.

Claude was in the small drawing room, sprawled on a settee. He did not get up as she entered but held out a hand to her. "Forgive me, darling, but my head is throbbing and I feel dizzy."

"Perhaps you drank too much wine," she said a little maliciously and took a chair nearby.

"I did not!" he exclaimed. "Come over here and sit by me. I want to be able to see you."

She started to draw the chair closer but he protested.

"Come and sit here." He patted a space beside him on the settee. "You're so adorable to look at and I'm terribly hungry for a kiss."

But she did not bend her head. "I'm sorry you have a headache. Maybe you should rest," she remarked casually.

"Not until I have made love to you, my beautiful."

"What gave you a headache?" she asked.

"Now stop talking about headaches. Put your hand on my head and it will get better."

"My hand is hot," she said. "It's so warm today. I have a headache too."

He exclaimed impatiently. "That's all we seem to be able to talk about!" Then he took hold of her and pulled her to him, kissing her passionately and ignoring her protests. When he slipped his hand into her bodice she slapped him.

"Now don't be a prude!" he said, and there was annoyance in his tone. "After all, we'll be married very soon."

"Then suppose you wait until we are!" she retorted with some irritation. "I want to talk to you about that, Claude."

"Nothing would please me more, my dear. If you're going to be so conventional then we'd better be married right away. The very sight of you inflames my senses."

He stretched out his arms to her again but she jumped up and away from him. Immediately he was on his feet, but instead of grasping her, he suddenly held his head and groaned.

"What is it?" Elise said, alarmed.

With one hand he groped for something to hold on to and then with a hardly audible, "Excuse me," stumbled out of the room. Elise stood looking after him with distaste. She was sure that he had drunk too much at dinner. She had noticed him fill his glass several times and had no doubt he had consumed several glasses of port as well. The way he swayed as he went from the room proved it to her. All her life she had known men who drank considerably, but she had no patience with those who did not know their capacity. Perhaps she could make this her excuse for breaking the engagement, she thought, and then was ashamed of herself. She must tell him the truth and without any more delay.

Several minutes passed before he returned and when he did he was so deathly pale that she softened a little.

"I do apologize, Elise. It's the voyage. It often affects me like this," he said.

"You, who are a sailor?" she said incredulously.

"Do you think sailors aren't seasick! Many of them are."

He sat down weakly on the settee and then laid his head back. "I must have caught cold. I feel feverish," he murmured.

"I'd better call your mother," she said.

"No. She's lying down. Bear with me for a moment." Gropingly he held out a hand and she let him take hers, but this time she pulled a chair close to the settee instead of sitting beside him.

"I'm sure I'll be all right in a moment. Forgive me." His face had turned a peculiar grey shade. She sat watching him, much disturbed. The afternoon lengthened and when she thought he was sleeping, she got up quietly preparatory to returning home. But he stirred immediately.

"Don't go, Elise," he said.

"I have to get home, Claude, before it is dark."

"I'll drive you home then." His voice sounded thin, and it seemed an effort for him to talk.

"No, you lie there. Your coachman can drive me home."

"No. I'm coming with you." He was adamant and she did not argue further.

During the drive he laid with his head on her shoulder and tried to talk but she could tell that it was an effort and did not encourage him. All the way she was conscious of the fact that she had failed in what she had intended to do. Tomorrow she would send him a note to call upon her and take care of the matter then.

He rallied when they reached the Manor House. "Please make my apologies to your parents. I will call and pay my respects tomorrow. Forgive me for such behavior, Elise. I don't know what has come over me."

"I do hope you will be feeling better tomorrow," she said and tried to sound kind.

"I shall be. May I call in the afternoon?"

"Please, do. I shall be expecting you."

Ann saw Elise getting out of the carriage and when Claude did not come in, drew the wrong conclusion. She met Elise in the hall and saw the troubled look on her face.

"Claude is ill," she began.

"Ill!" Ann said with concern.

"Yes, he has a very bad headache and I think was sick. He says it was the ship. Evidently he has never yet become accustomed to the motion."

"Oh?"

"And I accomplished nothing, mother. I was just going to tell him when he became ill. It's such a muddle! All they did was to talk about when the wedding would be. I feel such a hypocrite!"

"I was afraid you would have a difficult time."

"Claude will call tomorrow afternoon. He asked me to convey his apologies to you and father." She passed her hand over her brow. "I'm awfully weary and have a headache too. I think I will go to bed."

Ann felt her head. "Your head is hot. Get into bed and I'll bring you up some supper after a while." Together they walked upstairs and Ann helped her out of her clothes. She did not say any more. There would be time to talk later.

CHAPTER XXXI

ANTOINE WALKED ALONG the River bank on his way to supper at the Manor House. The sun was setting in crimson glory over the water and he paused several times to admire it. At intervals he stopped to chat with habitants who made friendly inquiries regarding the progress of his seigneury. Interest in this new seigneur was considerable and a matter of gratification to those on the de Courville seigneury. Antoine's cordial manner had made him popular and he had already received requests from new colonists who wished to settle on his land. Its progress was now more rapid, for three additional woodsmen had been obtained, this being in the form of a veiled apology from the first three because of their objection to Eric and Henry.

It had been Ann's idea to invite Antoine to supper, and when Paul had conveyed the message, he had hesitated for a moment, but in that moment had remembered Elise's words and had accepted. He had not seen her since that one visit to his seigneury but had heard from Paul that Claude de Ramezay was ill. This illness had spoiled Ann's plan. It was rarely that she was impulsive, but now she realized she had been foolishly impetuous. She had anticipated that by this time Claude would have come to see Elise and that she would have told him of her decision. Unfortunately, his fever had developed and they had not seen each other again. Ann's first thought had been that she should postpone her invitation to Antoine. When she mentioned it to Elise, however, she shook her head.

"I asked him not to stay away on my account," she told her mother. Her tone was listless. Ever since her return from Montreal she had been feeling wretched, and before supper time on this day her headache became so intense that her mother made her go to bed.

"Antoine will think I am doing it purposely to avoid him," she protested, but it was nevertheless a relief to lay her head back on the pillow. Rosalind, always her faithful attendant, applied cold cloths to her head, and this brought some relief.

Ann greeted Antoine warmly and expressed Elise's regrets that she was not well enough to come down. She saw his expression change and knew that, as Elise had feared, he thought this was an excuse.

"She did not want to go to bed, but I insisted," Ann explained.

"Of course," he said, more politeness than assurance in the words.

"She was afraid you would think she was doing it purposely." Ann met the challenge. "I knew you would understand."

Antoine smiled and again said: "Of course." He was disappointed, yet also a little relieved. Being in Elise's presence always disturbed him and left him depressed. At the same time he wondered why she had asked him not to stay away on her account and now made the commonplace excuse of a headache. She had asked that they be friends. He had expected that this might be the first step towards that. Could it be that she also was disturbed when he was near? This he felt was the answer, for she had shown him on the two occasions when they had met recently that she still cared for him.

As the others gathered waiting for supper, Antoine found an opportunity to talk to Eric. It was the first time they had met since the incident on the seigneury and Antoine felt he should make some explanation. He was relieved to find that Eric had taken no offense.

"You must have quite a little of that to contend with, monsieur," Antoine remarked sympathetically.

Eric glanced quickly across the room to where his wife sat talking with Paul and in a low voice answered: "Yes."

"I'm very sorry it had to work out that way," Antoine said.

"It was very generous of you to accept our offer of help in the first place," Eric assured him.

"Frankly, I did not think of it in any way except that you were guests of Monsieur Paul. I was most surprised that morning when the men came to me with their objections." He shrugged his shoulders. "Perhaps I don't think deeply enough about these things. Of course, I've not fought in any of the wars. I suppose I might feel differently if I had seen my people killed. My only participation in war was going with a ship to salvage what we could from the wrecked English ships."

"You did!" Eric's tone was surprised. "I didn't know you had done that." He turned and called to his son. "Henry, did you know Monsieur Antoine had visited the sight of your wrecked vessels?" he asked.

Henry joined them and said with an amused smile: "*My* wrecked vessels!" Then said: "No, I didn't know you had been there. Horrible sight, wasn't it?"

"Ghastly! By the time we reached there the bodies had begun to decompose and there was a vile stench."

They discussed the shipwreck and its causes until Ann called them to supper. Henry went up to get Rosalind, who was still sitting by Elise's bed. She was reluctant to leave and said anxiously: "She seems awfully ill, Henry. Her head is so hot and her face flushed."

"You'd better tell Tante Ann," he said. "Maybe she has a fever."

Rosalind did so before sitting down to the table.

"She hasn't seemed well since she came back from Montreal," Ann remarked, but did not discuss the matter further because of Antoine. As soon as supper was over she went to Elise's room, followed by Rosalind.

Elise was tossing and moaning and Ann hurried to her anxiously. "What is it, dear? Are you in pain?" She laid her hand on Elise's head and it was burning.

"I have awful pains in my back and legs," she complained.

"And . . ." She sat up quickly and Ann rushed for a basin. When it was over Elise lay back moaning.

Her mother studied her anxiously. "Stay with her, Rosalind," she said. "We must get a doctor."

She hurried downstairs and called to Paul. "I think you will have to go into Montreal and get a doctor. She has pains in her legs and back and has just vomited. I think she has a fever," she told him.

"I'll go at once," Paul said.

Before going upstairs again, Ann went into the drawing room to explain. Antoine listened anxiously and was a little ashamed of the doubts he had had before supper.

"Can't I go and get the doctor?" he offered. "Monsieur Paul may be needed here."

"Would you, Antoine?" Ann's voice sounded relieved. She called to Paul and told him Antoine's suggestion.

"That's good of you, Antoine," Paul said. "I'll have a horse saddled for you."

While he waited, Antoine asked Ann if she thought it was anything serious. Realizing his concern, she hid her anxiety and said: "Oh, no. Probably a cold or a fever," and she smiled at him with understanding.

Paul was back quickly. "I don't know where you will find him, Antoine, on a Saturday night. Dillon's probably."

"You want Dr. Menoir who took care of me, don't you?" Antoine asked.

"Oh, no. He's not here any more. He went back to France. It's Dr. Beret. He lives on St. Paul's Street, about five doors from Dillon's. It's a small white house," Paul told him.

"I'll find it."

"Go to Dillon's first, though," Paul repeated.

Antoine leapt upon the horse and said reassuringly: "I'll hurry back," and was off at a fast canter. He was glad of the activity, and as he thought of Elise his anxiety grew. He urged the horse to a fast gallop, slowing up only when he reached the Market Place where people stood in groups, gossiping. Outside the wine shops and taverns the crowds were thickest. With a ship in dock they were doing a thriving trade. It was only with difficulty that he could make his way through those who collected before Dillon's. He did not dismount but called to those nearest the door to find out if the doctor was inside. There was a goodhearted response to his request, for only an emergency could demand such a call and the lather on his horse testified to his having ridden hard.

When the answer came back in the negative, several gathered around him, volunteering directions as to where the doctor lived. Thanking them quickly, Antoine rode on a short distance until he came to the house indicated. There was a light showing through one window and, dismounting, he rapped at the door. He saw the light moving, and in a few moments the door was opened.

"I am looking for Monsieur le docteur," he said to the woman holding the tallow bowl above her head.

"He is not here, monsieur," she told him.

Antoine's heart sank. "Can you tell me where I can find him?" he asked, his urgency sounding in his voice.

"He was called to the lower town. He did not say where."

"Haven't you any idea?" Now his voice was impatient.

"It was a sailor who came for him. You might try the lodging houses."

Murmuring a hurried thanks, he threw himself upon the horse and started off again. This end of town was totally unfamiliar to him and badly lighted as it was, he had to go slowly. There were few people about, those who were abroad being at the taverns. He made his way to where he could see a light in a window. Two sailors came towards him, supporting one another and singing a bawdy song.

"Looking for Mère Carron's, monsieur?" one called out, but did not wait for an answer.

Antoine could guess what they thought he was doing there. It was useless to attempt to ask them whether they knew where the doctor was, so he went on until he saw three more sailors gathered outside another house. For all he knew it might be the Mère Carron's that had been mentioned, but he took a chance and made his inquiry.

The men were looking serious as they talked. They answered him politely: "Yes, monsieur, he was here but left a short while ago."

Antoine was beginning to feel hopeless and desperate. "Do you know for where?" he asked. "I am on urgent business."

"He went to the Chateau," one of them replied.

Antoine thanked them and galloped back. When he reached the Chateau, lights blazed in all the windows.

"Is Monsieur le docteur here?" he inquired of the lackey who came to take his horse.

"Yes, monsieur," he replied and Antoine gave a sigh of relief.

To the lackey who admitted him he said: "I want to see the doctor immediately."

The lackey bowed. "Yes, monsieur. He is with His Excellency. What name shall I say?"

"Monsieur de Brievaux. Please tell the doctor he is needed at once at the de Courville Manor."

"Yes, monsieur. Will you be seated?"

But Antoine did not want to be seated. He was too nervous over the delay and he paced the floor impatiently until Governor de Ramezay appeared accompanied by a thin little man.

"Good evening, Antoine," the Governor said cordially.

"Good evening, Your Excellency," Antoine said and bowed. "I apologize for disturbing you. I am looking for Dr. Beret."

"This is Dr. Beret—Monsieur de Brievaux." The Governor introduced him to the little man, who was fidgeting nervously. His appearance was anything but reassuring. Antoine bowed and received a jerky bow in return.

Mademoiselle Elise has a fever," Antoine said, addressing himself to the Governor.

"Elise?" The Governor looked perturbed. "When did this start?"

"She complained of a headache this afternoon and went to bed. After supper they found a fever had developed."

"It looks as though you are right, Dr. Beret," the Governor said. Antoine looked at him anxiously. "Dr. Beret has just come from below town. . . ."

"Yes, I tried to find him there," Antoine said.

"Several sailors there have the fever," the Governor went on.

Alarm made Antoine's dark eyes large. "You mean it's an epidemic?" he exclaimed.

"We don't know yet," the doctor said. He was looking scared.

"These sailors were all off the ship—the same ship my son came by. . . ." Governor de Ramezay explained.

"And Mademoiselle Elise may have caught it from your son?" Antoine's voice snapped. He knew he should have made some comment upon Claude's illness but he was too concerned to be polite. "She saw him the day he arrived, didn't she?" he asked and was a little ashamed of the accusing tone in his voice.

"Yes," Governor de Ramezay replied quietly.

"Then no more time must be wasted. Please come at once," Antoine said rather peremptorily to the doctor.

"But I've. . . ." the man began to protest.

"Go with Monsieur de Brievaux, doctor, and return here later," Governor de Ramezay said. "There's nothing more you can do for my son at present." His forehead was wrinkled with worry. "I'll call my carriage for you."

He sent a servant hurrying away, and recollecting himself Antoine managed to say. "I am sorry to hear Claude is ill, monsieur."

"He's very ill, Antoine," the Governor said gravely. "Dr. Beret has just bled him again."

The mention of bleeding made Antoine feel sick, not because of the mention of blood but because he hated the idea of Elise having to be bled.

The lackey returned to say the carriage was ready. The

Governor conducted them to the door. "Give my regards to the Sieur and Madame," he said. "Dr. Beret will give me the report when he returns and I will make further inquiries tomorrow. I am so sorry."

As Dr. Beret was about to step into the carriage, two men hurried up and intercepted him.

"You are needed, monsieur le docteur, at Dillon's," one man said. "A gentleman there has collapsed. . . ."

"And at Le Castor," the other man said, naming a tavern in the lower part of town.

The Governor's face went grey.

"I can't be in several places at once," the doctor said testily, alarmed at the prospect of being faced with an epidemic. "Get an apothecary," and he scrambled into the carriage. Antoine leapt upon his horse, impatiently urging the coachman to travel with all possible speed. There had been too many delays already and he was afraid the Governor might change the order.

The men looked after the departing carriage anxiously. "What are we to do, monsieur?" they asked the Governor.

"Do you know what the symptoms of these illnesses are?" Governor de Ramezay asked.

"This gentleman suddenly fell on the floor. . . ." the man from Dillon's began.

"Was he off the ship?" the Governor asked sharply.

The man thought for a moment. "I don't know. I suppose he might be."

"Did he have a fever and headache?"

"I don't know, monsieur. I was merely told to get a doctor."

"The sailor at Le Castor does," the other man said. "He was groaning and tossing something awful."

"Sailor!" the Governor exclaimed. "Go back to your places. Tell those who sent you that my orders are that these sick men are to be isolated. Keep them away from others at the taverns. Do you understand?"

"Yes, monsieur. And what about a doctor? That is what I was sent for," the man from Dillon's said anxiously. His patron was a gentleman and he expected a reward. The other man wasn't so concerned over the sailor.

"There are apothecaries in town. They must help until Dr. Beret gets back," the Governor said. As he turned back into the house his face was lined with anxiety. Not even to Dr. Beret had he voiced his fears, for to these was added the knowledge that the doctor was ill-equipped to cope with the situation.

At the Manor House, the doctor bled Elise from the right arm, while Ann and Paul watched anxiously. Downstairs Marguerite, Eric and Rosalind were sitting in the drawing room scarcely uttering a word, while Henry stood by the window deep in thought. Antoine paced up and down outside. He was too nervous to remain with the others. The moment the doctor came out he sprang to him.

"What do you think it is, monsieur le docteur?" he asked.

"I can't tell yet. We'll have to wait until tomorrow and see what develops," he said and hurried into the carriage. The little man was more than worried, he was in a panic. His knowledge was very limited and there was no other doctor in Montreal, if indeed, he could be called by that term. He had come to the colony as a barber and had only dabbled in medicine. He had studied what few writings there were upon the subject and having performed some minor operations successfully, had eventually given up barbering to devote himself entirely to medicine when Dr. Menoir had returned to France. But the most that his knowledge consisted of was a slight acquaintance with fractures and dislocations, without any understanding whatever of bone structure, and a dependence upon the established remedies of various herbs, bleeding, and blistering. Fevers frankly terrified him because of their contagious nature and the fear, that he would not have dared admit, that he himself might contract it.

Tomorrow? Antoine continued to pace up and down. How could he get through the night while the girl he adored tossed with burning fever that might be fatal?

Inside the house the others were equally restless. At times they all talked at once and then there were long silences. Henry alone remained aloof, staring out of the window but using every moment to recall to memory the teachings of Dr. Fitch of Albany. This young man had been Henry's closest friend for years. It was from him that Henry had caught the desire to be a doctor. Young Dr. Fitch was a man of advanced ideas, who had studied in London and obtained what meagre training was available. He had since made some experiments that were not always approved. Concerned over the narrowness and inadequacy of the medical profession and the manner in which his desire for reforms and progress had been scorned by more learned men, he had come to the New World in the hope that here he might have a larger field in which to develop his ideas. Attracted by Fitch's enthusiasm, Henry had spent hours in his rooms, studying the writings of the English physician, William Harvey, and the works of the eminent French physician, Ambroise Paré. He had accompanied Fitch on many of his cases, sometimes even assisting him. Dr. Fitch's chief interest had been fevers and their causes and he had expounded his views to his youthful friend. Now Henry was recalling those talks,

CHAPTER XXXII

THE NEXT DAY the doctor came to bleed Elise again. There had been nine more cases reported in Montreal and Claude de Ramezay's condition had become critical. Elise had now developed red spots on her face and a rash on the side of her thighs. The blood-letting left her too weak to move and she lay in a coma. Anxiously, Ann asked what could be done and the doctor shook his head in bewilderment. There was nothing that he knew could be done except let the fever run its course.

Perturbed not only over his own son, but over the spreading of the epidemic, Governor de Ramezay spent anxious days and sleepless nights. He had called in the captain of the ship but only after severe interrogation would he admit that the gentleman at Dillon's had been ill during the voyage and had left the ship with a high fever. Not able now to waste time berating the captain, the Governor had ordered him to submit a list of the passengers and crew. Isolated himself because of his son, he gave orders that soldiers were to comb Montreal until every person off the ship was accounted for. Some were already found to be stricken; others had not yet shown any symptoms. All that could be done was to isolate every one of them and those who were known to have had contact with them. But it was one thing to give an order and another to make sure it was carried out. At each house a soldier had to be posted to see that the people did not leave and spread the epidemic. Unfortunately, too long a time had already elapsed before the trouble was discovered and each day fresh cases were reported. Furthermore, to the general alarm were added consternation and indignation when it was found that a lodging house for sailors at the end of town was far more than its name implied! Many of the stricken sailors had already passed the fever on to the women there and they in turn had helped to spread it about the town. The Governor ordered the house closed and every one connected with it, whether stricken or not, thrown into the jail. There was a protest from the *directeur* of the jail but Governor de Ramezay was in no mood to listen to arguments. He ordered those who were ill to be placed in the largest cell and isolated there.

Then the vicious truth became known. The epidemic was not scarlet fever but smallpox. As the news spread through the town, every one became scared. Some tried to get away to friends living on outlying farms but the Governor had ordered all gates from the town closed and guarded. In some instances people stormed them in a frenzy of fear. Others sought comfort in religion and all day long the churches were filled. Even this proved to be dangerous, for there were those who had come to pray who later became stricken. People were ordered to remain in their own homes. The priests were kept busy all day as the toll of dead began to mount. Fearlessly the Sisters of the Congregation gave succor to those who needed it, taking care of the children of stricken families and giving shelter to many whose homes were isolated.

The Governor sent a message to Paul, asking him to keep those who had come in contact with Elise, away from the rest of the seigneury. Paul had not at first thought of the illness in terms of contagion and now he was alarmed. He took stock of the situation. The news that the epidemic was believed to be smallpox stunned him and he had to get control of himself before he could break the news to the rest of the family. When he felt calmer he went to Elise's door and called to Ann.

Ann's face was drawn and haggard, for none of them had slept since the Saturday night.

"How is she?" he asked, knowing that the answer could only be discouraging.

"Dreadful, Paul. The spots have increased and have now spread over her body and legs. Oh Paul, what are we going to do? Do you think it's scarlet fever?"

Paul did not answer the question. Instead he said. "Could

you leave her for a few minutes? I think we should have a family conference and decide upon a definite procedure. This illness may last for weeks and we must get things organized. You haven't slept for three nights and will collapse."

"But I must be with her, Paul," Ann said distractedly.

"I know, dear, but you will have to have some periods of relief. Can you leave her now for a few minutes? I will call the others up here. We can talk in this room. Then you can hear if she calls."

"All right." She went back into Elise's room. She was still lying in a coma, and, leaving the door open, Ann joined the others who had gathered in the room that formerly had been Jean-Baptiste's.

The lines on Paul's face were drawn and set as he braced himself for the news he must impart to them. "I have had a communication this morning from the Governor asking me to isolate all who have been near Elise so that the trouble may not spread to the seigneury. We must organize ourselves." He paused for a moment and then said: "This illness is not just a fever . . . it is . . . smallpox."

Horrified expressions were on all faces. Ann screamed and buried her face in her hands. For the first time that Paul could remember she lost control of herself, and as he held her to him, she beat upon his chest with both her fists.

"You must be calm, Ann," he said helplessly.

"But you don't understand, Paul! It will mean that her looks will be marred for ever. Our lovely child with those hideous scars! Oh God, not that." She sank down into a chair and buried her face in her hands. "Oh God, no," she pleaded.

"Perhaps it won't mark her," Paul said helplessly.

Marguerite and Rosalind were crying, too. Eric was holding his wife in his arms. Henry was staring out of a window.

"But you don't know, Paul!" Ann cried again. "I do. I saw the King many times. He had it when he was a boy and his face was all pockmarked. I have seen women in France wearing veils because their faces were left so hideous from it. Oh God, not that." She wept. "Oh, if only Claude had been taken ill before they had been together!"

Rosalind stole unnoticed from the room and went to sit beside Elise. She shuddered as she looked at the swollen, disfigured face but she would not leave her alone.

Ann had dropped to her knees and was saying her rosary and the others did the same. When she rose she said, in a voice that could hardly be heard: "I must go to her. Oh, my poor darling child," and the tears streamed down her face again.

"Wait just a moment, dear," Paul said gently. "We have to talk this over a little, yet."

Henry turned suddenly, having reached a decision. He came over to them and said: "Would you think me very presumptuous if I made a suggestion?"

Ann looked at him, her expression weary and hopeless. "What is it, Henri?" she asked.

He looked at his parents rather apologetically. "I know a little about smallpox. . . ."

"You do, Henri!" Marguerite exclaimed.

"Yes, mother. I helped Dr. Fitch during a slight attack in Albany. It wasn't an epidemic, only a few cases."

"When was this?" his mother asked.

"About two years ago."

"But I never knew it," Marguerite said. Eric touched her arm and signalled to her to let Henry talk. He had always approved of his son's interest in medicine and he was anxious to hear what he had to say.

"Go on, Henry," he said.

Henry turned to Paul. "This Dr. Fitch in Albany was my closest friend. I spent as much time as I could with him. As you know I have always wanted to be a doctor. Dr. Fitch has rather advanced ideas but he did save the lives of his smallpox patients and furthermore, in some cases, was able to prevent their being scarred."

"Oh, Henri, how?" Ann cried.

"If the patient can be kept from scratching the pustules and breaking them, there is a chance that they won't leave marks or at any rate not such deep marks."

"Do you know what Dr. Fitch did to prevent their being broken?" his father asked. His expression showed a deep interest.

"I have been going over it all in my mind and I believe I have remembered every precaution he took," Henry answered. Tear-stained faces were now turned to him with interest. Because he was the youngest of them all he was rather shy at placing himself in such a position and interrupted his statements to say, earnestly: "Please understand this is not a *cure* and my suggestions may not be of any value."

"At least you know more than we do, Henri," Paul said. "We are so entirely ignorant of what should be done. Tell us what you know."

Henry's expression became a little less anxious. "When the pustules begin to dry up an intense irritation will occur. It is then that there is danger of their being broken. This will not take place, however, for probably another week or ten days." Paul nodded. "It is those on the face that are of particular concern; probably most of the others won't show, though unfortunately the eruptions are usually more marked on exposed parts. Dr. Fitch covered the eruptions with strips of linen, soaked in *vin blanc*. When the irritation began, he bound up the hands and in some instances tied them down so that there would not be danger of scratching."

"Oh, Henri, if we can just prevent her having those awful pockmarks!" Ann cried.

"We can at least try . . ."

"Get some wine, Paul, and Marguerite and I will go and find linen that we can tear into strips."

As she started towards the door, Henry said.

"There are one or two more things. . . ."

"Wait a minute then. I'll get the linen and we can be tearing it up while we listen," Ann said and hurried out, returning in a few minutes with a pile of linen. "How wide should they be?" she asked.

"About so wide," Henry said, measuring off about four inches with his fingers.

Marguerite and Ann began to tear up the linen and Paul turned to Henry. "And now, Henri, tell us what else."

"Don't let them bleed her any more, uncle." His tone was pleading. "It will make her so weak and does little good. Not many physicians agreed with Dr. Fitch on this point but one day they probably will. She needs every ounce of blood to keep up her strength."

"I've heard that argument before," Paul said, "and it seems logical."

"I don't believe Dr. Beret knows anything else," Ann said. "He seems quite bewildered."

"Yes," Henry said. "I took the liberty of talking with him and he frankly admitted that he did not know what to do. That was when I decided to speak to you."

"I am glad you did, Henri," Paul said encouragingly. "Smallpox is highly contagious, isn't it?"

"Yes, and we are all in danger of having contracted it, especially Tante Ann and Rosalind." He looked around and said quickly: "Where is Rosalind?"

"Oh!" They all missed her then.

"She must have gone to Elise," Ann said.

Henry hurried out, alarmed. He found Rosalind sitting dejectedly by the bed watching Elise. When he remonstrated with her she looked up and replied: "Do you think I would leave her when she needs so much care?"

Henry laid a hand gently on her shoulder and said kindly: "No, dear, but please take the precautions I am going to suggest. I want you to come back into the other room and listen. I don't want you to catch the disease. You're important to me, you know."

She smiled gratefully at him. Henry stood looking at Elise for a few moments. It was the first time he had been in the room. Her face was highly flushed and on her forehead near the roots of her hair, showed several dark red spots. She kept tossing restlessly. He studied the spots closely. There was no question that she had smallpox and the worst development was yet to come. Would he be able to cope with it? He was afraid of the responsibility that he had undertaken. He knew more than the others, but did he know enough?

Rosalind watched him anxiously, seeing the drawn, worried look on his face. "Is she going to die, Henry?" she asked.

He shook his head slowly. "Pray to God, Rosalind," he replied. "She is in His hands. We can only do what little we know."

When they returned to the room the others were all discussing his suggestions. Ann looked at him with deep concern and asked: "How is she?"

"Very restless," he said and made no further comment.

"Now, Henri, what should we do to prevent us all being contaminated?" Paul asked.

Henry was thoughtful for a moment and then said: "This may all sound stupid but it may help. After you have been with her and handled her, immediately wash your hands in vinegar or if there is not enough of that available, *vin blanc* will do. Dr. Fitch says there is a germ that causes contagion. . . ."

"A germ!" Paul asked puzzled. "What kind?"

Henry looked at him apologetically. "I don't know. I am merely quoting Dr. Fitch. He didn't know either. He was trying to find out when I last saw him. But anyway, whether it is a germ or something else, the vinegar or wine will cleanse it from the hands and prevent it spreading elsewhere."

"That sounds logical," his father remarked, and Henry smiled at him gratefully.

"Also it may be on your clothes. Dr. Fitch used to put on a large apron rather like those you wear in the kitchen," Henry said to Ann.

"I have plenty of those aprons and every woman on the seigneury has a supply," Ann said. "They would let us have them, I'm sure."

"Of course they would," Paul said. "I don't know how the rest of you feel but I think we should follow Henri's suggestions."

They all agreed at once.

"I'll go and get all the wine we have and will send for more," Paul said.

"One last thing," Henry said. "Dr. Fitch believed that disease increased by having the windows all closed. He advocated having them open day and night."

"But with a fever wouldn't she catch cold?" Ann asked rather alarmed.

"Add more covers, she needs the pure air."

Marguerite put her arms around her son and said proudly: "Bless you, darling."

Henry kissed her and then said again. "All this may prove to be of no help. Don't count on it too much."

A discussion followed as Paul suggested they organize themselves into shifts to watch Elise. Ann continued to protest that she could not leave her but Paul was adamant and, furthermore, insisted that as soon as they had arranged their supplies of needed articles, she go and rest. Rosalind pleaded to be allowed to return now and remain until Ann should have had her rest and they agreed, although Henry was concerned because there were heavy circles under her eyes.

Paul brought up a supply of vinegar and wine and Ann produced some aprons. The vinegar and a bowl were placed inside the room and the aprons were left in a pile outside.

"I should like to bind up her face, if you will let me," Henry said. "Are there spots elsewhere. . . ." he asked, a little embarrassed.

"On her legs and . . . er . . . body," Ann replied.

"Will you bind those up, Tante Ann?"

She nodded.

Henry followed Ann, Marguerite and Rosalind into the room. Elise opened her eyes, bright with fever and stared at them. She opened her mouth to speak but no words came and she sank into a coma again.

CHAPTER XXXIII

As the news spread throughout the seigneury that Elise's illness was smallpox, intense fear spread with it. Mothers kept their children indoors watching them carefully. Every one tried to remember when last Elise had been near them, and those who had last had contact with her were extremely nervous. Any one who had a headache immediately took to bed and watched anxiously lest a rash appear. It was fortunate that after her return from seeing Claude, Elise had kept indoors, not being in the mood to talk to any one.

Antoine was in despair. Unable to be of any help due to the isolation, his days were filled with dread. He, too, had seen the ravages of the disease in France and without actual knowledge of the suffering she must be enduring, his imagination took flight and he was tortured by it. He spent long hours alone on the distant part of the seigneury, for to be with people meant having to listen to their discussion of the tragedy at the Manor House.

When Aunt Marie heard the news she at once hurried to the Manor and was indignant when she was refused admittance. Through a window Paul explained the situation to her, but still she was not appeased. She insisted that at least she be allowed to come and remain in the kitchen so that she could attend to their meals. Paul reminded her of her own children who needed her. "They can take care of themselves," she argued, but to no avail. Then he reminded her of her pregnant condition, but this did not placate her. Finally Paul set her the task of collecting all the aprons she could and she left a little happier, though still disgruntled.

Fear subsided a little when no further cases broke out on

the seigneury, and then thoughtfulness and friendliness became paramount. Each day the men brought over large pans of food that their women had cooked. Also, when Paul sent out a request for vinegar and wine they collected all they could obtain. Each day large supplies were brought and left outside the door. Though it was the busy season, they divided up the work on Paul's farm between them and his crops and livestock were well tended. The men carried back the news that the young English boy knew of some special cure which was expected to save the stricken girl. Many of them looked at each other rather guiltily when they learned that it was one of the English guests who might save Elise. One of the older men who had come to Paul with the delegation of protest, mumbled to his wife that perhaps they had been too hasty in their criticism.

The Manor House now resembled a fort preparing for a siege. After the one outburst, Ann had recovered and went calmly about making preparations, though the strain and worry she was feeling were apparent to all and Paul watched her anxiously. They divided the day and night into watches so that there were always two of them with Elise. Henry, however, frequently kept watch with the others, afraid that there might be a change that he would miss. Ann, too, took more than her share, and no amount of remonstrating by Paul could make her do otherwise. She would snatch a few hours sleep but all through the night she would keep going to Elise's room, so that there was scarcely an hour when she and Henry were not there. Few words were spoken by any of them. They dared not speak much, lest they voice their thoughts. The first days Eric and Paul would converse with each other when they happened to be off duty at the same time, and would derive some consolation from their pipes and an occasional glass of brandy, but as Elise grew worse they too fell silent. They would pace up and down outside, getting some fresh air, but always alert to see that no one from the seigneury came near them. Though it seemed that by this time none of them had contracted the disease, until the danger was over, they could never be sure.

The inactivity was galling to Paul, with so many things at this season of the year needing attention. Each day seemed endless. He wished so much that André could have been home, though he was glad to spare him the anxiety. Yet with André there he would not have been so depressed. But nothing short of disaster could bring him back at this time of year and they had enough disaster already. It would be many months yet, nearly a year, before they returned and how much had happened during their absence! Marguerite and Eric's visit, Antoine's return and now this smallpox epidemic. What was André going to find when he did get back? Elise meant so much to him. Would she ever be the beautiful, healthy girl she had been? These and other thoughts tortured him, thoughts that he could not dismiss because of his feeling of guilt. He had hoped that with Antoine's return all difficulties would be removed, Elise's engagement to Claude broken, and she and Antoine eventually married. Was God now going to punish him for that indiscretion of a score of years ago by taking away his beloved daughter? He scourged himself with the remembrance that had it not been for his belief that Antoine might be his son, this might never have happened. Elise would already have been married to Antoine and would not have seen Claude the day he arrived. "It's my fault, all my fault," he kept repeating to himself, and he could no longer go to Ann for comfort. Suppose Ann should also contract the disease and die? He would break into a sweat as these thoughts tortured him.

Elise's condition became worse. The fever had lessened to some degree but every hour the papules increased in number and size. Where there had been one, there were now several grouped together all along the hairline and around her mouth and chin. They were not as numerous on her body, though her legs and thighs were covered.

Repeatedly Henry and Ann changed the bandages. With hands that sometimes shook, he would lift off the linen strips while Ann stood ready with a freshly soaked bandage. There was always dread in their hearts as to what they would see as the bandage was removed. They would stare at the papules but they seldom made any comment to each other. All they could do was to wait and hope.

On the fifth day when the papules had so largely increased they filled with fluid and Ann could not repress an exclamation as she saw them.

"What does it mean, Henri?" she asked and her voice was filled with dread.

"It's all right," he said and there was some comfort in his assurance. "Tomorrow the center of each will sink in."

She looked to him for further explanation but he made no more comment, except to say: "We must be very careful how we bandage so as not to break them."

The next day, as Henry had said, each papule presented an umbilical appearance which remained for a couple of days. Then they turned to a nauseating sight as the central depression disappeared and each papule changed to a pustule filled with yellow, cloudy liquid.

"Oh, my poor child!" Ann exclaimed when she saw them and she could not restrain the tears that rolled down her cheeks. No one would now have been able to recognize the girl lying on the bed as one who had once been beautiful. Her features were highly inflamed and so swollen and distorted as to be out of all proportion.

"What will they do? Will they break now?" she asked.

Henry studied them, a deep frown on his anxious face. He shook his head. "No . . . if everything goes right they should dry up," he told her.

"How long will that be?"

"A few days, probably."

All through these days Elise was too ill to notice anything. Ann had tried to get her to take some of the soup that neighbors had brought, but she had no desire for it. Her throat was so swollen that she could not swallow, and when Ann held the spoon to her lips, she turned her head away, moaning with the intensity of her suffering. Much of the time she lay in a coma and it often seemed as though she had already slipped away to another world.

Much of the food that was brought to the house remained untouched. The servants slept in their own quarters away from the house and were isolated there since the orders had been received from the Governor. No one thought of regular meal-times, though Marguerite did all she could to keep the house running in orderly fashion. Only empty stomachs drove them to eat and then mostly it was to nibble on whatever was at hand. Henry ate little and slept less, even though his father tried gently to persuade him to look after his own health.

At the end of the week the crisis was reached and all that night Henry and Ann watched. The swelling had now increased to such proportions that there was danger she would be unable to breathe. The upper passages of her nose and throat were so obstructed that she had to struggle for every breath. Her eyes were so swollen that she could no longer open them and there was the fear, which Henry kept to himself, that her eyesight might be impaired. In an agony of doubt he kept changing the bandages, hoping that the cool wine would reduce the swelling. At times it was difficult to replace the dressings as she thrashed about in a desperate effort to breathe. Strange sounds came from her throat which Henry feared might at any moment turn to the death rattle. With each long struggle he found himself holding his own breath in unison with her efforts. Already so weakened, he feared her heart would not be able to stand all the strain, but valiantly she struggled against strangulation.

Dawn came in through the windows, as grey as their lined faces. Marguerite came in with Rosalind and Eric, who were to take the next shift. Silently they watched the struggling girl, their alarm pictured on their faces. Neither Ann nor Henry seemed to notice them. Quietly Marguerite told them breakfast was ready and they both shook their heads. She put her arm around Ann as she said: "You must rest, darling. Eric and Rosalind will take over."

"I can't leave now," Ann protested.

Paul had come in. "You must rest, dear," he urged. "I will watch and I promise you I will call you if there is any change. Come, dearest." He put his arm around her and drew her up. She leaned heavily against him, all her strength spent. She allowed herself to be led away by him.

Eric had his arm across his son's shoulder and was trying to persuade him to come to breakfast.

"Please bring me something on a tray. I must stay here," ne said. His strained eyes were bloodshot.

"But you, too, must have some sleep, Henri," his mother urged.

"Later perhaps—not now," he said and turned back to watch Elise. How long could she go on struggling like that? Wasn't there something that Dr. Fitch had done to relieve the suffering? He racked his tired brain and went on changing the bandages assisted by Rosalind, who had not said a word but was an efficient helper.

Again that night they watched. Henry had snatched a few hours during the day when exhaustion had necessitated it, but both he and Ann resumed their vigil that night. No one in the house slept. Some dozed in chairs; others paced the floor. From time to time Paul come to the door and looked in and went away again. Ann sat by the bed, her rosary passing through her nervous fingers. Henry prayed too—prayed for help in his ignorance and implored God to impart to man more knowledge that they might be able to help His suffering children.

Elise's struggles had lessened as she became worn out with exhaustion and her breathing was so light that it seemed she did not breathe at all. Tensely Henry listened for it and then showing panic for the first time, quickly lowered his ear to listen to her heart.

Ann watched him fearfully and in a whisper asked:

"What is it, Henri? Has she gone?"

He did not answer. Then he shook his head. "It is very faint . . . but . . . I think more regular," he said.

Ann fell on her knees by the bed. Paul came in and his eyes glazed with fear when he saw her. He looked at Henry.

"Is it over?" he asked in a whisper.

Henry was watching Elise intently. His eyes were so tired that he was afraid to trust them but it seemed as though the swelling had decreased. She wasn't struggling now, but lying in a coma. He was afraid to say what he thought, in case he should be mistaken. Ann stood up and Paul put his arm around her. All watched the girl on the bed.

Then Henry said: "I think . . . the crisis has passed," and his head drooped over the bed.

CHAPTER XXXIV

THE FOLLOWING DAY Father Joseph called and brought consolation to all by saying Mass from the steps of the Manor House. Isolated from Montreal, the habitants had all had to let two Sundays pass without going to church and it was a time when they particularly needed this comfort. Never before had Paul wished so much for a church on his own seigneury.

Father Joseph had spoken to Paul through a window and had wanted to come in. At first Paul had been tempted to accede to the request but he knew that if the curé had entered the house, those on the remainder of the seigneury would have been fearful of having him later in their houses. As word spread over the seigneury that Father Joseph would say Mass, they all quickly gathered and those within the Manor joined in through the opened windows. Henry and Rosalind took over the watch so that Ann should not miss the consolation which she so needed.

Father Joseph brought news from Montreal, and it was tragic. Hundreds had succumbed, including Claude de Ramezay. Also Dr. Beret, who had realized his worst fears and had contracted the disease. This explained why he had not come again to the Manor, a fact that had been noticed but not regretted, since they preferred to follow Henry's theories.

After Mass the curé visited every home on the seigneury and though his presence brought comfort, his news caused distress, for among those who had died were friends of the habitants. Father Joseph tried to comfort Antoine, for he alone, outside of the immediate family, knew of his love for Elise. Even the news of Claude de Ramezay's death brought Antoine only partial comfort, for as he had succumbed there seemed little hope for Elise.

For two more days Elise wavered between life and death. The reduction of the swelling brought some hope but this was immediately followed by a return of the fever. Though this was not so intense as the introductory fever, she became delirious, tossing restlessly as the fever devoured her. To the anxious watchers it seemed as though their world stood still.

Then the change for which Henry had been waiting occurred. The fever again abated and the pustules began to dry up. But with this the irritation began. Henry was hopeful that now the crisis had passed her life would be saved, but could they save her from permanent disfigurement? With the reduction of the swelling, her features resumed more normal proportions and her eyes were no longer forced shut. Her cheeks were sunken and the flesh wasted from her body. In the past few hours they had been able to get her to take a little nourishment and before the irritation became too intense she appeared for the first time in all these agonizing days to be more cognizant of what was going on. Intensely weak, she could not speak above a whisper and then only a few words at a time.

"I am very ill," she murmured. Henry was glad that Ann was in the room at the time. He could see that she could hardly restrain her emotion as Elise spoke. But her voice was calm as she replied:

"You have been very ill, darling, but you're getting better."

Elise's eyes looked wonderingly at Henry sitting there, haggard and drawn, but before she could ask the reason, she sank into a coma again. The news that she had spoken heartened them all and braced them for the second crisis they had to face.

The irritation increased. They bandaged her hands so that she could not use her fingers to scratch but she still tried to rub the bandages on her face. Each time she raised a hand they held it away from her face. The intensity of the itching drove her frantic and she writhed on the bed, rubbing her legs against the sheets and groaning with the torment. Not a single moment dared they leave her, for each pustule that she rubbed would become a scar. She turned and twisted her head, trying to rub her face against the pillow and when they prevented her, she fought them. The cruelty of it agonized them. They tried tying her arms to the bed but she tossed and squirmed so frantically that the restricting bands cut into her flesh. Then they loosened them and went back to holding her wrists. The shifts now had to be changed every hour, for the watchers were themselves exhausted by the vigilance that must be maintained.

"How long will this go on?" Ann cried frantically, and Henry could not answer her. He was now near collapse himself but he would not relax until he knew the danger was passed. And it continued for days, until she was too exhausted to make much resistance and lay there moaning and writhing. Nearly two weeks had now passed and the nerves of all were at breaking point.

At this time there came a diversion that momentarily distracted those on the seigneury. Antoine was sitting on the knoll where his house was to have been built, his axe lying by. He had tried to work but he had lost all interest in the seigneury. Young Philip arrived with the dinner pails for the men and after putting them down came to speak to Antoine.

"Maman's time's coming," he said. "I'm going over to get Mère Madeleine."

Antoine immediately jumped up and hurried to the house to see if there was anything he could do.

"Gracious me, no!" Aunt Marie said with a laugh. "This is no place for men. Be off with you. I've sent the children to Etienne's and you'd better stay over there a few days too."

"Don't worry about me," Antoine said. "You're sure there's nothing I can do?"

"Nothing. But wait a minute, yes there is. I don't want

them up at the Manor House to know about this. Ann has enough to worry about. Go tell Etienne and Pierre and the others that they're not to mention it. Impress it upon them. I'll be furious with any one who tells." She compressed her lips as she finished the sentence, to hide a spasm of pain. Beads of perspiration stood out on her forehead.

Antoine saw it and asked: "Shouldn't we send for a doctor?"

"Doctor! And where would you get one? Do you think if there were doctors in Montreal they'd come out here with an epidemic on their hands? Besides, we have no doctors."

"No, of course not. I forgot for the moment. But surely this is doctor's work . . ."

"Indeed it is not! I've sent for Mère Madeline. . . ."

"But can she take proper care of you?"

Again she laughed but it ended in another contraction of pain. "Don't you ever let her hear you ask that! She prides herself on her skill. There's not a baby on the seigneury at whose birthing she hasn't officiated. Now be off with you and forget it. You'll be having a family of your own one of these days and that'll be time enough for you to worry about a woman having a child."

Aunt Marie's frankness always shocked the other women on the seigneury, but Antoine liked it. Some of them had expressed their disapproval of the way she went over and chatted with Antoine's men when her condition was apparent, and others had hinted to her that she should not have Antoine at her house at such a time. They did not say very much because they knew the sharpness of her tongue. She merely ignored their remarks and had they repeated them she would have told them to go and attend to their own business. "Do they think I'm going to pretend to my children that babies are found under bushes!" she once remarked to Ann.

As Antoine reached the door she said: "Before you go, throw me that large towel there." He handed her the towel and then impulsively bent and kissed her forehead. It was hot and damp.

"God bless you," he said and left the room, his brow furrowed with concern. The moment he left, Aunt Marie looped the towel over the end of the bed and began to pull on it, screwing up her face with pain.

Antoine did not go back to the seigneury immediately. He walked down to the River and lit his pipe. When he saw Mère Madeleine arrive, accompanied by Pierre's and Etienne's wives, he felt easier. Aunt Marie was right; this was women's work, not men's. He smoked silently, thinking of her. There was a scream from the house and he jumped up, starting towards it, and then checked himself in time. "It hurts so that they scream," he thought, and perspiration covered his face. He did not wait for more, but started across the seigneury to carry out Aunt Marie's wishes that no word reach the Manor House.

Later that evening he stopped at the house. Brusque, jolly Marie looked very tender as she cradled the small form in her arms.

"Look, Antoine, my first girl," she said proudly.

Antoine looked down at the funny wrinkled little face and smiled. "I'm so glad," he said. "You wanted a girl so much."

"Indeed I did! Wait until Philip sees her!"

"Too bad he isn't here," Antoine said solicitously.

"Yes," she replied and sighed. She had been wishing that all the afternoon. Philip Boissart might be a rough, careless man but he was her man and she was lonely during all the months he was away, but she would never have let him know it.

"What are you going to call her?" Antoine asked.

"Elise," she said and saw Antoine catch his breath. "She's my favorite niece," she added. "What is the news today?"

He shook his head. "Not much improvement. The irritation still continues."

He left then rather abruptly to go and sit alone on his seigneury.

The next morning he had just begun work when several of the habitants arrived. He looked at them inquiringly, afraid that they might be bringing bad news.

"Monsieur Paul wants balsam fir," they told him. "Seems they are going to try some Indian cure."

Immediately Antoine was on his feet, delighted that at last he could do something to help. He called to the men who were working on his seigneury and at once they all set to work stripping bark and branches from the balsams that were so plentiful on his land. As each pile grew they carried it to the Manor House.

In the Manor House kitchen the men stripped the leaves from the branches and pounded them together with the bark, while Ann kept huge pots of water boiling. The bark had blister-like cavities that contained resin and when this and the leaves or needles were mashed together and boiled, the resulting infusion was said to be a cure for many diseases. While they waited for the liquid to cool, Ann asked:

"How did you learn of this, Eric?"

"During the two years I was a captive of the Indians," he replied.

"Some of their cures are better than any we know," Paul remarked.

"Indeed they are," Eric agreed. "When Marguerite and I were escaping you remember that she contracted fever. I tried this then and it cured her. As a matter of fact, she's had a return of the fever several times since and I have always used this."

"Pray God it will help now!" Ann said, desperation in her tone. She dipped her finger into the liquid. "Does it have to be cold?" she asked.

"Oh, no," Eric replied. He dipped his finger into the pot. "That should be cool enough now."

Henry and Ann hurried upstairs, leaving Paul and Eric to continue making the infusion.

Elise lay with closed eyes, moaning and stirring restlessly. She opened her eyes and gazed wearily at them. Ann bent over her.

"Darling, we have something that we hope will relieve the irritation," she said.

"Oh, God, I hope it will," she cried. "I can't stand this much longer." Her words ended in a moan.

Henry removed the bandages. The dried pustules now presented reddish-brown scars and he viewed them hopefully.

"They look better," he said. He took the soaked strips from Ann and laid them gently over Elise's forehead and round across her chin. Those by her nose they had not been able to bandage very satisfactorily. He dipped a cloth into the infusion and dabbed it over the spots.

"Is that soothing?" Ann asked, but Elise did not reply.

Henry left Ann and Marguerite to bandage the infected parts on Elise's body. Almost immediately she became quieter. Perhaps it was the balsam; perhaps it was only the power of suggestion. Perhaps the worst of the irritation had passed. But she no longer thrashed about the bed so hysterically.

For the rest of the day they continued applying the balsam-soaked strips. By night-time she was quieter and fell into a natural sleep—the first in all these agonizing days. Still Henry would not leave her, afraid that she would waken and be restless again.

The following morning brought the first ray of joy to the house. Elise wakened normally and recognized them all as they gathered to witness the answer to their prayers. She smiled wanly and her eyes that seemed sunken into her head, asked a question. Her small, emaciated body and hollow cheeks showed the struggle that she had had.

All watched tensely as Henry removed first the bandage from her forehead. Adhering to it were reddish-brown scabs, and even his tired, drawn face lighted up when he saw them. He heard the exclamations of those around him but was afraid to look where the bandage had been. Fearfully he forced himself to do so. Some scabs still remained but where others had been there were now white, depressed scars. He looked at them but made no comment.

"They're not like the marks on the King's face," Ann exclaimed. "They were deep, ugly scars."

"They are scars, though," Henry said, and his tone was disappointed.

"But those will fade, Henri, I think," Ann said.

"You think so?" he asked. He was so weary he could not think or remember. Deliberately he removed the bandage from the rest of her face. This, too, had scabs adhering to it, leaving the same white scars.

"What is it? What is wrong with me?" Elise asked.

Ann's and Henry's eyes met. Should they tell her? Ann braced herself. "You've had smallpox, dear," she said gently.

"Smallpox!" It was a cry of distress.

"But you are better, dear, and will soon be well," Ann said reassuringly.

Elise started to put her hand to her face but Henry caught it. "Not yet," he said quickly. "There are still scabs to come off."

"I shall be pockmarked?" she asked fearfully.

"I don't believe so," her mother replied. "There are marks now but I am sure they will fade in time so that they will be scarcely noticeable. We owe it all to Henri. He. . . ."

Henry did not wait to hear her explanation to Elise. Now that the tension was over, reaction began. Limply he dropped the bandages to the floor and left the room. He stumbled to his room and fell across the bed—and was asleep.

CHAPTER XXXV

BEFORE ELISE AND ANTOINE returned from their honeymoon in France, peace was declared. The Treaty of Utrecht was signed on April 11, 1713. Some said the Treaty was unfavorable to New France because the English received Acadie, Newfoundland and the Hudson Bay territory, leaving France only Ile Royale, some islands in the Gulf of St. Lawrence and certain fishery rights along the Newfoundland coast, in addition to the territory owned along the St. Lawrence River.

But to the habitant on his farm these facts meant little. Peace treaties were made by governments and he did not understand them. He had heard that these places existed somewhere to the east but that was all. What concerned him was the right to live peacefully with his neighbors, freed from the necessity of going to war and leaving his land and family. The Frenchman loved to dance and sing and be left alone to toil when he wished or to sit lazily in the sun with his pipe.

It was a peace that meant much and was to last for nearly a quarter of a century. It meant that new people would come to the colonies. It meant that the population of Montreal would be doubled and trade and industry would thrive. For nearly seventy years they had waited for it, and though its full import could not be realized for several years to come, it was the beginning of prosperity.

Paul with his beloved Ann; Marguerite and her yearning to be able to visit her family home without difficulty; André with his desire to explore; Philip and his jolly, carefree Marie and all their children; the habitant and his growing family; and Elise and Antoine starting a new life and looking forward to having children. To all of these the Treaty meant only one thing—the opportunity to live *in peace*.

344